SONGS
FOR
GHOSTS

ALSO BY CLARA KUMAGAI

Catfish Rolling

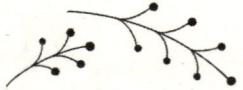

SONGS
FOR
GHOSTS

CLARA KUMAGAI

ZEPHYR
An imprint of Head of Zeus

First published in the UK in 2025 by Zephyr,
an imprint of Head of Zeus, part of Bloomsbury Publishing Plc

9 7 5 3 1 2 4 6 8

A catalogue record for this book is available from the British Library.

ISBN (HB): 9781803288086; ISBN (XPB): 9781035916962
ISBN (E): 9781803288062

Extract on page 179 from *Heroic with Grace: Legendary Women of Japan*, translated by Felice Fischer and edited by Chieko Irie Mulhern © 1991, Routledge. Reproduced by permission of Taylor & Francis Group.

Extract on page 421 from *The Tale of the Heike*, translated by Helen Craig McCullough ©1988, Stanford University Press. Reproduced by permission of Stanford University Press.

Every effort has been made to trace copyright holders and to obtain their permission for the use of copyright material. The publisher apologizes for any omissions in the above list and would be grateful for notification of any corrections that should be incorporated in future reprints or editions of this book.

Cover design: Cristina Bencina
Typeset by Ed Pickford

Printed and bound in Great Britain by
CPI Group (UK) Ltd, Croydon CR0 4YY

MIX
Paper | Supporting
responsible forestry
FSC® C171272
www.fsc.org

Bloomsbury Publishing Plc
50 Bedford Square, London, WC1B 3DP, UK
Bloomsbury Publishing Ireland Limited,
29 Earlsfort Terrace, Dublin 2, D02 AY28, Ireland

HEAD OF ZEUS LTD
5–8 Hardwick Street, London EC1R 4RG

To find out more about our authors and books visit WWW.HEADOFZEUS.COM
For product safety related questions contact PRODUCTSAFETY@BLOOMSBURY.COM

For my family

起きよ起きよ我が友にせん寝る胡蝶

Okiyo okiyo
waga tomo ni sen
nuru ko chō

— Matsuo Bashō
松尾 芭蕉

One

♩♫♪♪♩♪

Somewhere in the distance, a bell tolled. A wedding – no, a funeral. A dramatic ceremonial sound announcing the death of my relationship. Despite getting dumped on a street corner, my basic sense of dignity still hadn't kicked in; I couldn't help but watch him walk away. He didn't look back.

The pavement at my feet was littered with white flowers and, as a breeze shoved along, more floated to the ground. I caught a single bloom in my hand and stared at its delicate snowy petals and golden centre.

An old woman passed me, her walking stick tapping a rhythm. Her face was turned upwards and a flower landed on the lens of her sunglasses. She plucked it off.

'They only bloom for one day,' she said. 'But they'll be back next year.'

I didn't know if she was talking to me or to herself. I answered anyway. 'Not the same ones.'

She smiled in my direction and strolled on.

I turned towards home and my heart felt like it had been left behind, lingering on the pavement where two unremarkable paths met. Maybe someone would walk through that spot and feel a big waft of heartbreak; or they would see the flowers wilting, turning to dust in the wind.

———

'Everything okay, Adam?' Kate asked.

The kitchen was steamy and warm from the pot of potatoes on the stove. It curled around me thickly. Benny burbled in his playpen. I patted his soft blond hair.

'Yeah,' I said.

Kate was studying me.

'Everything okay with *you*?' I shot back.

She raised an eyebrow. 'Did something happen?'

I shook my head, trying to blur my features with movement. My face was always wide open, easy to read, useless for lying.

Kate hmmmed and said, 'Dinner's ready.'

I slumped at the table. She put a plate in front of me and sat opposite. Just me and her, again. And Benny.

'Where's Dad?' I asked.

'He has to stay on the base overnight.' Kate cut up her chicken in a disturbingly violent way.

'I see.'

We ate, thinking about men.

'I have to do some shopping later. Do you mind watching your brother? You can go out when I'm back,' Kate said.

I resisted the urge to correct her. *Half*-brother. 'I'm not going anywhere.'

'It's Friday. Don't you usually—'

'Not tonight.' Possibly not ever.

I could see Kate gearing herself up.

'Did you and Evan have an argument or...?' she asked.

Had we? Not over a specific *thing,* not about something one of us had done or not done.

I like you but I feel like you want something totally committed and I'm not in the same place. This is for the best, right?

It's just that I hadn't agreed with any of that.

'Not really. But. It's over.' My voice, appallingly, cracked.

'I'm sorry.' Kate reached across and touched my hand. I didn't move away, but I didn't hold her hand, either.

'I'm fine. Not fine. I dunno.'

Kate sighed. 'That's normal. You can wallow and eat ice cream and listen to sad songs. It was your first relationship so I can eat a lot of ice cream with you in case you don't know how to do that yet.'

I laughed a bit. 'Teach me your ways, mistress.'

A funny look flitted across her face. 'Don't call me that.'

'Master, then.'

She cleared her throat and smiled. 'You will be a worthy pupil. What flavours do you desire?'

'Chocolate, strawberry cheesecake, mint chocolate chip.'

'No green tea?'

'Don't like it anymore.'

'I thought it was your favourite?'

I shrugged.

Our third date had been getting ice cream and sitting in a park. *You Asians love green tea,* he'd said. I'd laughed awkwardly but then he'd kissed me and I forgot about it, just a small and normal joke.

Kate filled the sudden silence. 'I shall let the student guide the master.'

I pulled my mouth upwards. 'Thanks, Kate.'

Her eyes flickered the tiniest bit when I said her name. She still wasn't used to it after all these months. *Stepmother* obviously sounded too evil, so first name it was. But every time I said it I could feel the distance growing between us. It was strange – when Benny came, Kate and I had become closer in some ways, united in love of him. She hadn't changed towards me, but she was tired and her complete attention went to him; which was natural, he was a baby. *Her* baby.

I focused on my food, which tasted of nothing.

When we finished, I took the plates to the sink and did the washing up while Kate fed Benny.

'Could you do me a favour?' Kate asked. 'I was planning to ask your dad but seeing as he *won't* be back tonight...'

'Does it involve repairing something?'

'No.' Kate made an apologetic face. 'It does involve the attic, which I know you're scared of—'

'I am not!'

'The last time you went up there you wouldn't stop screaming.'

'A spider *went down my back,*' I said, reasonably. 'And that was years and years ago.'

Kate corrected me. 'It was two years ago.'

'I'm not afraid of the attic. I'll go right now.'

Kate reached into a cupboard and handed me a torch. 'Such courage, thank you.'

That was when it registered that I'd been manipulated. I sighed and put a hoodie on so nothing would skitter down the back of my neck.

The attic was dusty and cluttered – probably too stereotypical to be the start of a horror movie. After a few hundred sneezes, I figured I'd scared any poltergeists or monsters away.

I peered at each box, wiping away dust to read their labels in the dim torchlight. SKI WEAR. Since when did we ski? FISH TANK. I remembered that fish: a traumatic loss. Finally, KID STUFF. Kate didn't believe in specificity. I hauled it out. Behind it was a much smaller box, not cardboard but wooden. Despite the layer of dust, I could see the writing carved on the lid was Japanese. I squinted, trying to work out the characters. Tea, maybe? I opened it.

There was a particular smell of wood and something else herby, plant-like. Inside was a bundle wrapped in navy cloth. I unfolded it to find a slim book, no title on its worn grey cover. It was filled with handwriting. I held the torch close to the first page.

March 25th

So, Obaasama, you have died and left me. I am sorry to begin a letter in this way. However, these are my feelings and I have resolved to write the truth – as best I know it – here, to you. You always valued honesty and why should I lie to you? I would prefer to be direct than untruthful. Besides, I imagine the dead can see through the lies of the living.

For a second, I thought a bug was running over my arms but, when I checked frantically, I realised that it was goosebumps rising on my skin. I swallowed and turned back to the book.

> *It is unkind of me, and disrespectful too, to be angry that you have died, though months have passed. But I am here in this house on the hill, almost alone. Something has changed. I see strange things, Obaasama. There are whispers in the garden. I dream of music. Perhaps this is simply me wishing for you and the music you played. Your biwa is lonely without you, as am I.*

They were letters, or a diary written like letters. Or a *novel* in the form of a diary – that made more sense. The writer sure knew how to start with a bang. The book looked ancient. How did it get up here? It didn't seem like something Dad or Kate would read. Dad didn't pick up a book unless it was about a war, and Kate adored, bafflingly, both true crime and Jane Austen.

The writing on the box was Japanese; the letter in the book was respectfully addressing a Japanese grandmother. Maybe it had belonged to my mother.

'Adam, you alive up there?' Kate called.

'Yeah – found it!' I said.

My heart thumped. I untidily rewrapped the book in its cloth, and closed the lid. I scrambled down with everything, pausing in my room to shove the mystery box under my bed.

I brought the KID STUFF down to Kate.

'You're a brave boy.' She began rummaging around in it.

'What do you need it for?' I asked.

'Some of your old clothes might fit Benny soon – you had some adorable stuff.'

'That's – sustainable.' I inched towards the door. 'I have to do some homework, I just remembered—'

'Very studious of you for a Friday night,' Kate said absently, unfolding a tiny T-shirt.

I agreed and hurried to my room. I pulled out the wooden box but faltered after I opened the diary – what *was* a biwa?

I fumbled for my phone and read the first definition that appeared.

A biwa is a type of Japanese lute.

A musical instrument. How could that be lonely?

I began to read.

March 25th

... Your biwa is lonely without you, as am I.

Of course, I talk to O-Suzu and I am very fond of her. It is not the same, though. Not because she is a maid, but because I do not know if she has noticed any of the strange things. I have not spoken of them to her. O-Suzu is only five years older than me but she is so practical and clever. I am worried of what she might think and could not bear it if she resigned and left me. Mother is in Saga, taking care of her father. If I told her about these odd ideas she would be frightened. Uncle is not so far away but I do not think he will help me. Or rather he will assist me in the way *he* thinks best. For a priest he appears more occupied with this world than any others.

Obaasama, please help me. Is it you, causing these strangenesses I have sensed? Are other spirits or ghosts here? Can you ask if they are calling me, and why? I feel healthy and at only eighteen years of age I do not think I am in danger of becoming a ghost myself. But I cannot see the future.

I have been praying and burning incense and putting out salt but nothing seems to have any effect. Maybe this letter will. I cannot think of anything else. I am finding it laborious to think at all. I know you enjoyed letters, however, and perhaps you still do.

In any case, this has been some comfort to me. Perhaps tonight I will sleep.

~

March 29th

Obaasama, I must apologise for the letter I wrote to you. I was full of emotion. I am somewhat calmer today, or more tired. I did not sleep as I had hoped. My body hurt and my mind was flapping like a bird trapped or a butterfly caught between hands.

So I got up quietly and opened the outer door to the garden. I sat in the engawa and gazed at the shapes of trees and the glassy surface of the pond. The moon was thin as a fishbone.

I thought of you, Obaasama. What you would have said to calm me. And then, because I was dazed without sleep – or perhaps I *was* asleep, and only dreaming of wakefulness – I thought I saw your figure. An old woman wearing a grey handspun silk kimono, or perhaps it was not grey but grey in moonlight.

I called your name and you approached. I could not see your feet beneath the hem of your kimono. In your hand you held something. You were almost at the large flat stone set outside the door but your face was in shadow and your face used always to be filled with light. My fear became too strong and I fell back and shut the door fast and with force.

In the next room, O-Suzu called my name. I said I had wanted some air. Now I would return to bed. Good, she said. Yet I did not sleep.

When the sun was bright and there was no greyness left, I opened the door to the garden. On the large stone was an object, some kind of odd stiff leaf. Then I saw it was the plectrum used to play the biwa – a bachi. I looked at it for a long time before I picked it up. I knew it. It was yours, Obaasama. I had seen it in your hand many times, held firm to strike and strum.

I went to find your biwa, which I had not seen in some time. Before the end, you were too tired to hold it. You wanted to listen to me play, though I am not close to you in skill. The biwa case was closed tight. There was no bachi inside.

I called O-Suzu and asked if she had touched the biwa recently. She said, no. Not to clean it or check it or play it? I persisted. She repeated confusedly, no.

When O-Suzu had gone I picked up the biwa. There were no fingerprints on the lacquered wood, no marks on the slender half-moon openings. The four silk strings were strong and taut, the ivory frets firm in their places. I held it like a child. I saw in the case a piece of paper. *For you, Granddaughter*, it said. Your writing, Obaasama. So the biwa is mine. I held the bachi in one hand and the biwa in the other and I struck the strings just once. The sound echoed and I hoped you could hear it.

Two

♩ ♫ ♪ ♪ ♩ ♪

'Adam?' Kate called.

I jumped. 'Yeah?'

'I'm going shopping now.'

I tucked the diary away carefully and went downstairs.

Kate handed me Benny, attempted to smooth down her unruly red curls. 'Message if you need anything.'

Once the front door clicked behind her I considered getting the diary again – but old precious things and babies don't go well together. In the crook of my arm, Benny gurgled and yawned. It was so weird; I supposed it *was* a diary. It could be the first draft of a novel, but it didn't feel like that – no notes or crossings out. And there was something else; the feeling that the person who had written it had been *real*.

I got my phone out to message Evan and then remembered why I couldn't.

I messaged Sylvia instead.

guess who's been dumped

She replied, taylor swift?

close, I wrote. it is me.

Sylvia called immediately. 'Adam!' she howled.

'Shhhhh, Benny's falling asleep!' I whisper-shouted. 'Let me put him down.'

I took Benny up to his crib. When I was back on the couch, totally horizontal, I said, 'You may react.'

'What *happened*?' she yelled.

'Not really anything. I guess that was the problem,' I said.

'What did he say?'

'Apparently I'm not enough, but also too much.'

'He *said* that?'

'Not exactly. It's what he meant, though.'

Sylvia moved smoothly into attack mode. 'I suspected that he was not a logical thinker.'

I mentally counted down from ten and had reached seven when she said, '*But—*'

She was unfailingly and almost superhumanly optimistic. 'Maybe this is for the best. School ends soon and some hot college guys are gonna come home and they'll be studying, like, *philosophy*, but are also on the basketball team so they're tall. This can be your summer of fun.'

'That was an inspiring speech even though no guy like that exists in our town, let alone *multiple* guys. With those oratory skills and unfounded promises you're gonna make a supreme president.'

'I'm working on locking in the gay singles vote.'

'You have mine. I'll campaign on your behalf and tell the three other gay guys I know.'

'Every vote counts,' Sylvia said. 'That is *democracy*.'

I finally laugh.

Sylvia cheered. 'Best medicine! You wanna come hang out?'

'I'm babysitting, but Sunday?'

'Sure.' Sylvia paused. 'I think you're better off without him, Adam.'

'Huh. Love you, Syl.'

'Love you too,' she replied.

Sylvia's affirmations faded away. How could I be better off? I closed my eyes, exhausted by the answers I couldn't find.

Benny suddenly wailed, echoing my stupid miserable thoughts. I hauled myself off the couch and up to his room.

In the doorway, I froze. There was a *woman* there, standing over Benny's crib.

'Who are you?' I burst out. 'How did you—'

She raised her head slowly. Her hair was long and dark and straight, half-covering her face, a pale oval. Her lips moved, but I couldn't hear what she said. Benny quietened. Her eyes were like mine.

There was a noise from another room – my room – and I half-turned towards the sound, then remembered, caught myself and whirled back to the crib. There was nobody there, no woman, nothing. Only Benny, blinking his eyes, clenching and unclenching his little hands.

I felt dizzy. I spun around, as if the woman could have got past me. 'Is anybody there?'

Benny whimpered, but the house was heavily, terribly, silent. I gathered Benny up and looked into the bedrooms, then downstairs, but every room was empty. The front door was locked.

'It's okay now,' I repeated over and over, not sure if I was soothing Benny or myself. He was calming down, staring at me with his soft blue eyes.

And then the phone rang and I was on the couch again, arms empty.

I shot upright – *Benny* – but when I sprinted to the crib there he was, sleepily blinking, roused by my thumping footsteps. I snatched him up, holding him so tight he squirmed and complained. He was definitely real, but I pinched myself to be certain.

'It was a *dream*. I leaned against the crib, weak with relief. 'Just a normal terrifying dream.' Probably because of that freaky diary getting into my brain.

The phone was still ringing, so I went to it, clutching Benny.

'Hello?'

'Adam?'

It was Dad.

'Of course it's Adam,' I said. 'Benny hasn't learned to talk yet. Or, like, reach the phone.'

'Obviously not.' He sounded defensive. 'I was calling to see how you are. And Kate. And Benny,' he said.

'We're fine.' No way was I getting into any break-up details.

'I called Kate, but she didn't pick up.'

'She's shopping,' I said, instead of, *She's angry.*

'Then I tried your phone and there was no answer, so I was worried,' he went on.

'I fell asleep. And Benny was sleeping too. Safe and sound,' I said. 'But we're both awake now. Still... safe.' I shut my mouth before I could sound any more suspicious.

'Glad to hear everything's good.'

'Do you want to talk to Benny?' I asked.

'Oh, sure...'

I held the phone to Benny's tiny shell ear. Dad's voice was faint and uncertain.

'Hey there. Hope you're behaving yourself. I'll see you soon, little guy.'

When there was silence I took the phone back. Benny stared at me impassively.

'He's smiling,' I lied.

'That's great. I'll talk to you again soon.'

'Bye, Dad.'

I hung up. It was always painfully, unshakably awkward to have a conversation with him. It wasn't *that* weird, was it? Tons of people had bad relationships with uncommunicative fathers. That was practically The Classic Dad.

I'll talk to you again soon, he'd said. Not, *I'll be home soon.* Poor Kate.

'Poor baby,' I said to Benny.

Though Benny wasn't poor at all. He didn't have to do anything. We fed him and cleaned him and loved him. He had two real, living parents. He was blue-eyed and blond-haired and a perfect pinky white. Benny hadn't been dumped.

'Poor Adam,' I said.

⁓

Kate returned an hour later, hauling bags of groceries. I put my finger to my lips – Benny was back asleep – and took some of the bags from her.

'You're so good with Benny. He's always calm with you.'

'He finds me boring.'

Kate slapped my arm lightly. 'Were you mansplaining about why Yo-Yo Ma is overrated *again*?'

'It's just, why can there only be one famous cellist at a time?'

'You'll be famous,' she said. 'Then there will be two, which is *definitely* the limit.'

'No way. The next famous cellist is going to be some super-hot young woman. Not a chance that another Asian guy will get the spot.'

'You are half-white, remember,' Kate pointed out. 'And gay. Surely that will help.'

'Maybe the white part will,' I said.

An uneasy silence landed. I always did this. Said the wrong thing. Especially to Kate and Dad. I grabbed a bottle of fudge sauce from the bags.

'Does this mean what I think it does?'

'Yes! I'm going to make sundaes. I got tiny marshmallows,' Kate said.

'Nice.' I put cereal, beans, dry pasta in the cupboards. 'Dad phoned while you were out.'

'I spoke to him. Kate examined a jar of tomato sauce. 'He has to stay on base for longer than expected.'

He'd already been away for four days. 'That sucks.'

'He said he's not happy about it either,' she said shortly.

Dad had stayed at home for two weeks when Benny was born, but then was called away again. He kept talking vaguely about paternity leave, which he would take once things had calmed down. I didn't know what *things* were. There were no new wars, only the same old awful ones.

'If you being free and single means you're here to help on Friday nights then I'll make you sundaes forever,' Kate said.

That sounded bleak, but I didn't want to tell her that. Instead I asked, 'Is a baby a good wingman? Me and Benny could have Friday nights out together.'

'If you're not the dad then, yeah, sure. I feel like a dog might be more effective, but I encourage you to try.' Kate put an arm around my waist and pulled me into a brief hug. 'Thanks, Adam.'

'You don't need to thank me. It's big brother duties, a call which I will always answer.' I saluted.

'You look like your dad when you do that,' Kate said.

'Do I? 'Cause of my military posture?'

'The shape of your face is the same. You're as tall as him now. And your smile – it's like the one when he's *really* happy and gets that big grin.'

It was a good grin. Maybe because it was rare. 'I didn't think I looked much like Dad.'

'As you get older, you do,' Kate said.

Dad resembled an advertisement for the military back in the Second World War. He's got that corn-fed blond thing going on: tall and strong and with good teeth. I could be his shadow. Tall, but with almost-black hair, long brown eyes, skin darker.

Kate patted my arm. 'Choose a movie and I'll make sundaes.'

I went to the living room and stared at my face, reflected faintly in the black TV screen. Kate had listed our similarities so quickly, but I couldn't see them. Kate saw Dad in me because everything else was from my mother, a person she had never known but who was always here in a strange and silent way.

In the reflection of the TV, a flicker over my shoulder. A shape, a watching face. I wrenched myself around but there was nothing, no woman...

The TV turned on. I swung back, but it was only because I'd been holding the remote, and my hand was clenched stupidly tight around it. I concentrated on scrolling through movies until I landed on one that generally made me feel capable of having a fistfight.

Kate came in with a bowl in each hand. *'Mad Max?'*

'Mad Max: Fury Road,' I corrected her.

Kate sat on the couch. 'I thought we were going to watch something we could weep over.'

I didn't ask why Kate needed to weep.

'Post-apocalypse would help me. For perspective.'

I pressed play. The ice cream was so cold and sweet it made my teeth ache. That's why I was shivering, I told myself. Why I had to blink wetness from my eyes.

April 3rd

Obaasama, today I played your biwa. My biwa. I have been afraid to. But I kept thinking of the sound of the strings. In my dreams, I heard them. It was oddly hot today. Almost feverish. The biwa would be cool in my hands, I thought. So I took it out and held the bachi. I played a simple tune, thinking of you, Obaasama. As I did there was the feeling of something approaching, something that wanted to hear. I did not know what it was, why it wanted the music. There were soft footsteps in the hall. All the hair on my body lifted. And then the door opened and O-Suzu said, your uncle is here.

That was not what I had felt approaching. I asked O-Suzu to make tea and then I went to greet him. Uncle was the same, being important and correct in all things. He had hardly finished asking after my health when he told me it was not right for me to live here alone.

I told him I was not alone, that O-Suzu is my companion. But he said O-Suzu is a servant. O-Suzu is intelligent and has run our household for years now. As well as that, she knows about politics and fashion and Kabuki.

Uncle said these were trivial things, aside from politics, which was better for women not to think about. Good wife, wise mother, he said. That is what you should be.

I am tired of hearing this phrase from men like Uncle.

He continued to say we must work for Japan to make it one of the great nations of the world. It is unclear how O-Suzu and I discussing politics will hinder Japan's global status but naturally I did not say so.

Uncle suddenly said he had heard me playing biwa. He had thought it was you, Obaasama. He looked sad and I remembered that he had lost his mother. She would play for hours at night, especially in the summer. She told us it was her job, Uncle said, though she rarely performed for others. I said that Obaasama must have played for herself; at least that's what I always thought. Uncle whispered, for the ghosts. I asked what he meant. He said, your Obaasama's grandfather was a biwa-hōshi, a biwa player. He played heike biwa.

This stirred my memory; heike biwa was a variation of the instrument. I asked him to tell me more, but Uncle replied that it was of no importance to modern Japan. Old beliefs, old superstitions. Foreign religion! Shinto is the proper Japanese religion that honours ancestors and Emperor.

Uncle is displeased that we remain Buddhists when he has converted to Shinto, and before he could further complain about this matter I repeated, tell me about the ghosts.

Instead, Uncle declared it was time I married. I was dismayed. I was not ready and should continue my studies – I had been considering a women's college. And what about Mother? She must have some say in this.

Uncle said eighteen was old enough, and that I had enough education at the girls' school I had graduated from last year. It was my duty to marry and raise a family. He would write to my mother. I lied and said I had planned to study English further, which would be useful to a husband, particularly in Nagasaki. Many important men – businessmen, politicians – wanted wives who could speak some foreign language and have some knowledge of the West. I could support him. For a modern Japan, I said desperately.

Uncle reflected and finally said, that is not a bad idea. You do not have so much in your favour so these skills would be an advantage. He would look for an English tutor but would not put off matchmaking.

I bowed. It was the best that could be done. After Uncle left I went outside and walked up the hill. I looked out over the harbour to the ocean. I could see the horizon but I do not know how I can ever reach it.

Three

Who was she, the writer? The diary must have belonged to my mother but she couldn't have written it... This uncle of hers talked about *modern* Japan but presumably matchmaking had ended there decades ago. The girl who had written these words would be ancient by now. Or dead.

That woman by Benny's cradle came into my mind, her pale face and long hair — no, no. That had been a dream.

I reached into my desk drawer and took out a framed photo. I stared at my mother. Her bobbed black hair made untidy by the wind; her face shaped like a heart. She was holding me, a baby, her mouth in a sweet, lopsided smile. She looked nothing like the woman in the dream.

I rested my hand on the diary cover — my mother must have touched it too, turned the pages. This was something we could share, years apart; I had so little of her. But I could read these same words and if I could understand why my mother had kept them maybe I could understand her more too...

Kate rapped on my door. 'Adam, you've got to leave or you'll be late.'

'Come *on*.' I put the picture away before I opened the door. 'Let me skip this once. Nothing requires a mental health day more than a break-up.'

Kate refused. 'It'll take your mind off it.'

'It will *destroy* my mind. It's all I have left now that my heart is gone.'

'I'm not letting you stay in your room staring at your face. It's not good for your self-confidence.'

'Kate, that is the meanest thing you have ever said to me,' I said.

'Just get going!'

I sighed.

Kate softened her voice. 'You won't have to do Japanese for much longer. It's summer break soon, and then only one more year. I'm assuming you're not going to take it in university.'

'Hell, no.' The only Japanese I intended to encounter would be on restaurant menus and *Sailor Moon*.

'Stick with it and get some closure.' Kate clapped me on the back.

I'd been going to Japanese school every Saturday since I was thirteen, which is when Kate heard about it. Dad hadn't cared much – when I told him I didn't want to go, he'd actually sided with me.

Then I'd heard Kate and Dad arguing about it, her saying I needed to have *some* connection with my heritage. *You can't ignore it,* she'd said. *I thought you were the one that wanted to,* Dad had snapped back. Kate had been quiet for a long time, and I thought that she had lost the argument until I heard her sniff, and knew she was crying.

Anyway, Dad told me I had to go to Japanese classes. We had a big fight. I told Kate I hated her. I was ashamed, remembering it. But I'd been a kid. Every kid tells their parents they hate them on a regular basis, right?

I picked up my Japanese books, then added the diary so I could read it on the bus. I should use the time to go over my Japanese homework but there was no hope for me at this stage. And it wasn't like I was going to Japan any time soon.

April 7th

Obaasama, I have resolved not to give in to despair. It is less boring this way. I gave in to despair for the past several days and it was quite dull. O-Suzu scolded me for being silly and girlish. You knew this would come, she told me, so see what you can make of it.

I wrote to Mother myself and she replied that Uncle was no doubt correct but she would support me if I had some preference in the man I wanted to marry. She apologised for not being with me but I know it is important she nurse Grandfather. Saga is not so far away, but Mother has always been a little distant. I am glad of her support, though I do not think she has enough will to oppose Uncle.

Aside from despair, Uncle did give me matters to consider. You, Obaasama, and the biwa and Uncle's whisper of ghosts. You taught me how to play but not the history and meaning behind the songs. I have begun to practise, in daylight and with O-Suzu near me. I keep myself from the garden, yet I dream of figures beckoning, beseeching me to play in the moonlight. Is it a curse, Obaasama? Though I do not know why I have been cursed. What have I done, what can I do?

April 12th

Obaasama, I feel better today because Uncle has done as he promised. Thankfully it is not regarding marriage – as far as I know – but with an English tutor.

I was bewildered when the tutor arrived this afternoon. He asked if I had not been expecting him and I told him that Uncle can be somewhat forgetful about correspondence, which is true. We settled down easily enough, however.

This tutor reminded me of a heron, with his hair streaked with grey and his somewhat hunched posture, so O-Suzu and I privately refer to him as Sagi-sensei. Sagi-sensei enjoys lecturing. He is serious and rather boring, despite his stories being quite interesting. Sagi-sensei lived in America for some years, but was unable to return after a visit to Japan. While he had been away, the Americans had brought in a law to stop Japanese moving there. Sagi-sensei is still upset about this. He spoke at length about California. I suspect I will hear these stories many more times.

However, he is not a bad teacher. He said that I am not good at speaking or listening. Writing and reading English is easier for me, as I can use the dictionary whenever I need it, which is often. Sagi-sensei does not allow me to do that. Come now, he says, hurry up and get your words out. I become flustered and nervous but I suppose it is good to have a challenge.

Sagi-sensei has given me much to study. He brought newspapers from the Foreign Settlement. I have never been there, though Father went occasionally. Perhaps Sagi-sensei will take me. I must study now. If I fill my head with English grammar perhaps there will be no room for dreams.

Four

♩ ♫ ♪♪ ♩ ♪

I was so engrossed in the diary that I almost missed my stop. Hurrying off the bus, I was jealous of the writer's language skills – every sentence was so beautifully written that saying her English was 'not bad' was a staggering understatement.

I wished I could say the same for my Japanese. I braced myself as I entered the classroom.

'Adam-kun, ohayou gozaimasu!' Takane-sensei greeted me.

Takane-sensei was a jolly sort of guy, the kind of guy dogs really liked.

'Ohayou gozaimasu, sensei,' I mumbled.

'We have a new student this morning,' Takane-sensei said in Japanese. He gestured to a boy sitting by the window.

'I'm not a student!' the boy said, laughing.

'You're an *English* student, Jo-kun!' Takane-sensei replied.

'That's true. Sorry, sensei.' Jo dipped his head, grinning.

'Nice to meet you. I'm Adam.' I bowed self-consciously.

He stood up. 'Nice to meet you too! I'm Mori Jo.' He seemed to be fully Japanese, but with curly hair. I wanted to ask if it was a perm; it looked good. He kept speaking, too rapidly for me.

'One more time please...' This was my most used Japanese phrase.

'Ah.' He switched to English. 'English is better?'

'Japanese only!' Takane-sensei yelled.

I was saved by the entry of the four other kids in the class: Keisuke, Anna, Michael and Yuzuki. They were all better at Japanese than me – and way better at *being* Japanese.

They sat down with a clatter, greeting Takane-sensei and eyeing Jo.

'Ohayou, Adam-kun!' Yuzuki said brightly.

The rest of them *ohayou*-ed and I echoed it. They were nice. Well, Yuzuki was super nice, and the rest fell somewhere between pleasant and indifferent. Five was an annoying number for a class, and I usually ended up paired with Takane-sensei because I needed the most help.

There were *so many* reasons I did not like Japanese school.

Everybody shut up as Jo went to the front of the room. He bowed and proceeded to give a longer version of the introduction he'd given me. I stared at his mouth as if that would help me understand more. He had a nice mouth.

Jo was studying English here for a few months, staying with Takane-sensei, who happened to be his uncle. Takane-sensei had suggested he come along today to make some friends. He was seventeen years old. He liked baseball and music. He was from Nagasaki.

I felt a jolt. That was where the writer of the diary was from.

Takane-sensei called up Keisuke. Now we had to do our introductions, which despite being basic, made my stomach clench.

Keisuke was fully Japanese-from-Japan, but had been living in the US since he was twelve. He was a sporty type, always wearing a baseball cap backwards. We didn't have a lot in common.

Yuzuki was next, half-Japanese and half-Korean. She spoke Japanese *and* Korean fluently, but was so sweet I couldn't even be jealous. She had truly amazing skin. She tried extra hard with me cause I was half-Japanese too. We hung out every now and then and drank bubble tea.

Michael was Sansei Japanese – third generation Japanese American – and was obsessed with manga and anime, constantly drawing in his notebooks. He had the anime boobs down, anyway. The shading on them was disturbingly detailed.

Anna was Vietnamese but was born in Japan and lived there until she was ten. She wanted to go back for university. She was reserved and serious and had had a crush on Keisuke for years, which I sympathised with because he *was* hot in a dumb sports boy kind of way—

'Adam-kun!' Takane-sensei flapped his hand at me.

I mumbled my name, that I was seventeen, I had grown up here, I liked reading and swimming in the sea, I played cello. Jo watched me attentively. My introduction was shorter than everyone else's, so I sat down as fast as I could, before Takane-sensei made me say anything else.

Thankfully, he did not. He clapped his hands and started the lesson. Jo joined in. He was so cheerful, saying that our kanji writing was better than his, acting with enthusiasm for the boring practice conversations, laughing as Takane-sensei scolded him for using too much slang.

'But if they don't know wakamono-kotoba then they will sound old,' Jo protested.

During our lunch break we hung around in the classroom and I tried to follow the conversation, mostly about Japan and mostly in Japanese.

Michael droned on about Akihabara until Jo interrupted by calling him an otaku.

'What's otaku in English?' Jo added.

'Nerd,' Anna supplied.

'I prefer otaku,' Michael said stiffly.

Yuzuki shook her head, grinning. 'Such a nerd thing to say.'

I snorted.

Jo turned to me. 'Adam-kun, have you been to Japan?'

'I was born there. But I left when I was a baby.'

'You should come visit!'

'I want to,' I said unconvincingly.

'One of your parents is Japanese?' he persisted.

'My mum.'

'Do you speak Japanese with your mother?'

I shook my head. Everyone except Jo looked uncomfortable. Yuzuki bit her lip.

Keisuke saved me. 'You like baseball, Jo-kun?'

A flash of puzzlement crossed Jo's face before they began loudly arguing about teams.

Takane-sensei returned and we did grammar, reading comprehensions, writing. Finally, class was done, my brain entirely squeezed out.

I heard Anna inviting Jo to hang out and his loud '*Yes!*'. We left school, the afternoon warm and blessedly free of Japanese particles.

I said goodbye hurriedly, and Jo looked over his shoulder at me. He smiled so genuinely that I found one rising to my face in return.

April 19th

Obaasama, I am at my wits' end. Every night now I see them: shadows forming the figures of people, misty around the edges, but people nonetheless. They are shades of white and grey, faces indiscernible and yet capable of emotion, because how else could I feel their yearning? I think you are there too. It is as if you are all listening.

I do not want to play the biwa but I cannot stop myself because it is important, somehow. I try and try to capture the melody I have dreamed.

O-Suzu tells me the sound is too much to bear, though she has given up trying to make me stop altogether. She proposed I take biwa lessons as I am so eager to study these days. It is not such a bad idea.

I wrote to my old classmate Mumeo. Her father is a music scholar specialising in biwa, and she has often spoken of him. He is famous in Kyushu and Mumeo was proud of it. She replied today, inviting me to visit and speak with her father.

I will go, though I do not know what I will ask. Not about the dreams. But if he can help me find the music... it may help.

—

April 24th

Obaasama, I have lately returned from my visit to Mumeo and her father. I had not seen Mumeo since we graduated last year. She is as lively as ever and spoke excitedly about her recent engagement to a man from Osaka. I realised I have not spent time with a girl my age in a while.

After tea and many more details about Mumeo's life, her father joined us. He is just as talkative yet when I brought up the topic of biwa, he became quieter. Mumeo left us so we could speak alone. I explained that I played biwa only a little, but that you, Obaasama, had been a skilled player. I brought out my biwa and he examined it at length. I told him it had been in my family for at least four generations. He said it was likely far older than that, but unfortunately it is a heike biwa, which he did not play. He took out his own instrument, a satsuma biwa, bigger and longer-necked. He showed me a chikuzen biwa too, which has five strings rather than four and a small, narrow bachi.

He asked me suddenly if you had been blind, Obaasama. Bewildered, I said yes, that you had fallen sick and lost your eyesight before I was born. My great-great-grandfather had been blind, also... He asked how my eyes were and although they are fine, I became concerned. He told me I must have biwa-hōshi in my family, which was rather unusual... The style was an old and particular tradition yet some biwa-hōshi are little more than beggars, he said with disdain. Though this would not be the case for a reputable family such as yours, he added hastily.

Was I familiar with *Heike Monogatari*? he asked. I had read only a few parts of it, but I knew what it was: the long story of the Taira clan and the Minamoto clan and the war between them eight hundred years ago. The ballads played on biwa differ from the written account, he said. You have never heard them? I said no and then I said yes, because there came a recollection of you, Obaasama, sitting with your biwa and singing a kind of chant, recounting a story... He told me he could not teach heike biwa but would ask other teachers. There were few now, and as I was a girl there may be fewer willing to instruct me. Fifty years ago, there would have been many, now it was not popular, not modern, not fitting for the Meiji era...

I bowed and thanked him. I said goodbye to Mumeo. I took my biwa and came home.

April 28th

Heike Monogatari was among my father's old books, Obaasama. It is largely war and politics, of how Taira no Kiyomori wanted power and more power until he was mightier than the Emperor, and lost wisdom and virtue along the way. To the demise of his whole family...

There was an odd pressure, as though a typhoon was approaching. I plucked the biwa, closing my eyes to feel what it would be like to play that way, seeing with fingers and sensing the strings and feeling the bachi with my other senses. What else did you see that way, Obaasama?

37

Five

♩ ♫ ♪♪ ♩ ♪

I stopped to look up *Heike Monogatari* and found an extremely long Wikipedia article about it. In English it's called *The Tale of the Heike*, a twelfth-century epic about two powerful families: the Taira (also called the Heike) and the Minamoto (aka the Genji). They had fought for control of Japan, sparking the Genpei War. The main themes of the work were the samurai code of battle and bravery, and the Buddhist beliefs of duty and karma... I skimmed the page and saw summaries of its twelve chapters, a thousand characters' names and an instantly confusing plot, and my eyes blurred with boredom.

Did it actually have some mystical power? The writer of the diary believed that, but probably everybody did back then. Even though she hadn't written when *back then* was—

No. *She* hadn't, but that biwa guy had. I scanned the pages again – he had mentioned the Meiji era. I left the dull *Heike* summaries to find when that was. My excitement subsided when I learned that the era, defined by the rule of the Meiji

Emperor, had lasted from 1868 to 1912. I had narrowed it down to a forty-four year period that had ended more than a hundred years ago…

My phone lit up with a message from Sylvia.

see you at 2, i know you wont be late

I swore and started pulling on clean clothes. Sylvia didn't know everything. I was absolutely going to be late.

———

'Why can't you just let me eat two tubs of mint choc chip ice cream like Kate did?' I complained.

I didn't mean it. I was glad to get out of the house.

'Because I'm not your *mum*.' Sylvia wrenched me forward. 'Or *parental figure*. And mint choc chip is gross.'

I moaned like a humpback whale.

'Is that your sex noise?' Sylvia asked. 'Because if it is—'

'It is *not*,' I hissed.

We were in the middle of the street on a Sunday afternoon. People were staring.

'I'm not kink shaming. Everybody should make the sex noises that fulfil them. Listen, everyone—' Sylvia could not physically resist an opportunity to give a public speech.

Now it was me hauling her along. She giggled until I had to as well, and we staggered into our favourite taco place, trying to catch our breath as we looked at the menu.

Sylvia pushed me towards a table. 'I'm buying.'

'Then I'll have ten—'

'Your order has been the same for five years and it's *never* ten of anything! Sit.'

I got a table by the window. I'd had the same order for five years? I stared out at the street, wincing at the sight of stupid couples on their stupid little walks.

Sylvia banged a tray down in front of me.

I picked up a taco. 'Thanks, Syl.' I ate it fast, suddenly starving.

Sylvia watched me lick my fingers. 'All sorrows ease with bread, and are totally vanquished with tacos.'

'Is that a traditional Italian saying?'

'It's *my* traditional Italian saying.'

Sylvia's whole family is Italian, though she'd never been to Italy – and nobody grilled *her* about why. She could have a conversation in Italian with her relatives, could cook with them, celebrate special days; those things you do when you belong to a culture.

'How do you feel today?' Sylvia assembled her I'm-here-for-you-and-creating-space face.

I shrugged.

'Has he messaged you or anything?'

'Nah. We said we wouldn't.' *He* said we shouldn't. 'I don't know if this is a for-real break up or a break.'

'Like last time, you mean?' Sylvia asked.

I twiddled with the empty taco wrappers.

'I thought you guys explicitly agreed it was a break last time. You *knew*.'

'He just needs space again. Like, I get that,' I said defensively.

She looked so skeptical that I stood up before she could say anything else. 'Let's get out of here.'

Sylvia let me be quiet until we reached the pier. I rested my elbows on the railing and studied the murky water.

'I thought we were good together,' I muttered.

'He might have some other messed-up idea of what good or great is. Or,' Sylvia gave me a *solved it!* look, 'it was *too* good and he couldn't handle it.'

'I don't think that was it.'

'Some people love drama and think good is boring.'

'Am I boring?' I asked.

'No way,' Sylvia said. 'You're amazing and kind and thoughtful.'

I looked at her closely, her auburn hair twirling down her back, her glittering earrings and prettiness.

She scowled. 'Why are you staring at me like I'm a taco.'

And she was funny *and* she was smart.

I was wearing black jeans and a white T-shirt. I dropped my head onto the railing. 'I am so boring.'

'You are so dramatic is what.'

'You said some people like that.'

'I'm not those people. I don't think you need to change.' Sylvia put her arm around me.

We watched the water for a while.

'Let's walk,' I said.

We strolled along the boardwalk, watching a man chase a seagull which had snatched an entire bag of fish and chips out of his hand.

'You want to do something tonight?' Sylvia asked.

'Some hardcore moping?'

'I'm not doing that,' Sylvia said firmly. 'I'll allow you this weekend. But next week Tia's having a party, and we should go.'

'Will there be people there?'

'It's a party.' Sylvia pulled her phone out. 'Let's do a Google image search to check what that means.'

I grabbed the phone from her hand and held it above her head. 'What is Google?'

'Gimme my phone!' Sylvia reached for it but I was a head taller than her.

'What is phone?' I asked.

She yelled to the normal people nearby, 'He is a bully! Do not be complacent!'

'Okay, okay.' I handed her phone back. 'Don't turn a mob on me.'

'Are you kidding? Nobody even moved. It is not the violence of our enemies but the *silence* of our friends.' She glared at the innocent bystanders.

'They're not your friends,' I said.

'And they never will be!' she vowed.

'You were talking about a party,' I reminded her.

'Oh yeah. The party. You're coming.'

'Absolutely.' I was already planning excuses for next weekend, and the one after and the one after that.

'Then, my friend, we shall have a good time.'

'The best,' I lied.

We walked along, the seagulls shrieking overhead, searching for something to steal.

May 2nd

I had an unannounced and interesting visitor today, Obaasama. A biwa-hōshi came! And what a coincidence – the biwa-hōshi is a woman and said that she knew you, Obaasama! When I asked how, she replied only that like calls to like. She said that you were a gifted player and could have performed for audiences, but that you had a home and family to take care of.

The biwa-hōshi is pure in a way that I cannot explain. She is exacting and patient. She taught me the beginning of *Heike Monogatari,* and I played it again and again until she was satisfied. Now the words, she said, and though they were famous enough that I already knew them, I was afraid to sing. She did not ask why I was frightened.

Instead she sang while I played. She could tell where my fingers were and how I was holding the bachi by sound alone. For she is blind, and says she sees the world in her own fashion. I asked why biwa-hōshi are often blind and she said it was an old belief that those who could not see this world could look into the other; that they were a bridge. It took me some courage to ask her why this should be so important for those who play heike biwa. She told me because those who tell *Heike Monogatari* are not telling it only for the living; we tell it for the dead.

She said: I will come again and until then you must practise. Do not worry if you do not play perfectly. There are other things you may play, if you feel it is right. Listen and play with respect. I asked who I should listen to and she took my hand, the hand holding the bachi, and said I already knew. Be careful, she warned, for those that listen must be appeased.

~

May 4th

Obaasama, an uncanny thing – I wrote to Mumeo's father to thank him for sending me a teacher. He replied without delay and said he had not yet acquired one. He asked who had come to me. I am sleepy; I will rest and then compose a message in reply.

~

May 6th

Dear Obaasama, I am exhausted – yet sleep is beyond me. O-Suzu says I have been pale and distracted since the biwa-hōshi visited. My dreams are filled with figures of mist and some half-forgotten song. You are trying to tell me something. Why did you not tell me while you were alive? Perhaps you intended to – you were not so old, really; your illness was swift and sudden – but now there is something wrong with me. I am searching... for what? I am afraid. O-Suzu is telling me to lie down – she has brought me rice porridge like you used to make. How I wish you were here, real and alive and not the shadow I see in the dark when I close my eyes...

Six

♩ ♫ ♪ ♩ ♪

The shadow in the dark.

The back of my neck prickled. I resisted the urge to turn around, and prepared to read on before realising it was past midnight and now *Monday*. I had to finish literally all of my homework. I put away the diary with both reluctance and relief. I had work to do.

Monday morning was irritatingly bright and fresh. I got through my classes until lunch, the real test.

I wanted to sit where I could keep an eye out for Evan, but Sylvia knowingly pulled me to a table outside, as far away as possible. We waved over Art and Carmen and Rosie.

My eyes snagged on Evan as soon as he came through the doors. He sat with his friends, and joked and talked and ate as though everything was normal and nothing had changed.

'Um, Adam?' Rosie said.

They were staring at me.

'Huh?' I said.

'You and Evan broke up?'

'How did you know?'

'Because you're watching him like a sad puppy,' Art said. 'Also, Sylvia told us.'

'Sylvia,' I groaned, but my heart wasn't in it.

'You okay?' Art asked.

I shrugged.

'I always thought he was annoying,' Carmen said. 'Him and his sporty pals.'

'They play *tennis*,' Rosie cut in. 'They're not apex predators.'

Evan glanced over and everybody whipped their heads around to stare at the sky or the ground in highly indiscreet ways. I met his eyes before he looked back down at his lunch.

What did I expect? For him to run over and press me back against the bench to kiss me? That would be so hot. I lingered on the thought before I shook myself.

'It's over,' I said, half to myself, half to the table.

'We're here for you,' Carmen comforted me.

Art silently handed me a banana.

'Thanks,' I said.

My last class was orchestra. I sat with my cello, pulling it between my knees, my left arm looped around it. The cello is one of the few instruments you can hold like a person. That's why I wanted to play it.

We warmed up, my favourite sound. The instruments were waking, stretching, reaching out into the world. It made me think of the biwa in the diary, and the writer learning to play it.

Could music be a bridge to another world, to the ghosts she saw — *thought* she saw?

Mr Johnson tapped his pen against his music stand. He never had a baton. He started droning on about the percussion. I prayed that he wouldn't start his repertoire of mean jokes about drummers.

We finally started playing and then it was better — the smooth push and pull of the bow, my calloused fingers firm on the strings.

'Hold on, everyone,' Mr Johnson said.

I stifled a sigh. We rarely got to play a piece the whole way through because Mr Johnson stopped us after a single wrong note or the slightest hint of an incorrect change in tempo. We restarted. For a contented three minutes my cello hummed and sang. Then another stop. I rested my head against the side of the neck.

'That bad?'

It was Daniel, who played the violin and always sat on my right. He was pretty nice. And also gay. And Asian. I suspected he had a crush on me. Lately, he was a bit awkward when we talked. Blushing, avoiding my gaze.

'*So* tired of this,' I said. 'He's the worst.'

Daniel rolled his eyes in Mr Johnson's direction. 'Do you think he secretly hates music? Is that why he can't listen to it for more than two minutes?'

'I mean, I can't even listen to *him* for one minute—'

'Adam, you must be having a riveting conversation with Elwin,' Mr Johnson snapped.

'Sorry...' I muttered.

'I'm not Elwin,' Daniel said.

Mr Johnson peered at him.

'Elwin's on viola.' Daniel pointed at Elwin, who just so happened to also be Asian.

Elwin held up his viola and gave Mr Johnson a dead stare. 'Viola,' he enunciated.

'I know the difference between a viola and a—'

'A Singaporean?' Elwin asked.

Mr Johnson hmphed. 'All right, sorry about that... Daniel.' He shuffled away, adding, 'But both of you better stop talking and pay attention!'

One hundred years later, the class ended. I picked my stuff up, glancing over at Daniel.

He saw me looking. 'What a racist asshole.' He glared at Mr Johnson, who had cornered the drummer and was lecturing her. The drummer was definitely stoned.

'I mean, a violin and a viola do look pretty similar.'

Daniel didn't laugh. 'I guess so.'

We walked to our lockers.

'Sorry,' I rushed out. 'My brain is not with me today. I kinda got dumped last week so... Would've been nice to play and forget about it for a while.'

'I'm sorry to hear that.' He sounded sincere.

Daniel was becoming cuter and cuter.

May 10th

Obaasama, I am finally well enough to hold a pen, though my writing is slow and my fingers weak. I was ill for three days. I felt caught in a dream or some place between waking and sleep. I saw things... O-Suzu said I could not eat and drank only cold water. When she said she would call for the doctor I screamed and begged that she bring no doctor here...

So instead O-Suzu prayed to the ancestors. I have a memory of her opening the door to the garden to let in fresh air, and I saw it crowded with figures, as though a fog had come down from the mountains. You were there, Obaasama, holding the other ghosts back. But they were not enraged, they were lost. They were concerned for me. They did not want me to die. I could see them more distinctly than before. Some were dressed finely, others wore rags. Behind them were ghosts wearing armour, holding weapons.

My hand is tired. My head clouds too much to think. I feel compelled to play biwa but I do not think I have the strength to hold the strings down.

May 14th

I arose with determination and more strength today, Obaasama. I have been dwelling on what the biwa-hōshi taught me, yet I am reluctant to play... Will I become sick again? There is peril and I must protect myself.

I decided to confess to O-Suzu that you, Obaasama, were appearing to me in dreams, but made no mention of other ghosts. I reassured her that I did not believe you meant any harm. O-Suzu asked, if no harm was meant then why did you fall so ill? I had no answer for this; of course, O-Suzu saw it was because of my sickness that I was telling her this at all. However, she did not lose her head; she said she had known things were amiss and this was as good an explanation as any. I asked if she was not afraid and she said, no, not if it was you, Obaasama, who was appearing to me. Yet it was best to exercise caution when regarding spirits.

I was humbled by O-Suzu's good sense, though I refrained from speaking about the biwa and ghosts, because she would demand I completely stop playing biwa and that would be too sensible a solution for me to argue against. I suggested we go to the temple and O-Suzu agreed immediately.

We went to the temple where your funeral rites had been held, Obaasama, and Father's. We washed our hands and fanned incense over ourselves before praying. We requested to speak with the priest who performed your rites. I explained my situation – again, omitting the mention of any spirit but you, Obaasama. He said that ghosts appeared if they had business left undone or if they were driven by a strong emotion, such as jealousy or rage. The worst of these became hungry ghosts. I said that you had no such motivations. The priest asked if there was anything you had asked me to do. I hesitated before saying I thought you wanted me to play music. Then, because I was curious as to what the priest might know of biwa, I added that I was learning the *Heike Monogatari*.

The priest's expression dimmed. Have you not heard of Hoichi the Earless? I shook my head and he said, never mind, it is only a story. He asked if I was married, and was oddly relieved when I said no. Once you are married you will have less time for such activities and thoughts, he said. Young women are excitable, and many come here for help. Upon hearing this, I was glad I had said nothing of the other ghosts because doubtless it would have been dismissed as some girlish fear. Or worse, it might be taken far too seriously...

The priest was of the opinion my grandmother was merely concerned for me – this, Obaasama, is not untrue. The dead live on with us, he said, so respect them and pray for them. As a precaution he prepared ofuda talismans to keep unclean spirits away. O-Suzu appeared much comforted, which heartened me. I presented an offering and we went to the cemetery, where we cleaned your grave and put out fresh flowers.

As we left, I suggested we walk by the water so that we may have a cool breeze. We strolled beside the river, the dock visible in the distance. We do not go there, as it is rough and perhaps dangerous, though I would like to visit. There are ships from different parts of the world carrying different people.

We did see some foreigners: a group of three Chinese men, wearing silks of blue and black. As we crossed the bridge over the river, we passed two men who must have been from the American ships. Their uniforms were smart and shining. One said, good afternoon, ladies. I said thank you, it was certainly fair weather. This made the men stop. They were surprised. The other said my English was so good, would I stay and talk to them awhile? I considered it, out of curiosity, and we stood for a moment in the middle of the bridge before O-Suzu pulled me away. No, no, she said to the men.

She marched me up the hill and to quieter streets. What do you think the Americans would have talked about, Obaasama?

———

May 16th

Obaasama, forgive me for not finishing my previous entry. I became too tired to continue. Perhaps I am not as recovered as I thought.

When we returned home from the temple, I asked O-Suzu about Hoichi the Earless. I wonder if it was you who told it to me, Obaasama, for as O-Suzu recounted the story I realised I did know it. It happened not so far away in Amidaji. It goes like this:

Long, long ago, there was a biwa player called Hoichi. He lived in a little temple where he had almost nothing, but where the priest was a friend. Hoichi was a skilled player, especially of The Tale of the Heike. *One night,*

Hoichi went to sleep in his hut as a storm approached. The wind was rising and shrieked and tore about outside.

At first, Hoichi thought it was the wind that sounded like words. But there was a knock, and a voice called. Hoichi went to the door, where a gruff man waited. He was a samurai, sent by his master, who wanted to hear Hoichi play. It was late, but Hoichi did not argue, for it was best not to anger samurai or their lords. He was led to the daimyo, and Hoichi understood that he was powerful, for the house was large and there was the sound of many voices. Hoichi played, and the daimyo praised him. Hoichi guessed he must be old, by the age in his voice and his manner of speaking. The daimyo said that Hoichi's skill was such that even the oni must weep to hear him play The Tale of the Heike. The samurai brought Hoichi back and forbade him from speaking of the performance, as his lord was travelling secretly.

The next night the samurai returned, as his lord wanted to hear Hoichi play more. Hoichi was pleased and went to the daimyo's house and played and again the daimyo praised him. However, on this night the temple priest discovered that Hoichi was gone and was alarmed, for the weather was stormy. In the morning, the priest asked where he had been. Hoichi, heeding the samurai's warning, did not tell him. The priest perceived something unnatural was at work. That night he watched Hoichi's hut, and saw him leave after midnight. The priest followed Hoichi to the temple cemetery, where he saw him play his biwa, surrounded by nothing but gravestones. The priest pulled Hoichi away, in terror, for he had been tricked by ghosts.

Because Hoichi could not see; he was blind as all biwa players are.

The priest painted the characters of the Heart Sutra on every part of Hoichi's body, for this would render him invisible to the spirits. When the samurai came the following night, Hoichi sat motionless and silent as the priest had instructed. The samurai became enraged and hunted about the hut, but saw only Hoichi's ears, which he ripped off to take to his ghostly lord in vengeance. Hoichi still did not move, though blood ran from his head, covering the sutras on his body.

When the priest came, he was horrified and remorseful, realising he had forgotten to write on Hoichi's ears. However, the ghosts did not return and Hoichi's wounds healed. He continued to play and became sought after. His performance of The Tale of the Heike became famed; for Hoichi never forgot the spirits he had played for. After all, the story of the Taira is told so that the living will remember the dead.

This made me fear the ghosts in a way that I had not before. O-Suzu said that the Taira ghosts had been rich and powerful, and those people demanded obedience and took what they wanted. But *Heike Monogatari* begins with the lesson that the mighty cannot last, that everything must pass. I suppose the ghosts need to hear it because they would forget that, otherwise.

O-Suzu said perhaps Hoichi was a warning. She spoke lightly but I could tell she meant it. I argued that Hoichi played *Heike Monogatari* for a long time, and it was only once that he had fallen ill of the ghosts. What if he had played the third night, as the ghost had requested? O-Suzu looked suspicious though she did not attempt to dissuade me from playing. She merely asked if she should write a sutra on me, not forgetting my ears.

I asked if she knew all of the *Heart Sutra*. She confessed she did not. Neither did I, and we were rather embarrassed as it is famous. I do know the essence of it, Obaasama, though I do not understand it: *Form is emptiness, and emptiness is form.*

Seven

The week slugged by, busy and yet agonisingly slow. I had researched the Hoichi story and it was real – a real story, that is. It hadn't led me to any more information about the diary. All it had done was make me fear more for the writer.

And now exams were coming up, out of nowhere, and I spent every night cramming until I couldn't think straight. The diary kept intruding but I didn't have the time or concentration to read it... For some reason it took me ages to get through a page, probably because I wasn't used to reading cursive handwriting. Even so, I couldn't help but think of it, touch it. I wished the writer had signed her name. Then I'd know what to call her in my mind.

On Friday, Sylvia reminded me about Tia's party and ordered that I go. I lied and agreed.

In orchestra I asked Daniel if he was going to the party too. He was blushing one minute and being cold the next. I decided that was his flirting method and flirted back.

'I might go,' Daniel said. 'You?'

'Should I?' I said

'Do you like parties?'

'Not really,' I said honestly.

'Then... maybe you shouldn't force yourself?'

Shit. I'd forgotten the first rule of flirting: never tell the truth.

Mr Johnson glared at us and we shut up. He started to go on about the final exam, a solo piece performed in front of the class. My nightmare. I loved playing by myself, and with a teacher, fine, but solo in front of an audience was torture. That's why orchestra was good – I worked enough to ensure Mr Johnson didn't pick me out.

When the bell rang I went past Daniel and straight to Mr Johnson.

'Excuse me, about the final performance – do we *have* to do it in front of everyone?' I asked.

Mr Johnson tapped his pen irritably. 'Yes. That's why it's called a performance.'

'We didn't do that last year.'

'Tests get harder the older you get. They're *tests*,' Mr Johnson said tersely.

I hated him. 'Right.'

I went back to pack up my stuff. Daniel had gone.

May 20th

Last night, Obaasama, I took up the biwa and my courage and carried both to the garden. The story of Hoichi had been intended as a warning and indeed I fear the ghosts, yet I understood more clearly what it is they seek. And I had not been tricked like poor Hoichi; the biwa-hōshi had taught me. Though much remains unknown to me, I knew where it was I was going, and who I was playing for.

The garden was soon full of the mist and shadow left by the dead. My hands trembled as I held the biwa and shook as I played the first notes, so that the sound wavered. I thought of the biwa-hōshi and played the beginning of *Heike Monogatari*, and some of the ghosts came closer; those old warriors. I tried to be brave.

My voice cracked as for the first time I sang the words. I was not powerful like the biwa-hōshi; my voice was thin and had only as much substance as the ghosts. They still recognised it. A shiver went through them. They listened to my missed notes and clumsy fingers, my unsure voice. When I reached the ballad's end they waited. I had thought they would leave. The old ghosts had faded a little, the others remained. You remained, Obaasama. I could do no more. I bowed. I apologised and gave thanks. I closed the door. My fear had not left me. Had I done enough? But I slept well and did not dream, because outside the night was quiet.

———

May 27th

Obaasama, I thought that some of my troubles had eased... unfortunately that is not the case. Sagi-sensei came today and scolded me as usual for my slow English speaking, though personally I think I have improved. We had almost finished when O-Suzu informed us that Uncle had arrived. Sagi-sensei was alarmed – perhaps he thought his teaching ability was to be judged – but I explained that Uncle simply had a habit of visiting without notice.

Uncle began questioning my English progress and asked if I was ready for marriage. He directed this at Sagi-sensei, as if I was not present. I must have had an unhappy expression because Sagi-sensei said earnestly that any man would be fortunate to marry me. He added that in America women in good society were expected to converse about matters of the world, and knowledge was valued. Uncle said that we were in Japan, not America, and Sagi-sensei said yes, but Japan should be America's equal. Uncle replied, not equal but superior! Sagi-sensei agreed and then Uncle realised he had argued against himself.

Uncle announced that he had spoken to a matchmaker and potential husbands would be brought to us shortly. Sagi-sensei assured him that there would be excellent offers. Uncle looked doubtful. It was one of the rare occasions in which Uncle and I shared the same opinion. I poured tea and listened to Uncle and Sagi-sensei discuss the anarchists that had been executed several months earlier. Uncle became particularly animated about Kanno Sugako, the demon woman, as he called her. He went on to praise Japan's continued improvement of Chōsen.

Kanno is not exactly admirable though O-Suzu and I have read some of her essays and consider her ideas compelling – aside, that is, of murder. I know little of Chōsen or Japan's other colonies overseas, but I noticed that Uncle spoke about Kanno and women and the native people of Chōsen in much the same way: as though we are unintelligent and base. It may be my contrary nature, Obaasama, that makes me distrust Uncle's high opinion of what Japan does abroad.

After Uncle had finally departed, I asked Sagi-sensei if it was true what he had said about American women and he said, sometimes.

O-Suzu told me I may well get what I want. I asked if she meant my desire to stay unmarried and continue studying. She laughed and said no, certainly not, but a husband who has dealings with the wider world and wanted an intelligent wife. She said that was the best I could hope for. How have I become so caught, Obaasama, in these complexities of living and dying, bound to duties as if my life is not my own?

Eight

♩ ♫ ♪♪ ♩ ♪

'**K**anno Sugako,' I said aloud.

I felt a jolt of excitement: this was the first full name written in the diary. I grabbed my laptop and searched, and results appeared, along with a grainy black and white photo of a determined-looking young woman.

I read about her eagerly: a feminist journalist who wrote about gender equality – *very* cool. Okay, she was involved in a failed anarchist plot to assassinate the emperor... but hey, she had ambitions. And had been executed for them – in January 1911.

So this diary was being written in 1911. More than a hundred years ago ..

A piece of the puzzle, solved with a death. I tried to ignore the ominousness of that. In the rational light of my laptop screen, I clicked on link after link about Kanno Sugako, until I was led to *Reflections on the Way to the Gallows*, which she had written in prison. Another diary.

I found myself stuck on one line, and read it over and over:

*What are we puny things fighting about – in the
midst of eternal time and boundless sky?*

It gave me perspective. I decided I'd go to the party.

———

As soon as I got there I knew it was a bad idea. I couldn't see
Sylvia anywhere, and she hadn't read the message I'd sent
saying that I was on my way.

I wandered round to the big garden at the back where
there were trees and fairy lights, deckchairs and a barbecue.
Tia was handing a burger to someone and eating another
herself. She was a tall white girl who was captain of the
soccer team and always wore cute floral dresses, apart from
when she was playing a game. She regularly got sent off for
rough play and was generally feared after she told a ref she
would murder his dog.

'Hey, Tia, thanks for having me.'

'What's up, Adam,' she said. 'Wanna burger?'

'I'm good. Have you seen Sylvia?'

Tia chewed thoughtfully. 'Think I saw her in the garden.'

'Cool. I'll hunt for her.'

'Oh, and...'

'Yeah?'

'Sorry to hear you guys broke up.' Her face was sympathetic
and splashed with ketchup.

'Right. Thanks.' I backed away before she could ask me
anything else.

Did everyone know? I guessed Sylvia told her... I was
getting annoyed at Sylvia.

The garden was shadowy, and people were kissing behind the trees. Others were sitting on the grass or on blankets, but none of them was her.

I checked my phone again – she'd read my messages now. I sent another: *you in the yard?* It went to straight to read.

Was I interrupting *her* making out? There was a couple by the nearest tree, and I tried to peer at them without seeming like a pervert. It *was* someone I knew, but it wasn't Sylvia. It was Evan.

I knew I had to look away but I couldn't, like pressing down on a bruise. Somebody approached, tapping Evan on the shoulder, gesturing with a phone. The screen lit her face.

'Sylvia?' I said.

They turned: Sylvia, Evan and the other boy, whose hand was still on Evan's shoulder. It looked like I'd been spying on them.

'Adam,' she said.

'You didn't reply,' I said, stupidly.

Evan stepped back and the other boy turned out to be Daniel.

'Hi,' he said, having the decency to be embarrassed.

So he should be – had he gone straight after Evan when I'd told him we broke up? Or even *before* – maybe he was the reason why Evan dumped me. And Sylvia—

'Sylvia, why are *you* here?' I asked.

'We were talking earlier. I was about to go, and thought I'd say bye.' Her words were reasonable, which had the opposite effect of irritating me more.

'You interrupted a make-out session for that? And were you planning to avoid me and just leave?' A part of my rational mind whispered that it wasn't her fault but my anger stomped it out.

'I mean, I was going to *find* you—'

'Don't be mad at Sylvia,' Evan cut in.

'You can't tell me not to be *anything* anymore, remember?' I glanced from him to Daniel. 'Didn't take you long, did it? You are such a liar.'

Evan stepped towards me. 'Why's that?'

'You told me there wasn't anybody else, you just needed space for yourself. All that bullshit.'

'That wasn't a lie!' Evan said.

'Didn't look like there was much space between you and *Daniel*.'

'Hey, Adam, I'm sorry about this,' Daniel muttered.

'Were you pretending to feel bad for me the other day? And talking to Evan all along?'

'No...' he said, unconvincingly.

Evan moved closer until he was right in my face and I had to tilt my head to meet his eyes. I hated when he did that.

'Don't talk to him like that,' Evan said. 'He doesn't have anything to do with this. We broke up, and I'm sorry you're not happy about that. But it's over between us.'

'What do you have, yellow fever or something?' I hissed. 'Need someone more Asian than me?'

Daniel made a noise of discomfort.

'Adam, come on,' Sylvia pleaded.

Evan leaned back. 'What are you saying?'

'You know what I mean!'

'Just, please, stop it,' he said. 'You are so desperate.'

That was not a lie. The truth of it slapped me across the face. I put my palms on Evan's chest and pushed with as much force as I could muster.

He staggered and his eyes narrowed. He shoved me with fast, fierce hands and as always I was powerless against them. I stumbled and fell, the ground knocking the wind out of me, or maybe I couldn't breathe anyway. I sprawled, my hands gripping the grass, as Sylvia yelled at Evan to stop.

'I didn't push him that hard!' A sudden crease of worry crossed his face. He held out a hand to me but said, 'You started it.'

I picked myself up. My tongue felt coated with dirt even though my mouth hadn't touched anything.

Daniel was alarmed, his eyes moving between me and Evan. I was vaguely aware of people around, staring at us from the dim corners of the garden.

'You,' I said to Evan, 'can't do this to me.'

'All right, sorry I pushed you, sorry you fell over.' His voice was impatient and embarrassed.

Sylvia was at my side, glaring at Evan. 'Are you hurt?'

I pulled myself away. 'I'm going.'

She called after me but I was already passing the barbecue and its sickening smell of hot meat.

Tia was still there. 'You wanna burger now?'

'Thanks, but I've got to go.'

'Everything okay?' she asked.

'I fell,' I said vacantly, and then I left.

June 1st

I was reading *Heike Monogatari* today, Obaasama. Although it is long and full of men's names, I have become intrigued by the politics and battles. Amidst the long downfall of the powerful Taira there is beauty and honour, though I have lost count of the dead.

On an illustrated page there was a drawing, a strange butterfly that was familiar to me. It was the mon of the Taira clan, the family crest. Odd for such a mighty family to be represented by this delicate and pretty creature. I kept thinking of you, Obaasama. Had you shown me this picture? I recognise it in a way I cannot place.

June 4th

The biwa-hōshi came yesterday, Obaasama. Half in jest, I asked her about Hoichi the Earless and if it was a true story. She asked if a true story really exists. I thought and said that perhaps every story was both true and untrue.

She said: there is a balance. An understanding. An exchange. To tell a story, to know one, to receive one. A story heard is a story told. Those who die for a story must live through it. If she was speaking of the Taira family, I do not think they died for a story. They died from power and pride and *became* one.

When you pick up the biwa, what do you play? she asked. I told her I was practising the first ballads of *Heike Monogatari*. I also play the simpler songs I learned from you, Obaasama. She asked who listened to them. Ordinary people, was my best reply.

So you should listen to them as they listen to you. Ordinary people have stories, too. The Taira, well, they must be reminded of their tales and shown that they are remembered, she told me. Yet there are many without epics composed in their honour, I said, and those stories are not done. That is correct, the biwa-hōshi said. Surely it is not I who must finish them? I asked in some disbelief.

This frightened me, Obaasama. The biwa-hōshi merely smiled. How do I finish the story of another? I asked desperately. She said it depends on the story, and it was for me to think on. But I do not know, I said. Listen and learn, the biwa-hōshi told me. She was stern. I asked if that was what she had done.

She said, It is what I still do. I did not want her to go. I do not understand everything that she said. There is a kind of question, so I must find the answer.

—

June 13th

Obaasama, I dreamed of butterflies until I woke in the dark. Halfway between sleeping and waking, I went to the garden. I recalled the biwa-hōshi's advice: to listen. I saw you, Obaasama. There was something different about you, as if this was a special occasion. Then you were gone into the night. I returned to my futon, puzzled.

In the afternoon, O-Suzu brought me a roll of silk because a fabric seller had come calling with his goods. It was a blue-grey silk, patterned with chrysanthemums. She thought I might like it because of my name. I stared at it and all of a sudden I remembered. I told O-Suzu I had no need for fabric now.

I went to your old tansu, Obaasama. I opened it up, took your kimono out one by one until I found it. Your black tomesode, worn for formal occasions. I cannot remember when you wore it last. I unfolded it carefully. There, on the back below the collar, was the mon of the family you had before you were married. It was a butterfly. Not the same as the Taira mon, but simpler. It would have been difficult to recognize it as a butterfly, if I had not been thinking of it. Your mother had given it to you, Obaasama, as her mother had given it to her... How many generations of women had worn this? And now it is mine.

———

June 17th

So, Obaasama, you have spoken to me. I write this by dawning sun so I do not forget. When I awoke I did not at first know it was nighttime, for the room was filled with light, the moon round and the sky unclouded, and by that light I dressed myself in your tomesode – *my* tomesode. And in the garden, I lingered.

You came, Obaasama, wearing the same kimono, or your remembrance of it. Perhaps you had told me these words before and it was my fault for forgetting. You said:

Long ago there was a war, and as in any war there were soldiers who fled. They fled before battles in fear, and after battles in defeat. Some went alone, others brought their families. The victors hunted them, and so these soldiers hid. They went high into the mountains and deep into forests. There they settled. Years passed. Generations died and were born. Far from others, how could they know the war was over, that the victors had been defeated in their turn?

There were tales told by hunters who had come across these villages, who had met graceful women and strong men, speaking like nobles of some ancient time. Occasionally these men would return with a beautiful and bewildered wife, and these countryside families became known for the grace and refinement of their daughters. And people would say, Ah yes, their grandmother or mother came down from the mountains, you know... I heard the echo of your laughing voice, Obaasama. An image came into my mind: butterflies escaping the reaching hands of captors.

Nine

♩ ♫ ♪♪♩ ♪

Out of the corner of my eye I caught a quick motion, and my heart stuttered. I put the diary down slowly and turned to find nothing. The house had been empty when I'd got back, and I'd started reading to stop myself from reliving the party over and over. Evidently the escapism had worked a bit too well.

But then – again, a movement.

I'd forgotten to close the curtains. I went to my window. On the other side of the glass was a cobweb. A butterfly was caught in it. My breath rasped and stuck in my throat. I should break the cobweb and set it free, but I couldn't bring myself to open the window. A spider was already making its way to the butterfly. Spiders had to eat too, didn't they?

I couldn't watch, though. I backed out of my room.

And realised there were voices downstairs, footsteps...

'Adam? Are you here?'

'Kate.' I rushed down, relieved.

'And me.'

'Dad!' I said. 'I didn't know you were coming home.'

'Surprise.' He smiled.

'I'm going to put Benny down.' Kate tiptoed away.

'Heard you were at a party,' Dad said. 'How was it?'

'Not great.'

I waited for him to ask why, but instead he held up a paper bag.

'Are you hungry? We brought back leftovers.'

'No thanks.'

'Well, we can have dinner together tomorrow,' Dad said.

'Home for long?' I asked.

Kate rejoined us and answered for him. 'Till Tuesday.'

Dad nodded, glancing at Kate apologetically.

Kate was staring at me. 'Adam, you've got dirt all over your jeans.' She moved behind me. 'And your shirt. What happened?'

I'd forgotten to change. 'I tripped over in the yard,' I lied. 'It was kinda dark. I'm fine.'

Kate brushed at my shirt. 'Or were you rolling around in the grass with someone?' she teased.

'No!' I said, too fast and too angrily.

Kate's hands fell to her sides. Dad frowned.

The baby monitor crackled, and Benny shrieked.

'I'll go to him,' I said, to escape.

Kate opened her mouth but before I could find out if she was sorry or angry, Dad spoke over her. 'Thanks, Adam.'

I climbed the stairs towards Benny's reaching voice. He was tossing and turning, illuminated by nightlights. When he saw me his cries rose.

I cradled him and he quietened, but soft sobs hiccupped in his chest. He craned his head, seeking.

'It's just me,' I told him.

But as I turned I had the sick sensation of having lied, because there was a shape in the corner of the room – the figure of something like a person – it moved and a yell scraped from my throat.

'Adam?' Dad called.

'Come here!' I choked out.

I couldn't move.

The shadow came toward me, as if I had been speaking to *it*.

Dad entered. 'Is Benny okay?'

'It's—' Couldn't he see it? I spun and there was the empty room, filled only with tender light. I cast around frantically, touching the walls, checking behind the door.

'What are you doing?' Dad interrupted.

'There was something here – I saw...' I trailed off.

'Are you drunk?' Dad peered into my face.

'No!'

He pulled Benny from me. 'Your eyes are huge. Did you take drugs?' Suspicion loaded his voice.

'I didn't even have a burger!' This, I realised, was not the most logical comment to make.

'Sleep it off,' he said, disbelieving.

I opened and closed my mouth. I didn't know what to say, because now anything would make me sound high.

Dad watched me leave.

I went to my bedroom, flicking on the light as fast as I could. I tried not to think about the frightening things the writer of the diary had described, and the idea that they were coming for me. I couldn't shake it, though: the dread, the fear – and the *embarrassment* of being so afraid. Who could I tell, who would believe me? Even if they did believe me, what could they *do*?

I stood in the middle of my bright room trying not to blink, because every time the darkness of my eyelids descended it felt like I was lying in the grass again, the wind knocked out of me, all those eyes watching and nobody to help me up.

June 22nd

Obaasama, the other ghosts have begun to speak, as if you showed them that I can hear. Whether this is good or bad, I cannot tell. All I feel is a terror and wonder that I do not know how to express.

I went to the garden in the evening, earlier than usual. I perched on the big stone by the pond. There used to be koi, when Father was alive. I was in a melancholy mood, Obaasama. I did not play *Heike Monogatari*. I let my bachi drift over the strings and played an old song, a love song. The ghosts came nonetheless, and a figure stood out from the others. A girl who could have been the same age as me in life. Maybe that is why I saw her so easily. I asked, what do you want?

I did not expect an answer, but she spoke, and her voice was the wind in bamboo. It was difficult to understand her at first, but I heard:

We swore we would always love each other. I was married already... yet I could not stop myself. She was a painter. She painted me. I was on her brush and her paper. But my husband found them, found us... He burned the paintings and I burned too..

Her voice dwindled. I asked, what happened then? She repeated only, *I burned.* This was not any story but *her* story. She had told it and I had listened. Yet for her it was unfinished. She whispered, *Does she still love me? When she swore, was she true? She cannot see me...*

I could neither answer her questions nor tell a lie. I played the love song again, thinking about an ending that could give her peace. I sang, or chanted:

A picture does not live only on paper. It lives in the eye of the painter. It is in the hand that held the brush. A painter does not forget her painting.

This I felt was sincere, Obaasama. Do you think so? I have no wisdom or knowledge of what may be in the hearts of others, especially in love. The girl must have seen some truth in it though. She closed her eyes and her form became a breeze. I did not know if I had done harm or good. Has she gone onwards? I can only hope what I gave her was enough.

June 29th

I believe I am closer to understanding the task I have been given, Obaasama. Not every ghost speaks but I have begun to sense their wants. It is no secret; it is in all the stories I have ever heard and it is what the priest said, and the biwa-hōshi. They desire what is undone to be finished: to be given peace, to be remembered, to move on. There must be other kinds of ghosts – vengeful, enraged, restless – but those who come to me are lost and wandering spirits. I have begun to play folk songs of hometowns and returns. I sing lullabies to help children sleep, love songs.

I have even sung my old school song from simpler days: *If a diamond is not polished, it does not shine...* Once or twice I have chanted what I recall of the *Heart Sutra*, thinking of Hoichi and his poor ears. Each ghost knows what to listen for; there are stories in each and I do my best to tell them. When they are satisfied, they fade – not all, but a few every time I play.

July 3rd

I had peace and quiet for some days, Obaasama, until this afternoon, when O-Suzu rushed to tell me that a matchmaker was here. We were thrown into a panic. She hastily tidied my hair and straightened my kimono and obi.

The matchmaker and I introduced ourselves formally, making polite small talk until O-Suzu brought refreshments. I was unsure whether I should make a good or bad impression on the matchmaker. Perhaps if it was sufficiently bad he would refuse to match me with anyone.

The matchmaker asked if Uncle would join us soon. I said that I hoped so, but Uncle is a busy man and on occasion failed to inform me of his plans. The matchmaker realised that I had been unaware of this visit. I hurriedly suggested we discuss the matches he had brought. He hesitated but could not find a way to refuse. He had two men: a silk merchant in his forties and a bank manager in his thirties. The matchmaker showed photographs. The men looked extraordinarily dull.

I heard a voice at the door and went to greet Uncle but discovered it was Sagi-sensei, who had arrived for my lesson. I was rather flustered but brought him in because it meant I would not have to make conversation with the matchmaker alone.

The matchmaker rose as we entered the room. It was rather rude of him to be so relieved, but his face fell when he saw Sagi-sensei and not Uncle. Sagi-sensei, on the other hand, was intrigued and inquired about the potential matches. He truly is very nosy. Even Sagi-sensei did not seem impressed by my prospects. He asked if there were no men who had international connections as I had good English and would be a useful assistant. The matchmaker reluctantly said there was another man but...

I urged him to continue. He revealed that an American officer in the US Navy was interested in marrying a Japanese girl. Sagi-sensei was delighted. Perhaps you could even go to America! he exclaimed.

The matchmaker did not expect such a warm reaction. He detailed the American's income and career, both more than acceptable. He is twenty-eight years old. This is ten years older than me but the youngest man offered so far. The matchmaker wondered what Uncle would think, and we all fell silent and worried. My uncle is traditional, I said, but he often speaks of America's power and influence. He believes that Japan's relations with America are important.

This is true. I did not include that Uncle also complains that America is too strong and Japan must be careful of these relations. The matchmaker said he would suggest a meeting to Uncle I proposed that Sagi-sensei come too, as he is an educated man capable of conversing with the American. Sagi-sensei would also support me, though I did not say this.

The matchmaker agreed it would be helpful. I lied and said I would write to Uncle and explain what we had discussed. The matchmaker took his leave.

Sagi-sensei stayed for our lesson, though he reminisced at length about America rather than checking my writing assignments. After we finished, I sat down with O-Suzu. She said I was a trickster. I think she was proud of me. She warned me to be cautious, though, that Uncle would be angry when he found out. And this American could be a bad man.

But surely it is not too much to ask that I have some part in the decisions of my own life! Imagine if I could go to America. It would be exciting, Obaasama. It would be a whole new world.

—

July 7th

The ghosts have filled me with stories, Obaasama. They entrust me with what they have kept of their lives, sometimes good, often sad. For some I have given peace, if I can find an ending. Sometimes I simply promise to remember them and that has been enough. For those stories and questions I am helpless to answer, I try to calm them. Will these ghosts become the unquiet ones? What will they do to seek their own peace? I fear them becoming angry and seeking vengeance...

Obaasama, when did this begin for you? I knew you only as old and wise, so it is difficult for me to imagine you as a young girl. You must have had a teacher, your grandfather. Truth be told, I am occasionally vexed that you did not prepare me. Doubtless, it appeared I was not fit for this task. I showed no great talent for the biwa, nor any inclination for seeing ghosts. And I think you did not expect to die, which may be the only unwise thing I have known you to have done.

I have so many questions, still. When did this task begin? Why was our family entrusted with it? Is it a gift or a punishment?

Yet as I tend to the ghosts there comes what I can only describe as a kind of clearing of the atmosphere. It is as if the space becomes clean and pure, like blue sky after rain.

Ten

♩♫♪♪♩♪

I got to Japanese class with seconds to spare. I'd given up on sleep and read the diary until my alarm went off, and now my head pounced and my heart was still clutching in my chest. The ghosts were telling stories and the writer wanted to marry an American... I was full of dread and exhaustion but hadn't been able to stop myself turning the pages.

I slunk into my seat.

Yuzuki gave me an upbeat, 'Ohayo!'

'Hey Yuzuki-chan,' I said.

Jo was here again. 'Adam-kun, genki?' he practically yelled.

'Mmmm.' If I answered honestly – *Nope, in fact I may pass away at any moment* – it would only invite more questions. I didn't ask Jo if he was genki. Genki burst out of him like a strobe light.

Takane-sensei chose this moment to start class. I struggled through, keeping my head down and my eyes on the textbook. We were almost finished when Takane-sensei made some announcements. He talked about our class 'graduation', which would be him giving us a homemade certificate in front of our parents and then everybody eating Japanese snacks.

There was a final thing, Takane-sensei said gleefully. He announced that there was a homestay opportunity. At his brother's house in Nagasaki. One of us could go this summer! We just had to apply!

Everyone murmured enthusiastically. A great way to hang out in Japan. Good to practise Japanese. Summer was such a fun time. Watermelons! Matsuri! Fireworks!

It probably would be cool, except for the homestay part – and the speaking Japanese part.

I muttered my usual excuses not to hang out, but had an urgent craving for something cold and sugary. I decided to pick up a consoling bubble tea and go wallow in bed for the rest of my life. Perfect. I had almost escaped the school when I bumped into Jo, emerging from the bathroom.

'Adam-kun! Where are you going?'

'Getting some bubble tea, then home,' I said. 'Aren't you hanging out with everyone else?'

Jo scrunched his face. 'I said some not nice things about the Yomiuri Giants so I think it is best to stay away from Keisuke-kun.'

This sentence was entirely incomprehensible to me.

It did not slow Jo down. 'I like bubble tea! Is there somewhere you recommend?'

'There's a place just down the street...' I said.

Jo nodded eagerly.

I gave in. 'Why don't you come along.'

Jo kept up an incessant stream of chatter that flowed in and out of Japanese and English, and I joined in when I had to. After we ordered, Jo sat at a table expectantly. I vowed to suck down my tea as fast as possible.

'Is something wrong?' Jo asked, sudden and blunt.

I shrugged. 'Boy trouble.' Then I tensed. I didn't know how Jo felt about gay stuff. Despite the incredible queerness of anime and manga, I knew that Japan wasn't exactly leading the field in LGBTQ+ rights.

He blinked at me uncertainly.

I pushed away the uneasy tension that always roiled in my stomach at times like this. 'I'm gay. I like guys.'

'I see.' Jo's eyes darted away, his face otherwise expressionless.

'Do you have a problem with that?' It came out more aggressively than I intended.

'No, no! It's – good.' He blushed.

'Good,' I echoed. The knot in my stomach dissolved. One of the knots.

'What is the trouble?' Jo pressed on.

Why not tell him? He was an impartial observer. I gave him a basic rundown, attempting to speak Japanese until halfway through, when I gave up.

Jo was an attentive listener, only interrupting to check an English word or help me out with a Japanese one.

'What is yellow fever?' he ventured.

'When someone is into Asians,' I explained. 'In a weird creepy way. Girls get it a lot from white guys.'

Jo said optimistically, 'Maybe your ex likes people who play music.'

'String instruments, famed for their horniness.'

'Do you play piano? Piano is sexy,' Jo said.

'It definitely is not.'

'You can lie on it,' Jo pointed out.

I burst into laughter. Jo grinned.

'Practical,' I conceded. 'Do you play any music?'

'Some taiko.' He air-drummed, a straw in each hand. 'But my family isn't so musical.'

'Oh, are you one of those guys who wears a loincloth and doesn't have sex?' I asked.

Jo looked blank.

I consulted my dictionary. 'Who wears a... fundoshi.'

'Ah. No. That's the group called Kodō, I think. They are...' He shook his head in a way that could mean *impressive* or *bananas*.

I googled *taiko Kodō fundoshi* and a photo of a man's muscular, sweaty back appeared, holding wooden sticks above his head, about to bring them down on a huge drum. We stared at this image for a few seconds.

'*Hot*,' I said.

Jo was blushing. *Was* he okay with gay stuff?

'If you come to Japan, you could see taiko,' he said.

'Actually,' I said, 'do you know the biwa?'

'Not much. You like biwa music?'

'I'm... not sure,' I said. 'I just learned about it.'

'You should apply for the homestay!' Jo insisted. 'Then you can come and find biwa.'

'My Japanese is horrible.'

'It is not good,' Jo agreed. 'That's why a homestay would be helpful. Here my English has become much better. I live in Nagasaki too. So you would have a friend there.' He looked at me with such earnestness, but it was the way he had said *friend* that made me reply.

'Why not?'

And that wasn t all that would be in Nagasaki: the diary writer was there – *had been* there. A coincidence. Nothing more.

When I got home I dodged Dad and Kate and went straight to my room. I put my headphones on. I hadn't listened to biwa music yet for some reason – well... I knew the reason: fear.

The songs that appeared after a basic search had Japanese titles, so I chose randomly and held my breath.

The sound of the instrument surprised me. It wasn't exactly melodic and had an almost buzzy timbre, but without the vibrating resonance of a guitar. There was a series of twangs that came from separate notes, which stopped as an undulating voice sang. It was a man, and the singing was closer to chanting or intoning. When he finished, the music began in earnest, building to quicker arpeggios and rolling strums. It was unlike any western music I had ever heard. But what had I been expecting? Something mystical and otherworldly, that would conjure ghosts, or calm them.

I heard a noise, beyond my headphones, and pulled them from my ears. It was voices in the next room; Kate singing to Benny. The living, because the dead couldn't sing. They couldn't – it was impossible. I wished I didn't have to remind myself of that.

July 15th

Uncle came today, Obaasama, and was irritated that the matchmaker was not here. He became even more irritable when I told him the matchmaker had visited the previous week. I do not often think that my father and Uncle are similar but I must say they shared a certain absent-mindedness.

However, Uncle revealed that the matchmaker had already sent him details about the potential matches; more detail than I had been given. I could not hide my annoyance. I am the one to be married, not Uncle. The silk merchant is a widower with four young children, and I suspect more in need of a childminder than a wife. The bank manager is the youngest of three sons. When Uncle said his name, O-Suzu gave me a warning glance. I asked if she knew him and she mentioned rumours that the men of that family indulged in gambling. Uncle muttered that the background check had not been completed yet. I said that our name was good, and I had no desire to pay for another. Uncle hmphed but did not argue because, after all, we have the same name.

I said, what about the American? Uncle cursed the matchmaker and said he did not want a foreigner in the family. I told him that a high-ranking officer in the Navy of a powerful nation was no dishonour. With some recklessness, Obaasama, I said that Father would have approved. Uncle said my father had been a weak fool; his death had proved that.

I was furious. I said Father had been wise enough to teach me to open my mind and not fear what I did not know. Obaasama would agree, I said. Uncle told me I had no way of knowing that and I replied yes, I did. I was suddenly aware that the ghosts had gathered. Uncle had an odd expression on his face. He fell silent. I told him I would seek my mother's counsel. Uncle said he would wash his hands of it, which I do not believe.

I feel a kind of power came to me, Obaasama, that the ghosts of you and the ancestors came. Yet now as I think on it I cannot tell if you were warning Uncle, or warning me.

＿＿

July 21st

Obaasama, I received a reply from my mother regarding the matchmaking. She promised to visit as soon as she could, but she trusted my opinion. I imagine other mothers would be more involved. Mother, though, has been quiet and tired since Father died. She does not find the city pleasant. She prefers the slow life of the countryside, in the house she grew up, where her own father needs care.

To my surprise, she did not warn me away from the American. She stressed the importance of meeting him and being informed of his background.

No doubt I am moving with too much speed, Obaasama, but I think it best not to give Uncle time to change his mind.

I sent word to the matchmaker that Mother has given her approval, and we would have an omiai to formally meet with the American to see whether he is suitable. If he is not, I am not sure what I will do...

In any case, I must practise my English.

⁓

July 30th

Well, Obaasama, the omiai was extremely interesting.

The best thing was that Mother came. She arrived this morning. She seemed smaller since the last time I saw her, at New Year. She was as gentle as she always is. She brought me one of her kimonos, light purple dyed in the Amakusa Sarasa fashion, with a beautiful intricate pattern.

The hotel where we held the meeting was pleasant, one of the few near the Foreign Settlement which often caters to foreigners. We had a private room. There were eight people: myself, Mother, Uncle, Sagi-sensei, two Americans, an interpreter and the matchmaker. Sagi-sensei was in good spirits. Mother was quiet as usual, but smiling. Uncle was angry but silent. The matchmaker and the interpreter were nervous. The American is a lieutenant, a good rank. He brought his friend, also a lieutenant though of a lower grade. The Lieutenant calls him by his first name, which I feel is rather too casual. I shall refer to him here as Mr S—. They both wore their uniforms, dark blue with gleaming gold buttons.

The Americans said hello in Japanese, then spoke only English. The interpreter was busy and Sagi-sensei was eager to help translate. I sat opposite the Lieutenant. I was more nervous than I anticipated. He is a person I may spend all the years of my life with.

The conversation moved faster than I was accustomed to, but I understood most things. They spoke about the weather and America and the unusual things in Japan. The Lieutenant spoke about his education and family and duties in the Navy. The interpreter relayed this to Mother and Uncle, with the matchmaker relieved with each good detail. Everybody was drinking sake.

The Lieutenant said that he had been told I could speak English. He did not look at me when he said this. I told him that I could speak English, though I was not at all accomplished. However, it was easier for me to speak if I was spoken to. The Lieutenant and his friend were surprised rather than offended by my rash words. Mr S— smiled. Then the Lieutenant leaned across the table and said suddenly that he knew me, that we had spoken once in passing.

I recalled the two Americans O-Suzu and I had passed on the bridge. What a funny chance! The Lieutenant said he was sorry he had not recognised me at once, when it was that encounter that had prompted him to consider marrying a Japanese woman. Mr S— said it was true and that the Lieutenant had been quite taken by that mysterious young lady.

I was lost for words, aside from saying I was hardly mysterious. The Lieutenant spoke to me far more after that. I think he was pleased with me. His eyes were often on me; blue eyes, Obaasama. I have never been so close to eyes like that.

Dinner finished and we wished each other goodnight. The Lieutenant hoped to see me soon. When the Americans left, Uncle said they were rude and terrible.

The matchmaker said he understood, though the Lieutenant had exceptional qualifications, the best we had been offered. Sagi-sensei, predictably and helpfully, was of the opinion that they were decent men.

Mother said that she was not familiar with Americans, but the Lieutenant was a strong and lively man. He could give me a future full of opportunity. I was surprised that Mother said this. It was what I had been thinking too.

And now here I am, Obaasama. I cannot tell what will happen next. Yet meeting those Americans again... It must be some sort of fate.

Eleven

'Hey Adam,' Kate said, on the other side of my bedroom door.

'Hey.' I slid the diary under my pillow.

'We're going for a walk on the beach. Want to join?'

'No.'

There was a silence. 'Can I come in?' she said.

'I suppose.'

She came in. 'You seem... tired.'

'You mean I look like crap.' I'd had another horrible night, waking every couple of hours to switch on my lamp and listen to silence and see nothing at all.

'Your dad said you've been acting a bit weirdly.'

'I wasn't high at that party!' I said.

Kate chose her words with care. 'You've had a tough time lately and haven't been yourself. If it's because you've been using anything then—'

I did not want to sit through a lecture. 'I swear to you I had not taken any drugs. Or alcohol.'

'Really?' she asked.

'*Really.*' There was no way I could tell her what I'd seen, or thought I'd seen. In the sunny light of morning, it would sound ridiculous. I half-wished I *had* taken drugs, that I could blame it on them.

'Tell me what happened at the party then.'

Kate was trying so earnestly to be patient and attentive that I was about to spill my sorry guts.

Then Dad called, 'Kate, how *much* time can Benny spend lying on his tummy?'

She sighed, her motherly care diverted to this important baby development question.

'Nothing happened,' I reassured her.

'In that case you're coming for a walk with us!' she ordered.

'I'm sorry I snapped at you,' I added.

'Oh, I'm used to *that*,' she replied, and left my room to care for Benny, and for Dad.

———

'Morning,' Dad greeted me. He was reading an actual physical newspaper.

'Hey.' I made myself a bowl of cereal and concentrated on eating it.

'You're coming with us?' he asked.

'Yup.'

'Good, good.' He turned a page with a rustle.

Kate popped her head in. 'Frank, could you check the baby bag has nappies?'

'Sure!' Dad cast his eyes around the room uncertainly.

'The bag's probably in the buggy,' I said.

'Right.' Dad went to the front door. He returned a second later.

'By the back door,' I told him.

'I forgot,' he said.

I ate my cereal. Dad rummaged for a while, opening and closing cupboard doors. I knew better than to say anything.

Eventually, he reappeared. 'All set!' he called to Kate.

We packed ourselves into the car, along with the buggy, the baby bag, the back-up baby bag and snacks. I leaned my head against the window. The ocean came into view, surprising me as it always did, even though I knew it would be there. We parked in a half-empty lot near the beach.

'Let's walk to the lighthouse,' Kate said.

Dad put the baby carrier on like a horse saddling itself up. Benny nestled against his chest.

I licked the salt from my lips. I wanted to be in the water, to submerge my body in something huge, that would envelop me and let me rest against it.

It was easier to be quiet here, with the waves and wind and seabirds wheeling above. The lighthouse was a smooth and spotless white; even close up it was blindingly clean.

'Photo!' Kate took a selfie with Dad and Benny. 'Adam, get in.' She took some more photos, then turned her phone to show us. 'Me and my boys.'

I felt out of place in those photos, like some tourist they had met on their day out. A stranger stepping into the frame and interrupting a young family.

'Should we go to the top?' Dad said.

'Is there a lift?' I asked.

Kate chuckled and tugged my arm as if I was joking.

My calves were burning before we got halfway. Everybody was gasping. I would have laughed if I'd had enough oxygen in my lungs.

When I finally made it to the top, I didn't look down. I knew how my stomach would lurch. The horizon was heaven, a place that could never be reached.

'You want me to take him?' Kate offered, and Dad strapped the baby carrier onto her.

Kate walked around, crooning. *My bonny lies over the ocean, my bonny lies over the sea...*

'Do you miss being on a ship?' I asked Dad.

'Sometimes,' he said. 'But even Navy guys get seasick.'

'I thought that got drilled out of you.'

'Yeah, and then you end up feeling sick on dry land.'

I tried to keep this rare talkativeness going. 'How many times have you crossed the Pacific?'

'On water... I can't remember,' he said. 'I crossed by air too. The last time to bring you back.'

It was unusual for Dad to volunteer anything like this, anything related to my mother. 'Did you know it would be the last time?' I asked.

He shook his head. 'I didn't know anything. In fact, I came back knowing less than I had before.'

'What do you mean?' I must have been too eager, because Dad blinked as if he hadn't been aware of what he'd said.

'Sometimes when you learn something new, all it does is tell you what else you have no idea about.'

'About Japan?' I persisted. 'Or about my mother?'

'Your mother...'

I couldn't tell if Dad was confirming this or repeating my words.

'It didn't turn out the way I thought it would,' he said. 'I was young. I hadn't even considered death.'

'It must have been a shock,' I ventured.

Dad nodded at the sea, as though the waves were the ones talking to him, not me. 'I felt so terrible. Still do.'

Terrible was a weird word to use.

'Kate told me you broke up with your guy,' Dad said.

Kind of Kate to pretend I had done the dumping.

'You'll get over it,' he went on, a statement of fact.

This was such father-son-manly talk. I wasn't used to it. For some reason, I said, 'Did you and Mum ever break up and get back together?'

His brow furrowed. 'Why are you asking that?'

I shrugged, feeling stupid. 'Guess I'm just holding out hope.'

'Don't do that. Best to move on,' Dad said forcefully.

I wasn't going to get any more sympathy. Maybe Dad felt bad because he gave me a tight, sad smile.

Kate returned to us. 'Benny's going to need a feed soon.'

'Let's go down,' Dad said.

And down we went.

August 1st

The Lieutenant visited us today, again bringing Mr S—
as friend and chaperone. The matchmaker apologised for
requesting another meeting so soon, saying Americans are
not patient.

I poured the tea and gave them sweets. The Lieutenant
has been in Japan since spring and he finds it very pleasant.
I was surprised that he has been here such a short time and
already wished to be married. The Lieutenant said wistfully
that he wanted a home after so long at sea. Mother asked
the Lieutenant and Mr S— about their hometowns. The
Lieutenant grew up on a farm surrounded by endless fields;
a prairie. Mr S— said he was from a city called Chicago,
where there was so much snow and wind in winter that
occasionally the vast lake froze.

It was easier to observe them today. The Lieutenant's face
is always smiling or laughing, opening up. His hair is fair and
wavy. Mr S— has auburn hair and brown eyes with flecks
of green, and his skin is not so white as the Lieutenant's.
His expression is often thoughtful; he observes everything.

I commented on how they had careers on the sea despite
having grown up far from it. Do you love the sea? I asked.
The Lieutenant said sure, unless you get seasickness. I told
them that I often contemplate the sea, though I have never

been on a boat. It is gorgeous and sometimes frightening; when the tsunamis come it is as if the sea is jealous of people. But it never stays, because perhaps it is only from far away that land seems beautiful.

The Lieutenant told me I had an admirable way with words and Mr S— asked if I wrote poetry. I was embarrassed and said I merely enjoyed reading it. Mr S— said he would be pleased to give me a book of English poetry. The Lieutenant quickly added he would give me poetry too. I thanked them both sincerely.

Mr S— asked Mother if he could see the garden, and she happily agreed. She brought the interpreter and I could hear them naming plants and trees. She has taken rather amusingly well to Mr S—.

The Lieutenant moved close to me and clasped my hands. I stopped myself from pulling away. He said I was a charming girl and he had taken a liking to me. I was taken aback by this forwardness, and was reminded how different Americans are to Japanese. All I could do was thank him.

I was grateful for Mr S— and Mother returning just then. Mr S— said that the garden was beautiful. He said this in Japanese, which was a great delight to me and Mother. He said he was studying. Like me with English, I said. He told me that my English was much better than his Japanese.

The Lieutenant said perhaps we should learn together, giving me a smile of such boldness I could not help but laugh. We parted ways quite merrily. Obaasama, perhaps this will work after all.

August 3rd

Mother left this morning, Obaasama. She has returned to care for Grandfather. I think Mother misses Father more when she is in this house. But it is because I miss him that I stay.

Mother said I would have an interesting life with the Lieutenant. This is a rather evasive statement, in my opinion. Mother worries about me here, without a guardian. Did I know people told peculiar stories about me, studying like a scholar, playing old music all alone?

Of course I know.

She said the Americans would not, and that was good. She appeared worn out and I regret that I am a source of anxiety for her.

Obaasama, if you have any counsel to give, I would welcome it. I did my best to have a choice in who I marry but now find that choices themselves are even more bewildering.

I have some time to decide, though, as it will be Obon soon, and time for us to honour our deceased ancestors. I have requested we wait until afterwards before proceeding with further meetings or correspondence. This may be cowardly of me but it is true, Obaasama, that I must attend to the dead.

Twelve

t was weirdly difficult to close the diary, as if my hands didn't want to listen to me. But I was too anxious to continue; I was restless with tension. My fingers itched so I took out my cello to distract them.

I tightened the bow, rubbing its horsehairs with resin, allowing this ritual to relax me. I leaned the cello against my chest, pegs and scroll tucked behind my left ear, its weight and smell and resonance a comfort.

My test was next week and I hadn't even played the piece the whole way through. I settled my music on the stand, drawing out each note and beading them together. Halfway through my fingers stumbled on a phrase, and I played it slow, over and over, repetitions sinking into my skin.

'Adam.'

I jerked. Dad was in the doorway.

'I knocked,' he said.

'I didn't hear you.'

'Benny's going down for a nap, so could you take a break for a while?'

'He likes cello.' Well, he didn't *hate* cello.

'I suppose if you're playing lullabies. That's not what you're playing, though.' Dad laughed half-heartedly.

'It's Bach, Cello Suite No. 1 in G Major,' I explained. 'It's a... challenge.'

'Even more reason to take a break!' Dad said.

I sighed and lowered my bow. It would do no harm to listen to it a few times.

'Thanks. You want a coffee? A juice?' Dad offered.

'Nah, I'm good.' I stood up and the diary caught my eye. 'Oh, actually—'

'There's orange juice, tomato juice, pineapple—'

'Tomato? No, I mean...' I picked up the diary. 'Have you seen this before? It was in the attic.'

His eyes widened. 'That... Your mother read it. She didn't write it.'

'I know *that*. Did her mum or grandma write it?'

Dad shook his head. 'No – well, I don't know. Probably better not to touch it.'

'Why?'

He said quickly, 'I just mean, it's so old you might – damage it.'

'Have you read it?'

'Obviously not. I'm surprised you're interested in it.'

'It's... different. Did Mum ever talk about it?'

'She wouldn't tell me anything about it.' Dad turned and left, closing the door behind him.

I stared at the door in surprise. What could be in the diary, that Dad had been curious enough to ask about, and that my mother refused to tell?

I decided not to listen to Bach; I needed to hear *Heike Monogatari* and not just random songs. Nowhere seemed to have the full performance of it so I settled for the woman who had the most videos on YouTube, and pressed play on the first. The beginning notes thrummed out on the biwa and every part of me tuned in, in a way I hadn't before. The woman's voice was solemn, the rich notes plucked like punctuation. I couldn't understand the lyrics, because of how they were delivered or because they were a form of Japanese I had no grasp of. It was still mesmerising.

The sound quality wasn't great, though, because there was static or distortion – almost like something else playing on my laptop. I paused the video and for a few beats I could hear the noise: a murmur, as if another voice was whispering along. It stopped. I unpaused the video and this time the noise was gone. I shuddered, glancing around my room, but the only thing listening was me.

August 6th

Obon approaches, and no doubt you and the ancestors are preparing for your travel, Obaasama. O-Suzu and I are readying the butsudan, where we will lay offerings and burn incense and pray for our dead. You used to tell me about the ancestors I had never met, how they were coming to visit, ensuring that we were safe and living well. I can see that for myself now.

The garden is thronged with ghosts. Some cannot find their descendants, or have none left. I have had to ask around and look through records for such lost families. A few I found, but most I could not. Then I must tell those ghosts that they may consider me a daughter, that I will hold them in my memory. I smile and sing cheerful songs to comfort them. They are soothed. I must accept their fear and sadness too. That is part of my duty and I understand more and more that it is also a gift, though I still do not know why it is I that must do it.

Yet I am weary, Obaasama. O-Suzu has come to say that I look over-warm and should cool down. She is anxious I will lose my looks before an engagement is decided. It is indeed hot... I will rest and ask her to sing to me, because I have a need to be comforted as well, by someone in the land of the living.

August 10th

Obaasama, I try but I can steady neither my hand nor my breath. I am sorry if this is difficult to read—

When I opened the doors to the garden, there was a feeling as if lightning was about to strike. The ghosts were faint, muted; as if they were afraid. I became afraid too, for what a ghost must fear, the living must surely fear more. So I was prepared, a little.

You must have seen such ghosts before, Obaasama. It was a horror, the thing that came. I could not even tell what manner of human it had been; perhaps even it did not know any longer. It came howling, a decaying green, eyes black with no white left in them. Its mouth stretched across its face, its neck thin and long, leading to a stomach bloated with starvation, and that was what made me recognise it: a hungry ghost. But hunger was a pale word, Obaasama. Hunger is what my stomach feels when my supper is late; this ghost was ravenous in its soul. It came towards me and stopped at the large stone before the engawa, and the stone began to blacken.

I could not even scream. My biwa I clutched tight but could not play; what use was music? I asked, what is it you want? It shrieked and I thought the sound would kill me. Yet I understood what it was saying:

You have forgotten! Sent to that island... I was forgotten once and then once again! My bones returned but they do not rest... I slept but have woken... I remember but you do not!

CLARA KUMAGAI

I have never heard a ghost like this. Its voice was desolate. It was a stony beach and icy waves. I struggled to answer. I whispered, who are you? It only screamed and reached for me. If there had been no salt at the doorstep, no ofuda above the door then it would have entered the house - perhaps ripped the flesh from my body.

I prostrated before it, my face to the floor. It wailed and cried, and I wept from fear but also from pity. I wondered only if I would die. When the ghost fell silent I dared to raise my head, but all I saw was the dawn breaking and the ghost paling before it. It turned its face to me, mouth deep as hell and I knew, Obaasama, that it would return.

~

August 11th

I am alive, somehow. The only reason I know is because I can pick up my pen and turn the pages of this book... I am fatigued, Obaasama. Dread has made me hollow... The hungry ghost has both less and more power than I thought. Less, as it cannot touch me; more, because it will return and return until I calm it or until I have been worn into a shadow myself...

It came last night and screamed, and it must be only I who can hear it. The other ghosts do not come and I am glad; they should stay away from this haunted place. I should tell O-Suzu to go too...

I can hear the voice of the hungry ghost still – it echoes in my mind...

You have forgotten me... alone... on the island... I lost count of months and days... I survived on salted water... to see my family once more... but they are dead before me... I am forgotten...

The words were familiar, Obaasama. I have heard them before; or not the words but the story behind them...

My body is empty but I cannot eat. I fear to hunger...

August 12th

Obaasama, I have done my duty. I would lie down and perhaps never rise again yet I must write to you, in case my mind clouds later...

Yesterday I decided I must go to the temple, for this was beyond my power. I wondered what the priest would say; he had warned me about Hoichi the earless monk. Then on the memory of the monk I stayed. A monk, haunted – I had read it...

I turned to *Heike Monogatari* and located the chapter. Three men had plotted to overthrow Kiyomori, the Taira leader, and were exiled to a lonesome island far from the capital. But when Kiyomori's daughter became pregnant she was haunted by the vengeful spirits of those wronged by the Taira. The solution was to honour those ghosts to calm them, and forgive the living, and so two of those exiled men were pardoned. The other was left behind, the monk Shunkan. He tried to climb into their boat but was pushed away, and there alone on the island he wasted. He was at last visited by a man once employed in Shunkan's household, but when told of the death of his wife and son, he stopped eating the little food he had. He died. Shunkan's only remaining family, a daughter, became a nun and prayed for him, but when she passed there was nobody left.

Her prayers, Obaasama, must not have been enough to calm the hunger he had in life and death. For hungry ghosts are those who, when living, had destructive appetites for more than food; or they are the forgotten dead, longing to exist if only in memory. This ghost could be either or both. If I have some drop of Taira blood in my veins then perhaps that was why he had come to me...

When the air sparked I knew the fury of the hungry ghost had grown and felt such terror, I feared I could not do the task set before me. It came screaming and starving.

The salt at the doorway dissolved as if in boiling water. The paper ofuda singed. I knew I could not keep the ghost out any longer, for it was the third night, and so close to Obon when ghosts gain power...

I began to play biwa, the sound weak and feeble, as if that abominable mouth was eating it up, leaving only scraps of noise. I closed my eyes and sang.

I recited the story of Shunkan as best I could, for I did not know the ballad. If this was not Shunkan it would not be appeased – such a wretched tale would only enrage it to more cruelty...

But it began to quieten. It was listening. I glimpsed a starved man, sanded and salted, hair wild from the sea-wind – a spirit feeding on sound, on the nourishment of memory...

I played until my voice was hoarse and the story of Shunkan had ended. While the ghost was still, I lit incense and bowed my head. I said, I remember you. I ask you to hunger no more. I beg that you rest.

I thought it would speak again, but that mouth had closed – neck shortened, stomach sated – it had had its fill.

And when the sun rose the ghost raised its head and drifted apart in the light.

I must stop writing, Obaasama. I fear other hungry ghosts will come, in time. How terrible it would be, to become one.

I will not think of it. I will rest too...

Thirteen

♩ ♫ ♪♪ ♩ ♪

My hands left damp marks on the page. I was sweating, breathing hard as if I'd just run miles, except I was cold instead of hot. Because it was fear – though this ghost wasn't real, couldn't be…

Even so, the handwriting was ragged and scrawled in places and faint in others – terror radiated from the paper. If I didn't think it was real, it didn't matter; she did.

I exhaled as slowly as I could manage, gripping the solid wood of my desk. I couldn't tell if I was the only thing hungering, and I was too afraid to eat. I put a hoodie on and got into bed, but I couldn't thaw the deep cold in my bones. I shivered and shook myself to sleep.

Next morning was Monday, which was bad, but at least I was warm again. I showered away the sweat and nightmares and stuffed a piece of toast in my mouth as I left. As I opened the front door Sylvia pounced from behind a bush.

I yelped. The toast fell out of my mouth.

'You can't avoid me,' she said.

I hoisted my schoolbag over my shoulder and started walking. I would ignore her.

'I'm super thankful you're not being irrationally angry with me,' she went on.

'I am!' I snapped, setting a record for the shortest silent treatment ever. 'I mean, I'm not!'

Sylvia didn't gloat. 'Explain.'

'I thought you were on my side but it felt like you were on Evan's.'

'I'm *always* on your side!' she protested. 'I knew if you saw them you'd be upset. And I didn't want anybody to be upset.'

'For once, Syl, you did not succeed.'

'My unblemished record is no more, thanks to you.'

I couldn't help out ask a stupid question. 'You think I'm that sensitive?'

'You were so sad, Adam,' Sylvia said. 'I didn't want you to be more sad.'

'You achieved that, cause I was way more pissed off than sad.'

'Is that it? You seem kinda...' She scrutinised me. 'Not yourself. Pale. Stressed.'

I'm reading something so freaky it's making me hallucinate, I did not say. 'Stress,' I confirmed.

Sylvia slung an arm around my waist. 'I love you.'

'I know,' I said.

She took a breath and I knew what was coming.

'I never expected you to get violent,' she said.

'I was mad. I couldn't stop myself.' Shame twisted tentacles around me. 'No. I could have. I didn't want to.'

'I'm very, very glad you're aware of that,' Sylvia said.

'Are Evan and Daniel boyfriends?' I asked.

Sylvia tensed.

'I want to know before I talk to them.'

'I don't think so. Daniel felt weird...'

I felt weird too. 'Evan used to say stuff about me being Asian all the time,' I said, aiming for explanatory rather than defensive. 'Not insults exactly, but comments. Jokes.'

Sylvia was outraged. 'Those are micro-aggressions.'

They *had* felt micro — tiny splinters I could never brush away but couldn't bring up either. Evan probably didn't know that, though, and he'd never *really* been unkind to me.

'I'll apologise,' I said quickly. 'I love you too.'

Sylvia squeezed me and any misplaced anger at her drained away. Shame filled the space it had left behind.

—

I got through the day, my body shuddering occasionally, until Art asked if I was getting sick. I didn't think I was, but there was a pang in my stomach that disturbed me, making me wonder exactly what the writer had meant when she'd said that some hungry ghosts had *destructive appetites for more than food.*

What was I hungry for? Attention? Love? When did that go from being normal to being destructive?

'You're definitely coming down with something,' Carmen said at lunch. 'You're kinda pale.'

'Yeah, might be,' I mumbled.

'You're probably starving,' Sylvia said.

I flinched. 'How do you know?'

'You lost your breakfast in all that screaming you did,' she reminded me.

'Right,' I said, too relieved.

Art gave me an energy bar, which I gratefully accepted.

'And I didn't *scream*,' I added.

Sylvia laughed and I didn't mind because that was normal, everything was normal, everything was fine.

August 15th

I have returned from the Spirit Boat Festival, Obaasama,
half-deaf as usual yet rather restored. It was good to be
around so many of the living. There were many beautiful
boats and a few humorous ones. I watched the parade with
some old classmates, and it was as if our school days had
come again. We even sang our old school song! I found I am
behind with the goings-on lately. They told me that Fusae
has gone to study at the women's school in Ochanomizu,
which I am envious of. Natsuko pretends not to notice old
classmates since she married, as her husband's family are an
old and high-class family. I reminded them that Natsuko is
the governor's daughter and scarcely spoke to us at the best
of times. Sayuri visited Tokyo last month and said it was
entirely too sprawling and crowded.

Unsurprisingly, they had heard of my own potential
engagement. Nagasaki is not so big a city and the matchmaker
had been asking around about me and my family. My
classmates are accustomed to some of my peculiarities,
as they call them. They attribute it to the foreign books
Father and I read and a somewhat liberal upbringing, treated
more as a boy than a girl. They have many questions they
want answered if I do marry the Lieutenant, some of which
embarrassed me and which I will not recount here.

I must go to the ghosts, for they will be excited too, on such a night. We must all be calmed.

~

August 16th

I played in the garden until sunrise, Obaasama, as I think you are aware. O-Suzu was not here to scold me to bed, as she has gone to stay with relations for Obon.

I was glad and sad to see you, Obaasama, and Father too. And to meet the aunts and uncles and great-grandparents and other relatives I have only heard of. A man came forward, your own grandfather, Obaasama. His eyes were milky white. He said:

Long, long ago, our ancestors were at war. They played biwa for the family they fought for, because those who cause wars need to know that they are right, that their deeds will be recounted. Yet when our defeat became inevitable, our ancestors fled. They had something to live for, because they knew that stories must survive. Much was lost during that war, emperors and treasures, but without the ballads we would never have known. So they ran and took their biwas with them, and when it was safe they left their hidden villages and played their songs. They had to show the ghosts of the war that they were not forgotten; they had to appease those who haunted them.

But we knew that it is not only the rich and powerful who deserve commemorating. It is our duty to respect the dead and that is why they come to us.

Now this is your duty, granddaughter of my granddaughter.

When he finished speaking the night was in a hush. I helplessly asked, but must it be *me*? Why? And you answered together, with words as familiar as the bachi in my right hand, as set as the hardened fingertips of my left.

You said:

Because we are like a dream on a spring night. Pride falls and all that prospers decays. We are dust in the wind.

And one last whisper:

Because we must remember.

A gust blew through the garden, sweeping away the deepest dark of night. The sky brightened and dawn came as though it had waited as long as it could and would wait no more. The sun rose on a garden filled with butterflies and they flew off like an illusion, borne away by the irresistible wind.

<hr />

August 20th

Since Obon has passed I feel more tranquil, Obaasama. The weather has cooled slightly. A fresh breeze has been blowing from the ocean. There are fewer ghosts. None are hungry. My biwa playing has become easier, knowing why it is that I must do it. As I play I think of our ancestors who composed these ballads so long ago. I can feel a connection between me and them, a long string taut and resounding with a drawn-out note.

I would be almost at peace if it were not for the breeze turning to a gale and carrying news with it: the Lieutenant was disregarding the etiquette of a third meeting. He would be honoured if I married him.

My plan has succeeded. To tell the truth I have no other choice I can think of.

So I will agree. Obaasama. I will say yes.

Fourteen

'We are dust in the wind,' I whispered.

Some questions *had* been answered, no matter how fantastical they seemed. The writer and I both finally knew why the ghosts were coming, and why she had the responsibility of helping them. I put the diary down, content with this rare moment of resolution.

I went to my cello, woefully unprepared for the exam. At least I was playing for Mr Johnson and not some demon spirit. Right?

I drew my bow across the C string and the cello hummed, sonorous and deep.

I was roused in darkness, reeled out of sleep like a fish on a hook. By a sound – a high soft strum – I looked towards my cello, leaning against the wall.

I swallowed and switched on the lamp, squinting against the sudden light. I thought I saw the strings on the cello vibrate, as if they had been struck—

Benny cried, and I jolted up, scrambling out of bed in case *something* was near him. By the time I reached his room Kate was already there, soothing him.

'He's just hungry,' she whispered. 'Go back to bed.'

Benny nuzzled at her. I rubbed my eyes and returned to my room. I put the cello back in its case and got into bed. I put earplugs in. I didn't turn off the lamp.

Miraculously, I made it through another day without seeing either Evan or Daniel. Sylvia wasn't pleased when I told her this as we trudged out of school, likely because I sounded too happy about it.

'I'll apologise, Syl, I will. Tomorrow.'

'You better. Hey, when's your music final?' she asked.

'Next— no, *this* week!'

'That's a great distraction,' Sylvia said in her pep-talk voice.

'I would kill you if I didn't need my hands to play cello.'

She scoffed. 'As if *you* could kill *me*. I would bite your face off.'

She crouched into a wrestling stance, so I simply picked her up before she could grapple me. She laughed and drummed her hands against my back.

'Beating someone else up now?'

I put Sylvia down. *Of course* it was Evan.

'We were just agreeing that Adam would never defeat me.' Sylvia's smile was forced.

'What *is* Adam capable of?' Evan asked.

I couldn't tell if this was a taunt or – Evan's eyes tracing me up and down – a flirtation. 'I don't know,' I said.

Sylvia opened her mouth.

I cut in before she could say anything. 'Syl, you should go on ahead.'

'All right...' She left with a warning look.

'I'm sorry,' I said in a rush. 'I shouldn't have pushed you. It was wrong, *very* wrong.'

Evan shrugged lazily. 'I pushed you back.'

'And knocked me over,' I couldn't resist saying, because he didn't apologise for *that*.

'Self-defence.' He came closer. 'You can't go around saying stuff about me being racist.'

'I never said that.' This wasn't the time to explain the nuances of racism and fetish.

'We all knew what you meant,' he said. 'And I'm *not*.'

Evan wasn't exactly mad. He was anxious, and intense in a way I'd seen before, a way that made me a little scared, a little excited.

'You're stronger than I thought.' He squeezed my arm as if measuring my muscles, testing my bones.

'You don't expect much of me,' I replied.

He released me. 'Is that what you think?' Before I could respond he turned away, saying, 'I'll see you around.'

I didn't move. I was confused by what that had been: attraction or anger or a challenge. But I wanted him very badly. My hand reached for my arm, placed itself on the ache he'd left.

September 14th

Obaasama, I am married. How odd that I woke up this morning my normal self and by evening had become a wife.

I wore the kimono my mother had worn at her own wedding. It was red and lucky with cranes. The Lieutenant wore his uniform, burnished with medals. I had thought we would be married in a church as the majority of Americans are Christians. We do have churches here in Nagasaki that are more accepted these days.

However, the Lieutenant had no wish for a ceremony, so we simply completed the necessary papers. I used my hanko, and as I did I realised I needed a new one, with my new name. One stamp of ink and the surname I had carried my whole life was changed. What a small and simple thing! Mr S— and the matchmaker were there as witnesses. It was strange that people had to see it happen for it to be real.

The Lieutenant held my hands and kissed my mouth. I am aware this is a Western custom but it was unexpected nonetheless. I could not prevent the heat rising to my face. The other men looked away.

We went to a very fine restaurant afterwards. Sadly, Mother could not attend as Grandfather had taken a fall several days before and she had to nurse him. Uncle did not

come. He did send a short message: *I do not approve.* I wish
you had been there, Obaasama.

I invited O-Suzu instead, though it was slightly odd
for her to attend. But many things are odd now, so I may
as well do as I want while I can, and O-Suzu did not need
much convincing. The meal was delicious but I found it
difficult to eat. The Lieutenant and Mr S— were in high
spirits, laughing and talking exuberantly. However, they
asked me questions and told me stories, which I related to
O-Suzu. I think they are good men.

Then we returned home. The Lieutenant will live here,
when he is not on the ship or called away to his duties. He
is in the bath now. O-Suzu laid out the futons. Then she
brought two little cups of plum wine. She drank with me
and told me what would happen. I knew this already but
I was glad O-Suzu spoke to me about it. I asked what she
thought about the Lieutenant. She said that she did not
think he would try to hurt me, and I felt relieved. Then
she said, sometimes things hurt anyway.

I understand that. It is true. But I must admit I did not
want her to say it. Tomorrow would be sunny, O-Suzu said.
She took the cups and left.

I think the Lieutenant has finished his bath. I will put
my pen and paper away.

—

September 15th

O-Suzu was right, Obaasama. It is sunny today. The Lieutenant has gone out on business and will return in the evening. The house is quiet again.

I feel shy to write about last night but I think I should remember it. You are acquainted with these matters, Obaasama, yet you may consider it vulgar to speak of. Though you are dead, so beyond those feelings, I imagine.

Last night, after I had put away the notebook, the Lieutenant returned from his bath. His skin was pink and his damp hair was a dark gold. He was dressed in a yukata and I was glad of it, because he looked less imposing than in his military uniform. The yukata was wrapped the wrong way, however, so I gestured at his obi. Undo it, I began. He said, my goodness, you are eager.

I realised what he meant and was so embarrassed I covered my face with my hands. I said no, it was only the yukata should not be closed that way because it is how we dress the dead. He did not know that and apologised repeatedly until I lowered my hands. I confess, Obaasama, that I was more nervous and unsure than I had expected. The Lieutenant asked suddenly if I knew any American songs. Surprised, I admitted I did not.

He said he would teach me one that he liked singing. He sat on the futon and when I sat beside him he put his arm around me. He sang a sweet simple melody and indeed he has a handsome voice. I was somewhat indignant – did he think I was a child?

Yet it calmed me. He taught me the words and I sang along. You sing well, he said. When you come to America with me, you will learn even more songs, he promised. He kissed me and I enjoyed this more, in private. I kissed him back. He watched me as I took off each piece of clothing. I wanted him to look away but he did not. He did not have to; he could look at me any way he wanted now.

He touched me all over, as though he wanted to make sure he had every part of me, telling me I was very pretty. He took his yukata off impatiently. He told me to lie down. I asked for the lantern to be put out and he did so, which I was grateful for. I wanted him to slow down, to wait a few moments, but it was hard to say anything else. He asked if I was all right but he was not looking at my face. I said yes because I did not know what else I could say.

I do not know how to write what happened next; perhaps I do think it is shameful... There was blood on the sheet afterwards. He said that was normal. I offered to take the sheet away but he said it was fine, that we should sleep. He said he was happy and asked if I was happy too. I said of course.

He put his arm around me, warm and heavy. He fell asleep but I lay awake for a long time. I thought about the blood underneath us, about how I would wash it out.

Fifteen

y face was hot. It felt too private, reading about the writer's wedding night. I wasn't only embarrassed; I was angry. The Lieutenant... He had basically assaulted her. Was that just the way it had been then? No talking, no asking what a girl wanted or didn't? Just because they were married? For all the writer's honesty there were things she didn't want to say. But what did I know? And what did it matter, because it was over and done with, long ago. I rested my hand on the diary.

'I'm sorry that happened to you,' I murmured.

I closed my eyes tight and kept very still, because I had felt a change in the air and I didn't want to know what it was. I shook my head.

'I'm sorry,' I repeated, and waited until whatever was there had gone.

I realised that, for the first time, I had accepted that *something was there*, and that scared me more than anything else.

The day before my music exam, I slumped at the kitchen table with my wrists aching and my head thudding a tempo. My other exams had fallen by the wayside, because if I failed them it would be nice and private.

Kate watched me stuff spaghetti into my face. 'Should I be worried?'

'About my arms falling off? Yes.'

'I'll glue them back on,' Kate promised. She twirled her spaghetti. 'Are you going to apply to any music schools next year?'

'Hadn't thought about it.' I had, and dismissed the idea. There was no way I was good enough.

'You should.'

From his high chair, Benny triumphantly hurled his bowl of mashed banana to the floor. I got up before Kate did. 'Finish your dinner,' I told her. 'Enjoy the fruits of your labour.'

'That baby is the fruit of my labour,' Kate said.

I snorted and picked him up. 'Sorry I haven't been hanging out with you much this week, Benny.' I planted a kiss on his forehead, leaving a tomato-sauce mark on his milky skin. I wiped it off with my sleeve before Kate noticed.

'Is the cello keeping him awake?' I asked.

Kate shook her head. 'I bet it's soothing. He's been listening to it even before he was born.'

'Dad said...'

'What?'

I booped Benny's nose. 'Nothing. Doesn't Dad want me to study business or economics or science?'

Kate put her fork down. 'Has he said that to you?'

'No.' He hadn't said anything to me. 'I figured he'd want me to have a more reliable career.'

'Your dad will support you. You should follow your talent.'

'I might follow it to dead ends. Or playing in subway stations. Or to... Europe,' I said.

'You want to study abroad?'

There was an odd note in Kate's question. Would she be happy if I went far away? Even if it meant she had less help with Benny, would it make her life simpler?

'We can think about it,' Kate said, and I became conscious of the fact I'd been staring at her, not replying.

'If you want to,' she added. 'I'm not about to become a stage mum.'

I gave her a tentative smile. 'You'd be a good stage mum. You have that competitive streak that would make you ruthless.'

'I do not! May I remind you that we didn't even make you do your recitals.'

'Maybe you should have. It could have helped me with my crippling social anxiety.'

'Or made it worse,' Kate pointed out, without reassuring me about my social skills, which was rude. 'I didn't want to make you do anything you didn't want to.'

'I thought that's basically what being a parent is.'

'I didn't want you to hate me,' Kate said softly.

I looked at Benny instead of at her. 'I don't hate you.'

She came over to us. 'What instrument goes best with cello?'

'Violin?'

'Then I'll *strongly* encourage Benny to play that. And you can play together.'

'That'd be nice.' I meant it. That would be the kind of thing brothers do.

November 18th

Obaasama, I have been a married woman for several months now, and writing less often because of this adult life. My days are spent managing the house and studying, and most evenings I am with the Lieutenant or out with his friends. When the Lieutenant is called away for duty or other engagements I enjoy the peace of the house. Of course, I continue to do my duty for the ghosts.

I have been telling some of their stories to the Lieutenant, and Mr S— too, for he is often with us. As a result, Sagi-sensei recently declared that my English has become quite capable. The Lieutenant and Mr S— tell stories too. The Lieutenant's are often about hunting and adventures of war, which are not exactly dull, but the stories Mr S— tells are rather better. He said his mother was a skilled storyteller of tales from her home country. There are surprising similarities between these stories and my own, but I suppose love and death are the same no matter where you go.

Yesterday, I recounted to them a story the ghost of an old man told me several weeks ago:

Not so long ago and not so far from here, there was a farmer. He was a good man, but not so good a farmer. In his fields he became distracted by the sweet birdsong.

If he grew a perfect apple, he gave it to his grandmother to see her smile. If a fox made off with his tofu he did not give chase because it was well known that foxes love tofu but are unskilled at making it, not usually having human hands.

All in all, this farmer was loved but not wealthy. It so happened that his youngest child fell sick and the medicine prescribed cost money. The distraught farmer went out to harvest his crops and hunt in the forest to find something to sell. He found his fields were overrun with weeds (how could he cut such pretty blossoms and starve the bees?) and he was as bad at hunting as ever (who could kill such a graceful deer?). The farmer became angry at himself. He sank to his knees and cried out, how I wish I was different!

A passing fox heard him (a fox plump from stolen tofu) and asked how he would be changed. The farmer said, I wish I was a tough man who did not lead his family to illness and poverty. The fox thought about turning him into an oni or changing him and his family into wolves. Luckily, this fox had learned something of kindness from the farmer himself. The fox said, you idiot. Why would you not wish for your child to recover?

The farmer said, oh yes, that would be a better wish. The fox sighed and said, of course it is. I will make your child well, and here is how. Go to your most beautiful field, where butterflies gather. There is a rare plant with gold and purple petals. Pick its leaves. Then go to the stream behind your house, pure and bright because you kept it clean for the frogs and fish. Collect a pail of water. Make okayu with that water and those leaves, and feed it to your child.

The farmer was grateful, and promised tofu for as long as the fox should live. The okayu the farmer made was delicious and his child soon recovered, and was in fact stronger than ever. The farmer built a shrine for the fox and faithfully left out tofu every evening.

Word spread of his healing okayu and people began to come, pleading him to cure some ailment or another. The farmer happily made the okayu, requesting no payment, but the people gave gifts of rice and sake and well-made cloth. So the farmer and his family lived well, as did the birds in the nearby trees and the flowers in his fields and the fish in clear water.

The farmer lived to be one hundred years old. Upon his deathbed, he told his youngest child – now grown and with children of his own – to always leave tofu for the fox, and to be kind to the animals and the land. He did so, and the family prospered.

But he forgot to tell his own children this, and they became more concerned with money. They cleared the fields to harvest more of the purple and gold plant; they spread fertiliser that muddied the stream; they neglected the tofu. Rather than becoming richer, the family became poorer and, what is worse, forgot to be kind.

The farmer, worried even in the next world, returned as a ghost. He appeared and said, you idiots. Clean the water, let the plants grow and, most importantly,

remember to give tofu to the fox! For wise foxes live to be
a thousand years old, and remain hungry.

And so the farmer's children's children did as he said.
The okayu healed once more, and the family remembered
kindness and the fox became fatter than ever.

The Lieutenant and Mr S— enjoyed this story immensely,
for it is rare I tell a humorous one. I had not told everything,
naturally. In fact, after the farmer had appeared to me, I
sent an unsigned letter to his family scolding them for their
behaviour. The farmer had done something that no other
ghost had done before, and came back to say that my letter
had sufficiently frightened his grandson and that all was
returning to what it should be. And then his ghost merrily
disappeared, leaving behind a smile in the night.

Sixteen

I n the music room, everybody else was tuning up calmly. Suddenly I *did* hate Kate for not making me do those awful recitals. I'd have to tell her that plan of hers didn't work out after all.

Daniel sat in his usual seat beside me, and the silence between us was a long, drawn-out note.

Mr Johnson stomped in, barking instructions like a hell hound. 'We'll go by rows! Starting from the back.'

I'd be almost at the end. Better than the start.

'What's the delay, Julie?' Mr Johnson beckoned her forwards.

Julie trooped up with her trumpet. She played as if she was a medieval herald, declarative and demanding. A trumpet was not shy. When she finished we applauded.

Mr Johnson clapped three or four times, less applause and more a *chop-chop, hurry up* sound. Next was drums, then piano, clarinet, flute, bassoon, French horn, the strings. With each my heart increased its rhythm, drowning out the breathy flute, the low call of the viola.

'You next.' Mr Johnson crooked a finger at me.

My hands were unsteady, slipping on the neck of my cello, on the bow. I took a deep breath, drew my bow across the strings and began.

I could feel it straightaway; it wasn't right. The time was a touch off, the move from one note to the next edged and clumsy; all I could hear were my errors and not the music. I clenched my jaw and made the mistake of glancing up and caught Daniel wincing the tiniest bit. He hadn't winced when Evan had reached out to him; I'm sure he wouldn't wince when Evan drew him in.

I pushed and pulled the sound out, and thoughts of the diary writer intruded: her playing, her power. Whether it was real or not, delusion or fantasy, I wanted that.

I played angrily almost, a middle finger directed at Daniel and Evan and horrible Mr Johnson. For a few bars it felt good, as if I was alone and strong, until I missed a note and faltered. The stumble stretched out until it had become a silence. I had stopped.

'Well,' Mr Johnson said. 'I think you had better leave it there.'

I slunk back to my seat, eyes down. Mr Johnson called for the double bass, but I could only hear my disjointed playing.

Then Mr Johnson declared unceremoniously, 'That's it then! Good job, most of you. Go away, have fun, have a mediocre summer etcetera. Dismissed!'

There was a collective sigh and the chatter and clink of people packing up their instruments. I stuffed my cello into its case, desperate to escape.

I couldn't help passing Mr Johnson on my way out.

'You'd better practise over the summer,' he said. 'You sounded like you were playing a lullaby for half of that. I mean, the half you played. You're distracted.'

I could only say, 'Sorry.'

'What do *I* matter?' he scoffed. 'Respect the music. And yourself.'

I didn't know if that was a motivation or an insult.

A lullaby. He was right. I needed strength and confidence and power. I felt a spike of resentment towards Dad and Benny, for making me be quiet; making me fail.

When I got home I was glad Kate and Benny weren't there. I stood at the bottom of the stairs and looked up.

There, the shape of a person lit by slanting sunbeams.

I climbed the steps as if controlled by something not myself, willing the figure to move, or to disappear between one blink and the next. But it stayed, outlined in the motes of dust suspended in the air.

This was wrong. It was bright ordinary daytime – these things couldn't exist in such mundane light. I waved my hand and the dust swirled and then there was nothing, just particles that had been caught and held too long in my overactive imagination.

'There's nothing here,' I said loudly and firmly.

I got to my bedroom, trying my best not to run. On my desk, open, lay the diary. Though... hadn't I shut it, placed it back in its box? Maybe Kate had found it, or, or— No. I was distracted, by its ramblings of ghosts and long-ago superstitions – and I was exhausted from my exams, sleep-deprived.

I shoved the diary into its box. It was cursed. It was driving me mad.

I went to the living room and turned on the TV and the lights, even though it wasn't dark. I stared through whatever comedy was playing on the screen, swinging between belief and disbelief. I waited to feel safe again; waited and waited.

November 29th

A typhoon has been and gone, Obaasama, and left behind an unseasonable heat. The poor Lieutenant did not take well to this sudden change in weather, and Mr S— was only slightly better. With nothing else at hand, I proposed a story.

The Lieutenant wondered how this would help and I said that in summer ghost stories kept us cool. Mr S— said, shivers up your spine. The Lieutenant moved his fingers up my back and neck to show me the meaning. I trembled and laughed. I had an urge to run my fingers up Mr S—'s neck in turn but of course did not do so.

I explained that Obon is during the summer and that is another reason why we tell ghost stories, because it is the time when the dead return to this world. The Lieutenant said he did not believe in ghosts and I told him that they did not need his belief. He gave me a piercing look and I wished I had not said that.

I called O-Suzu to bring in a paper lantern. I put out the other lights, and the lantern threw shadows on our faces. I told them:

There was once a young lord, brave and handsome. He knew the loveliest ladies, and the merriest music and the tastiest sake, for he lived for pleasure. One night, rather late, he became lost in the streets and heard music being played. It was a shamisen, a beautiful and lonely melody. He followed the sound, and came to a house dark except for a single lamp, which lit the figure of a woman.

He was taken by her beauty and called out, asking her name. She said he could call her the Lady of the Lantern, and she would call him the Lost Lord. They spoke and he was enchanted, and they fell in love there and then. The Lady of the Lantern asked if he would return the next night and he said yes. He promised a hundred times over. He returned home in the light of morning, as the lanterns of night were extinguished.

But after he had slept and woken he was empty, and thought it must have been a dream. He had been drunk, after all. When night fell he looked at the lanterns and set aside his promise and went to bright houses where lively music was played. Yet no matter how much he ate or drank, no matter the pretty ladies, he felt empty that night and every night after, till he was half-mad trying to fill himself up.

And so he returned to the house, but there was no shamisen and no lantern lit, no lady. He stopped a passerby and asked if a lady lived there. The passerby said, ah that elegant lady died not long ago, all alone. The young lord wept, for now his heart would never be full. Every night he returned to the house; every night until Obon.

It was then he saw a lantern lit. His lady was there, alive and beautiful. He cried out in joy. She said she had

CLARA KUMAGAI

been *away but it was customary to return to one's home during Obon, so that the dead may be honoured.*

He stayed that night with her, and the next night and the next, until his absence was noticed. His family sent out servants to seek him, and it happened that one asked the very same passerby that the young lord had questioned. The passerby remembered the young lord, and relayed their conversation to the servant.

Then the servant felt cold fear, even in the swelter of summer. He went to the house and in the falling darkness saw the flicker of a single lantern. He called out but only silence answered, and so he opened the door. There he saw the young lord, lying on the frayed tatami, a sweet smile upon his face. Embracing him was a figure in a kimono once made of the finest silk, now torn and faded; once worn by a great beauty, now a rotting skeleton with bony arms around her love.

The servant cried out and ran to the young lord, but it was too late, for he was cold and dead. The skeleton withered away until there were only scraps of silk beside a broken shamisen. All was lit by that single lantern, and it was too terrible a scene for the servant to look upon. He picked up the lantern, filled with two uncanny flickering lights, and he blew it out.

Mr S— said he did feel cooler. The Lieutenant agreed that it was a horror story right enough. I asked if he had been frightened and he said, no, no, not at all. The story did not have such a bad ending, I said. The Lieutenant replied that it was entirely bad, because everyone was dead! But dead for a beautiful reason, I suggested. Mr S— said it was beautiful in a story but would be only a tragedy if it happened in real life.

But, in the end, it was about love.

Seventeen

♩ ♫ ♪ ♪ ♩ ♪

I rubbed my arms; I was trembling too.

I had slept restlessly, half in fear, half in some kind of nervousness that I couldn't name until I recognised it as suspense. When I did sleep, I dreamed of the sound of papery fluttering wings, trapped and frantic. Then I'd wake, my eyes pulled to the desk, and the diary, until I gave in and started to read.

The stories within stories in the diary were giving me a weird feeling, almost vertigo. The real and unreal was becoming blurred, but I couldn't tell if that was the writer or if it was me.

I got a message from Sylvia.

Beach!

Right. We were hanging out. The saltwater would be good for me. I needed something indisputably *real* to clean my body, soothe my spinning head.

'It was bad. Like, keep-you-up-at-night bad,' I told Rosie as I handed her the sunscreen.

'I bet a million dollars it was better than you think.' Her hands spread the cool lotion on my back and when I shivered I thought of lanterns and skeletons.

'Adam choked,' Sean said to Rosie, grinning down at her. I wouldn't have invited him but the beach hang ended up including our entire class.

'You play the *bassoon*,' I said.

He scowled. 'Somebody has to. Coming for a swim, Rosie?'

'I don't date bassoonists,' she told him.

He stomped off.

'Harsh,' I said. 'You would totally date him.'

Rosie watched him do a belly flop. 'Ugh, I know.' She got up. 'Coming in?'

We waded into the water and once I was out far enough, I dived beneath the surface, the cool shock soothing me and waking me up at the same time. I floated on my back, held between the blues of sky and sea. What did some dumb test matter? The sky had seen trillions of tests happen, and billions of other fools failing them. Once I felt reassuringly insignificant I swam back in.

'Cleansed?' Sylvia said.

'Yes. And starving.' I sat on my towel and tore into the snacks I'd brought, then passed a bag to Sylvia.

She started munching. 'You wanna keep hanging out? We can go night swimming.'

'We should have a fire.' I didn't want the darkness here. 'We can dance around it,' I added.

'Very pagan,' Sylvia said approvingly. 'Sean and Art are gonna get some drinks.' She stretched out. 'Have you made any plans for the summer? Art said his place is hiring.'

'You think I'd be a good waiter?' I asked.

'You're a polite young man. Though you'd better work on your fake smile.'

I bared my teeth at her.

'Like I said, work on it,' Sylvia told me.

We lay around, chatting about nothing with each other and whoever was close by. When the sky bloomed purple I got up and scoured the beach for driftwood to ensure the night was kept at bay. Sean and Rosie lit the pile we made and the flames leaped, eager and blazing. More people arrived, and the hang turned into a party.

I felt happy, and then giddy after a drink was passed to me. This summer would be good. There would be plenty of days like this, with ocean and fire and friends.

Someone offered me another drink and I took it, gulped and spluttered. I wandered into the flickering semi-darkness, needing to dilute it. I found water and added some to the concoction in my cup.

Then I saw Evan. He was crouched by his bag, the light of his phone screen making his face glow.

I paused behind him. 'Hey there.'

He twisted around and squinted up at me. 'Adam?'

'Yeah.' He couldn't see me as well as I could see him. I liked looking down on him.

He stood unhurriedly. 'Having fun?'

I shrugged.

He took the cup from me, brushing his fingers against mine. 'You mind?' He sipped and made a disgusted noise. 'How am I gonna get that taste out of my mouth?'

'There's drinks going around.' But all I could think of was his mouth.

Evan grinned as though he knew it. 'I've been thinking about you.' He rested a hand on my hip.

'You have?' My voice was too hopeful.

He leaned in and kissed me, making my head spin more than any drink. He drew back to say, 'I want you to understand that the Asian thing – that's not why I like you.'

The present tense of *like* fevered through me.

'And Daniel?'

'What about him?' He trailed his fingers along my jaw.

That didn't feel right but his hands did, his mouth did. We lay down on the nearest blanket. Above us the stars quavered silver in the inky sky, and this was almost perfect. One of Evan's hands curled around the back of my neck.

'You know what I liked?' he murmured. 'When you fought with me.'

I had an idea of where this was going, but I still asked, 'Why are you telling me this?'

Evan's hard tightened. 'Wanna fight me?' His words were teasing but I could hear the seriousness, see the excitement in his eyes.

I felt excitement too, and a twist of unease. 'I don't know...'

'Come on.' He kissed me again. One hand on my neck and the other on my wrist, holding it against the blanket and the sand.

It felt good, being held there, assured that he wanted me. He tightened his grip.

I shook my head to stop his mouth. 'I don't want to.'

He moved his lips to my ear. 'I won't really hurt you.'

'What if I hurt *you*?'

Evan laughed in a way I didn't like. 'You won't.'

'Why do you want me to try?'

'It could be fun. It's hot. It's just experimenting.' He said, low, 'Don't be so boring.'

'I'm not—' But I supposed I was. Lots of people found this kind of thing hot, and that was fine for them, but Evan's hands were too strong, holding too much force in them. I gasped into his mouth, half in pain and half in something else. I wanted to give in; I wanted to fight. What would it be like to struggle against him, to hit him with all my strength? It would feel *good* – and then I panicked, because that's not what I wanted to feel good about.

'Don't!' I shoved myself up and pulled away.

Evan sat back heavily onto the sand.

'Shit, don't make such a big deal out of it.' His casual carelessness didn't conceal his alarm.

'I'm not. That's not okay, to...' I wanted to say, *to do things like that* or *to ignore someone saying no.* 'To say I'm boring.'

'Right, you're not boring, happy now? But you're afraid. You always hold back and wait, and then you sulk around instead of doing anything,' Evan shot back.

It was a surprising hurt, true in a way I hadn't thought about so starkly before.

'It was nice, before,' I said weakly. 'We can do that.'

Evan hesitated, as if he was about to return to me but he turned towards the fire. I thought of loves and lanterns flickering against the dark and he became nothing more than the shape of a boy outlined in flames.

———

The salt and wood smoke was a heavy perfume on my skin. I had drunk more before I left and the taste of alcohol on my tongue was both sweet and sour. I could hear the TV on in the living room and hoped Kate was dozing in front of it. I went to the kitchen and reached for a glass but my hand fumbled and it fell and smashed on the floor.

'What was that?'

Of course, Dad was home this weekend, *of course,* he was awake.

'Nothing! Just a glass,' I called back. I grabbed the dustpan and brush and swept the shards up, but the splinters escaped. They twinkled at me, tiny stubborn constellations.

'Careful.' Dad was crouching beside me.

'It's fine,' I mumbled.

He stiffened. 'Look at me.'

I met his eyes.

He sniffed. 'Another party?'

'I don't go to that many parties. School just finished, you know that?' I got up, too fast, and had to lean against the counter.

'Get me some paper,' he said.

I lurched in and out of cupboards until I found a paper bag. He took it from me and wrapped up the broken pieces. He got another glass, filled it with water, and handed it to me. I gulped it down and Dad refilled it silently.

'Sit,' he commanded.

'I'm gonna go to bed.'

'Not until you sober up a bit. I don't want you choking on your vomit.'

'Ugh, okay.' I sat down heavily at the kitchen table.

Dad sat opposite. 'Adam, you can't behave like this.'

'Like what?' I asked, trying to sound innocent and only sounding dumb.

'You know exactly what. Being rude to Kate, coming home late, not helping out. You told Kate you weren't high after that party but I don't believe that, especially now—'

'Not helping *out*?' The unfairness of this slapped me closer to sobriety. 'I babysit, I change nappies, I go shopping – but how would you know? You're barely here!'

'I'm working to support our family.' Dad's voice was composed but his cheeks began to redden.

'Sorry, sorry! Can't remember which poor country's getting bombed but clearly it's more important than us.' My rage came swift and spiky.

'Obviously I want to be at home—'

'It's not obvious,' I cut in.

'—but work needs me and—'

'Kate and Benny need you too!' I couldn't bring myself to include *and me* because it wasn't true. I didn't need him.

'That's why I'm relying on you.' Dad's voice had changed, become solemn. 'You're the man of the house.'

I laughed; this was genuinely funny. 'What decade are you living in? Is this even my house?'

Dad frowned. 'What do you mean?'

I ignored his question. 'You don't believe it, either. That I could be the *man* in this house. That's not my place.'

'I don't know what place you're talking about,' Dad said.

'Oh, just being good and quiet and not causing a fuss. Blending in. The usual.'

Dad blinked.

'You have a *real* son now. And my job should be to take care of him. Why should I be taken care of?' I didn't know how these words were forming, but I was spitting them out before I could make them more logical. I had never practised this argument or these lines, the way you do when you prepare for a confrontation. I'd never thought there'd be one.

'That's not true! Dad was angry too.

'It's true you've never thought about it. Or that you pretended otherwise.' I kept my eyes locked on his, willing him not to look away.

Dad raised his voice. 'You belong here!'

I wanted to say, no, I don't, but where else could I belong? I had nowhere else; I knew nothing else. I thought of the diary suddenly, and it was as if the lights flickered – but surely it was my drunkenness making the world waver at the edges.

I tried to get a grip on myself. 'Tell me,' I said, 'about my mother.'

Dad's eyes narrowed. 'What?'

'Start with how she died.'

CLARA KUMAGAI

'You already know.'

'Tell me again,' I demanded.

'She died in a traffic accident.' Dad's voice had lost its strength.

'Where? How?' I fired at him.

'She was outside the train station. A car hit her. The driver was an old man. He shouldn't have been driving.'

I had been told this. But I wanted to know more, know every detail.

'Where was she going?'

'Why are you asking me this all of a sudden?' Dad said.

He was hiding something. 'Do I need a reason to ask about my own mother?'

The lights flickered again, and when Dad looked up at them I knew I hadn't imagined it.

'Go on,' I told him.

Dad glanced at me, the lights, the table. He shook his head as if to clear it. 'She was waiting for us – we were late coming back, you and me. I'd taken you out to meet Kate—' His eyes darted to mine, startled, and I didn't understand why until his words fully sank into my brain.

I leaned forward. '*Kate* was there?'

This I had never heard before.

Dad's hands bunched into fists. He at least looked ashamed. 'Yes. I was with Kate then.'

'You were *cheating*!' I yelled.

'It was complicated,' he mumbled. 'Your mother and I weren't really together anymore... We were living in different countries and—'

152

'And my mother knew it was over, did she? You told her the truth?'

'I'd told her it wasn't working, it was time for us to face up to that.'

'Both of you,' I sneered. 'Why was she waiting then?'

'To pick you up, I told you!' Dad snapped.

But all I could see was a woman standing, watching for a man and their child. What came was what killed her.

'She died waiting for you. And for *me*. You were going to leave her,' I choked out. 'If she hadn't died, where would I be?'

'You'd spend time here and in Japan. Grow up in both places.' He was not convincing.

I caught my breath. I felt cold. I felt nothing for him. 'Liar.'

Dad slammed his hand on the table. 'No. I admit I did not tell you *everything* but it's difficult—'

'You think it's easy for me? Growing up here, like this?' I gestured to my face. To my whole body.

'What you don't know can't hurt you,' Dad said hoarsely.

'The biggest lie,' I spat. 'I know nothing. If you don't think that hurts then you don't know anything either.'

I wished I was still drunk but everything sparkled with clarity, as hard and sharp as the broken glass that had been swept away.

December 22nd

Obaasama, I am full of conflicted anger at the Lieutenant. He has complained about the time I spend studying and playing biwa. I told him that this study has enabled me to speak to him and he said, Well, your English is good enough now. I said it may be good enough for him but not for me. Did your husband think you existed only for him, Obaasama?

Well, what's the use of that music you play at all hours? he asked. What is the use of music, I repeated, and he seemed to notice the foolishness of his question. Let me play for you, I said, so you may see its *use*. It was not incorrect to say I was furious.

I fetched my biwa and opened the doors and sat before them, facing the Lieutenant with my back to the garden. I set the lantern beside me and left the rest of the room in the blue of the night. The moon was in shadow. I struck the strings of the biwa and began to sing.

It was one of the most famous ballads of *Heike Monogatari*: Kumagai Naozane's killing of the Taira warrior Atsumori. Even in my anger I felt the vengeance and sorrow echo from the strings through my heart. I sang:

Naozane heard from the castle
a flute being played

a wondrous melody
ringing like jewelled bells
like a deer calling in moonlight
or a goose crying across the blue skies
it rustled with the wind in the pines by the sea
and sang of the weariness of the world

The Lieutenant held up his hand, but I did not stop. I sang about Kumagai meeting Atsumori, and their fight amongst the waves. And Kumagai, about to kill Atsumori, saw his young face, the same age as his own son – a cherry blossom opening in spring – and stayed his hand. Yet behind him other Genji warriors came, and Kumagai knew he must kill Atsumori or be seen as a traitor. So he swung his sword and cut the flower from its stem. Kumagai removed the boy's armour and found in it a flute, and realised that it had been played by Atsumori.

Even the heart of a warrior
feels the vanity of this changeful world
he discarded his sword, his bow and arrow
and donned the robes of a monk

The Lieutenant stirred for the first time in many minutes, and rubbed a hand across his eyes as if they had blurred. I felt then, the ghosts assemble behind me, the warriors recalling their own regrets and deaths. Stop, the Lieutenant whispered. But I had to sing to the end.

Naozane prayed
and in the depth of his heart felt sorrow
felt sorrow from the depth of his heart

Enough, the Lieutenant said, but the final notes of grief were already echoing away. That is enough, I repeated, and I knew the ghosts were withdrawing. The Lieutenant's eyes stayed on me but I could tell he could sense them.

A feeling came over me, not fear, which I am accustomed to. It was power.

I asked the Lieutenant if he had enjoyed the music. He muttered that it was not the sort of thing he listened to, songs about death. He had understood its message, Obaasama, though I had sung only in the old Japanese of these ballads. He could have been recalling soldiers who had died, or soldiers he had killed. I told him he did not have to listen, but he would not stop me playing. The lantern flickered.

He said he would not listen, then. In fact he would not be close enough to hear it, for he was being called away for duty next month. I asked for how long and he said he was unsure. However, I would have the freedom to play as much as I pleased while he was gone, he said, even more freedom than he already allowed me.

I had a rush of unexpected emotions: relief and sadness. But can freedom truly be given from one person to another? It seems to be a thing that can only be taken away.

January 8th

Obaasama, I think that Mr S— is aware of the ghosts that visit me.

Last night a storm came without warning, and Mr S— arrived with it, as if the wind had swept him here. He had arranged to have supper with the Lieutenant, who had not returned – I assumed because of the weather. It was a surprise that Mr S— had come despite it, and he was equally surprised to find the Lieutenant absent. He wondered if he should leave too, but the weather was so fierce that I insisted he stay.

We talked about this and that, in Japanese as well as English. I enjoy addressing Mr S—'s questions about the Japanese language, as he makes an effort to understand the answers. He is a good companion to study with. Eventually we ate, setting aside the Lieutenant's portion should he arrive. It became late and Mr S— said he must leave, but the rain was falling as if the gods were angry at the earth, and the wind was stronger than ever. I recommended he sleep here. The Lieutenant would think nothing of it; it was his doing that Mr S— was here at all. Mr S— listened to the wind howl and accepted.

O-Suzu laid out a futon for him and I gave him one of the Lieutenant's yukatas. He thanked us and said he would sleep if the tempest let him. I informed him I would play biwa, which might hide some of the noise outside and he told me not to worry, he was not a child anymore. Yet, Obaasama, out of his uniform and in the yukata he seemed younger and for the first time I saw that Mr S— is not so many years older than I am.

O-Suzu went to bed without delay because storms make her head ache, and Mr S— followed suit. I went to the engawa, closing the door behind me. How extraordinary it was, to see the ghosts light as mist and yet unmoved by the gales wresting the trees around them. It was rather wonderful to play with such weather as accompaniment.

It was because of the noise of the storm that I did not notice the door behind me had been opened by a meddling gust... and then I heard Mr S— say, who are you playing for? I hastily shut the door to the garden. He asked if a person had been there and I said no. Mr S— said that it was not so strange to play for people not there. The sound carries, he said.

I saw him in the half-light and thought how different he was from the Lieutenant, gazing at me keenly with his green-speckled eyes. I apologised for disturbing him and he said this was not disturbing, only something he had not encountered before. He told me there was much in the world that he did not understand but that did not mean they could not be true. I held the biwa to my chest and a string twanged as though speaking for me. Mr S— said he should return to bed, and he was sorry for startling me.

I went to my futon too, considering his words. When I rose in the morning he had already gone, leaving behind a note:

Forgive my rudeness for departing without a farewell, but I have early business to attend to. I beg pardon for imposing last night, and for any perplexing things I said. *Blame the storm! The Lieutenant would laugh at my odd ideas so I shall refrain from speaking of them to him.*

Thank you for your kindness.

I want to ask him more of the things in the world he has seen, and what he does not yet understand.

Eighteen

♩ ♫ ♪ ♪ ♩ ♪

An insistent rhythm kept time with a hectic whirl of images: watchful eyes, a raised sword, a flute played by the weeping wind...

Until the beat resolved itself into the knocking on my bedroom door.

'No,' I croaked.

This was ignored. Kate barged in with a cup and a plate and a determined expression.

I squeezed my eyes shut. 'I said, no.'

'I'm acknowledging that you said that and I'm going to ignore it. Eat. I'm not lecturing you about drinking because, quite honestly, I don't care.' Her voice was grim.

I peeled one eye open. She placed the cup and plate on my bedside table

'We'll talk after your graduation,' she said.

Twin revelations seeped over me: what I had discovered from the fight with Dad and that my Japanese class graduation was today. I was genuinely torn between which was more awful.

I put my hands over my sore face. 'Why are you making me go? It's not even a real graduation.'

'I guess it's all I can do for you.' She didn't wait for a reply, which was fine because I had nothing to say to that.

This was going to be a terrible day.

———

Takane-sensei loved being MC. I had no idea what a proper graduation in Japan was like, but I suspected it wasn't quite such a comedy show.

'And now, our juniors!' Takane-sensei announced.

I shuffled up with a stuck-on smile and thanked Takane-sensei when he presented the certificate with a flourish. Back in my seat, I stared at the paper Takane-sensei had printed from the school computer, wondering if I'd truly passed when I only felt failure.

After the real, actually graduating class had been applauded, everyone mingled, heading to the next room where there were platefuls of onigiri and mochi and a mum furiously making takoyaki.

'Congrats,' Dad said.

'Dunno if it's much of an achievement,' I replied under my breath.

Takane-sensei materialised. 'Yes it is, Adam-kun!'

I bowed. 'Thanks to sensei.'

Takane-sensei noticed Benny and cooed and made some objectively hilarious faces until he was rewarded with giggles.

Takane-sensei pointed to Benny's T-shirt. 'Ah, is that Futa-kun?'

It was a cartoon of a grinning, anthropomorphic building. A speech bubble from its mouth said, 'Fu-ta' in Japanese.

Kate said, 'I don't know – I just thought Benny should wear something Japanese to support his big brother. It's funny, isn't it?'

Takane-sensei asked, 'You've been to Fukuoka?'

'Oh...' Kate glanced at Dad, who frowned.

'Was that mine?' I asked, remembering the KID STUFF box.

Dad pretended to think. 'Must have been.'

'My mother bought it for me,' I said slowly.

Kate cringed. 'I didn't realise – it would have been too small for you when—'

If things had been different, if Kate had been my mother, I would have looked just like Benny.

'How cute,' Takane-sensei said, heroically attempting to break the tension.

Yuzuki, with some social awareness superpower, came over and grabbed my hand.

'Photo,' she explained, and took me to pose for a hundred class photos.

Michael handed me the molten hot takoyaki his mother had made, cautioning me to let them cool down. Anna and Keisuke appeared to be arranging a date, at long last. I found Yuzuki, deep in conversation with Jo. Maybe they were setting up a date too, which made me irrationally jealous.

Jo noticed me watching. 'We are all going for pizza, Adam-kun. This time, you have to.'

I held my hands up in surrender. 'Take me to the pizza.'

Kate tapped me on the shoulder. 'Benny's tired. We'll see you at home.'

'Can't wait,' I replied.

Dad gave me a warning look.

First, we had to tidy up and stack chairs and thank everybody over and over again.

'How are you doing?' Yuzuki asked, as we hoisted a table together.

'I can't feel parts of my body, is that normal?'

'Which bits?' she asked.

'My brain, my heart. But my hair hurts.'

'I think that's a hangover.'

'I think that's my life.' We set the table down and hefted another. 'What's up with you and Jo?'

Yuzuki raised an eyebrow. 'Jo is not into me.'

'I dunno...'

'I *know*. He's—' Yuzuki shut her mouth.

'What?' I persisted. 'Got a girlfriend?'

'No.' Yuzuki looked shifty.

'*Oh*. I see.' I stared over at Jo with renewed interest.

'Stop it,' Yuzuki hissed. 'Don't say anything!'

'I won't. I'll just smooch him.'

'I'll just kill you then.'

'Honestly, oneesan? That would be a mercy.'

At pizza, everyone was chatty and giddy enough for me to inconspicuously smile along. Michael and Yuzuki were visiting Japan over the summer, Anna was doing an internship, Keisuke was going to play baseball until he died or school started again, whichever happened first.

'What're you doing, Adam?' Anna asked.

'Oh... getting a part-time job and wondering where it all went wrong.'

Everyone laughed. Jo glanced at me seriously, as if he was the only person who could tell I wasn't joking.

We stayed in the restaurant about an hour too long, then everyone hugged and otsukare-d and dispersed. I headed towards the bus stop until I heard someone call my name. It was Jo.

'You've got it.' He beamed at me.

'What?' I asked.

'The homestay.'

The homestay. I'd totally forgotten about it. 'How do you know?'

'I recommended you. You will be staying with Toshi-ojisan, another uncle of mine. He is my mother's brother. Takane-sensei's brother,' he explained.

'Wow. Thank you.' I was a fool. Obviously I'd be the one to go – everybody else had been to Japan before or had their own actual homes there.

'I think you will enjoy it,' Jo continued. 'And I will be close by.'

'Oh. That's good.' At least I'd have one English-speaking person to talk to.

Jo examined me. 'You don't seem happy.'

'I'm... not,' I confessed. 'But not cause of the homestay. It's other stuff.'

'The boy trouble?' he asked.

I winced. 'Also family.'

'So it would be good for you to have a holiday. It has helped me.'

A homestay did sound better than my other idea, which was *run away and never return.*

'The food is delicious in Nagasaki. And it is beautiful. But hot.'

'I like hot weather.'

Jo was skeptical. 'It is *very* hot. Like... mushi atsui. You know?'

'Nope.' One of the many, many words I did not. I was going to have to cram *so* hard.

'You'll learn it soon,' Jo said ominously. 'But I will meet you there!'

'That would be good. I have literally no idea what to do.'

'Great!' Jo said.

'Is it?' Panic was setting in, but he was already bounding away.

'See you in Nagasaki! Mata ne!' he called back.

'Mata ne,' I repeated. I checked the meaning of mushi atsui on my phone. Humid. I could deal with that. It was just everything else I had to worry about.

January 12th

The Lieutenant and I have recovered from our argument, in no small part because I play biwa only when he is not at home. He speaks of leaving with regret, which I confess I share. I have grown fond of his company. The Lieutenant is full of life and energy, at times almost too much for this house, yet it will be empty without him. He assures me that he will return in no time at all.

Yesterday he asked for a happy story, such as a romance. I do not think happy stories and romances are the same, Obaasama. He admitted that tragic love stories are the most popular. *Romeo and Juliet* and so on. I do not know them and requested he tell me. He said it is complicated to recount but he would look for a copy for me to read.

At that moment, O-Suzu came in to say that Mr S— had stopped to visit. Mr S— entered and said he hoped he was not bothering us. He glanced at me cautiously as he spoke and I smiled to show it was no trouble. The Lieutenant told him no, there was nothing to do in any case. I suspect the Lieutenant is the kind of person who arrives somewhere and immediately thinks of the next place to go. No doubt this is the life Navy men lead, but the Lieutenant has a restless nature.

I informed Mr S— that I was about to tell a love story that had some happiness in it. O-Suzu brought sake and I poured it for the men and then I began:

Long, long ago there was a weaver and a cowherd who lived in the sky. The weaver was a princess and every day she made cloth by the river in heaven. She worked diligently and never met anybody and her father, the king of heaven, felt sorry for her. He introduced her to a cowherd, a young man who took care of the white cows on the other side of the river. They loved each other at once, so much that they did not want to do anything else but be with each other.

Eventually, there was no cloth and the cows wandered all over the sky. The king of heaven became angry at these neglected duties. He separated the weaver and the cowherd and their hearts too, were sundered by sadness. The weaver wept and wept until her father relented, and agreed she could meet her cowherd on one night every year.

However, when they went to meet they saw they had no way to cross the river. The weaver was so desolate that a flock of passing crows took pity. They formed a bridge and let her walk across their backs to meet the cowherd. The weaver and the cowherd had their one night together, full of joy and sorrow.

If it rains, though, on that one night, the crows cannot fly to heaven. The weaver and the cowherd cannot meet. Their tears mix with the rain and fall to

*earth, so that even we are sad. So every year, we must
hope the skies are clear.*

The end? Mr S— asked. I guess there is no end, if it happens
every year, the Lieutenant said. But I wouldn't want my
marriage to depend on the weather. And only meeting once
a year! I said this is what makes it so romantic. You're more
patient than I am, the Lieutenant told me. I disagreed, in
fact I am thoroughly impatient. The Lieutenant asked Mr
S— if he was satisfied, even though the story did not end
happily ever after.

Mr S— was of the sentiment that not many good stories
for adults end happily. Happy endings make us feel better,
though, the Lieutenant said. Is that what you want stories
to do? I asked.

He said yes and Mr S— said no. Mr S— asked my
opinion. I enjoy stories that make me feel something new,
I said. When I was younger I thought only of the love story
between the weaver and the cowherd. But there are other
kinds of love. The weaver's father loves her, even when
he is angry. The crows love. Even the cowherd must love
his cows.

Mr S— opened the doors and gazed up. The Milky Way,
he said. That's what the river in heaven is. The Lieutenant
and I joined him. The stars glittered in the cloudless sky.
Mr S— gestured to two bright twinkling points. Yes, I said.
There is the weaver. There is the cowherd.

Stars! the Lieutenant said. They are stars.

They are also stars, I said.

January 17th

The Lieutenant will leave tomorrow. He is quite downcast, which surprised me, Obaasama. He has become even more affectionate than usual. I have promised to write him letters and he has promised to do his best to reply.

He has asked Mr S— to take care of me while he is away. O-Suzu and I are more than capable of taking care of ourselves, as we did before the Lieutenant came, but I did not protest. In truth, I am glad that Mr S— will continue to visit, and that the Lieutenant is in favour of it.

The Lieutenant is calling me, Obaasama...

Nineteen

'So,' Kate said.

We were at the kitchen table. Dad, Kate and I, a triangle of tension.

'You and your dad spoke last night.' Kate visibly steeled herself. 'The circumstances could have been—'

'Sober?' I supplied.

'Better,' Kate corrected. 'But we should talk more. I want to be open with you, Adam.'

She genuinely did, even though it was hurting her. Dad nodded, his eyes sliding from mine to Kate's. A rapid rush of anger spun my head.

I turned to Dad. 'Why is Kate the one doing this?'

He deflected as he always did. 'We're a family.'

'You already had a family,' I replied.

In the doorway, a silhouette coalesced. Dad glanced over his shoulder.

'Did you see something?' I whispered.

'What? No, I just...'

I made myself focus on Dad and Kate even as my skin crawled and my heart beat in my ears. 'Did she know you wouldn't stay? Did she love you?'

The shape shimmered.

'I—I don't know,' Dad stuttered.

Kate interjected calmly. 'Adam, there are other questions that we could answer better.'

'What did *you* know?' I shot at her.

She swallowed. 'I knew about you. And your mother. I had no idea what would happen.'

'But you knew what you were *doing*, didn't you? That Dad already had a wife. That he was cheating on her with you,' I insisted.

Kate blinked very fast. She didn't deny it. She reached for my hands. 'I love you, Adam.'

It came from guilt, though, that love.

'I don't love you.' My mouth felt numb, because my words were so cold, so frozen.

Kate removed her hands from mine abruptly, pushed herself away from the table. 'I've done *so much*. I've tried—'

'You have, more than *him*—' I amended.

'—for both of you, and it's so hard!' Kate cried. 'Do you think I don't know you're not mine?' She gritted her teeth. 'You want some apology – I'm sorry I *tried*.'

And I felt sorrier than I thought I could.

Dad turned on me, voice low and furious. 'You are behaving terribly.'

'You think Kate's only talking to me?' I said, incredulous.

I willed Kate to speak up, but she only bit her lip and dropped her head.

'You know what it's like to be left behind?' I asked hoarsely.

Neither of them answered.

The silhouette in the doorway resolved like a picture coming into focus. A woman in a dark kimono, so transparent that I rubbed my eyes – but she remained, faint but *there*. She was a ghost, a real ghost. I held in a scream and then almost laughed, feeling entirely deranged.

I had to get out of this house.

'I'm going to Japan.' I stood up. 'I'm going for the summer, and you're not going to stop me. I'm going home.'

Even as I said *home*, I knew it wasn't true. It was just a word to hurt them.

I walked towards the woman. She waned away as gradually as the certainty that crept over me: she was the writer of the diary, and by reading her words I had brought her back.

I held my breath and stepped through the space where she'd been, bracing for a chill. But the air was warm – hot, even. The heat left by the summer sun.

February 7th

The Lieutenant has been gone for three weeks, Obaasama, but Mr S— visits me regularly. We converse or read together and it is calm and unhurried. I speak in English and he replies in Japanese and we correct each other's words, and exchange new ones. Though he may not be as practised as Sagi-sensei at explaining grammar and so on, he is an enthusiastic teacher.

Mr S— is learning to write in Japanese. I taught him the alphabets, which he is exasperated by. Why so many? he exclaimed. However, he is determined with brush and ink, drawing increasingly elegant characters. I asked if he ever painted, and he said he used to. He asked if I painted and I said, no. Ah well, you are a musician so it would be unfair if you were talented at painting too, he told me. Mr S— said I must play for him soon. I warned that biwa was difficult for foreigners to enjoy, and Mr S— replied that not every foreigner shares the same opinion as the Lieutenant. It seems the Lieutenant had spoken of my playing, and not in a flattering way.

Mr S— noticed my silence. I would truly enjoy it if you played, he said. I heard you that once, but— He stopped. He asked, is this better? pointing at what he was practising, the character for *sea*. I gave some advice and watched him write *sea* over and over. It made me look out at the horizon and wonder about the Lieutenant's ship. But he will not return for another few weeks.

Long ago, in the imperial courts, people would conduct romances through letters and poems, I said. They might not see each other's faces for a long time. So a person's handwriting was important. It could be intimate.

Mr S— stared at my brush, my hand. Perhaps you can know a person by how they write, he said. Though, I added, *what* they write is more important. Your writing is beautiful, he said.

Thank you, I replied, but we should remember that you cannot read Japanese. He grinned and said, true. He asked if the Lieutenant writes me letters. I said he does, though he is irregular with his correspondence. I revealed that his handwriting is untidy but charming nevertheless.

I suppose that's him, Mr S— said. I saw that his hand had rested against the wet ink on the paper. Be careful, I chided. I raised his hand. His palm was rough but the inside of his wrist was smooth. I felt his blood move quick beneath his skin.

Ah, he said. He did not take his hand from mine. I did not let his go.

Then he touched my cheek, lightly. Oh no, he said in alarm. He pulled his hand away hastily. I put ink on your face, he said, his eyes wide and worried. That made me smile. We are like children learning how to write, I said.

He gave me his handkerchief, apologising. I said no matter, all was well, but my heart was uneasy. I was not sure precisely what we were talking about. He was agitated, and said it best he leave.

After he had gone, I took out my mirror. On my cheek, beneath my eye, there was the faint mark of his fingerprints.

February 13th

Obaasama, I am confused. It is about Mr S—. When we are together there are moments when it feels as if something will happen, though I cannot tell what it will be.

There is guilt, too, for when Mr S— is here I do not miss the Lieutenant. Or occasionally when Mr S— is here it reminds me of the Lieutenant and I become conscious that I have *not* thought of him.

O-Suzu said it may not be proper for Mr S— to visit so often. It was the Lieutenant who asked him to, however. O-Suzu cannot dispute that. And who cares about what I do? Mother and I write regularly but her concern is only if I am healthy and taken care of. The neighbours may gossip but I am accustomed to that. They gossiped when all I did was read and play biwa.

But, Obaasama, in my heart I am troubled and the source of it is Mr S—, who has done nothing wrong. I will go play biwa, and try to distract myself with the troubles of the dead.

February 19th

Mr S— visited today. This time I watched my feelings, Obaasama. He was unusually quiet, and several times he did not hear a question I asked, or made silly mistakes in his Japanese. Eventually we lapsed into silence.

Mr S— abruptly enquired as to whether I was excited. I was plainly bewildered and he asked if I had not received word from the Lieutenant. He is returning? I asked. Mr S— said yes, and added that he had been told by another officer, and it was natural that a command would travel more rapidly than a letter to me.

Oh, I cried, that is good news. You are happy? he asked. I will be glad to know he is safe, I said. And I confess it can be lonely here. I have even come to miss going out and those noisy American parties. No doubt I will stop missing them once I attend a few again. Will I have to attend so many parties in America? I asked.

The Lieutenant has said you will join him in America? Mr S— asked. Yes, I said, though I am unsure when. Do you want to return to America? Occasionally, he said. Japan is so different and difficult to understand but that is also why I would like to stay and learn. It is because of the little Japanese I have that my superiors want to keep me here longer.

It would be strange if I go to America and you remain here, I said. Many strange things happen in the world, Mr S— replied. It is one unexpected thing after another.

He appeared as though he was about to leave, and I found myself not wanting him to, so I proposed we read some poetry, for practice.

He agreed. I wrote out a poem and then read it aloud.

Hana no iro wa
Utsuri ni keri na
Itazura ni
Waga mi yo ni furu
Nagame seshi ma ni

I don't understand it, he said. Except the first line. *The colour of the flowers.*

It took me some time to write it in English. When I finished, Mr S— thought it sad. I concurred; there is a perception that the woman who wrote it is regretting her lost youth. The poet was Ono no Komachi, famous for her writing and her beauty. Once, there was a long drought and she was asked to help because her poetry was so powerful.

They asked a poet to help with the weather? Mr S— asked. I said, she wrote a poem so sad that it rained.

Mr S— asked what the poem was and I said I did not know; maybe it was too sad to be remembered. If people continued to read it, it might never stop pouring.

Mr S— said it was enough to imagine the poem, then. We spent a while imagining it, and were astonished when, shortly afterwards, it began to rain.

March 4th

The Lieutenant returned several days ago. I was nervous, Obaasama, because I wondered if the time apart had changed anything. Yet when I went out to greet him, I was quite delighted to see him. He was pleased to see me too. He lifted me off the ground and carried me into the house.

We have been meeting his friends since, dining and drinking. He said it was no fun being away. He gave me gifts of sweets and books, and a pretty western style dress. O-Suzu was thrilled to see it and begged to try it on, which I allowed without hesitation.

The Lieutenant asked if Mr S— had taken care of me while he had been away. I think my face did not change but my heart moved faster. He was very kind, I said. But I can take care of myself, and O-Suzu does the rest.

The Lieutenant laughed and agreed that O-Suzu is highly capable but it is good there is a man about that he can trust. If I ever... He stopped speaking. I asked him what he meant. He said, never mind, darling.

I have been left wondering about many things.

Twenty

♩ ♫ ♪♪ ♩ ♪

I leaned my head against the aeroplane window, letting the vibrations judder through my head. I wished they were strong enough to shake away the airport goodbye, Dad distantly infuriated and Kate struggling to get past the guilt I could see in her eyes. I'd ignored them both, hugging Benny instead.

Dad and Kate hadn't argued about the homestay – why would they, when it was such convenient timing? They wouldn't have to think about me for the rest of the summer, forget my troublemaking and all that fuss about things that had happened so long ago. And it was good for me too, obviously. I was leaving them and my messed-up relationships behind. And the spookiness too, I hoped...

I had kept myself from the diary after that last awful conversation with Dad and Kate, shaken by how clearly I had seen the woman in the doorway. But I couldn't leave the diary behind; what if Dad or Kate found it while I was away? Dad hadn't been happy that I was reading it and, knowing him, he would get rid of the diary and pretend it had never been there...

It had felt safe enough to take the diary out on the plane and, as soon as I'd begun reading, the words possessed me once more. And now here I was with the writer, who had fallen in love with Mr S— and didn't seem to know it yet.

There were hours to go. It was my turn to cross the ocean.

April 1st

The plum blossom has come and gone, Obaasama, and with it the Lieutenant. It was a sudden departure, a week ago. He said he had received urgent word that he must go to Yokohama, and after that he would be sent somewhere abroad. I cried and was surprised that I did.

The Lieutenant consoled me. I asked when he would return and he said only that he may be away longer than last time. I could not prevent from asking if he would not bring me with him.

He was taken aback. I asked if he had given any more thought to my moving to America. The Lieutenant said, but your home is here, and I don't even know if I'm to be sent to America this time. You would not enjoy it there, he continued. I told him he did not know everything that I enjoyed. Unfortunately we had an argument after that.

In the end, he said he would try to find out the likelihood of his being stationed in America again, and the preparations that would be necessary if so. This is vague consideration but I was forced to agree, as it was his last night and I saw that this was not a thing to be solved quickly.

When I saw him off there was some distance between us. From my hill I watched his ship leave the harbour, and the distance between us grow.

April 5th

I have been restless, Obaasama. I had not seen Mr S— for a while, so I wrote him a letter a few days ago. Yesterday he arrived at the house unannounced. I enquired if he was all right because he appeared agitated. He said that he had been busy and apologised for not writing a reply.

I asked if he would like to read or write together but he said he would be a poor student today, and I did not press him for an explanation. At last I said, You asked me to play biwa for you. If you would still like that... He said he would, very much.

I fetched my biwa and returned to see that Mr S— had opened the doors to the garden. I decided it fitting to play a ballad about poetry. Tadanori, one of the Taira, returns to the capital to present a poem of his to a famous poet, saying that if it was preserved then he would not regret his death, whether it be in the mountains or the western sea.

And so my thoughts went to the Lieutenant. Was he on water or on land?

I sang:

Shiga, the city of water rippling
is in ruins
but the mountain cherry trees bloom
like always

As I finished, I looked at Mr S—. His face was bright and intent once more. I have never heard your voice like that, he commented, so low and strong. It's... He trailed off. Unnatural? I suggested. Or too manly?

Powerful, he said. I took this as a compliment, because I think he meant it as such. There is so much more singing than playing, he continued, and I am afraid I could not understand much. But I felt the sadness...

It is sad, and you are sad too, I ventured. He sighed, saying he has never been any good at hiding his emotions. No, you are not, I agreed. Can you tell me what it is? Your husband, he said slowly. I was suddenly frightened. What has happened? I took his hand. Is he dead?

Mr S— looked at my hand and then my face. He is well, he reassured me. He wanted me to tell you that... Mr S— glanced away. He has been ordered away for longer than expected, he continued, and might not be able to write you often. I did not expect to upset you so much, Mr S— added.

I did not expect it, either – oh, that sounds odd, I amended. He is my husband. I *should* feel that way. He is your husband, Mr S— repeated. I removed my hand from his and attempted a smile. Mr S— returned it, but he was concealing something, I could tell. I would have asked him more if I had not distressed him enough already. You shall have to continue visiting me, I said, and forgive me for burdening you if the Lieutenant is away a long time.

Mr S— promised me he would, that if anything he was more of a burden on me. He looked as if to speak, then stopped. He bowed and said he never intended to hurt me

I said I was not hurt at all. He said he would try his best to ensure I never was. My husband is grateful to you, I said. I noticed his jaw clench. No doubt he is, Mr S— said in a strange tone.

I have been writing since he left. There was much left unspoken. But I have no more to write, Obaasama, until I understand more.

———

April 12th

It is some early hour of the morning, Obaasama. I am writing because I hope it will help clear my head.

Yesterday Mr S— and I went to view the cherry blossom, now in full bloom. We walked beneath the trees and discussed the poetry about cherry blossoms that I had given him. There were many people strolling about and others having picnics. I should have thought of a picnic, it would have saved us some distress...

We stopped at teahouses nearby but they were full, so I proposed tea at home, as it was not far away. O-Suzu was out doing errands so I made the tea myself, though Mr S— said we could wait for her. I can make the tea, I chided him. You must think I never do a thing here. I never imagined you making dinner, Mr S— said.

What do you imagine me doing, then? I asked. Mr S—'s face changed. I poured the tea without speaking. He did not look at me. The room was in a hush. Sometimes I imagine you doing things, I said, to break the silence.

Like what? Mr S— asked. I imagine you reading my letters and seeing my mistakes, I said briskly. I was relieved when he smiled. He said he hadn't realised I had such an anxious mind. I imagine you reading poetry too, I said. And you writing back to me, your hands holding the brush so tenderly and carefully.

I broke off. It was as if I had confessed a dreadful secret but was not exactly afraid. It was as if I was in a dream. Mr S— reached for me as if he was asking a question and I touched him in answer. His face was close to mine. He whispered my name. I meant to say his name too, but instead I kissed him. His arms went around me, pulling me close. His mouth hungry and mine too, hungrier than I knew it could be. I shook, unmade with desire.

He felt it, stopped and asked if I was all right. I said yes but all at once I was upset. Oh no, he said. I should never have – I thought... He took his hands from me. I do, I said, but I cannot. I know, he said, and I can't either and now I've done a dreadful thing.

It is not dreadful. It is just too late, I said. Yes, he agreed. I wish we... He shook his head. I won't ask you to keep this a secret from your husband. But I will not tell him. Unless you want me to.

No, he cannot have everything, I said. I suddenly felt angry at the Lieutenant, though I should have been angry at myself, or Mr S—.

I'll go, he said. I'm sorry. I felt a pain in my heart. We can still write to each other, I said. That would be permissible, would it not? He said yes.

I closed my eyes so I would not have to watch him leave. It is terrible, Obaasama, I know. I put a hand over my mouth to stop myself from telling him not to go.

~

April 18th

After writing several letters to Mr S— with no reply, I at last received a response from him. I am distressed beyond my own belief. How can it be that we have such feelings that only make their strength known when the world outside comes to meet us... It is almost frightening, that such emotions may be roused and then unable to control; as if a part of myself has become separate and mysterious to me.

I must return to the letter, Obaasama. It was polite but not long. Mr S— is to be stationed elsewhere and will leave Nagasaki in a few days.

I replied immediately, telling him he must come and say goodbye. The ink from my pen spread across the page in an unsettling way, as if I had no command of the words I meant to set down. It is not a good idea, but I cannot bear for him to leave without a farewell. The self I cannot control would not allow it and I am at its mercy.

~

April 21st

Mr S— left a short while ago. When he arrived I said I was glad that he had come, that I was not sure if he would.

You asked me, so I did, he said. It seemed hard for him to look at me. I began to say what I had planned to say: You are a dear friend to me, so I wanted to see you once more before you left.

I thought perhaps you would rather not, Mr S— said. I wrote you, I said. You sent me poems to read and translate to English, like a responsible teacher, he replied. I told him I must not be a good teacher if he had not understood the poems.

He averted his eyes. It would be a pity to say goodbye in this manner, I said. So I will try to be polite despite my vexation at you. He laughed suddenly. I can't say you are trying very hard, he said. That's rude of you, I replied, but I smiled behind my hand. It was good to laugh with him again. Will you go to where the Lieutenant is? I asked. No, not to America sadly. I'm being sent to China, he told me.

My laughter disappeared. The Lieutenant is in America? I asked. He told me he was being sent elsewhere. Mr S— seemed at a loss for words.

I do not hate it here, I went on, but I have been wanting to see the world. Mr S— said softly, I am sorry I can't show you more.

I wish— I began to say. Mr S— had almost uttered a wish when we kissed. I wondered what he might have said. That other self within me whispered, *I wish it was you who had been taken with me on the bridge. I wish I was married to you instead.* I swallowed these wishes and felt them roll through my body.

Mr S— caressed my wrist. I wish you would write to me, I said instead. I will, he promised. I could not stop looking at his mouth. Will you return? I asked. I hope so, he said. But for now it's better than I am not here. Not near me, I suggested. He kissed my palm. Your hand can always reach mine, he said.

I went to the door with him. A foreboding came over me, saying goodbye to these men with only their promises to keep me. My hands clutched at each other, wishing and wishing they were holding his.

Twenty-one

♩ ♫ ♪♪ ♩ ♪

My eyes were damp. I quickly chose a random movie to play on the tiny screen before me, so I could pretend I was having aeroplane emotions. My heart hurt for the writer, trapped in her own doomed love story. Surely, she would divorce the Lieutenant, plainly such an unreliable liar... or Mr S— would return to her and they would live and love together, because what did the writer care about proper society anyway?

As I turned the next page, an announcement instructed us to buckle our seatbelts. We were about to land.

—

I stepped out of Nagasaki airport and staggered. The damp heat hit me, so heavy and fierce that for the first time I understood a word with my whole body: mushi atsui did not mean *humid*, it meant a thick wet wool blanket that was also on fire.

'Ah – are you okay?' Toshi said.

'Hot. So. Hot,' I gasped. 'Is it always like this?'

'Oh no,' he said. 'It will be hotter in the afternoon. And every year now, it becomes hotter.'

I wanted to weep, but all the liquid in my body had turned to sweat.

Toshi led me to a square white car and I breathed a sigh of relief when he turned on the air con.

'About fifty minutes to home,' he told me. 'Please, relax.'

I tried to observe Toshi discreetly. He was Takane-sensei's older brother, probably in his early fifties. He had springy greying hair, a stocky build and an expression of cheerful concern. He told me he was half-retired, whatever that meant. His English was pretty good, and he had switched to it when he'd heard my stammering replies to his Japanese. He must have learned to be patient with dreadful Japanese from other homestayers; that's what he would be getting from me.

We drove along a smooth highway, where almost every car was white. I glanced at my phone but had no coverage. Toshi tapped his fingers on the steering wheel; they were surprisingly long and elegant. The land on either side became green. A mountain rose on my left.

'Have you been abroad a lot?' I asked.

Toshi nodded vigorously. 'The last time was about ten years ago. I went to San Francisco and LA.'

'You liked it?' I asked.

He smiled broadly. 'In LA, I saw Tommy Lee Jones.'

'That's... cool. Are you a fan?'

'He's Boss coffee,' Toshi said cryptically.

I couldn't summon up the energy to ask about this and we fell into silence. Eventually the road left the trees and fields, and entered a city.

'This is Nagasaki,' Toshi declared.

The buildings lining the road were tall, and I tried to read the signs as we passed them: ramen, a coin laundry, an izakaya, an array of convenience stores.

'Chinatown is that way.' Toshi gestured out of the window, and I glimpsed an embellished red gate. 'It's famous. The oldest Chinatown in Japan. We'll visit.'

The car chugged upwards as the streets narrowed, commercial buildings turning into houses that fitted together like jigsaw pieces. Toshi maneuvered into a tiny lot and parked tidily.

'We are here!' He leaped from the car and hauled my suitcase out. 'This way.' He headed up the hill.

It was *steep*. We only had to walk past four or five houses, but by the time Toshi opened a front door, I was a sweaty blob. I followed him into a narrow hallway in front of two steps that led into the rest of the house.

'Tadaima!' he called. *I'm home.*

There was a distant response of, 'Okaerinasai!'

'This is the genkan,' Toshi explained. 'Please take your shoes off. In a Japanese house we always do this.'

'Of course,' I said, as if this wasn't the first time in living memory that I was in a Japanese house. I was immediately stricken with the fear of what my socks smelled like.

Toshi left my suitcase at the bottom of a staircase, then led me through to a compact kitchen that opened on to the dining area. There were some framed photos on the walls, a TV in the corner, fresh flowers in a vase, an electric fan humming a breeze. I edged towards the fan.

A middle-aged woman came in, with short, neat hair and very thick lensed glasses. 'Adam-san?' she said.

I straightened up. 'Hello! Nice to meet you.'

'Hajimemashite. My name is Junko. Yoroshiku onegaishimasu.' She bowed sedately.

I bowed clumsily back. 'Sorry, Junko-san. Yoroshiku onegaishimasu.'

Junko continued speaking Japanese. 'Otousan, were you speaking English? and I recalled that married couples often called each other okaasan and otousan.

She raised an eyebrow at Toshi.

'A little,' he admitted.

Junko gave me a look of unmistakable sternness. 'Japanese only, Adam-san.'

'I understand.' Hopefully they too would understand once they heard my Japanese.

Toshi gave me a tour of the house, which didn't take long because it was not big. There was the kitchen and dining room, a tatami room with a family altar in the corner, a bath, a toilet, a neat garden out back. Upstairs were bedrooms, doors closed except for mine. It was simple and nice. A western style bed, a desk, a window. An air-con unit.

'This was my daughter's room,' Toshi said.

I hoped his daughter didn't mind, but there was no sign of her here.

He went to the window. 'Look.'

Rooftops dappled a descent towards a river, and beyond them were mountains and the glint of the ocean.

'It's beautiful,' I said.

Toshi smiled. 'Don't be nervous,' he whispered in English. 'This is your house. We are your host parents.'

I bowed gratefully. 'Thank you.'

'Are you hungry? We will have dinner soon,' Toshi said.

'I'll come down.'

'Take your time,' he said, and backed out.

I closed the door and had to force myself not to collapse on the bed. I unzipped my suitcase and pulled out the gifts I had brought. Takane-sensei had recommended 'local specialties' but nothing local seemed especially special so I'd brought chocolates. I put on fresh clothes and went down, arranging Japanese in my mind.

Toshi and Junko were sitting in front of the food spread out on the table.

'I'm so sorry!' I hurried into a chair. Soon *really* meant soon.

Junko waved her hand. 'Please, don't worry.'

I awkwardly handed the chocolates to her. 'A present, it's small.'

Junko took it with both hands and bowed over it. She proceeded to speak in the slowest, simplest Japanese I had encountered outside a textbook. 'It looks delicious. Thank you!'

'Thank you!' echoed Toshi.

The two-hand thing. I should have presented it to her nicely like that, not basically flung it at her.

Junko began filling our bowls with rice. She pointed out the dishes: katsu, steamed vegetables, a fresh salad. My mind was a total blank of things to say. I stuck to making yummy noises, which I didn't have to fake; the food was delicious.

'Jo-kun is excited to see you!' Toshi said.

'I'm looking forward to seeing him too,' I said fervently. Jo would help me out. He had to. It was his fault I was here.

We finished dinner. Toshi cleared the plates and I offered to wash them but he shooed me away. Junko discreetly asked if I would like a bath and I accepted enthusiastically.

'I'll prepare it,' she said, and went off before I could ask what that meant.

Toshi produced a melon and cut slices that we ate with miniature forks. It was sweet and almost obscenely juicy.

'A Kumamoto melon,' Junko told me.

Kumamoto was in Kyushu, the same big island Nagasaki was part of. The only other thing I now knew about it was that they had good melons.

A melody played from another room and Junko beckoned me to follow her to the bathroom. There was a tiny stool and a basin, a shower head in front of a mirror, a deep, almost-square bath. I guessed the mirror was to ensure I didn't miss anything.

'First, wash your body.' Junko mimed washing gestures. 'Afterwards, get into the bath.' She gave me some towels and an encouraging nod and then left.

I hunkered down on the stool and soaped myself, washing away the travel and miles layered on my skin. The bathwater was so hot I suspected it was some kind of test, but I inched in and my stiffness eased, defeated by the heat.

Then the bath started talking to me in a tinny voice. I panicked and pulled clothes on over my damp body.

I panted into the kitchen. 'Toshi-san. The bath... talked?'

He grinned, went to the bath and pressed some buttons on the panel, giving an explanation in Japanese that my brain refused to process.

'I'm a bit... I want to sleep,' I said.

Toshi nodded understandingly. 'Please, go to bed.'

'Good night,' I said.

'I hope the bed will be comfortable.'

'Thank you. I'm glad your daughter does not need it,' I said.

There was a pause.

'Yes,' Toshi replied shortly.

Junko was kneeling at the low table in the tatami room, reading papers and making notes.

'Junko-san. Good night.'

She nodded. 'Sleep well, Adam-san.'

I fell into bed. I glanced blearily at my phone – I'd forgotten to ask about Wi-Fi. Dad and Kate might be worried. Whatever. Let them. I shoved away a pang of homesickness. I wasn't sure if being here was better, but it couldn't be worse.

June 10th

I have been unwell of late, Obaasama. I had not had visitors in some time, until Fusae contacted me – Fusae who studied at the women's school in Ochanomizu. She lives in Tokyo but is married now, and had come to Nagasaki with her new baby to visit family.

Fusae's company was energetic and stimulating. Her husband has a good position as a bureaucrat and their social circle includes several foreigners. She has been attending English classes and wanted to discuss my own studies.

I said having an English-speaking husband had greatly helped, and it was a pity that avenue was not open to her. She laughed and said yes, it would be good to save on tuition but she was fortunate her husband was supportive of her education. She asked how I was feeling and if I needed to rest. I blamed the weather, and she agreed, saying it was difficult in my condition.

And so, Obaasama, I felt exceptionally foolish and began to weep. Poor Fusae was alarmed and called for O-Suzu. Then poor dear O-Suzu started to cry and so did Fusae. All of us, weeping! It was quite a funny scene, and I had to laugh. Truly it is rainy season, I commented. They saw the humour and presently we recovered.

Fusae and I spoke more, until she took her leave, making me promise to write to her.

O-Suzu, red-eyed, prepared me a nourishing meal. I sent her off to rest, for she seemed as worn out as I am. I sat down to write to Mother of my pregnancy, but caught myself staring at the paper and thinking only of the Lieutenant. And of Mr S—.

I gave up and went to the garden. The ghosts came and I played lullabies, the kind you sing to little children to send them to sleep.

July 8th

Rainy season is over, Obaasama, and I have finally returned to my diary. The last month was wearying and it is only now I am strong enough to put pen to paper and set down my thoughts.

And what thoughts do I have? I scarcely know. I have been absorbed in the practicalities of the body rather than the world of the mind. No doubt that is why I have been unable to reply to the Lieutenant and Mr S—. I have received one letter from the Lieutenant, vague and hastily written, which vexed me. The two letters from Mr S— were brief and shy. He commented only on the poems I had sent him before his departure. They expressed what I had been feeling and I believe he understands that now.

I did write to Mother, who imparted much wisdom. She intends to visit soon. She counselled I delay informing the Lieutenant until I was certain that all was well. This was welcome advice, I must say...

I am tired again, Obaasama... I have been tending to the ghosts, though *Heike Monogatari* does not feel right to play at this time, with its stories of death and glory. I have been singing old village songs, of home and harvest. It will be Obon before I know it – the cicadas are singing of it – the ghosts will assemble.

August 11th

I am sorry that weeks have passed with nothing written, Obaasama. I sense that you are close, though, as it is almost Obon. O-Suzu and I are preparing the butsudan, and marvelling at how a year has passed in such a slow and fast way. Looking back at the last Obon, I feel that person I was then was so young. I rather miss her...

I did reply to both the Lieutenant and Mr S–. General news and hopes of his continued safety to the Lieutenant; thoughts of poetry to Mr S–. I did not tell either of my condition. Instead, I asked if they would be returning to Nagasaki soon, but neither have answered satisfactorily.

I have been writing, as promised, to Fusae. Her letters, like her, are lively and full of interesting news. O-Suzu is always excited to hear of the goings-on in Tokyo. It makes me feel that Nagasaki is altogether rural.

I have also resumed lessons with Sagi-sensei. It is important for me to keep up with my English, and to tell the truth, I am glad of his company. He has been most kind, and I regret my earlier criticisms of him. However, he is as exacting as ever with his assignments and corrections.

If I fail to write regularly, please forgive me Obaasama. I will see you at Obon.

———

August 21st

The weather is cooling, at last. I was so glad to see you, Obaasama, and Father too, at Obon. I am sorry for crying so much, but be assured that some of those tears were happy. You were such a solace. I hope that I gave solace, in my turn.

I received an unexpected visit on the last day of Obon, from the biwa-hōshi. She had come to teach the end of *Heike Monogatari*. It was about Tokuko, the mother of the emperor, who cut her hair and became a nun – the last of the Taira clan. It was a secret text, this ending.

As the biwa-hōshi sang, a dreadful fear mounted in me. When Tokuko spoke of the death of her child I could listen no more. Why must you play this? I cried. The biwa-hōshi put her strong fingers on mine and said, it is about redemption. What you must learn to see is hope, even when all is despair.

The biwa-hōshi said I would understand later. When I wept, it was at the story and the skill of her playing and not out of pity for myself. I thanked her when she had finished and promised I would practise.

O-Suzu and I watched her walk down the hill, slow but sure. I wondered aloud when she would visit next and

O-Suzu sighed. Though it was not yet evening I felt the ghosts gather round and then, too late, I realised she would not come again.

———

September 24th

The leaves are turning, Obaasama. What can I say that you do not already know? The trees are yellow, brown, deepest red. It is the time of year to eat and read and I have been succeeding well at both. Everyone assures me this is quite right – even Sagi-sensei, which made me smile. We have been reading different stories of late: ones for children, by Hans Christian Andersen and Charles Perrault and the Grimm Brothers. Some are similar to Japanese folktales, and even to the stories the ghosts tell. It makes me wonder whether there are only so many stories in the world...

I have been relaying these thoughts to Mr S—, who is my constant correspondent. The Lieutenant's letters have become even less reliable. I still have not told him everything.

The breeze is crisp, the colours of leaves brave in defiance of the coming winter. I feel hopeful, despite everything...

Twenty-two

♩ ♫ ♪♪ ♩ ♪

The writer was *pregnant*. I could feel her optimism and fear rise from the page, as if the ink had been suffused with it. Would the Lieutenant be back before she gave birth? I tried to be optimistic too: maybe he *would* take her and his child to America...

I got up and opened the curtains. I'd been awake for hours, thanks to jet lag. The sun had just risen, sparking light from roofs and windows and the waves beyond. This was the same sea that the writer of the diary had watched, perhaps from not far away...

And by the desk the woman emerged into view, like a photo developing from blankness to image. With her came a sense of unreality, as if the rules of the normal world had glitched and shattered. She raised her eyes to mine. Her hair was pulled back, her kimono dark, her face a pale moon above it. The sunlight shone through her. She cast no shadow.

My body lost all sensation, but I heard myself say, as if from a great distance, 'You're *here*.'

Her mouth moved silently. I shook my head and she seemed to understand. She glanced at the diary.

'You wrote that, didn't you?' I whispered raggedly.

She nodded.

'Who are you? What is your name?'

She raised a hand, extended a finger and moved it through the air, as if casting a spell. Her mouth opened again, wider, and the descriptions of the haunting hungry ghost came back in a vivid swoop of horror.

I leaped away until the back of my knees hit the side of the bed and I half-fell onto it. 'Don't hurt me—'

She lowered her hand. Her face flickered in a terrible, utterly unnatural way, and then she was gone.

I knew she would return. I had brought her with me. I had brought her home.

⁓

Breakfast was rice, tofu, miso soup and another stuttering conversation. I was unsettled. My hands shook and I dropped my chopsticks and Toshi quietly set a spoon before me. I shrivelled with embarrassment and then asked about Wi-Fi.

Toshi gave me the typical old-person password of a long string of letters and numbers. 'You want to talk to your family?'

'Yes,' I lied.

He looked at me kindly. 'Ah, maybe a little lonely.'

I wasn't sure if he meant me or my family. I didn't think either was true.

I messaged Sylvia first.

I'm in Japan and wtf is going on
don't understand anything
not even the bath

Then I messaged Kate.

Hey. Got here no problem but tired from the flight.

Hope everything's good.

My phone immediately lit up with a call. I sighed and answered.

'Hi Kate.'

'We were worried when we didn't hear from you...'

'Jet lag,' I said.

'Are you okay?'

'Physically, mentally or emotionally?' I asked.

There was an uncertain silence.

'All are fine,' I said at last.

'I'm glad.' Kate's voice was determinedly upbeat. 'Send us photos!'

'Yeah.'

'Call us soon. Benny misses you. Tell us if you need anything.'

'Give Benny a kiss from me. Bye.'

I went back into the kitchen, where Junko was at the table with a pile of documents and Toshi was tapping on his phone.

'Your family are well?' he asked.

'Yup. Not lonely.'

There must have been something in the way I said this that made Junko look up from her work. 'Adam-san, will you tell us about your family? Why don't you show us a photo?'

Junko had strong teacher vibes, which I could see would make her both an excellent host mother and the bane of my life. I sat beside her and Toshi leaned over inquisitively. I showed them the selfie Kate had taken at the lighthouse and introduced her and Dad with the basic details: name, age, hometown, job, hobby. Junko corrected a word every now and then.

She pointed at Benny. 'Cute baby.'

I said eating and sleeping were Benny's hobbies. I didn't know how to say 'pooping'. Junko and Toshi's eyes flickered between the photo and me, not wanting to ask.

I gave in. 'Kate is not my mother. When I was small my mother died.'

Toshi and Junko nodded gravely at this but didn't say they were sorry or anything. That was fine. It was sometimes uncomfortable when people were too sympathetic.

'My mother was Japanese,' I added, in case they weren't aware.

'Where is your mother's hometown?' Junko asked.

'Um.' Why hadn't I asked Dad where my mother was from *before* I'd come to her country? 'I can't remember...'

'That's all right,' Junko replied.

'Adam-san, will I show you the neighbourhood?' Toshi asked.

I didn't want to go out into that heat, but I also didn't want to stay in the bedroom and be haunted.

'Let's go,' I said.

October 30th

The ghosts are gathering close, Obaasama. I was frightened
at first, but I detect no threat... I think it is because life and
death are two sides of the same coin. They see the boundary
between worlds, between flesh and spirit.

One told me a story today. She said:

*Long, long ago, there was a small shop on the edge of a
town. The shop sold various household goods, including
mizuame, a syrup fed to babies. The shopkeeper was a
quiet man. One cool autumn, a woman began to come
to his shop. She visited every night, shortly before his
shop closed and just as darkness came. She was thin
and pale. She would point at the mizuame and with
her hands show the amount she wanted: only a little.
She paid with dirt-covered coins but the shopkeeper did
not mind; money was money.*

*Once, the shopkeeper asked if she lived nearby but
she did not answer. Next night, he asked if there was
a new baby in her family, but she did not answer. The
night after that, he asked if she was well, but she did not
answer. However, she looked troubled. The shopkeeper
thought she wanted to speak but had been warned not
to. Her home, he assumed, must not be a good one.*

The shopkeeper was quiet but he was also kind. When next he sold her the mizuame, he took a lantern and followed after her. Down the narrow streets and through the shadows, he followed, until he saw the woman enter a cemetery. She turned to look at him. She nodded and said with her hands, come. So the shopkeeper went.

He followed her past graves until finally, she stopped before a large tomb of a once-wealthy family. The door of the tomb was open... and the woman went inside.

The shopkeeper inched forwards, step by step. He held the lantern high. Then he heard a sound – a child, crying. He ran inside and there was a baby, alive. There was the woman, dead. She must have been buried too early, and the child born even as the mother died. Beside her were the pots which had once held the mizuame. The baby saw the shopkeeper and stopped crying, and laughed in the light.

And so you see: love is stronger than death.

I took the story to be a comfort, Obaasama. I told the ghost, yes, love is indeed stronger than death. And she smiled and faded away.

Twenty-three

♩ ♫ ♪♪♩ ♪

My throat was tight with sadness and horror. I was sick of how the writer spoke of love and death, always together, as if they couldn't be separated. As if dying for love was a beautiful thing... 'Is that why you died?' I whispered, and then covered my mouth.

Why was I *trying* to talk to the ghost? I shut my eyes so I wouldn't see her develop out of nothing.

The doorbell rang.

'Adam-kun?' a voice called.

It was Jo.

I rushed downstairs and almost threw myself at him. To my surprise, he hugged me.

'Adam-kun!' he said. 'Long time no see!'

It did feel like I'd seen him in a different age. 'Long time no see,' I agreed.

Toshi and Junko were also happy to see him, in a way that made me suspect they were glad someone else was here to take care of me. They launched into an animated conversation, of which I caught one word in ten.

Jo asked me a question, then saw my face and repeated it at about one-third the speed: did I want to see more of Nagasaki with him.

'Please,' I said.

'Great!' Jo declared, as if there'd been a chance I'd refuse.

Jo reminded me to say *ittekimasu* as we left.

'Itterasshai,' Junko and Toshi replied in unison.

Once we were outside, I said in English, 'Jo, please help me. I don't understand Japanese and never will.'

Jo laughed and thankfully replied in English. 'That's what I said in America. Don't worry. Junko-obasan and Toshi-ojisan have helped many homestay students. Your Japanese will get good!'

'Have they had anyone as bad as me before?'

Jo thought. 'I think one was almost worse.'

I supposed this was comforting. We headed downhill, amid a cacophony of buzzes and shrieks.

'What *is* that?'

Jo was momentarily confused, as if he couldn't hear a thing. 'Ah, the *miin-miin, miin-miin*?'

Whatever onomatopoeia that was, it did sound like the noise around us.

'It's semi,' he said.

'Semi,' I repeated.

'Cicada. It's mating time.' He gestured to a bug that resembled a big dry moth, resting on a telephone pole.

'It must be extremely horny to be making that noise,' I said.

Jo grinned bashfully and then laughed enough to make me feel funny; enough to make me laugh too.

'So where do you want to go?' he asked.

'Toshi already showed me a temple and a café, two conbinis... I don't know much about Nagasaki. I meant to do more research but...' But I hadn't.

'Is there anything you need?'

'Oh – a SIM card!'

'We can get that. Ah.' Jo stopped walking. 'We should speak in Japanese. Or Junko-obasan will know,' he said ominously.

'Ugh. Okay.' I agreed that Junko would somehow know.

Jo switched to Japanese, and it took me a moment to understand he was asking me the same things he'd just said in English. I could do this. It was a lot easier to talk to Jo, maybe because his English wasn't perfect either, or because of the enthusiasm he gave off in generous waves.

We rode the tram into the city centre, Jo pointing out landmarks. We went into an electronics store, blaring jingles and announcements and staff calling, *Irasshaimase!* I chose a SIM card and paid, needing some prompting from Jo to understand the cashier.

Afterwards, we walked through the streets and Jo patiently answered my questions.

'What's that?' I asked over and over.

'Pachinko. A sort of pinball game.'

'Snack bar. Like... a bar where women talk to you.'

'Gacha gacha. Um. I don't know what gacha gacha is in English. But you can get funny toys there.'

I'd been on family holidays abroad, but here everything felt foreign in a new way. I could puzzle out some of the signs or catch a few words of a passing conversation – I would *almost* understand, until Jo made a comment like, 'That bakery is famous for chiffon cake but it only opens on the second Thursday of every month,' or, 'The battleship island is especially popular,' and then I had to recalibrate my brain to form a logical question.

Eventually, I began peering at stuff like benches and cars and asking what they were and Jo started laughing.

'Want to eat?' he asked.

I did.

We went to a plain corner restaurant, where Jo showed me how to work the ticket machine. The soba was delicious, simple and refreshing. I tried to copy Jo's slurping and almost choked to death.

Afterwards, we walked along the pier, the water moving sedately and the sun sliding towards the mountains.

'You feel okay?' Jo asked.

'Tired but... I'm glad I'm here,' I said.

'It's better to be in Japan?'

I thought of Dad and Kate and Evan. Then of the ghost, here, and still said, 'Anywhere is better than home.'

'I see,' Jo said.

'I didn't mean that – I'll tell you about it some other time, if you want,' I said quickly. 'I'm happy I'm here, really.'

'I understand.' Jo gazed at the boats, the shape of islands in the distance. He turned back to me and his face was like the bay: open and hopeful. I didn't care if he was just being polite or if he'd forgiven me; I was glad to see it.

'Now,' he ordered, 'say all that again, in Japanese.'

May 18th

How strange to open up this diary after so long, Obaasama! Reading some of my last letters to you is like returning to a novel I read long ago... Yet it has not even been two years. It has passed swiftly, for the most part. There have been countless moments of wonder.

My son is more than a year old. Haru. He is full of energy, and clever. O-Suzu and I are constantly busy with him. He is like O-Suzu's child too. She says he is lucky to have two mothers. Some neighbours say it is a pity, but we require only food and shelter, really. And stories. Haru has all he needs.

Though I am afraid that he has not much more than that. My days are full enough, with Haru and the household and playing biwa for the ghosts, but I am considering looking for some work, most likely teaching. The Lieutenant's allowance does come, but not always on time, or less than usual.

Mr S—'s letters remain regular. He is determined to continue his Japanese learning and says I remain his best teacher. I still see his hands holding his brush, sweeping ink thoughtfully across a smooth page. I do not tell him that. I do not tell anybody that, except for you. You are good at keeping secrets, Obaasama.

Fusae and I write to each other frequently. She continues to relay gossip from Tokyo – O-Suzu would be outraged if she did not – but our conversations have turned to the latest writers and journals. She sends me issues which feature writing by women, whom we have both come to admire. It is only at such times I wished I lived closer to Tokyo, so that I may meet such women.

It may be because of this that the urge to write has returned to me. There is another reason. I am not sure why I did not write it first but it is difficult, somehow.

The Lieutenant is returning, at last. He is as bad at writing letters as ever, but in so many he promised he would return soon. And so, despite my occasional doubts, I always thought he would return next month, or the month after. Which is why I never wrote to him about Haru, despite my mother and O-Suzu urging me to. I wanted to tell him in person, let him see with his own eyes. The Lieutenant will know soon enough.

—

May 28th

It has been an eventful day, Obaasama. Mr S— was here.

I had just laid Haru down to sleep when I heard O-Suzu's cry of shock. There Mr S— was at the door, somewhat darker, wearing a new uniform. His eyes were the same, as was his smile. He said he meant this to be a surprise but it appeared he had frightened us instead. I wanted to say that my heart had leaped in an entirely different way, but I held my tongue.

We laughed and forgave him. He presented gifts and a beautiful pen. I saw it and thought of you, he said. I bowed to thank him and to hide my face. I asked him why he had not informed me he was coming and he protested that he had but must have outrun his letter.

O-Suzu brought tea and we exclaimed over the treats he had brought: little cakes and candied pineapple. Mr S— had brought them from Hawaii, where he had been sent after China. He described Hawaii to us, a place made of islands, full of beauty.

When O-Suzu had gone to prepare some food and we were alone, Mr S— said he was happy to see me. He asked me if I had been well, and I assured him I was, that the lack of men about did not worry us in the slightest. He laughed, seeming relieved. He told me I looked different, as though I had grown up in some way. Mr S— said he had felt it from my letters too, and was glad I was writing to him more frequently.

I told him I was glad he was here so I did not have to write to him at all. He smiled, the green in his eyes appearing the brighter because it had been so long since I'd seen them. I had to look away. I felt as though I was losing some control of myself.

Mr S— asked if I still wanted to go to America. I replied that I certainly wanted to see more of the world and asked if he did too.

I don't know, he said. I would like a home. Will you leave the Navy then? I asked. I intend to, he said. I don't like it. They tell us that America is powerful and must remain so but... He sighed.

This was also what our newspapers and politicians and even ordinary people say, more and more these days. They think Japan should rule all of Asia and perhaps it could happen, with so much attention and money currently devoted to war.

Hawaii, though... Mr S— continued. It's beautiful. The people are kind, even to an American like me. I've often thought how you would like it. You would be able to watch the ocean there, too.

He touched my chin and raised my face towards his. He smelled like the sea.

I had thought we had settled into a friendship; that he had forgotten. That my feelings for him were gone. Yet there we were, again. All those unspoken things between us. He reached for me and I let myself rest, for a moment, in his embrace. His mouth was against my neck, just below my ear. I can feel it still.

Wouldn't you come with me? he whispered.

I pulled away. I cannot, I said hoarsely. The Lieutenant has said... Mr S— was taken aback. The Lieutenant writes to you, then? Irregularly, I replied slowly, for his surprise struck me as odd. Do you not?

Not for some time, he admitted. We had a disagreement. You were not aware he is returning in a few days? I asked. Mr S— shook his head, no, no. And half to himself muttered, so he is coming back after all...

Before I could request an explanation, Haru cried. Mr S— heard, and I saw understanding dawn on him.

We listened to O-Suzu soothing Haru, telling him not to cry. Her footsteps neared and she opened the door with

Haru in her arms. Haru-kun wants Okaasan, she said. I opened my arms and Haru flung himself into my lap.

This is Haru, I told Mr S—. I could not meet his eyes.

After a moment, Mr S— shook Haru's plump hand gently. He said, nice to meet you. You are a lovely child.

Do you see? I asked. Yes, I'm sorry, Mr S— said and tried to smile. So that is why the Lieutenant is returning?

He does not know about Haru yet, I said, so it will be a surprise. Ah, Mr S— said, that's not... The Lieutenant is... well you know how he is. I should have told him, I am aware, I said. Not only that, Mr S— began.

Haru started to weep. I tried to hush him but he would not calm down. Will you come visit me again? I asked. We can talk more.

I should never have mentioned anything, Mr S— said, I am sorry. I will come, if you ask me to. I will, I said. I wished that Haru had not cried when he did. There were so many things I wanted to tell Mr S— but I knew it would do no good.

I will always ask you, I said.

～

June 2nd

The Lieutenant came back today, Obaasama.

He had sent word ahead. O-Suzu and I were up from daybreak, cleaning and freshening the house. While she prepared a special meal, I fixed my hair and dressed in the kimono the Lieutenant liked best. I tried to put Mr S— out of my mind. I made sure Haru's face was clean and shining. His hair is light brown and his eyes are dark blue, but otherwise he is as round and sweet as any Japanese baby.

Your father is coming, I told him. Be as polite as possible. He rolled on the tatami and giggled at his toes. I became increasingly anxious. I could not laugh or play with Haru, and so it was a relief when it was time for him to nap.

The Lieutenant was late. When I opened the door he said my name as if he had not been certain that I was real. I bowed low. Stop, no need for that, the Lieutenant said. He had forgotten Japanese customs after being so long away.

He came inside and took my hands, looking down at me intently. As pretty as ever, he said. The Lieutenant also appeared unchanged, strong and handsome.

Come, I told him. We sat down. He was still holding my hands but did not kiss me or pick me up as he used to do, which I was grateful for.

It has been a while, hasn't it? he said. Quite a while indeed, I agreed. Yes, I am sorry about that. You know how it is... he said. I asked how long he would stay, and that I hoped he would not leave soon.

He did not answer, but asked if I had been lonely. You shouldn't be alone, a young girl like you, he said. I am not so young anymore, I told him.

The Lieutenant was nervous, which surprised me. You are home again, I said, be easy. I must apologise for not writing to you more, he said abruptly, and in more detail. You have been very patient. Oh, I have had my impatient moments, I replied.

Your English has become even better, he told me. I
thought you might have forgotten it since I left. I study, I
reminded him. And in America I have no doubt my English
will seem poor. I watched him carefully as I said this. He
glanced away. My uneasiness grew.

Mr S— has remained a good friend, I said. We exchange
letters to practise English and Japanese. He was here a few
days ago.

Was he? the Lieutenant asked in a cutting voice. What
did he have to say? My heart quickened. I was foolish to
mention his name. He told me about Hawaii, I said carefully.
Yes, that's where he was. Nice place to be. I haven't seen
the fellow for some time, the Lieutenant said.

Did you have an argument? I asked. We had a falling-
out, he said. That man is altogether too sensitive to be in
the military. I was suddenly afraid he knew of what had
happened between Mr S— and me.

A lot has happened since I left, the Lieutenant said, and I
do have an important thing I must tell you. My unease grew
stronger so I interrupted by saying, as do I. I called for O-Suzu
and she came, carrying Haru. This is Haru, I said. Your son.

The Lieutenant's face paled, then flushed. He did not speak.

Haru-kun, this is your otousan, I said, and I gently
pushed him towards the Lieutenant. My son? the Lieutenant
asked. He is mine? Of course he is yours, I replied, with a
touch of anger. Look at him. Look at his eyes.

Blue eyes, the Lieutenant said. They are like mine, aren't
they? How old is he? He is more than a year, I answered.
Why didn't you tell me? he asked.

I believed you would return soon, as you promised you would. Then I thought it better to show you, I explained. It's a shock, the Lieutenant said. He's an adorable kid. But a shock...

Are you not happy? I asked. The Lieutenant suddenly picked Haru up. Haru shouted but did not cry, then stared at the Lieutenant and laughed. He knows who I am, the Lieutenant said.

The Lieutenant gazed at Haru with wonder. I had been uncertain of his reaction, but this made me glad. He looks like me when I was a baby, the Lieutenant said. Hair's a bit darker but really just like me. My son, he repeated. So you are pleased, I said.

The Lieutenant stared at me as if he had forgotten I was there. Yes, but... the situation is complicated, he said slowly. What situation? I asked.

The Lieutenant spoke fast and fractured, saying, When I came here, to Japan – I knew I would be away from America for a while. I get lonely easily, it's my own fault. A fault of many men.

I do not recall breathing as he spoke. My heart did not beat at all.

And you! he said. I never saw a girl so pretty. We had a good time, didn't we? I should have been clearer when I left but I just didn't want to make you sad. I see now it would have been better to do that...

Tell me, I said.

The Lieutenant looked at Haru, not me. The thing is, I'm married, he said. To an American girl. Our families are friends. When I went back she was different from what I remembered. A lovely young lady, really.

I said, You are married to me.

It's not the same as an American marriage. The laws are different here. It's easy to get a divorce, isn't it? he said.

So you came to divorce me? I asked.

I thought I ought to tell you face to face. He declared this as if it was deeply worthy and good of him. I asked why he had gone to the bother of marrying me if he had thought it meant nothing. Why could he not have paid women whose job it was to keep men like him company?

He told me to calm down. I wanted more, he said, someone who—

You wanted to be loved, I finished for him. He did not reply. Instead he said, I thought you had an idea. Or that Mr S— informed you.

Mr S— knows? I asked. And that was a knife sliding smooth into my heart.

I've taken care of you, though, the Lieutenant went on. Plenty of other fellows up and leave without a goodbye.

If you divorce me, I suppose that will end, I said. The Lieutenant beamed into his son's face saying, But this baby...

Give me Haru! I cried. I pulled Haru from his arms. He is my son, I told the Lieutenant, he is mine. He's mine too, the Lieutenant said, you can't deny that. I told him to leave.

Don't shout so, he said. Let's talk. I thought I might stay here tonight. Get out, I said. It is my house and my family's house. It is not your home.

O-Suzu slid open the door. She was holding a tray of food but I think she had come to see why we were raising our voices, why Haru was wailing. The Lieutenant looked from her to me. He was angrier than I had ever seen him. But I was angrier than I had ever been in my life. If my biwa had been near I would have reached for it, I would have called every ghost down upon him.

I will return, the Lieutenant said. We have business to finish.

Now I am waiting, Obaasama, and writing this beside Haru as he sleeps because I cannot bear to let him out of my sight.

—

June 3rd

I am relieved I can write to you here, Obaasama. I wrote letters to the Lieutenant and tore them up. I wrote a letter to Mr S— and tore that up too.

O-Suzu is at a loss. She is enraged and sorry, but she reminded me that I should have told the Lieutenant about Haru immediately. Maybe then he would have come back sooner. Everybody knew foreigners were like this... I shouted at her until she went away.

The Lieutenant returned in the evening. He had composed himself and said he had an idea and I could make the decision. So I listened.

The Lieutenant proposed that he bring Haru to America, where he would raise him. What about me? I asked. Wouldn't it be easier for you to get married again without a child? he said. Do you want to move to some other city? I'll help set you up, he offered.

You promised you would take me to America. Was that a lie? I asked.

He said he wanted to, but it was impossible. Only taking Haru is possible, I said. The Lieutenant nodded. I asked what his wife would say.

Stay here a moment, he told me, and he went outside. I already knew what was going to happen. I followed him out because I did not want her inside my house.

Oh, she said. Hello. She introduced herself, speaking slowly.

I spoke as slowly back to her. You must be the lovely American girl, I said. She was taller than me. Her hair was a shade of blonde that was almost orange.

This is my wife, the Lieutenant said. We have that much in common, I replied. This situation is... unusual, the wife said, but I am your friend. I told her not to speak to me as if I was a fool. I think I said this calmly, but I cannot entirely remember. I may have shouted it.

I see, she said, I won't, then. My husband has told me about the child. Other women would be cross but I'm not. He would have a good education, the best opportunities.

I asked what prompted such selflessness, as it would be apparent that Haru was not her child. The wife flinched as if I had struck her. We want a kid, the Lieutenant said, but the doctors told us—

The wife interrupted him to say that she wants a family more than anything. I told her that was what I wanted too.

You can still have one, the Lieutenant said, and it would be easier to find a husband this way, wouldn't it?

Why would I want another one? I asked. The Lieutenant spoke as though he could not hear me. I can see you're struggling here, he went on, and how will you afford school and books and everything a growing boy needs? You could send more money, I said. The wife shook her head. I need that money for my own family, the Lieutenant argued. This solution would make life easier for you and Haru.

I asked where Mr S— was. Why do you want him? the Lieutenant asked. Because he understands me, I wanted to say, and because perhaps it was not too late. Instead I said, I would like his opinion because I have little knowledge of American laws.

I sent him away, the Lieutenant replied coldly. It was time for him to go and I'm his commanding officer.

I could neither speak nor think. You must leave me, I said.

You have to give an answer. You know what the right decision is, the Lieutenant said. Give her some time, the wife advised. We will return.

I went inside and held Haru. I thought about him and his future, about what he could do, what I could do. I have been trying to imagine his life, all the possible ways he could live. How can anybody decide this?

What will I do, Obaasama?

—

June 5th

All the absent men have visited me, Obaasama.

Uncle came today, to my shock. He is changed since last I saw him. He is old and hunched and worn. He had gone to Taiwan last year, setting up a Japanese shrine. He said it was proceeding well, and Japan would soon control the rest of China too. However, it was more valuable for him to be here, encouraging Japanese to go settle in the colonies. The native people in Taiwan were stupid, he declared, and he had not been prepared for the work required to convince them of the superiority of Japan's rule and religion.

There was a note in his voice, Obaasama, that told me he had not liked what he had seen; likely that the people of Taiwan were not stupid in the least. Uncle resembles Father; what exists in his mind is better than the real world. He moved the conversation to Haru. He wanted to see him. Haru, sweet boy, hid behind me and peeked at Uncle from under my sleeves. Even Uncle could not help but soften.

But he said, the child does not pass for Japanese. I asked why he should. Uncle said that Japan's strength was in its bloodline and purity. I did not see how this related to Haru and told him so. He replied that this would not be a good place for Haru as he grew older. I asked why not, when he had a good home and people who loved him. I knew what he meant, though, and I could feel my fury rise, as it had risen when the Lieutenant had been here.

Uncle said he knew that Haru's father had returned and what he had proposed. He too thought it best that Haru go to America. He spoke with an urgency that chilled me. You think I am being cruel when I talk of purity, Uncle said, but I am not the only one who thinks so. I am your family and I am trying to protect you.

I was alarmed, and asked if someone wanted to hurt Haru. No, he said, but life will not be easy for him here, or for you. In America, there are many kinds of people and he would have a father of status.

And I have none, I said. Uncle was not without pity when he replied no, you have none. I will have less than nothing without Haru, I said. Uncle told me that it was not about me, that I must stop being selfish. This was about my son.

I could not help but cry. Haru came and touched my wet cheeks and I held him close. Uncle turned away, but he had spoken the truth. And how am I to fight the truth, Obaasama? It is as cold and unyielding as the winter sea and I cannot make it disappear. I wanted to pick up my biwa and summon the ghosts, but what could they do? For this is about life, and what is yet to come.

I am hollow. I am full of pain. I can write no more.

Twenty-four

♩ ♫ ♪ ♪ ♩ ♪

I couldn't stop crying. My breath hitched and I wasn't able to wipe away my tears fast enough, so I turned my face to the pillow and let it soak up my useless sorrow.

'Adam-san?'

Junko was standing in the doorway.

'Sorry.' I didn't even try to speak Japanese. 'Did I wake you?'

She shook her head. 'What's the matter?' she said in Japanese.

Fine then. I answered in Japanese. 'I read a sad book.'

She didn't look like she believed me. She left and I lay down again, hoping that was the end of it. But she returned a minute later with what resembled a big white Band-Aid and laid it gently on my damp forehead. She smoothed it, carefully brushing my hair back, and a coolness spread across my skin. I wanted to tell her I was too old for that but didn't know how.

'Sato gokoro.' She gave me a small sympathetic smile.

'Thank you.' My voice was hoarse.

She gazed at me for a beat longer, then left the room, closing the door softly behind her.

I reached for my phone and looked up sato gokoro. Homesickness. Written with two kanji: the first meaning village, or a parent's home; the second kanji meaning heart.

~

I awoke abruptly in the grey of what could be twilight or dawn. I orientated myself: this bed, this room, this country.

The woman was back. She was by the window. The diary was open on my chest. Above my heart.

I sat up slowly and slowly she looked at me.

'What do you want?' I whispered.

Her lips parted and closed. Her eyes intent, probing.

I held out the diary, opened on the last page I had read. She drifted closer. We both looked down and my eyes filled and overflowed onto the yellowed pages.

Writing appeared, stroke by stroke, drawn in my tears as though they were ink.

I cannot rest
where did the story go?

The words dried and disappeared. I gazed up at her and our tears were like dark mirrors.

'You want me to find it?' I asked.

A noise, low and mournful. A ship's horn. The woman was stopped by the sound, and suddenly she was by the window again, staring out. The horn sounded once more and it was as if it tore her apart into nothingness, the air rent by her vanishing scream.

~

I stayed up until it was time for breakfast, when I slunk down, mortified.

Junko was putting dishes on the table.

'Thank you for last night,' I mumbled to her. 'I'm embarrassed.'

'Not at all,' she said briskly. 'It's normal."

I was interested in how many normal seventeen-year-old guys she knew.

We ate in awkward silence. This time she let me wash the dishes and then I declared I was going for a walk.

Junko said, 'Air would be good for you.'

It would, no matter how molten it was.

'Ittekimasu!' I remembered to say, before I left.

'Itterasshai!' Junko replied.

When I was a safe distance from the house, I video-called Sylvia.

'Adam!'

'Syl... am I glad to hear your English-speaking voice.'

'So you still can't understand the bath?'

'Some friendships take longer than others!'

She giggled. 'What are you doing?'

'I'm just walking around – I haven't done any exploring on my own.' I started zigzagging through the narrow streets, organised without rhyme or reason.

'Tell me everything,' Sylvia said.

I did – apart from the diary, the sobbing, the ghost – halting occasionally to show her things: a tortoiseshell cat, futons draped over a balcony, the torii gates marking a shrine entrance.

'Your turn,' I said, when I'd finished describing Kumamoto melons.

'Nothing's happening here.' Sylvia then complained for fifteen minutes. It was soothing until she mentioned Evan.

'When did you see him?' I asked.

'A few days ago. I met Rosie and Sean – who are officially a *thing* – and he turned up. He's pals with Sean.'

'Huh.' Evan and I hadn't spoken since that night.

'Did something happen at that beach hang out?' she asked bluntly.

'We made out a bit, I told you.'

'Evan was kinda weird about it.'

'Go on.' I reached a tiny park, and sat on a bench under a tree's scant shade.

'He said you –' Sylvia made quote fingers '– "freaked out", and asked if you'd said anything.'

What had Evan done? Pushed boundaries, came on too strong, but nothing had *really* happened. I'd sound over-sensitive.

'It was – lack of communication,' I said, humiliated by what I wanted to say, what I couldn't.

Sylvia sighed. 'I think that was the main problem you guys had.'

'Our main one?'

'It seemed tough for you to talk openly with Evan,' she amended.

'About some things,' I mumbled.

'And that's normal!'

I thought of Dad, sitting across the kitchen table from me.

'Is it?'

'You're in *Japan*, Adam. Evan is a million miles away.'

But now Evan was here too, smuggling himself into the country inside my brain.

'Don't message him,' Sylvia warned.

'Obviously not.'

'Is everything else okay?'

'Yeah, though... I wonder if the house is haunted. I've been having... messed-up dreams.' I tried to laugh.

'Dreams – sure but ghosts do not exist,' Sylvia said firmly. 'I bet it's the new food and heat and jet lag giving you nightmares. What are they about?'

It was a bad idea to tell Sylvia, scientific sceptic. 'Can't remember,' I lied. 'I better go, but talk soon?'

After we hung up I stared at my phone for a second. Then I messaged Evan.

so you think i just FREAKED OUT?

I considered insults to add, but before I could, he replied.

well yeah. but i know why

why? I shot back.

I watched dots appear and then disappear and felt a kind of satisfaction.

Then he wrote, **can we talk?**

It would be better to ignore whatever shitty explanation he had, or simply avoid his anger.

I video-called him.

Evan answered, but said, 'I didn't mean right now.'

'I didn't want to wait.' I wanted the upper hand. 'What do you have to say? Or do you prefer talking to my friends behind my back?'

'I don't prefer it. I wanted to find out if you'd care if I did,' he said flippantly.

I rolled my eyes. I'd walked right into it. 'Why?'

He took a breath. 'Because I wasn't sure you'd listen to me.'

'I'm listening,' I replied cautiously.

'I acted badly at the beach and... I'm sorry.' Evan, uncharacteristically, sounded both sincere and uncomfortable.

'Where did this come from?'

'I was told how I'd messed up. Pretty harshly too.'

'By who?'

Evan screwed up his face. 'Daniel.'

'Daniel?' I repeated in horror. 'That was private—'

'Like you don't talk to Sylvia about me?' he scoffed.

'It's different, you and Daniel!'

'Why?'

'I don't have sex with Sylvia!'

'We haven't— Hang on, didn't you have a thing?'

'Are you guys going out?' I interrupted.

Evan exhaled. 'He didn't want to. Because of the beach.'

I was speechless with confusion.

'He was pretty disgusted at me,' Evan said finally.

I was sorry for every mean thought I'd had about Daniel. I collected myself. 'You didn't listen to me. I wasn't... comfortable. That's not okay.'

'I know.' Evan wasn't contrite enough to hide his impatience. 'I sort of lost control.'

'You wanted control.' As I said it I recognised that's what I had wanted too, when I'd pushed him in the garden.

Now Evan did look ashamed. 'Yeah,' he said.

'Well. Thanks for saying sorry. And thanks to Daniel, I guess.'

'We aren't talking anymore.'

I tried not to appear too pleased.

'It would be nice to talk to you, though,' he said. 'Sometimes. If you want.'

My idiot heart softened. 'That would be nice.'

'Bye, then.'

'Bye, Evan.'

I sat there, disconcerted, too hot to think. I wanted fresh coldness; I wanted the ocean.

I sent Jo a message.

are there any nice beaches nearby?

July 14th

The house is silent, Obaasama. My mind is twisting full and empty. I intended to write more here but this pen is heavier than I can bear. Mr S— gave me this pen. He is out of reach. Everyone is, except the ghosts. I will rest again. I will pray. Please listen.

—

August 27th

O-Suzu tells me I must write, Obaasama. She means letters, but I am writing here instead. Fusae has written to me, and the Lieutenant, and Mr S—. I can only open Fusae's letters, but cannot form sensible sentences in reply.

I prefer to read books these days. I have read dozens in the past months. They carry me to different places. I do not have to think about this life. I can have others instead.

I will attempt another letter to Fusae. Please help me, Obaasama, if I have not already taken all the help you have to give.

—

September 23rd

Dear Fusae came to Nagasaki, Obaasama. She was visiting relatives but it was also out of concern for me. The letter I had finally written her was many pages long. I tried to explain everything – almost everything.

She called to me yesterday and asked about Haru. Hearing his name hurt. The Lieutenant sends letters. I do not have the strength to read them. I told Fusae that Haru is safe and content in America and it is better if I let him live his new life. Fusae said this was also my chance to start over. She was concerned about me doing nothing but reading and playing biwa. I said that I never thought that a bad life, even before. She insisted I needed some company. She is determined to introduce me to some women in Nagasaki – New Women, as they are called. I must say this interested me more than anything else in the past months.

Maybe there is a new life for me. Maybe it is time to kill my old foolish self.

Twenty-five

♩ ♫ ♪♪ ♩ ♪

'**K**ujirahama,' Jo said. 'That's where we're going.'

I followed him obediently to the tram and then we changed to a bus. I didn't notice how much I'd zoned out until Jo asked, 'Are you tired?'

I'd been staring out of the window, not seeing anything. 'Yeah but... Sorry. Just thinking.'

'About what?'

Exes and ghosts and lost children. Instead, I said, 'A diary. A Japanese girl wrote it. She was from Nagasaki, actually.' Jo was the first person I had told, apart from Dad, and it felt like revealing a deep secret.

He was intrigued. 'A Nagasaki writer! What's her name?'

'I... don't know. It's a *real* diary.' Or entirely *un*real.

'I'd like to see it.'

'Sure.' But I didn't want him to. It was private.

'It's—' Jo said a word in Japanese.

I repeated it – guuzen – and checked the definition.

'Coincidence.' That was too flimsy and accidental for what it felt like, though.

We got off the bus and walked the kilometre to where the sand began, revealing a dazzlingly gorgeous beach. It wasn't big but it was tropical and uncrowded, trees rising around a gently curving shore.

'Wow! It's like Hawaii!' I cried.

'Have you been to Hawaii?' Jo asked.

'No! Have you?'

'No.' He grinned.

We trudged barefoot through the soft sand until it became firm and cool, and then I couldn't help but run, because it felt so good beneath my feet. Jo sprinted after me, and in the middle of the beach I threw down my bag and tugged off my damp T-shirt and shorts.

Jo bent forwards to tug off his jeans, his back bare and smooth. He straightened up and I saw the muscles of his shoulders, his chest firm and strong as he turned towards me. I averted my gaze quickly.

'Race you!' I cried.

We dashed into the waves, gasping and yelling at the first fresh grasp of water. I marvelled at how much warmer this side of the Pacific was, backstroking lazily until Jo splashed me and I splashed him back.

I swam until I was exhausted. I stretched out on my towel, glad to be drenched in a light that dispersed dark shadows.

'It's so quiet,' I said.

Jo propped himself up on his elbows. 'It's crowded at the weekends, until September. But when I was a child my mother wouldn't let me swim after Obon.'

'When is that, exactly? And why not?' I asked.

'Obon is August thirteenth to fifteenth. She said it was dangerous because of the kurage—'

I consulted my dictionary. 'Jellyfish.'

'And,' Jo added, 'the ghosts.'

'Ghosts,' I echoed.

'Obon is when the dead come back,' Jo explained, 'to visit family and so on.'

'I know,' I said softly.

'Some travel in the water, through the sea.'

'They can catch you? They're bad?' I asked.

'Not all bad. Some are lost, or lonely,' Jo said.

I rubbed my arms.

'It's a story,' Jo assured me.

'I'm thinking about the jellyfish,' I told him.

He grinned knowingly.

'Do you swim after Obon now?' I asked.

'Sometimes yes,' he said.

'And sometimes no?'

'If you want to swim after Obon, I'll come with you. I'll keep the jellyfish away,' Jo promised.

Which meant I'd have to protect him from ghosts. I looked at him, golden and beaming. I *did* want to protect him; not because he needed it but because he said he'd do that for me, and I believed him.

November 21st

I have become braver, Obaasama, and I must thank you for enduring so much The New Women Fusae introduced me to have helped. They are a passionate group. There are less than ten of us, but we meet and discuss writing and ideas and the world.

The last time we met, we spoke of literature and fear. Should some books frighten us? Should we be afraid of writing certain things? One woman believed that literature was a place to escape terror. Another argued that literature should capture *all* emotions. Another said that it is a bad state when people fear books.

I agreed with them and had no new opinion to offer. I could think only of the letters from Mr S— and the Lieutenant, which I had still been unable to open. Those were the words I was afraid of. After the meeting I came home and vowed to be brave. I began to read.

First, the letters from the Lieutenant and his wife. They call Haru, *Harry*. Harry was healthy, strong, quick and clever and speaking English like any American child his age. Some of the Lieutenant's letters were more messily scrawled than others. In those, he wrote about missing me, recalling memories and personal things that I read through swiftly and put away. I hope he is not drinking too much;

it would not be good for Haru. At some point, his wife's letters replaced his. Perhaps she learned what he had been saying to me. She said she loves *Harry* very much.

There was a photo: the Lieutenant, his wife and Harry. Harry is dressed in western clothes, three years old and standing straight and serious. I held it to my salted heart.

I had to stop reading then, Obaasama. I cut the photo apart until only Haru was left but then I wept because it looked as if he was all alone.

December 3rd

Today, Obaasama, I read the letters from Mr S—. His first letter apologised for not coming to say goodbye, but the Lieutenant had him sent away from Nagasaki at once. He could not refuse an order from a superior officer.

He begged forgiveness for not revealing that the Lieutenant had married. When he learned of the engagement he had urged the Lieutenant to be honest, and they had quarrelled. He feared that if he told me I may not believe him and think he was only trying to drive us apart. But when he returned and saw me, he mistakenly assumed that the Lieutenant and I had separated...

After the apologies, the letters became more like the correspondence I was accustomed to. He had returned to Hawaii. He set down thoughts on poetry, recalled our conversations, the matters we had discussed and argued about. These letters are similar to the ones I write to you, Obaasama.

I should be ashamed to admit it, but what is the use of that? I confess I miss Mr S— more than the Lieutenant. I cannot say it aloud but I will write it: I want him. I began to consider what he had asked me, about going with him to Hawaii.

But then... Oh, Obaasama, there was another letter. Mr S— said that after writing for months with no reply, he was surrendering the dreams of us he had still harboured. He presumed I remained loyal to the Lieutenant, and if that was my reason for not replying then I need not fear his feelings any longer. It came to me that Mr S— was unaware that the Lieutenant had left me and taken Haru. Mr S— said he would continue to write as before, even if I did not answer, in the hope of preserving our friendship. He implored me to understand and forgive his directness.

I read the next letters with a falling heart, until my foreboding was confirmed. Mr S— was engaged. He was leaving the Navy but staying in Hawaii and marrying a woman there. She was Japanese too. I would like her, he wrote. She was intelligent and kind; witty but not as fierce as me. He promised to describe the wedding celebrations in a future letter.

I did not know he thought I was fierce. I did not even know there were pieces of my heart yet unbroken; those sorry fragments are shattered now.

O-Suzu came and asked what had happened. I told her that they were all gone. It was nobody's fault but my own. O-Suzu let me lie weeping in her lap. She stroked my hair. She said all things must go in the end. Did I not learn that from the poetry I read? From the flowers I saw in their different seasons?

The flowers return every year, I said.

O-Suzu replied, not the same ones.

~

December 15th

I washed my face and composed myself this morning, Obaasama. I picked up the pen Mr S— had given me. It is a symbol of the past but that did not mean I could not keep it. It truly is a beautiful pen.

I congratulated him on his engagement, or his marriage if he was married already. It sounded as though he had found a good woman. Ferocity was not a positive trait to have. I told him about the Lieutenant and Haru. I explained how unhappy and ashamed I had been, and that was why I had not read his letters until recently.

I described the winter weather. Winter appears bleak but gifts time for rest and sleep. By spring the world would be fresh and growing once more.

~

April 6th

Though I have not written here in some time, I feel this an appropriate place to record this news: my first article has been published, Obaasama. I received a copy of the magazine today, which is written almost entirely by women and is not about housework or child-rearing, but about the ideas and experiences women have. My article is not so shocking. It is about *wise mothers*. How are we meant to be wise if we are not educated? How can we understand the world if it is kept from us? True wisdom must be earned on one's own, not learned by rote from men.

I was satisfied to see my writing in print, though I did not use my real name. I will be even more disapproved of by the neighbours if they learn what I am writing about. I will consider this my new self.

Twenty-six

S o Mr S— had abandoned the writer too. I was furious. Why hadn't he told her about the Lieutenant and let her make up her own mind? All the fighting she had to do to preserve some scrap of freedom, even when the choices given to her were between bad and worse.

Still, my own heart hurt for the romance between her and Mr S—, broken by tangled words and silences. At least she was publishing her own writing, expressing her ideas. It was a weird feeling, knowing that it wasn't only me who had found her on ink and paper...

And Haru was with his new family in America. How had that been for him? Well, I had an idea. I wanted to see that photo of Haru, the one the writer had cut apart. I thought I knew what he looked like: he looked like me.

'Adam-san, you enjoy reading don't you?' Toshi asked me. 'Do you have other hobbies?'

I guessed Junko had informed him of my breakdown.

'I like music,' I said feebly. Who didn't like music?

'If you are interested in opera—' Toshi began.

'I'm not,' I interrupted hurriedly. 'But I play cello.'

His face lit up. 'I play music too. Do you know shamisen?'

'No, but... Will you play for me?'

'Ah, Okaasan doesn't like the noise anymore so I don't play often.' Toshi sounded sad.

This didn't bode well for his playing ability.

'Junko-san isn't here,' I pointed out.

'Yes...' Toshi glanced around furtively.

I smiled. 'Please?'

'Come.' Toshi brought me upstairs, to what I'd assumed was another bedroom.

We entered a room lined with bookshelves and immaculate boxes of records, a worn armchair beside a record player. It was cosy and secretive, like seeing into a new corner of Toshi's mind. He brought out a case, opening it with a flourish to reveal a stringed instrument: long-necked, three-stringed and with a squat, squarish body.

He took it out and said, 'Shamisen!', then produced a plectrum that resembled a small, smooth spatula. He settled in the armchair and spent a few moments listening and testing the strings, then struck a chord.

I pointed at the plectrum. 'Is that a bachi?'

Toshi raised an eyebrow. 'You do know some Japanese instruments!'

He began to play. The sound surprised me: quick and twanging and banjo-like. The tune was exuberant, Toshi's hand sliding up and down the neck with assured speed, the bachi plucking with swift precision.

When he finished, I applauded. 'That was brilliant!'

Toshi shook his head but beamed. 'You enjoyed it?'

'It was fun!'

'You thought Japanese music was all serious?' he asked.

'Well...' I stared at the bachi. 'Do you play biwa?'

'No, not many play these days. You're interested in biwa?'

'The heike biwa,' I said.

He looked disconcerted. 'Very traditional. Old. How—'

Downstairs, the front door opened.

'Tadaima,' Junko called.

'Okaeri,' Toshi and I replied.

Toshi put the shamisen away as Junko peered into the room. 'Listening to music?'

Toshi dodged the question by saying, 'Adam-san plays cello.'

'How nice,' she said. 'Do you need to practise, Adam-san?'

'Not *really*...'

'Jo-kun's friends play music!' said Toshi, in a *eureka!* tone. 'You should meet them.'

Junko nodded approvingly. 'Good idea.'

'You can make friends! I'll ask Jo-kun.' Toshi whipped out his phone.

'No! I mean... wouldn't that be troublesome?' The prospect of trying to make friends through *cello* flooded me with panic.

'They would be delighted to meet someone like you,' Toshi said.

I didn't know what that meant, but it was too late to protest.

'It will be great,' Junko pronounced with finality.

I was defeated.

Junko's gaze landed on the shamisen case, and she almost winced. Toshi noticed and ushered me out of the room. I didn't ask him why, not only because I couldn't phrase the question, but because I knew pain when I saw it.

March 26th

I have neglected to write to you over the past year, Obaasama. Most of my words have gone into stories and essays and letters. The rest are sung for the ghosts, as ever. But I have encountered some success in my publications, and usually have a piece to write or edit.

My poor mother has passed away, after a swift illness. I went to Saga to be with her. Her gentle voice had become a whisper. I had not been a very good daughter and I apologised to her. She held my hand and said it was only that I was different, that I had been good even when she did not understand me. Excuse me, Obaasama, my tears have smudged the ink...

There, I have wiped my face and the ink has dried, for now.

Mr S— and I continue our correspondence. He reports that his wife enjoys everything I write and that I am what some men might consider a bad influence. Not him, he declared. I suspect, however, that my influence on his wife does not always work in his favour, which makes me guiltily pleased.

But why am I writing about Mr S—? There is another topic more pressing. Fusae introduced me to a man, a magazine editor and an admirer of my work. We have met several times: he is rather older than me and, having lived in Europe, has liberal ideas. He lives in Fukuoka but is moving to Tokyo and has asked me to accompany him as his wife. I am aware this turn of events appears quite wonderful. An educated man who would support my writing, who would marry a divorced woman! O-Suzu certainly thinks so.

I do not know if I love this man, however. I cannot help but think of Mr S—, and even the Lieutenant. I have changed so much since then, but still I cannot let the past go.

Nevertheless, I think it is time. I am sorry to leave this house. Will you come with me, Obaasama? Will the ghosts be able to find me? I beg you, tell them I will listen and play for them no matter where I am.

Twenty-seven

♩ ♫ ♪♪ ♩ ♪

A nd just like that, another year had passed for her. It was good, I supposed, that she was so busy with real life that she wasn't writing in the diary all the time, but I missed the detailed entries. She was growing distant; or maybe she was simply growing up. And this man, her new husband *sounded* like he would be good for her. She deserved that.

I was turning the next page when Jo bounded into my room. I hid the diary hurriedly.

'Adam-kun!' he cried in Japanese. 'Let's meet my friends!'

'What, *now*?' I said in alarm.

Jo switched to English and lowered his voice. 'They're excited to see you and hear you play. They're meeting today so it's good timing.'

It was *worse* that they were excited. 'Do they know my Japanese is awful? That I'm not even that good at cello?'

'I told them you were very good at both!' Jo said, as if he really believed it.

I moaned.

'Kana-chan was in Australia last summer so she has some English.'

'You'll be there too, right?' I said.

'No, no.' Jo waved his hand nonchalantly. 'I'll meet you afterwards.'

I moaned at a more intense pitch.

'I was nervous when I went to your class,' Jo said. 'But you were all kind. I was happy I did.'

'That was different.' What I meant was, *Jo* was different, with his bright friendliness, so unlike me.

'They will like you,' Jo said.

'How can you be so sure?'

'Because I—' He shrugged and half-turned away. 'I know.'

So I trusted him.

—

Jo delivered me to the rehearsal room and then disappeared. I was an abandoned child on their first day of school. Luckily, 'everyone' was only four people the same age as me: a string quartet. I floundered in Japanese as we made our introductions.

Kana (viola) took charge. She'd studied in rural Queensland, and spoke English with a drawl that I couldn't help finding adorable, especially because she swore like it was punctuation.

'Shit,' she said, 'your Japanese is worse than Jo-kun said.'

I wondered if she had acquired this directness in Australia, and if so I made a note never to go there.

'I don't know why he said it was good!' I protested.

'Oh, that's Jo-kun,' Kana said, fond and dismissive.

'Hare otoko,' said Shion (first violin).

I understood the words – *sunshine boy* – but not the meaning.

'Wherever he is, the sun appears,' translated Sakurako (second violin). She spoke curtly.

'That's true!' I said. 'But... it's already so hot.'

They cheerily agreed it was hot, far too hot.

'Was Jo-kun playing funny buggers about you playing cello too?' Kana asked.

I gaped. 'Playing *what*?'

'Sorry,' Kana apologised. 'I was speaking Australian.'

That was hardly an explanation. All I said was, 'I can, but Jo hasn't even heard me.'

'Would you like to play?' Ruka was the cellist and the quietest. He swept his fringe over his face shyly.

'Can I listen to you first?'

'Fine, but we're only practising.' Sakurako's voice was abrupt, but she put her chin into the violin's rest as if she was laying her head in the lap of someone older and wiser.

'We're not very good,' Shion warned.

They were very good. They played Schubert with a lovely ease, strings lacing and harmonising like a tapestry being woven. They hadn't lied when they said they were practising; there were a few slips and mistakes, but they met each other's eyes when that happened, acknowledging and correcting.

'You're amazing!' I burst out, when they'd finished.

Everyone looked gratified and protested *no, no*.

CLARA KUMAGAI

'We've played in the orchestra circle since junior high school, but became a quartet last year,' Kana said.

Ruka proffered his bow. 'Your turn.'

I wanted to refuse more than ever now that I'd heard how good they were. Yet my hands longed to hold the bow, to let sound tremor through me.

'You don't mind?' My cello was so personal to me that it felt like an invasion of privacy when anybody else touched it.

'Please,' Ruka said.

I settled down with the cello, simultaneously familiar and unfamiliar. I drew the bow back and forth across the strings, listening to this cello's voice.

'I'm not good at performing,' I told them.

'Please relax,' Shion said.

They gave me encouraging smiles, except Sakurako, who looked skeptical. I began an easy piece that I could play in my sleep. It was soothing, to be with a cello again; I'd missed it more than I'd known. I finished without any noticeable mistakes and received a round of applause and praise.

It was my turn to say *no, no* except I meant it.

'You can play something more difficult, I think,' Ruka said unexpectedly.

'Maybe,' I admitted.

'Next time,' he said.

'What next time?' I asked.

'You should play with us. Wouldn't you like to?' Shion said.

'But— I'm not as good as you. Aren't you a quartet?'

'Ruka will be away so we actually need you,' Kana said.

'Perhaps you're too busy with other friends,' Sakurako suggested.

I was unsure whether she was giving me an out or trying to dissuade me.

'I'm not,' I answered, deflated.

All I did was have mostly awkward conversations with Toshi and Junko, and cling to Jo whenever he was around.

'Good,' Shion said. 'We'll see you tomorrow then.'

'We have a performance next month. You'll catch up!' Kana said.

'What?' I spluttered. I was betrayed; it had been a set up.

January 20th

It has been years, Obaasama. I assumed I had thrown this book away, but I must have taken this box with me from Nagasaki to Tokyo and back again, though I cannot recall it. I read my first letters to you and felt some admiration for my younger self, despite her numerous confusions and mistakes.

The bundles of letters are here too, from the Lieutenant and his wife and Mr S—, old and yellowed. At least fresh ones arrive from dear Mr S—, but I have not heard from the Lieutenant or his wife in some time. I had become worried. Until last week...

I received a letter from my Haru. I held the paper to my face to make certain it was real. He introduced himself as if I would not know him. As if twenty years was enough to make me forget. *I am your son*, he wrote. He is in Japan to work at a university in Tokyo. He wants to meet me. He wants to know why I did what I did.

He is angry. I am a little afraid. What if Haru is full of hate; what if he has grown up to be a man like the Lieutenant?

My husband is no longer living, yet I can hear what he would say: *Stop thinking and do it.* But my other son, Hiro, the son of my husband and I... I do not think I should tell him. He is studying in Kagoshima. My husband knew about Haru but I did not speak often of him. Even when letters came from America, he did not ask. He accepted it as a different part of my life, one that did not concern him.

I will meet Haru. Give me wisdom, Obaasama, give me courage.

~

April 10th

Haru has departed, Obaasama. He told me to call him Harry but I cannot. He will always be Haru to me... Did you see him bow at the butsudan? He was raised Christian but I am glad he is respectful of ancestors and traditions not his own. Or rather – these *are* his traditions. It is only that he does not know them.

After he left, I sat playing biwa. I had taken it out to show Haru, wondering if he had any memory of the music. He said no, until I picked out a lullaby, and then he closed his eyes and murmured yes, he remembered that.

I should start from the beginning of his visit, not the end. Haru is tall but not as tall as his father. His hair is light brown, his eyes darker. It took me some time to find my voice at first, but when I did, I found myself saying that he had had blue eyes as a baby.

Mother and Father told me that so many times, he replied. They sure did love my blue eyes. I asked if they did not love his eyes now. Seems not, he said. I began to understand more about him and what his childhood was like.

Your English is damn good, he said. I said it was not as good as it had been, with fewer chances to speak it since leaving Tokyo. Dear Sagi-sensei is no longer here, having passed several years ago. I am more used to writing and reading English.

Haru had heard I was a writer, and was disappointed when I told him my published work was only in Japanese. He said a translator might help him. He is studying Japanese architecture as well as lecturing on western engineering and has some translators assisting him.

I was grateful he had had a good education, as the Lieutenant promised. Haru said he had studied a lot. He had not had many friends.

I often preferred to be alone, too, especially as I had got older, I told him. So I get it from you, he said, that's funny. I did not see the humour. No other Jap kids in my neighbourhood, he explained. I wasn't popular.

That was painful to hear. Not only for him, but because he resented me for it. I told him that marrying a foreigner did not make me popular either. He did not believe me. In America, you'd be lucky to get a guy like Father, he said. Apparently, the Lieutenant told him we were never married. He said the same to me in the end, I told him. Yet we still needed a divorce.

You're not how he described, Haru said, I thought you'd be quieter. Your father is not the best listener, I replied. And I was young then, but I have learned to say whatever I think of.

He sure does prefer talking to listening, Haru said. I asked about the wife. Haru said she wasn't his wife anymore, that they had separated. He had a new wife now.

Another wife? I asked. It came out more bitter than I intended.

I've only met her a couple times. My stepmother was good to me, though, Haru said. I am glad, I said. I thought she would be. You didn't know, he replied. She could have treated me horribly.

Yet she did not So why are you angry? I asked. It was stupid of me to say that, but I had become angry too.

His voice rose. You gave me away. You never tried to contact me. I was your child!

Your parents and I exchanged letters about you. You think it would have been better for you to stay with me; America must differ greatly from Japan. Women can raise their half-foreign child alone and be respected. Is that so? I asked.

Haru did not reply.

I calmed myself and whispered, It nearly killed me, letting you go. Haru told me he'd never heard about the letters. I should have written to you directly, I told him. But I did not know if you would want that. I thought it best to let you be with your new family.

But you're my family too. Aren't you? he asked. Haru's face reminded me so much of the Lieutenant, who could be furious or selfish and yet still ask for love. I glimpsed Haru's lonely childhood in his eyes.

I am and always will be, I said. In this world and the next. Did anybody ever tell you that love is stronger even than death?

Twenty-eight

♩ ♫ ♪♪♩ ♪

I was too happy and jealous to read any more. But there was something I didn't understand: hadn't Haru returned? So what was the end of the story the ghost of the writer was looking for? I wanted to ask. I was close to calling out to her, but the image of her screaming mouth returned to me. I thought I heard a ship's horn. I didn't look at the window; I turned away and rushed out.

When Toshi saw me he asked, 'Would you like to eat Chinese food today?'

'Yes!' I said gratefully.

We took the tram to Chinatown. It was my first time crossing under the red, ornate gate. I'd been expecting something bigger but it was only a couple of blocks of restaurants and shops with Chinese clothes, food or medicine.

'For a long time, Chinese people could do business only in Nagasaki, not in other places in Japan,' Junko said.

Right, Japan cut itself off from other countries for hundreds of years, until the Americans arrived with big ships and big guns. Chinatown seemed a bit rundown and shabby, but long ago it must have been foreign and fascinating. The diary writer could have walked these streets, peered into the shops, eager for unfamiliar food.

We went into a restaurant, were seated and handed thick menus. I kept asking Toshi and Junko for the meanings of words, and when the waiter came I just asked for his recommendation. He was handsome, so when he pointed out a dish, I just agreed. He followed up with a lot of questions that I didn't understand, so I kept saying yes until he shrugged and wrote it down.

Toshi said, 'Impressive, Adam-san!'

'Uh, thanks,' I replied, puzzled. 'Do lots of Chinese people live here?'

'I think so,' Junko said. 'But for a long time, Chinese people had to live in—' she said a word I didn't recognise.

'Compound,' Toshi supplied in English.

'Dutch people too,' Junko said. 'In Dejima.'

'You can visit it. There's a museum,' Toshi said.

'And Americans?' I asked. 'What about them?'

'They didn't have a compound,' Junko said, 'they came later.'

'You're interested in history?' Toshi asked me.

'Well, Nagasaki history. Especially from around one hundred years ago.'

'That's great!' Toshi said.

Junko looked at me curiously. 'Why then?'

I hesitated, but then the waiter arrived. He placed dumplings and noodles in front of Junko and Toshi and with a flourish, set down a steaming, scarlet hot pot before me. So this was what I had ordered.

'Itadakimasu,' Junko, Toshi and I said to each other.

I took a spoonful of soup and a couple of bites of vegetables, said it was delicious, and then my mouth caught fire and my face melted. Junko and Toshi watched in alarm as I choked down a glass of water. I glared at the waiter, whose face was a mixture of hilarity and remorse.

'Are you all right?' he asked.

'I am dying,' I said, 'you killed me.'

He looked stricken until I smiled, pretending my lips weren't burning, regretting having mentioned death.

He said, 'You'll get used to the spice. It's delicious.'

He was too cute to argue with. 'I think it's becoming less spicy.' Or else the numbness was taking the pain away. I was *drooling*. I looked accusingly at Toshi and Junko.

'You said you wanted it spicy,' Toshi said apologetically. 'That's why I was impressed.'

Junko was laughing, Toshi trying not to grin. I laughed too, and then we ate.

July 7th

I am afraid, Obaasama, to write to you. If this is discovered I will be a person of suspicion, harbouring traitorous thoughts about my country. Yet I cannot prevent myself from writing, though I have ceased publishing. Almost all letters have been stopped. They are read by the army, I think. They decide what we should know and what we can tell others.

Haru returned to America before things became perilous. However, the last I heard from him was that it was becoming dangerous for Japanese there. I hope he is safe. He has his father's name, after all; his father's respectable past in the Navy. Surely, that will be worth something? But it fractures my heart that I have lost him once again...

I was able to write Mr S— for longer. There are so many Japanese in Hawaii it was not so unusual. But after the harbour attacks those letters come no more.

And Hiro, my thoughtful, cautious son, is fighting. He is a soldier and day and night I fear for him. He promised he would be careful but what good are promises in times such as these?

They tell us the soldiers are brave and noble and that fighting for Japan is a most honourable duty. Uncle said this, years ago, and here is what it has become. There is war across the world. Everything burns.

I have returned to writing poetry but there is nowhere to publish it, unless the poems are about glory and the Emperor. Fusae said we can start our own magazine after the war. I long for that day.

I play biwa, feeling as though I am in a place outside of time. I have truly become a woman from a Heian romance, or from some strange tale. The garden is thronged with ghosts. They are hungry, they come limping and screaming. They are dressed in blood and what they thought was honour. They come from Manchukuo, Chōsen, Nanjing... The stories they tell me – I cannot write of them here. They speak of their own deaths and I do my best to ease them and send them home. They speak of the deaths they brought to others and I struggle to absolve them. The things that have been done...

It sickens me, Obaasama. *Heike Monogatari* made beauty out of battles, but I can find no goodness or art in what the ghosts tell me. When I read the newspapers and listen to the radio I recognise what they are – lies, lies...

And last night I had a dream, Obaasama: I dreamed that I was sitting in the engawa, gazing at a sunny, warm morning – then my vision turned white, a piercing blinding white. It burned. Is it a premonition? Will I become blind as you did? I suppose I will become a biwa-hōshi of old if so. Yet there was something wicked in this kind of unseeing, for I woke screaming. O-Suzu hurried in, and I stammered that it was only a bad dream, but she asked if I had been hurt. I did not understand until she brought a mirror and I saw the skin around my eyes was red.

O-Suzu laid a cool cloth over my face and asked about the dream. All I could say was that it may have been the future.

And so, Obaasama, I have decided to pack up this diary. I do not want it to be discovered or destroyed. I will bring it to my husband's old family home in Fukuoka and hide it there. I considered remaining there, in the countryside. But Nagasaki is my home and I will wait until Hiro returns, at least.

I will go soon, so that I may return here before Obon begins. There will be so many ghosts to attend to. I will beg for their help. All my dear ones are lost somewhere in the world. I want to find them but I do not know how. But the dead have power, as you do, Obaasama. They can still help the living.

Twenty-nine

♩ ♫ ♪♪ ♩ ♪

That was the end. There was no more, only a few empty pages. I flicked through them frantically, passing my hands over them as if there were hidden words I could polish back into sight.

'Where are you?' I breathed.

This time she listened. She arrived like dissipated smoke returning to the moment after its candle had been blown out.

I bowed. 'I finished your diary. What happened, afterwards?'

She touched her eyes. Her mouth moved. I wished I could cry again, so she could write in my tears, but I was too distressed; tears couldn't release this pressure in my heart.

'Haru,' I said. 'Did you find him again?'

She shook her head, her eyes so vivid with sorrow they almost lost their transparency.

'Are you looking for *me*?' I whispered, the irrational question I couldn't help but ask.

She drifted nearer, her hands reaching for my face. My skin prickled but I couldn't tell if it was from fire or ice. She bowed her head, slow and sad.

'It's not me? But...' *But I'm your son,* I wanted to say, even though I knew it was both true and untrue.

She had pity in her eyes. This ghost felt sorry for *me*.

'Go away,' I said.

Her expression flashed, fierce and bitter. I flinched, remembering what she was, and her shape loosened until it was part of the unfathomable night. My tears gathered, too late to be of any use.

—

Jo came over after breakfast, as I had asked him to. We went to my room, where I immediately began speaking in English.

'This is weird,' I warned. 'Remember the diary I was reading?'

I showed it to him, hesitantly.

He took it gently. 'It's old.'

'The first entry is in 1911, and the last one must be during the Second World War.'

Jo thumbed through the pages. 'You read all of this?'

'I've just finished. Took me longer than I thought.'

'So your reading is much better than your speaking! This is a little difficult even for me,' Jo said.

'She writes in this old-fashioned way—' I stopped. 'What do you mean, my reading is better?'

'Better than how you speak Japanese.'

'But it's in English.'

'Adam-kun.' Jo tilted his head. 'It's in Japanese.'

I coughed out a laugh. 'No...'

Jo stared, holding out the open diary. Like an optical illusion, a trick picture where one image was the negative of the other, I saw it. The diary was full of Japanese, in flowing, beautiful ink.

For an instant, I could see the hand that wrote it, but when I blinked there was nothing else there. Jo watched me, expecting an explanation.

I swallowed several times before saying lamely, 'I got confused. Between Japanese and English.'

'That has happened to me, once or twice,' Jo said agreeably, but his eyes were doubtful.

Not like this, I wanted to say. 'I want to find out who wrote it,' I said instead. 'I don't even know her name.'

Jo's voice was soft. 'The writer is probably dead.'

'I *know* she's dead, but I need to find out who she was. What happened to her. If she has surviving family they should have this diary.'

'Where did *you* get it?' Jo asked.

'It belonged to my mother.'

'Don't you think your relation wrote this? Your grandmother, great-grandmother?'

'I thought that,' I said, 'but no.'

'A mystery.' Jo was curious. 'Did your mother ever talk about it?'

'She died when I was a baby...'

'Your mother's family might know,' he suggested.

For some reason, this had never occurred to me – that my mother had a family that could be my family too. I knew I had no living grandparents, but Dad had never mentioned aunts or uncles.

'I can help you!' Jo offered.

'Please,' I accepted gratefully, 'because I have no clue where to start.'

'We'll do it together,' he said.

We stood, smiling at each other. Jo started to read while I compiled a list of what I knew. It wasn't much.

Writer's name unknown
Date of birth, 1892/3
Lived (and born?) in Nagasaki
Mother lived in Saga with her own father (unwell)
Father dead, mother died (1915-ish?)
One uncle, priest
Educated (school unknown), tutored by Sagi (real name
*   unknown)*
Played biwa, taught by an old woman (name unknown)
Became a writer, published in some magazines
One servant/companion, O-Suzu
Married a Lieutenant in US Navy. Divorced by him.
One child, Haru, raised in the US, an engineer
Friends with Mr S— member of US Navy (also a
*   lieutenant, lower-ranked)*
Married a Fukuoka man, moved to Tokyo
Had one other son, Hiro
Returned to Nagasaki (1930s?)
Date of death unknown

Too many *unknowns*.

I skimmed through my list for something tangible. 'Jo, where is Fukuoka?'

'In Kyushu.' He showed me a map.

It was in Japanese, and I saw, with a sinking heart, that I couldn't understand it. It was only the diary I could read, because the ghost had wanted me to.

Jo explained the geography: Fukuoka was Kyushu's northernmost prefecture, separated by a sliver of sea from the southern tip of Honshu. Below and to the west of Fukuoka was Saga, and beneath Saga was Nagasaki.

'The writer lived in Nagasaki. Her mother and maternal grandfather were in Saga, and her second husband was from Fukuoka.' All neatly in a row.

'Have you been to Fukuoka?' Jo asked.

Takane-sensei had asked this same question, when Benny had been wearing clothes that had been mine, long ago.

'Actually,' I said breathlessly, 'I think I have.'

That night I did what I'd been avoiding since I'd got to Japan: I called Dad.

'Adam, it's good to hear your voice.' Dad sounded like he meant it.

'I've been busy,' I lied.

'Well, it's good you're busy. How's everything?'

'Hot.'

'So humid it'd take your breath away, I bet,' Dad said nostalgically. 'You been to the onsen?'

'Not yet.'

'They're boiling too. Incredible feeling.'

'I think I'm bathing in my own sweat every time I step outside, so...'

'Ha! Well, it can't get worse then, can it?'

I hated it when people said that because everything, in my experience, could somehow get worse. 'How's Benny?' I asked.

Dad rambled about the new noises Benny had learned, then put him on the phone in an attempt to demonstrate them. Benny refused to perform.

When Dad took the phone back I said, 'I want to ask you a few things.'

'Go on.'

'Where was Mum from?'

He hesitated, either in surprise or because he was trying to remember. 'Fukuoka prefecture... something-shima.'

'An island?'

'No, it *wasn't* an island. Why?' he asked guardedly.

'My host parents asked me. It felt weird not to be able to tell them.' This was not a lie. 'Did Mum have any other family?'

Another silence. Then, 'A sister.'

I had an aunt.

Dad coughed. 'We're not in contact.'

I wondered whose idea that had been. Dad volunteered nothing more. I plunged on.

'Remember the diary I found in the attic?'

'Uh huh.'

'Can you tell me *anything* about it? Did Mum ever say where she got it?' I asked.

Dad swallowed audibly. 'No. She was sort of obsessed with it, tracking down the writer. She had it when... It was in her bag when she died. So I brought it home.'

'Oh.' A disorientating sadness brushed through me.

'Why are you asking?'

'I read it. It was written by someone in Nagasaki, so it seems like the right time to find out more,' I said.

'That's lucky.'

Unlucky, I wanted to correct, but it was deeper and stranger than that.

'If you remember anything more, will you tell me?'

'Itoshima,' Dad said suddenly. 'That's where your mother was from.'

'Ah,' I said, 'thank you.'

I stared at the diary, imagining it so close to my mother when she died, almost angry that it had survived when she had not.

Thirty

♩ ♫ ♪♪ ♩ ♪

'It's a cello,' I said, unnecessarily.

Junko eyed the case I'd slung off my sweaty back. 'I see.'

'Shion's sister lent it to me.' His sister hadn't played cello since going to Tohoku for university, and apparently didn't mind me borrowing it.

'That was kind.' Junko tapped her pen against a book, one of the few signs of discomfort I'd seen from her.

'I'll only practise when you're out,' I offered. 'If you don't like the sound.'

Junko frowned. 'The sound is fine.'

I tried to fill the sudden silence. 'What are you reading?'

'I'm translating.'

'You're a translator?' I asked. 'With what language?'

'English, of course.'

I gaped. 'You're fluent in English?' I said, switching to English.

'Speak in Japanese, Adam-san.' She was smiling faintly. 'I can't say if I am fluent, but I'm good enough for the job.'

'This whole time,' I moaned, back in Japanese.

'What does it change?' she asked.

'I sound so stupid in Japanese.'

'You're not stupid. You are learning,' Junko corrected me. 'Would you like lunch?'

'Can I help you?' I asked.

'Certainly!'

I brought the cello to my room first, where I took it out and gazed at it. Would I hear it in the night again, being played by some unseen hand? The thought was slightly less terrifying now that I knew what the ghost wanted. She hadn't appeared for the past few nights. Hopefully knowing that Jo and I had started investigating was enough to calm her.

Junko was washing vegetables when I joined her in the kitchen.

'Do you like somen noodles?' she asked.

'I dunno. I've never eaten them.'

'It's a tasty summer dish.' She handed me an apron.

Junko was as adept at teaching recipes as she was at teaching Japanese. She related a hilarious range of onomatopoeia: saku-saku for crispy, gari-gari for a crunch, gutsu-gutsu for a bubbling pot.

'Without those words, I don't know if I could describe food,' she said. 'But they are the most difficult to translate.'

I peeled the carrots. 'What do you translate, Junko-san?'

'Instruction manuals, websites, sometimes books.'

'Do you ever see English and Japanese at the same time?' I asked.

'What do you mean?'

'Nothing,' I said. 'I don't think I could translate anything.' Not without the help of a ghost, anyway.

'If you work hard, yes.' Junko passed me a cucumber. 'Do you ever live in a book? When I translate a story, I have to be in it. Then I bring it into myself, and *then* I bring it out in Japanese.' Junko did some miming to help me understand this. It looked vaguely like childbirth.

I laughed. 'No, I couldn't.' But wasn't that what had happened with the diary? The ghost had come into the real world – but she couldn't speak. She was untranslatable.

'You can,' Junko said firmly, and then demonstrated how I was chopping the cucumber wrong.

Toshi returned home and exclaimed at how wonderful a job we were doing. He set the table and we sat down.

We chatted until a lull fell, and then I said, 'I spoke to my father. My mother was from Itoshima.'

'That's not far away!' Toshi said.

'And... I have an aunt.'

Junko's brow creased. 'You just learned this?'

'Yeah,' I replied, hoping they wouldn't ask why.

'You could meet her,' Toshi said.

But did *she* want to meet *me*?

'Think about it,' he advised.

I nodded. Maybe that's what he and Junko decided to do as well, because the rest of the meal was quiet. It felt private somehow; each of us turned inward, away from each other and towards something else I didn't know.

Jo came by the next afternoon.

Toshi and Junko were pleased to see him. It was impossible to be *displeased* to see Jo. When they started talking I was reminded how slowly they spoke to me in Japanese. I was half-speed at best.

Junko said, 'This project sounds interesting.'

My eyes darted to Jo.

'Nagasaki history project,' he clarified, 'for your school assignment.'

'I *love* school assignments,' I said. 'We'd better get started.'

We escaped to my room, where I related what I'd learned from Dad.

'So your mother might have found the diary in Itoshima,' Jo said, excited.

'But how...'

Maybe my aunt knew.

Better to start w th what we had.

'Is there a way to check marriage records?' I asked. 'Probably there weren't that many Americans marrying Japanese people in 1911...'

'A person's koseki would have that,' said Jo. 'It's a family register. But without a name I have no idea how we could find it.'

'The Lieutenant, then. The military has records but there'll be a lot of lieutenants. My dad might help.'

Jo sat and read the diary while I messaged Dad.

Could you check military records for me? I'm searching for someone, I wrote.

Who? he replied.

A lieutenant who served in 1911.

Need more than that. Name?

I groaned aloud. **Dunno. Can I call you?**

At work. Will get back to you...

When?

I watched the typing dots appear and disappear.

'Useless!' I said.

Jo raised his head. 'Your father can't do it?'

'Won't. Or doesn't want to.' I slapped my phone on the desk with more force than necessary.

'Is your father not... helpful?' Jo asked.

I laughed. 'That's one way of putting it.'

Jo nodded sympathetically but didn't question any further.

'What about your family?' I asked. 'Do you have siblings?'

'An older brother. He's at university.'

I gave him a sidelong glance. 'Do you get along with each other?'

Jo was puzzled. 'We are brothers.'

This somehow conveyed a *no*.

'What about your brother?' Jo asked.

'He's a year old so for now we get on well. He cries but I don't take that personally.'

Jo smiled. 'You like babies?'

'I dunno. I like *him*.'

'Was it strange? To get a brother now...'

'A bit. He needs a lot of attention – I mean, he's an actual baby. The family has been kind of different with him.'

'Are you lonely?' Jo asked.

I looked away. 'I'm happy for Dad and Kate. They wanted a kid for a long time. Now they have a real son.' This was self-pitying, but it wasn't a lie either.

Jo said hesitatingly, 'Sometimes I feel my brother is the real son. He is what my parents want him to be. I'm...'

I caught my breath. Jo hadn't *told* me he was gay, and sometimes I'd wondered if Yuzuki had misunderstood.

'...different,' Jo finished.

'You're their son, though. Like, one hundred per cent. I'm not,' I said shortly.

'I wanted to say that I understand your feeling,' Jo said.

'It's not the same,' I replied. 'Thank you, though.'

All of a sudden, I wanted to hold him. I reached out involuntarily before letting my arm drop.

Jo didn't move. 'I—' he stopped. 'Let's go out. You should see more of Nagasaki.'

'The diary...'

'We'll come back to it,' he promised.

Outside, the afternoon was softening.

'Show me Nagasaki then.'

Jo and I climbed the steep steps framed by stone torii gates. I was full of the tomato ramen we had eaten, topped with eggplant so tender it melted on my tongue. We reached a shrine, but Jo didn't stop there. He took me to a souvenir shop, where he bought two round-trip tickets.

'The cable car to Mount Inasa! It's the third best night view in Japan,' Jo said proudly.

Japan loved a listicle. 'Who decides these things?'

'I don't know,' Jo confessed. 'But it's true.'

We secured a spot at the back of the cable car so we could watch the buildings shrink as we ascended. Jo had timed this perfectly; the sun was about to kiss the horizon and the sky was blushing in anticipation.

We disembarked at the top and climbed the circling stairs of the observation building to the deck. Jo was smug at my gasp of appreciation. We stared out over the city, the mountains and the water, and watched the sun slip away. For a second I was light-headed with the sense of the earth turning beneath my feet.

'It's beautiful,' I said, hushed.

We strolled around to take in every angle, and I was struck by a sudden longing to be in nature.

'Can we go to a lake? Or hike in the mountains?' I asked.

'We can go wherever you want,' Jo said.

His words struck me somewhere in my chest. I crossed my arms on the railing and rested my head on them. Jo leaned forward and let his arms dangle over the edge.

'You're being very kind,' I said.

'It is comfortable to be with you, Adam-kun. I don't know many people like you. I feel... safe.' He said this without looking at me.

I understood the meaning beneath his words, and that there was something neither of us could articulate here, among all these people. I touched his hand and when he didn't move away, I held it lightly, ready to let go.

His fingers laced themselves with mine. We stayed still, gazing at the illuminated sprawl of the city. It was entirely dark.

After a while, Jo cleared his throat and said, 'Should we return?'

In the cable car, we descended serenely. We didn't say a word.

At the shrine, among trees shrouded with shadows, I took Jo's hand once more. He exhaled shakily. His lips parted. I touched my mouth to his. The kiss was gentle until his fingers tangled in my hair, and then it thrilled. An electric hum tremored through my body, from mine to his and back again. The cicadas buzzed and thrummed around us, filling the dark with the call and response of desire, and the night view dazzled behind my eyelids.

Thirty-one

'Adam-kun?'

I blinked. The quartet were staring at me. 'What?'

Kana said, 'Were you asleep?'

'No, I lost concentration. I'm sorry!' I said.

'You didn't sound bad,' Shion said, 'only... lost.'

I *had* been lost – playing with my eyes closed, thinking about Jo.

'You need to pay attention,' Sakurako snapped.

We started again, and I focussed on my bow, the strings, the reverberations of longing sound. I couldn't help replaying the kiss with Jo, as though I was scoring a scene from a movie. We were meeting later to talk about the diary; hopefully we could intersperse that with more kisses.

We finished rehearsal and despite nobody saying anything, I got the distinct impression that I hadn't played well enough.

Ruka said timidly, 'It's not easy. You just need to practise.'

'I will,' I promised.

Ruka was going away next week, and I was anxious about the space that would be left by his kindness and by his cello. I'd have to take over for real then.

Sakurako tutted, which I tried to ignore.

Everybody else went in the opposite direction together, but that was okay. We weren't exactly *friends* yet. We were just playing music together.

⸺

The house was empty when I got back, so I settled down in the bedroom and played as loud as I dared. The sound echoed through the house, and remembering Mr Johnson comparing my performance to a lullaby, and Shion's *lost* comment, I played aggressively, fierce, as if the cello wanted to fight. Would the ghost hear? Would it draw her like the music of the biwa?

I finished, panting slightly, and became aware that someone was in the doorway.

'You came back,' I said.

'Of course.'

I twisted around. It wasn't the ghost – it was Toshi.

'Do you always play like that?' he asked.

'I was trying something different.'

'May I listen?'

'Sure. It's Schubert.'

I began, glancing at Toshi, who occasionally tilted his head, as if he could better listen from one ear or the other. I lowered my bow at the end of the section.

'There's more but...'

'I can hear your style,' Toshi said. 'That's important.'

'I don't think *I* know what that is,' I admitted.

'It's easier for somebody else to hear. Like it is easier for another person to see all of you.' He gestured in a way that indicated he meant both body and mind.

I asked, 'But you don't play with other people often?'

Toshi looked regretful. 'I used to play with Okaasan. And my daughter. I taught her – she was so good, since she was small. I wanted her to go professional.'

'Your daughter must have got her talent from you and Junko-san,' I said.

Toshi glanced away. 'Yuna-chan doesn't think of it that way. She stopped playing.'

'Why?'

'She... lost her good memories of it,' Toshi said.

I wasn't sure if this translated to something like amnesia. 'What do you mean?'

'Yuna-chan is adopted,' Toshi replied.

I didn't know how this related to music.

'We told her when she was twenty. She was an adult. We thought it was a good time to tell her.' Toshi lowered his eyes. 'She didn't understand why we had not told her before. She felt that we had not been truthful.'

'Well,' I said, 'you weren't.'

Toshi looked at me sharply, but his voice was resigned. 'Sometimes truths are hard to tell. We were worried. Adoption is not so common in Japan.'

'Oh. It's pretty normal in America. My friend Art is adopted.'

'How is your friend Art?' Toshi asked. 'And family?'

'Good. Happy. Normal...' I hoped Toshi wouldn't ask me to define *normal*. Art had always been aware he was adopted – his parents were open about it and he met his birthmother regularly. The most unusual thing about his family was that they went birdwatching together once a week.

'Your daughter might just need some time,' I offered.

'That was five years ago,' Toshi said.

Shit.

'I apologise,' Toshi said formally, before I said anything worse. 'I'm sorry if you feel uncomfortable.'

'It's fine! I understand.' I put my hand on my heart. 'Honestly, I do.'

His face softened. 'Thank you, Adam-kun.'

He had almost left the room when I asked, 'But why won't your daughter play music?'

'Ah... Every year we enjoyed going to a festival in Okaasan's hometown, Shimonoseki, and playing shamisen together. We told her when we were there. She wouldn't play with us and left.'

'That's why Junko-san doesn't like the shamisen,' I said.

'She lost her good memories too. I don't know why we chose then to tell Yuna. But the festival is held to remember a family and a battle from long ago, perhaps we were thinking of that...'

There was a screech. I had jerked the bow against the strings. 'What family? What battle?'

'It is called Dan-no-ura,' Toshi said. 'The last battle of the Taira family.'

I became aware that I was gripping the cello's neck very tight.

'It happened at sea, a long time ago,' he said. 'During the Genpei War. The Taira died there with their emperor.'

'I know,' I breathed.

'You do! How?' Toshi asked.

I could only stare open-mouthed at him, trying to find an answer.

After a second, he said, 'I have kept you too long from practice. Excuse me.' He shut the door tactfully.

Something had been answered, a mystery I hadn't even tried to solve.

—

When Jo came over we grinned at each other shyly, and as soon as he'd closed the bedroom door I leaned in for a kiss. He granted me a brief one before breaking away.

'It's a little weird, here... in my uncle's house,' Jo said.

I rolled my eyes. 'It's *my* room.'

'It's Yuna-chan's room,' Jo corrected.

My nosiness momentarily eclipsed my urge to kiss him. 'Do you talk to Yuna?'

'Yes, often.'

'Toshi told me about her,' I said cautiously.

Jo was surprised and wary. 'He doesn't talk about her much.'

'He misses her,' I said.

'So do I. She was more like my big sister than my cousin,' Jo replied.

'Would Yuna mind if I kissed you in her room?' I teased.

Jo grimaced.

I touched his cheek. 'I'm joking. We don't have to do anything.'

His visible relief made me feel guilty.

He picked up the diary. 'We could tell Junko-san and Toshi-san about this. They could help.'

I hesitated. 'When we have some more information, yeah.'

I didn't want more people to read it. Jo hadn't even finished – he only read when we were together.

Jo shrugged, either agreeing or choosing not to argue. 'I checked about the koseki, but you can only request your family's, not a stranger's. Women also leave their family's koseki to become part of their husband's, so that makes it even trickier.'

'That's old-fashioned.'

'Yes,' Jo said glumly.

'So the koseki would be the Lieutenant's.'

Jo pulled an apologetic face. 'If you are a foreigner you do not have a koseki. If a Japanese marries a foreigner they add a note.'

That must be what my own mother's koseki looked like. Dad and I were just notes. 'That's stupid.'

'It's an old system. Japan thinks the family is the most important. More important than one person,' Jo explained.

'That's *really* stupid,' I said.

'You think so?'

'What if your family doesn't want you?' I asked.

'That doesn't mean they are less important.'

'Yes, it does,' I argued.

'For you, maybe,' Jo replied.

This had moved beyond a social lesson to something personal. 'Different for everyone,' I relented, not wanting it to become a fight.

Jo must have felt similarly because he changed the subject. 'Records might also be lost or destroyed.'

'By who?'

'By the war or the bomb.'

'Right,' I said soberly.

The atomic bomb was the only reason I knew about Nagasaki in the first place. I had had a vague idea that it would be a sad or eerie place, but it wasn't. I hadn't connected it with the here and now, with the living, breathing city.

'We all learn about the A-bomb here. Do they teach it in America?'

'A bit. That and Pearl Harbour. More Pearl Harbour,' I admitted.

'We don't learn much about that,' Jo said.

I sighed. 'Makes sense.'

'Have you gone to the museum yet?' Jo asked.

'I will. *We* should do something more fun.' I wanted so badly to touch him.

Jo could tell, because he leaned away from me, but he was smiling. 'Come on then.'

―

I kissed Jo in a hidden corner between two buildings until we were breathless, and then he dragged me out.

'Japanese people don't really kiss in public,' Jo said.

'Some people... societies... just aren't about the PDAs.'

'What's a PDA?' Jo asked.

This was a nice thing about speaking in English – I could teach Jo rather than stammering through endless questions in Japanese.

'Public display of affection. Holding hands, kissing, being touchy-feely. My ex was like that so I got used to it,' I said.

'Weren't you ever worried?' Jo asked.

'Our town is pretty liberal. A few times people said things, or they would stare or look offended. Nothing ever *really* happened.' Even so, there was always that lingering feeling, that whisper of caution in the back of my mind, whenever I held hands with Evan or he kissed me. *Someone somewhere thinks this is disgusting and wrong. Someone might hurt us.*

'What about here? Japan's conservative and all, but would people be homophobic?' I asked.

'Yes, they could be. Like in school—' Jo broke off. 'It's becoming more normal. But we can't marry. Some politicians say we are sick,' he said distantly.

'Things will change.' My words floated, empty.

'I hope so but... Do Junko-obasan and Toshi-ojisan know about you?' Jo asked.

'About being gay? I didn't tell them. Should I?' I hadn't been avoiding it but the situation hadn't exactly arisen. I knew from experience that blurting out *I'm gay* with no context could be awkward.

'You don't have to. You can,' Jo mumbled.

'Would they be bad about it?'

'No, but... For me...' Jo swallowed.

'You're not out to them?'

He shook his head.

'To your parents? Your brother?'

Jo shrugged unhappily. 'Sort of.'

I wanted to hug him but settled for gently bumping my elbow against his. 'It can take time.'

Jo's eyes were full of worry and hope. 'How much time?'

'I wish I could tell you. It'll be okay, though,' I reassured him, because I couldn't bear to tell him otherwise.

We walked alongside a narrow river and over a double-arched bridge.

'This is called Spectacles Bridge,' Jo told me.

I saw the reflection in the river; the symmetry forming glasses frames with circular lenses, the kind John Lennon used to wear. 'I see!'

Jo pointed at the walls that banked the water. 'There's a stone shaped like a heart. Can you find it?'

I searched, squinting. The light rippled across the water, making me scrunch up my eyes. 'Give me a clue.'

Jo, uncharacteristically, refused. 'You have to find it yourself.'

We walked on to Dejima, which was where Jo had decided we should go. The old Dutch compound wasn't actually an island, and now it was a reconstruction of storehouses and a few residences made to look old.

'Must have been tough, being stuck here,' I said.

'The Dutchmen were here for business, they didn't stay long. A few years,' Jo said.

'Some might have been here for pleasure,' I teased.

Jo looked doubtful. 'There were some Japanese women who had children with foreigners. I think they weren't treated so well.'

'I'm sure they weren't,' I said flatly.

Maybe the diary writer *had* done the best thing for Haru.

Jo changed the topic. 'The Portuguese also did business in Nagasaki. They brought castella cake and tempura.'

I was surprised. 'But tempura's so... Japanese.'

'Now.'

'That's cool.' I was inexplicably pleased.

We ambled around, discussing what it would have been like to live here, hundreds of years ago.

'You'd look cute wearing a kimono,' I told Jo.

He looked me up and down in a way that made me laugh. 'You would too,' he declared. 'Have you ever worn one?'

'Nope.'

'We should wear yukata for the next matsuri!' he said.

'You'll have to dress me.'

We both seemed to have the same thought about dressing and *undressing*. I wanted to reach for him, for him to reach for me – but we behaved and showed no affection even as I thrilled with every glance and smile.

Leaving Dejima, I imagined what it had been like when guards were here. Would they have let me pass, seeing me as Japanese? Or would they have stopped me, a foreigner, and kept me in my place?

———

I was woken by the music. The ghost was embracing the cello as if it was a person long-lost. Her transparent hands plucked at the strings. Each note reverberated longer than it should.

'We're looking,' I told her softly. 'Please, wait.'

She didn't seem to hear me. She frowned in concentration.

In the ripple of the notes, I heard her; cello was the instrument most like the human voice, and she was trying to use it as her own.

what I
do not know
you must
remember

The notes died away.

'What if I don't *have* anything to remember?' I asked frantically.

Her fingers clutched feebly at the strings.

time is
coming
going
I will be
lost

'Lost, how? Where? Tell me your name and—'

Her eyes became frightened. The cello twanged in distress. Her body blurred and her mouth opened as if trying to swallow the room – grasping towards me...

A cold, anguished noise on the edge of my hearing; a chill as if winter had exhaled. A string on the cello snapped. The ghost was gone. And, once again, I was afraid.

Thirty-two

I was twitchy, on edge, wary of shadows. The ghost didn't even need to haunt me herself because those final frightening moments lingered behind my eyes like a nightmare. She was changing, but into what? Time pressed against me, but I didn't know the deadline, or what I was supposed to do before it came.

So it made no sense that I enjoyed how each day passed quickly, with the burn of pressure and practice with the string quartet, which had increased since Ruka left; in the whirl of excitement and giddiness with Jo. He was sharing the city with me like a gift, as though he had made it himself.

'I'm falling in like with him,' I told Sylvia.

'I can tell. You've been hiding it well but my powers of perception are laser-like,' she said.

'Yeah, yeah.' I *had* been talking about Jo non-stop.

'Have you considered that you're falling for the one queer guy who speaks English?' Sylvia asked.

'It's more than that! Anyway, don't you say that choice is an illusion?'

'That's in terms of consumerism,' Sylvia corrected. 'Though you are *consuming* him, right?'

'I mean... Not totally? He isn't comfortable making out in his uncle's house, and I haven't been to his. His parents are – strict.'

Sylvia scrutinised me. 'Is he in the closet?'

'You weren't joking about the perception lasers,' I said.

'Doesn't require lasers. Be careful, please.'

'Jo's not going to mess me around because of that. Evan came out when he was basically a toddler and he—'

'I didn't mean it like that,' Sylvia murmured. 'Only that it might be more complicated.'

'What's *un*complicated?'

Sylvia forged on. 'Has he said he likes you?'

'I know he does.' I hated that I was answering in that way.

'Adam...'

'Can we not do this?' I pleaded.

Sylvia bit her lip and relented.

I wished I had a better answer for Sylvia, that I could have said, *Yes, Jo told me he likes me; he can't keep his hands off me; he doesn't hide me; he wants me.*

I went to the cello but every note was spiky and jangling, like my brain.

I messaged Evan, asked if he could talk.

Sure, he replied.

'I'm gonna ask you something,' I said, when his face appeared on my phone screen.

He instantly looked worried but said, 'All right.'

'Why did you break up with me?'

Evan's worries had apparently been confirmed. 'Do you honestly want me to explain again?'

'It wasn't that satisfactory then so...'

He sighed. 'It was like something was missing. I wanted more.'

I pushed. 'This is so vague. More what?'

'You're not going to enjoy this,' he hedged.

'Probably not,' I agreed.

'Excitement? Or—' Evan grasped for the word and I remembered how he had grasped for me.

'Passion,' I finished.

Evan half-smiled. 'Sounds like a romance novel, but yeah. I don't mean sex.' He caught my expression and said indignantly, 'I don't!'

'You wanted me to do more.'

'If you know this already why make me say it again?' he asked impatiently.

'I didn't know it then.'

'You never said what you wanted to do. You could have, I wouldn't have stopped you,' Evan protested.

'You didn't really ask me,' I said.

'Don't wait to be asked!' he shot back.

'Sometimes you have to, Evan!'

Neither of us spoke for a while.

Then I said, 'That did clear stuff up for me.'

'I told you you wouldn't like it. And I didn't either.'

'I can be more confident. Assertive.'

'Are you trying to get back with me?' he asked.

I gazed at him, his face on the screen small enough to fit in my hand. I couldn't tell how many fractions of joking he was.

'I'm motivating myself, that's it,' I said.

'Uh-huh.'

I knew by his tone he didn't believe me.

'I have to go,' I said.

'If that's what you want,' he replied, mocking.

'It is.' I hung up.

I could be assertive. I could do whatever I wanted.

———

I opened my curtains, yawning. And froze, my mouth still open, hanging in a rictus of horror. The windowsill was strewn with fragile bodies: butterflies, all dead, piled like soft leaves from some dying tree.

I couldn't even scream. I picked up my notebook and opened the window, brushing the butterfly corpses off the sill and into a gust of wind that swept them away. I slumped against the wall. The edges of my notebook were dusted with a dull iridescence. I opened it to the list of unknowns about the diary, as long and unanswered as ever.

I was seized by a paralysing urgency. I sat in front of my laptop and searched — for what? I scoured the diary once more for clues but finding out anything about its writer appeared increasingly hopeless. And if every clue or record *had* been destroyed, as Jo had wondered...

At lunch I was desperate enough to ask Toshi and Junko about the atomic bomb.

'It was very sad,' remarked Junko, a massive understatement.

'My grandmother's sister died,' Toshi said sombrely. 'The rest of the family escaped. But a few relatives passed when they were still young, from the sickness afterwards.'

'I'm so sorry,' I murmured.

Junko said, 'My father's family was in the countryside, but they could see the fires and the smoke. They said it looked like hell.'

'I thought it was a long time ago,' I said. 'But it wasn't, really.'

'For some it's history and for others it's yesterday,' Junko said. 'That's how memory is.'

'You can't escape it,' Toshi added, 'either way.'

We ate quietly until Junko asked, 'You've heard of Obon, Adam-san?'

'It's next month, isn't it?'

'There's a special festival that only Nagasaki has. Shoro Nagashi,' Junko told me.

'It's a parade to remember those who have died,' Toshi said. 'We always go.'

Time is coming, going. You must remember.

'What?' Junko was staring at me.

I had spoken aloud. 'I read that... Obon is the time for remembering. What if we don't remember them?' I asked. 'The dead.'

'They are unhappy,' Toshi said.

'Sometimes they become hungry,' Junko murmured.

My breath caught. Is that what would happen to the ghost...? She would become hungry if I didn't find her descendants, to remember her? Like the monk Shunkan that she had written of, hunting and never becoming full...

'Adam-san?' Junko prompted.

I jumped. 'Yes?'

'I said, would you like to go to Shoro Nagashi with us?'

'Yes, please. Will your daughter come home for it?' I asked, not thinking.

'Perhaps this year,' Toshi answered eventually.

'I'd like to meet her,' I dared to say.

Junko glanced at Toshi, who met her gaze and sighed.

'You could also think about your family,' Junko said.

'My family?' I doubted Dad's ancestors would appreciate that, in their Christian heaven. But my mother...

'You could ask your aunt,' Toshi suggested.

Dad hadn't given me any information about her. I'd have to ask, and hope he could give me answers.

The Peace Museum was on a hill, so I was dripping sweat when we entered, which felt disrespectful. In the lobby were tourists, both foreign and Japanese, and high-school kids in uniform being admonished by their teacher for speaking too loudly.

Jo had been reluctant to join but I'd said I needed company and kissed him until he was convinced. I was pleased with my powers of persuasion.

We entered the exhibition and I instantly understood Jo's reluctance. There was a room with a reconstruction of rubble, a statue of a Christian saint with a mutilated face. There were displays of melted glass and coins, torn clothing, twisted pieces of metal. There were photos of bodies. I read the information plaques over and over, unable to comprehend this destruction.

Periodically, Jo pointed something out. That was a street we had walked down; this had been a child's toy; this was a painting a survivor had made, all blood red and black smoke.

Information boards had timelines of what had led to this, as if war was logical. Placenames snagged my eye:

1895: Japan annexes Taiwan

and

1910: Japan begins to occupy and rule Korea (then called Chōsen)

and

1937: the Japanese army carries out the Rape of Nanjing. Casualties are put as high as 300,000 though this is disputed by some Japanese historians, who argue that it was closer to 40,000

My head swam. *Arguing.* As if 40,000 was not so bad. The diary writer's uncle came to mind, saying Japan was improving Asia, teaching and helping other countries. He had spoken of Chōsen and Taiwan. And during the war ghosts had appeared, telling the writer of terrible things. They had been in Nanjing – they must have been monstrous, evil—

I staggered on. I passed a screen, where a Korean woman was talking about the aftermath of the bomb, her husband rubbing salt on the intestines that had spilled from his wounds.

Someone else watching said, in an English accent, in unmistakable disgust, 'America.'

'Are you all right?' Jo asked.

I wasn't, and I couldn't tell if it was because of the sickening details or shame or anger. I was an inheritor of all this guilt and pain.

'The memorial hall is not like this—' Jo began.

'I want to go,' I interrupted.

Outside, I gulped oxygen, but it settled in my lungs heavily; my entire body was leaden, my head thick and slow.

Jo rubbed my back. 'It's okay.'

I swept my palm across my eyes. 'No, it isn't.'

Jo's hand kept tracing slow and steady circles. 'I know.'

The group of school kids appeared. They must have been sweltering, the boys in high-necked dark coats with two rows of gold buttons. They weren't raising their voices anymore.

People were not evil. They were ordinary, capable of evil acts. And my horror only increased.

'Do you feel angry at America?' I asked Jo.

He thought. 'Not the America now, but the America then. Their army. The people who ordered the army. I feel angry at the Japan then too.'

'That's... fair of you.'

I reached for his hand and watched him hesitate, checking swiftly if anybody could see us.

'Would you like to get food?' he asked.

The thought made my stomach churn. 'I'd like to go home. I need to be alone for a while. I'm sorry I made you come.'

Jo was concerned. 'You should rest.'

'I will,' I said.

But that wasn't what I wanted to do. What I wanted was to talk to my father.

—

Dad picked up the third time I called.

'Adam, I'm at work – is this about the officer you were asking about? I can't—'

I ignored him. 'Can you tell me more about my aunt?'

'That's what you're calling about?' Dad sounded annoyed. 'It's not a great time—'

'You know when would've been a good time? Ten years ago,' I said.

Dad exhaled. I knew the expression he was making as he did his *I'm-being-calm* breathing: jaw clenched, eyes slightly narrowed.

'I want her address, her phone number, everything,' I continued.

'Why?' he asked.

'Because she's my family and I want to meet her.'

'She won't want to see you,' he argued.

I barrelled through that pain. 'When was the last time she had the chance to? Somehow I don't think it was recently.'

'No, but she—'

'Maybe I'll make a better impression than you.'

'Look, she wasn't thrilled your mother was with a foreigner. Me being in the military... For some reason she didn't like that.'

'Some reason?' I half-yelled. 'You know where I was today, Dad? The museum of the atomic bomb! What you did to us—' I bit off the end of that sentence.

There was a stunned silence on the other end of the line.

'I didn't do anything,' Dad said icily.

'You're in the *military*!'

'That war was over before I was even born, Adam!' Dad raised his voice. 'And I suppose you learned about what Japan did during the war? The atrocities?'

I flinched at the word, its accuracy. 'I know Japan wasn't innocent!'

'And where is this *you* and *us* coming from!'

'I don't want to be like you,' I said simply.

I couldn't hear Dad's calm breathing anymore.

'I'll send you your aunt's details,' he said, from far away. 'So you can find the family you want.'

All I could see were flames.

———

I squinted sleepily at my phone, silencing my alarm. There was a gossipy message from Sylvia, an anxious one from Jo, a photo of an ice-cream smeared Benny, from Kate.

And a message from Dad that made me sit straight up in bed. It contained only three things: my aunt's name, address and phone number.

Thirty-three

♩ ♫ ♪ ♪ ♩ ♪

I slumped blearily into my train seat. It was 7 a.m., because Toshi had insisted I get a full day in Itoshima. My aunt's name was Mayumi and when I called the number Dad had given me, she hadn't answered. Junko had recommended I send a letter, but I didn't have the patience to write it or to wait for a reply.

I decided to doze, though as soon as I closed my eyes my brain showed a montage of the numerous ways this could go wrong. I put on my headphones and stared out of the window instead, listening to Schubert and biwa in turns.

In Fukuoka I transferred in Hakata Station, modern and bustling with people. My next train was on the airport line, and I momentarily considered going to the other side of the platform, getting on, flying home. It was stupid but probably less stupid than my current plan. I watched that train leave and got on mine. The next and final train was two-cars long and only half-full. Outside, buildings gave way to greenery. When I left the station – just a platform and a waiting room – there were a few houses and then nothing but fields.

It didn't seem like a taxi was going to pass by, but it was only a thirty-minute walk. At least it was cooler than the city.

The fields were a lush green which turned out to be rice, stalks growing in mud and water, narrow streams trickling between the fields. There were dragonflies everywhere, like volleys of disobedient arrows.

The unhurried beauty calmed me. Sure, my aunt would be surprised. But pleasantly? It would be a reunion!

I turned down a side road to a cluster of houses. The one my map directed me to was large and old, with a tiled roof that curled at the ends and an impeccable garden behind its white wall.

I had an unexpected urge to call Jo or Sylvia, even Dad. But what would I say? I gritted my teeth and rang the doorbell. It chimed and echoed inside. The seconds stretched and with each I relaxed a fraction. If nobody was home then there was nothing else I could do...

'Yes, yes,' someone called distantly. Footsteps shuffled closer.

Damn.

A woman inched open the door. 'Hello?' she said in Japanese. She was in her late forties, hair cut to her chin, mouth a straight line; she did not look like my mother.

'Hello,' I replied stupidly. I had already forgotten what I had rehearsed. 'Koga Mayumi-san?'

'Yes,' she said suspiciously.

I bowed. 'I'm Adam. I'm sorry to bother you. My mother was Koga Ai. Your sister...'

Mayumi recoiled, and I thought she was going to close the door. Then she came out, very suddenly. She searched my face the same way I was searching hers. Her eyes were wide, mouth parted, her whole expression soft with shock. Now she did resemble my mother.

'Ai's son?' she breathed. 'Kai?'

Kai was my middle name, my Japanese name. Nobody called me that.

'Yes. I'm sorry to surprise you—'

'How did you know to come here?' she asked.

'My father gave me your address. I wanted to meet my mother's family.'

Mayumi spoke fast, sounding almost annoyed.

'Can you repeat that, please? My Japanese isn't good.'

'Why now?' she said slowly.

'I'm here for the summer. It's the first time I've been back in Japan.'

'Your father told you about me recently?' She wasn't annoyed; she was furious.

'Yes,' I said wretchedly. 'I asked him.'

She gave me a long stare full of anger and sadness. 'Tell your father it's too late.' Mayumi stepped back inside and shut the door.

Yes, it was too late. I wanted to tell her that I despised my father too. I wanted to bang on the door so I could see the ripple of my mother again.

I turned away blindly, back to the rice fields. A sudden movement made me stop, and my eyes cleared enough for me to see a white heron spread itself into the wind and fly away.

I watched it land in the next field, clean and elegant and out of my reach.

In Hakata Station I tried to buy omiyage for Junko and Toshi. Jo had schooled me in this: always bring back a gift when you go somewhere, preferably food. I figured this was how everyone in Japan knew about the specialties of each region. But the station was too crowded, full of people knowing where they wanted to go. I escaped through the nearest door.

I walked aimlessly. The streets of Fukuoka were different from Nagasaki's – broad and gridded, the buildings newer and taller. Fukuoka Tower loomed overhead, reminding me of the tiny T-shirt that had been mine and now belonged to Benny.

A park appeared almost magically: walking and cycling paths ringed a glassy lake, bounded by trees. I collapsed onto a bench and cradled my head in my hands. Dad had been right, but it was *his fault* that he had been right. What had he done to make Mayumi hate him so much?

And what about me? There was no way to even think that without a whine. I was her sister's kid. Though it might be that Mayumi hadn't got on with my mother, either. There was so much about my mother that I didn't know, and how was I supposed to find out if no one would tell me?

I rubbed my palms into my eyes. I scrolled through my phone, needing to talk but not to anybody who'd ask about the visit. I couldn't bear to explain such a humiliating rejection.

I video-called Evan.

He answered, confused. 'Adam?'

I tried and failed to muster a reassuring smile.

'Everything good?' he asked.

'No,' I said honestly, 'not really.'

Evan sat up and I saw that he was in bed. He was shirtless, and tilted his phone hurriedly so it showed him from the shoulders up.

'Early night?' I asked.

'I have work tomorrow morning but – yeah, there's not much going on here,' he admitted.

'I'm jealous.'

Evan raised an eyebrow. 'Of me in bed?'

'Of not much going on!'

He grinned. 'Liar.'

I shook my head.

His expression changed. 'What's wrong?'

'It's too weird and complicated to explain. It's family stuff and – being here is hard,' I breathed deeply, trying to steady myself, 'and I'm alone.'

'No shit, it's hard. You're a million miles away in a totally different country. I couldn't do it,' Evan said.

This surprised me. 'Yeah, you could.'

'Wouldn't even want to. It's cool you're doing it, though.'

'Really?'

'I think it's brave.' Evan coughed as if embarrassed to concede this. 'And if you feel like you can't – so what? You're there.'

'Thanks. That actually makes me feel better.'

And it did. I wouldn't have been able to take Sylvia's determination or Jo's sunniness or Kate's cheerleading. Evan was blunt and frequently cynical, but he was never falsely positive.

'Could we just talk for a while?' I asked. 'Tell me what's going on. Make me glad I'm not there.'

'I can do *that*.' He launched into mundane and instantly interesting drama.

I gossiped along, saying things like, 'She had that fight months ago,' and 'Obviously that's messed up, they're cousins.'

When Evan finished, he said, 'Feel better?'

'Kinda.' I *wanted* those low and ultimately inconsequential stakes. I wanted normality. I still, like an idiot, wanted Evan.

'Show me Japan,' he said. 'I'll pretend I'm on holiday with you.'

'It's my first time in this city. I'm just passing through.'

I turned my phone camera around so that he could see the park, and walked around the unruffled lake, chatting idly. I reached a red pavilion, then continued on to another area where steep stone walls rose from the grass.

'Fukuoka Castle Ruins,' I read from a sign.

'Cool,' said Evan. 'I love castles.'

'You do?'

'I was super into medieval stuff as a kid. Knights, quests, samurai, honour—'

I rolled my eyes. 'Why is honour always associated with Asians?'

'I don't mean that,' Evan cut in. 'Honour, chivalry, heroism – that's everywhere. Everyone can have honour.'

'You're right. They can. Should.'

I crossed a bridge arching over what was apparently a moat, but so thick with lotus flowers it resembled a meadow.

'This might be the best holiday I've ever been on,' he said. I laughed.

'Seriously! I've never been out of the country. Don't even have a passport.'

'I have two,' I boasted.

Evan's face closed. 'Greedy.'

'Sorry, I—'

'I'm kidding. This isn't a bad way to travel. I mean, it's free.'

'I'll show you Nagasaki, if you like,' I offered. 'I know it better than here.'

'I'd like that.' Then he said, 'I miss you.'

'Oh,' was all I could muster in reply.

'Are you seeing someone over there?' Evan asked suddenly.

'Sort of.' Jo and I hadn't discussed what we *were*. By the general rules of dating, that meant it wasn't official.

Evan said, 'You're coming back, aren't you?'

'Definitely.'

'So it's a holiday thing.'

'I'm not sure what it is,' I replied truthfully.

He softened. 'It's been good talking to you like this.'

'We should have talked more, before.'

'You think it's too late?' There was a note in his voice that I couldn't identify, then I realised it was disappointment.

'I thought so,' I said cautiously.

'We could see how things are, when you come back,' he suggested.

'You want to get back together?'

He took an audible breath. 'I still like you. Honestly? I like you even more now.'

And that was what I had longed for – to be told this, easily and directly, to be *wanted*. No doors closed, nobody pulling away. A smile spread across my face, covering the guilt.

'I didn't stop liking you. So... yeah. When I'm back...' I said.

Back at home, at school, so far from Japan and Jo, in my real and normal life – Japan would be a memory, a dream. I might never return here; right now, I didn't even want to.

'When I'm back,' I said, 'let's try again.'

Thirty-four

'How was your aunt?' Junko asked.

'She was surprised. She...' I grasped for words.

Junko and Toshi waited expectantly.

'... was nice.' She probably was, to other people. 'We talked.'

Junko was, perceptively, not satisfied with this. 'Will you see her again?'

'Oh, yeah. Sometime soon. She's busy. We'll see,' I babbled.

Toshi beamed. 'It's good you met.'

I knew Junko didn't believe me, but she didn't pursue the topic.

We sat down to dinner, but my appetite had gone. I kept missing what Junko and Toshi said, and eventually they gave up attempting conversation. When I told them I was tired and should go to bed they didn't argue, despite Junko glancing unhappily at my full plate.

I entertained and discarded the idea of messaging Jo. I thought of Evan and felt ashamed, thought of my aunt and felt worse. A headache was condensing behind my eyes, so I closed them.

—

I thudded awake in a sweaty panic. My sleep had been delirious, broken by snatches of songs and shadows. I'd missed my alarms and felt groggy and sick. I saw the time and swore, grappled into my clothes and lugged the cello downstairs.

'Adam-san?' Junko emerged from the kitchen. 'You should eat.'

'I have rehearsal,' I told her, grabbing my backpack, though my headache hadn't gone away. It was in fact worse, but I couldn't fall even further behind.

As soon as we started playing, I knew I should have stayed in bed. My fingers were clumsy, my headache thumping a rhythm that contradicted the tempo. I scrabbled through until Shion called for a break, which we all agreed to with varying degrees of relief and exasperation.

I went to the vending machine outside and bought a Pocari Sweat, pressing the cold bottle to my forehead but feeling too nauseated to drink it. I hauled myself back to the rehearsal room and paused at the doorway, mustering my remaining energy.

Shion, Kana and Sakurako were talking in low voices.

'... he just needs to practise more,' said Shion doubtfully.

'He's not serious,' hissed Sakurako.

'He's on his holidays, isn't he?' Kana said.

'The concert is going to be awful. We should get someone else,' Sakurako said.

The only reason I didn't turn and leave was because the cello was in the room. I entered, and an embarrassed silence ensued.

'I'll go home.' I concentrated on packing away the cello.

'Let's finish,' Kana said uncomfortably.

'Sakurako-san is right. You should replace me.'

Sakurako's arms were crossed. 'You don't care about this. I can hear it when you play. There is no feeling in your music.'

That stung. 'I d dn't ask to play with you. I only came because Jo wanted me to.'

'We only let you play because Jo-kun asked us,' Sakurako shot back.

I threw my hands up. 'That's not my fault.'

'It's because of *you* that Jo-kun—' Sakurako bit off the rest of her sentence.

'I'm not making Jo do anything,' I replied.

Sakurako gave me a look of deep disgust. 'You're trying.'

Kana and Shion were watching as though we were playing a violent game of tennis.

I was too exhausted and infuriated to ask what she meant. 'Whatever. I'm leaving.'

I ignored Shion and Kana's pleas and got out. I'd call Jo and find out what Sakurako was insinuating. She was such a *bitch*.

Outside was white-hot and unbearable. I swiped clumsily at my phone to call Jo.

'Giving me a tour of Nagasaki today?'

I squinted at my screen. It was Evan, once again in bed and shirtless. This time he didn't tilt his phone to hide that.

'I didn't mean to— You were the last person I called so...'

His voice was smug and teasing. 'No need for excuses. You can just say you're tired of your holiday guy.'

'Tired,' I repeated. 'I mean, no, not of him.'

Evan peered at me. 'You all right?'

'I'm not feeling great.' I was boiling and freezing. 'I might have a fever. And there's other stuff...'

'Get yourself into bed.' He waggled his eyebrows.

'I do need bed. Or medicine...'

'Too bad I'm not there or I'd tuck you in,' Evan said.

My heart was beating too fast. My head swam. 'That would be nice.'

'Who's that?'

I turned, dizzying myself. Jo was right behind me.

'Oh, hey – someone from school.' I held my phone behind my back. 'What did you hear?'

Instead of answering he asked, 'Did you finish practice early?'

'I'm not playing with them anymore. They don't want me to.'

'What?' Jo said, bewildered.

'What is up with Sakurako? She's been horrible to me since day one. Does she like you?' The words poured out, accusatory as a jabbing finger.

He held up his hands. 'We're friends. She wants to keep me safe, I think. She knows about us.'

'Is she homophobic?' That would explain a lot.

'No! But in the past, we—'

'I get it. But she shouldn't take it out on me.'

'I told her you are nice, you wouldn't do anything to hurt me.' Jo's voice was flat.

A heavy silence swayed between us.

'The person you were talking to. Is he a friend?' Jo asked.

Evan's voice blared from my phone. 'I'm still here!'

I hadn't ended the call. I fumbled at my phone in a panic and it was because I was shaky, my hands sweaty, that I dropped it with a clatter. Jo picked it up and stared at the screen.

They saw each other, Jo and Evan, and I wanted to die.

'You're the holiday guy, then,' Evan said.

'Who are you?' Jo asked.

'I'm Adam's ex,' Evan replied with all his lazy confidence, which I'd always found kind of hot, but hearing it directed at Jo made me wince.

'Well... Are we exes, Adam?' he continued. 'Or—'

I grabbed the phone from Jo's unresisting hand.

'Enough.' I hung up, but not before catching a glimpse of Evan's expression, which didn't match his tone. It was resentful, hurt. I couldn't make sense of it, of anything.

Jo waited, his cheeks red, his eyes dark.

'He's a guy from home. We used to go out, and we're talking again but... He told me he likes me. And I like him too,' I blurted out. 'We – you and me – don't have any rules about other people so it's not as if I'm...'

Jo was looking at me with such incomprehension that for a moment I couldn't tell what language I was speaking. It was like the diary again, the English overlaying Japanese, except this time it was only confusion and no clarity.

'I don't want to hurt you,' I said, hating that now Sakurako was right.

'You told me about him before. Your boy trouble.'

'Trouble,' I echoed. 'Yeah. He is.'

'It's all him?' Jo asked evenly.

'No. Me too, but I...' My thoughts and words stuck to themselves. 'Look, I'm trying to be honest.'

In Japanese, Jo said, 'I don't understand.'

I kept going in English. 'Why are we hiding everything? Why does everyone keep lying?' I was shouting, not just at Jo but at Dad, and my aunt, at Toshi and Junko.

'We don't always have to say everything. We can keep things inside. Sometimes we do it for others.' Jo's tone was fierce.

The ghost appeared without warning, a shadow of a shadow, like an afterimage burned into my eyelids. Behind Jo, watching me.

'What do you want?' I asked her brokenly. 'I can't find what you're looking for. I can't help you...'

She was gone then. There was only Jo and Jo's eyes, brimming with betrayal.

The cello was too heavy for me, and why had I even brought my backpack? It had nothing in it of use.

Not true.

I took out the diary, thrust it at Jo.

'Take this. Read it all, if you want,' I muttered. 'I can't...'

I stumbled away. Around me, butterflies flew and died, dissolving on the pavement before my darkening eyes.

Thirty-five

♩ ♫ ♪♪♩ ♪

I had heatstroke, Junko told me. She scolded me gently. I had walked around in the sun too much in Fukuoka the day before, exhausted myself, hadn't eaten or drunk enough water. She put cool gel packs on my neck and underneath my armpits, and gave me endless bottles of Pocari Sweat.

When I finally came to I was drained and weak but my fever was doused. I was dredging up the strength to get out of bed when there was a knock on the door.

Toshi poked his head in. 'Adam-san, how are you feeling?'

I sat up. 'Better.'

He looked relieved. 'We were so worried. Heatstroke is dangerous!'

'I've never had it before.'

'Please never get it again,' Toshi said sincerely. 'I'll bring you food.'

I remained in bed and unwillingly remembered what had happened yesterday. Quitting the quartet, Evan, Jo – and how I had spoken to him. I felt sick again, this time with shame.

I'm so sorry, I messaged Jo.

I was too cowardly to write anything else. He didn't reply.

—

I stayed in my room that day, and the day after. I messaged Evan to say I was sick and avoided his calls. I ate with Toshi and Junko. I didn't offer to help cook. Whenever they asked how I was, I said I was recovering, but tired.

I *was* tired. I was exhausted.

The ghost didn't come, and I was glad of it. Maybe her time had run out before I could do any more. Or she went where the diary went. Which meant she was with Jo... But he didn't reply to any of my messages, and what could I even ask him? *Are you being haunted?*

I wanted to talk to Sylvia about Jo, though I knew she couldn't resist an *I-told-you-so*. I needed sympathy. I called Kate.

'Adam!' Kate said. 'How's everything? You've been busy...'

I'd dodged a lot of her calls. 'I'm less busy now.'

'What happened?' Kate asked instantly.

'Well...' I related the whole debacle.

Kate said levelly, 'I think you were a bit – thoughtless.'

'I'm aware.'

'You took your frustrations out on Jo, which wasn't fair. You always—' Kate cut herself off. 'You've done that before.'

Kate meant I'd done that to her – but that wasn't true, I hardly ever shouted at her or argued... But then who needed shouting, when you could simply close a door in someone's face?

Into this silence, as if she read my thoughts, she observed, 'You haven't said much about your aunt.'

'She didn't want to talk. She hates Dad, and by extension hates me,' I replied.

'Your father is aware of that, which is why he didn't tell you about her.'

'Have you met Mayumi?' I asked.

'Once.' Kate's voice was pained. 'She was upset. Understandably. She was protective of her little sister, your mother. I think she's someone who loves deeply.'

'If you were her, what would you want?'

'I would want my sister back,' she said.

And I couldn't do that.

'You need to decide what *you* want,' Kate said, 'that's what's most important.'

'Right. Thank you, Kate.'

Decide what you *want.* I did need to do that, but it *wasn't* the most important thing. Jo had talked about shielding others by keeping stuff inside, but that didn't feel right either – at least not for me.

I stared out the window, over the city I'd just begun to know, and felt more lost than ever.

⁓

The sound wrapped around me, pulling me from sleep with such slow sadness that I woke half-crying. It was the shamisen. I followed the source of the music, expecting Toshi, or the ghost.

But it was Junko in the music room, her fingers plucking and pleading.

I listened for a minute before whispering, 'That's beautiful.'

Junko didn't stop or raise her head. 'I didn't think it would wake you.'

'I don't mind,' I said. 'I want to listen.'

'I'm out of practice,' she said.

'If you're playing for yourself then I think it doesn't matter.'

'I'm playing for...' She finally looked at me.

'Your daughter?' I ventured.

Junko's hand tightened on the shamisen's neck. 'I'm reminding myself of her.'

'When did you see her last?' I asked tentatively.

'Several years ago. We speak on the phone but it's only small conversation.' Junko's voice was small too.

'Sometimes it's difficult for me to talk to my father,' I offered. 'I'm often mad at him.'

'Does he—'

I didn't understand the rest of her question.

'Does he deserve it?' Junko spoke in English, stepping out of her teacher role for once.

'I think so.'

She reflected on that. 'Will you always be angry at him?'

'I don't want to be. But maybe a part of me always will.'

'Some feelings never go away, do they?'

'Why did you tell your daughter... the truth? Did she suspect?' I asked.

'No. She was shocked. But we owed it to her, I thought.'

Owed was a weird word. It wasn't wrong, though. A secret was a debt. It depended on who or what you were in debt to: another person, or shame, or pride.

'Sometimes I think I should have told her after I died. Then I could have had a happy life with her.'

I almost smiled, but Junko wasn't joking.

'I bet she'd feel angrier that way. More betrayed.' I tried to sound confident, but a happy life sounded so good.

'I wouldn't be there to be angry at,' Junko replied calmly. Then, abruptly, 'What about your father's wife?'

'Kate. I'm not mad at her... It's complicated. I know she loves me.' I thought of Benny, her own sweet, real child. 'But I'm harder to love.'

Junko looked baffled.

'Some people are just easier to love,' I explained. 'Like Jo. He's like sunshine. I... We...' I shut the hell up.

A kind of understanding dawned on Junko's face, informing me I'd outed myself, and worse, I'd probably outed *Jo*.

'I hope your daughter can come for Obon,' I blurted.

Junko strummed a dissonant chord.

'I should go back to bed,' I said.

Her voice floated to me as I walked away, the final notes of that song she'd been playing.

'Her shamisen is here. She left it behind. She said she'd never play again.'

—

In the blunt light of morning, I vowed three things: to focus on the diary, contact my aunt again and leave Jo alone. At least romantically. It was better that way. I wanted to be friends but that was it. Jo was too good for me.

I told Sylvia.

'Obviously you're *good enough*,' she said. 'But yeah, might not be the moment for a committed relationship. You're not there much longer.'

'We weren't really committed.'

'I think it's pretty loose until The Talk,' Sylvia said.

'Same. But it could be different here.'

'And different for Jo,' Sylvia added. 'If it was his first sort-of relationship.'

'Yeah.' I switched topics. 'What's going on over there?'

'Sean and Rosie broke up two days ago and reconciled this morning.'

'They're a dynamic couple.'

'I send a message to Rosie every day: *did you break up again y/n.*'

'Economical,' I said appreciatively.

'I have no time for all that.'

'Did you get more hours at work?'

Sylvia looked glum. 'I'm studying. Writing torturous application essays.'

'Already?'

'It's not that early!' she said. 'You'd better not leave it too late or you'll be freaking out and writing about when you overcame failure or some crap.'

'I can't think of any situation like that.' Cello, relationships, Japanese fluency... Nope, no overcoming any of those.

'Think of it as a creative writing exercise. You have a list of schools, at least?'

'Kate suggested I go to music school.' I snorted.

Sylvia raised an eyebrow. 'What's so funny about that?'

'I literally just got kicked out of a string quartet.'

'If you get back into it then that's a good example of overcoming a failure. Boom. Essay topic!' Sylvia said.

'It's highly disturbing that that is your reason.'

'I'm a utilitarian. Think about your failures,' she said menacingly.

'Got lots to mull over then,' I said.

Sylvia hung up before I could ask her to prove me wrong.

I *had* been thinking about the string quartet, but the memory of Sakurako made me fume. Kana had sent me a message saying sorry, which I had responded to with my own apologies. As to whether they'd find another cellist – that was their problem. I had my own to deal with.

I began, in my appalling Japanese handwriting, a letter to my aunt.

An hour later, I had lost the will to live. I had accumulated pages of errors, smudges, and lines of kanji I'd practised over and over in an attempt to make them uniform and neat. My hand throbbed.

I stared at my pathetic letter and brought it to the living room.

'Junko-san... Thank you for talking to me last night.' I tried a respectful bow and held out the letter in both hands. 'Could you please help?'

Junko scanned the paper. 'There are many mistakes.'

We sat at the table among Junko's stacks of documents.

'So your meeting with your aunt did not go well,' she said.

'No,' I admitted. 'I want to try again.'

Junko corrected each grammar mistake and misspelling. She taught me the right phrases to politely ask and humbly say.

'You should apologise here.'

'Again?'

'Yes,' she said sternly.

I did as I was told.

'This will do,' she eventually conceded. 'I'm glad you are not giving up.'

'Thank you,' I said.

As I stood, my eye snagged on a page at the top of one of Junko's stacks, on a fragment of writing. No: a poem.

I read it aloud softly:

The color of the flowers
Has faded away,
In vain
I spent my days in this world
Gazing at the long rains falling

Junko was staring at me. 'You said you couldn't translate.'

'What?'

'You read it in English,' Junko said.

It was my turn to stare at her, then at the poem. And like the diary, I saw the overlay of languages: it was written in Japanese.

'Ah, I... I read it somewhere. The translation,' I invented. But it *was* familiar, in some way. 'I can't remember who wrote it, though.'

'The poet is famous in Japan. And abroad. Ono no Komachi of the Heian period.'

'Yes!' That was it – the writer had told Mr S— about her.

Junko was still looking at me strangely. 'But you said a particular translation. There are many – that's what I'm working on.' She picked out several pages and handed them over.

I skimmed through them. At the top was the poem in Japanese, and below were translations into English, each by a different person, none exactly the same.

'It shows the variety of possible interpretations,' Junko explained.

I was gripped by the feeling of being *close* to something, some answer. I checked each translator's name until...

'Who's this?' I pointed, hoping Junko didn't notice the tremble in my finger. But my voice trembled as I said, 'Taira Chyōko.'

'I hadn't heard of her before this. I suppose not much of her work has survived.' Junko paused. 'Yes, that's the exact translation you said.'

The writer's surname was Taira.

'Chyōko... What does that name mean? How do you write it in Japanese?' I asked.

Junko wrote out two kanji. 'Ko is a common kanji ending girls' names. It means child. The first one is the same as chyō-chyō.' She looked at me expectantly, a teacher testing a student.

'Oh,' I said. 'Butterfly.'

Thirty-six

♩ ♫ ♪♪♩ ♪

Junko, unfortunately, had been correct; there was barely anything to be found about Taira Chyōko. Aside from that translation credit, she was cited in one academic article, where her stories were described as *scandalous*, which made me oddly proud. She had written honestly about life as a woman and a mother, though there was no mention of her children. The article discussed other, more famous women writers and the feminist Japanese publications they had contributed to. I vainly looked for these magazines but only a few pages appeared, not even written by her. I couldn't find any personal details: no family or date of death.

And there was the nagging sensation something wasn't entirely right, because Taira couldn't have been her maiden name. If she was related to the Taira, it was through her grandmother, and the name would have been lost in her marriage... Unless Chyōko's second husband was a Taira? That would have been so notable that surely she would have mentioned it in the diary, but it was the only explanation I could think of.

At least I had a solid place to start. I looked until my eyes were heavy, for hours, finding no end.

When my phone buzzed it was a welcome distraction.

You up?

It was Evan.

I bit my lip. I'd put this off for too long. I video-called him.

'I *am* up. And I'm sorry I haven't called you sooner,' I said.

'Feeling better then?' he asked.

'Heatstroke is more like a heatslap.'

A corner of his mouth raised but he didn't laugh. 'It was nice to meet your holiday guy.'

'No,' I said, 'it wasn't. You wanted to start a fight.'

'I was telling the truth. Were you?'

I was silent.

'Did you have a fight, then?' Evan asked.

He sounded *hopeful*.

And I was furious. At him and myself. 'Why did you say you like me more now?'

'Because I miss you.'

''Cause I'm not there. I was seeing someone else. And you're bored.'

His lip curled. 'I'm not threatened by your summer fling.'

He was lying, and once that might have made me triumphant. 'I didn't say that's what he was. You didn't ask me how I felt. Again.'

'That's not the same as the beach thing!' he said defensively.

'You're *treating* me the same.'

He shook his head, but the anger had drained from both of us.

'I'm not saying I've behaved well either.' I struggled for words. 'I haven't been very... honourable.'

He scoffed. 'You're a knight now?'

'You said everyone can have honour.'

Evan glanced away. 'I guess so.'

'It sounds dramatic, yeah. You were the one who made me think about it, though. Honour is doing the right thing, isn't it?'

'It's having your beliefs and holding yourself to them. Being worthy and respectable,' Evan said.

'I'm not exactly thinking of respectability.'

'The respect of others. Respect for yourself.'

'Yeah. I'd like that. I don't think I have it.'

'Then neither do I,' he said, subdued.

'Well, it's not too late. I mean, I hope not. That's why I'm talking to you. *Telling* you what I want.'

'There's lots of stories about people losing their honour, or fighting to get it back,' he said. 'You have to prove you have it. You have to earn it.' Evan met my eyes. 'I get it.'

'So do I,' I said, 'now. And I don't think we should get back together.'

'It's the holiday guy, huh.'

'Not anymore.'

'You had your own Daniel moment?' Evan, understandably, was smug.

'Daniel should be our code of honour,' I said.

Evan broke into laughter. 'For the moment. Until we find our own.'

Another thing to search for. I could find it. In the end, the answer lay with me.

———

When my alarm went off it was uncannily dim, even though it was mid-morning. I clambered out of bed and opened the curtains, expecting a sky dark with an oncoming storm. But I couldn't see clouds, not even any sky, because my window was covered from the outside.

I blinked, trying to comprehend what it was – what *they were:* insects, all over the glass – a horrible palpitation of thin legs and the dull undersides of wings. I banged the window with my palm and they took fluttering flight: butterflies, a hundred of them, in every colour. The shadow cast by them lifted and, as I staggered back, their papery bodies withered and blew away into nothing.

I tried to calm my heartbeat, waiting for the shudders to cease. Numbly, I opened my laptop, but nothing had changed since last night; the only crumbs I'd found were references to Japanese feminist writers in academic papers that I couldn't get hold of. Maybe I could go to a university, use the library there?

Or I could go to a school. The writer had studied here in Nagasaki, and wouldn't a school have documentation of their students, especially notable ones?

I looked up *schools for girls Nagasaki.*

There were only three. I could go to them! My excitement ebbed at the thought of walking into a high school and asking about students. Even if they were long dead, it seemed creepy. There was nothing else I could think of, though.

I went to beg Junko for yet more assistance in my bizarre request, but she was on the phone, murmuring in another room. I circled the living room restlessly, my mind circling too, between names and connections and missing people...

I paused to examine the photos on the bookshelves, finding Yuna. That was surely her as a child, dressed in an elaborate kimono.

The front door opened and Toshi called, 'Tadaima.'

'Okaerinasai,' I replied automatically.

He joined me. 'That is for Shichi-Go-San. A ceremony for children. Yuna-chan was five,' he said fondly.

I didn't comment on the photo of a teenage Yuna playing shamisen, brow creased in concentration. I pointed at a class photo, Yuna wearing a uniform and holding an embossed folder, surrounded by other girls. Only girls.

'Her graduation,' Toshi supplied.

'Did Yuna-san go to an all-girls' school?' I asked slowly.

'She wanted to,' Toshi said, as if he thought I'd have a problem with that. 'She said more girls could be leaders in activities and circle groups. Once Yuna-chan makes up her mind it is not easy to change it.'

'That's good,' I replied, distracted by the eeriness tingling over me. Because there was a piece of information I hadn't checked: whether these schools were running back in 1911. 'Has the school been open for a long time?'

Toshi nodded. 'It's the oldest girls' school in Nagasaki.'

Of course it was. 'I want to talk to Yuna-san,' I said.

My frantic tone made Toshi pause.

'Why?' It was Junko, stepping into the room.

'I'd like to ask about... her high school experience.'

Toshi and Junko appeared equally disconcerted.

'Can't you ask Jo-kun about that?' Junko asked.

My mind was devoid of any excuse good enough to persuade them to call their estranged daughter and request that she talk to me, a teenage boy, about her time in a girls' school.

I came clean. 'This is a long story but...' I explained about the diary, omitting the ghost, the butterflies, the things that could be dismissed as me losing my mind.

'How interesting!' Toshi exclaimed, when I'd finished.

'I'd like to see the diary,' Junko said.

'Jo's reading it,' I replied regretfully.

'I'll call the school,' Toshi declared.

'That would be amazing!'

I waited as Toshi spoke on the phone. Junko, understanding the conversation, looked increasingly discouraged.

He hung up and sighed. 'I spoke to the principal, but it seems he is new and reluctant to help because he doesn't know us. I told him our daughter attended the school but even so... He has never heard of this writer, anyway.'

I groaned.

'If I find anything more about her, I'll tell you,' Junko said, seeing my disappointment.

'If there is any other way we can help, please ask us,' Toshi added.

'I will. Thank you both for all your help,' I said.

They had been helpful – they had helped me so much. That was why I couldn't bear to ask them to do what was most painful to them: contact their daughter.

i know this is weird, I messaged, but could you talk to Yuna for me

Jo replied, no doubt because it *was* such a weird request. why?

it's about the diary, I replied.

He called a minute later. 'Yuna-chan is connected to the diary?'

His voice stirred something in me: longing.

'Not exactly.'

I tried to explain.

'I'll ask her,' Jo said, once I was done.

I hadn't expected him to agree so readily.

'I need to know about the diary as well,' he said.

The tone of his voice prompted me to ask, 'Have you been... seeing things?'

Jo's breathing hitched. 'No,' he denied, and then more loudly, 'No!'

Which meant he had. And didn't want to. I had a foolish stab of jealousy, that the ghost had gone to him.

'You can talk to me,' I said, 'about anything.'

There was a pause and I thought Jo really *would*, but he said, 'I'll tell you what Yuna-chan says.'

All I could reply was, 'Thank you.'

———

A day later, Jo messaged me.

Yuna has helped.

Thirty-seven

♩ ♫ ♪♪ ♩ ♪

I wished Jo was with me. Not only because he'd be *here*, but also because it would be less perplexing if an actual relation of Yuna had come to the school too. I hadn't wanted to tell Toshi and Junko that I'd essentially gone behind their backs.

There were no students, though for some sadistic reason the teachers were still there. I entered the main building, situated high on a hill overlooking the city, and followed signs for reception, where a middle-aged woman was patiently watching a fax print out. I paused. I had never seen a fax machine in the wild before.

I said, 'Excuse me? I'm a friend of Yuna.'

The secretary did a double-take. 'Adam-san?'

'Yes, nice to meet you.'

The secretary launched into what I deduced was a story about Yuna singlehandedly running the school festival. She looked at me expectantly and I gave an uncertain laugh, hoping that was the right response. It must not have been because she said slowly and simply, 'I remember her! Such a lively girl. Shall we go to Takahashi-sensei?'

She led me through the corridors, insightfully not even attempting to give me directions. She knocked on a door. 'Sensei?'

There was a distant scuffle. The man who emerged looked about eighty, with horn-rimmed glasses and a moustache. He gave off Hayao Miyazaki vibes, minus the perfectionism.

The secretary introduced me. 'This is Adam-san. He's the exchange student doing research.'

This magical combination of words appeared to cast a spell of helpfulness on adults.

Takahashi peered at me. 'Please, enter.'

The secretary hightailed it back to her fax machine and I launched into my standard disclaimer of being bad at Japanese.

Takahashi cleared his throat. 'I speak some English...'

'That's great!' I said in relief.

'It was good to hear from Yuna-san. She was a determined student. Stubborn but *respectful*.'

I got the impression Takahashi was disrespected often.

'Tell me more about what you need,' he continued.

'I'm looking for Taira Chyōko, who I think graduated from this school in 1909 or 1910.' I showed him the kanji of her name.

I'd hoped he'd recognise it, but of course it couldn't be that easy. 'She was a writer, and I found a diary she wrote. It is an important document which should be returned to her family but I can't find any information about her.'

Takahashi frowned. 'I doubt her school records will help with this.'

'Taira is her married name. I think. So finding her maiden name would be very useful,' I explained.

'This is strange,' Takahashi said gruffly.

'*I know*,' I said fervently.

Takahashi hesitated, unconvinced.

'If you have a lot of work, I understand. You probably want to do your grading and classwork.' I glanced meaningfully at a teetering pile of reports.

Takahashi flinched at the sight of his work. 'I can take a short break.'

I bowed low. 'Thank you very much.'

We set off to a room full of filing cabinets and ledgers lined up on bookshelves. I'd been hoping for some sort of computer system they could use to find past students. But no. I was in analog.

Takahashi surveyed the shelves. 'You start at this end.'

He began to pull out files. I followed suit. The ledgers were yellowed with age and the print was tiny and faded. I examined the page, aware of Takahashi flipping speedily through.

Takahashi said wistfully, 'I researched this way in university. It is slow, but so fun.'

I mentally crossed history off my list of potential majors.

A few characters on the page in front of me became recognisable.

'This is Chyōko, right?' I showed Takahashi.

'Endō Chyōko. Entered the school in 1908, when she was twelve years old.'

I calculated her age. 'I don't think that's her but I'll note her information.'

Takahashi's brow furrowed. 'I'm not sure...'

'It's from such a long time ago,' I pleaded.

Takahashi relented with a shrug. He was the kind of teacher who would tell you to read a chapter of the textbook and then go to smoke a cigarette outside.

I scribbled an approximation of Endō. Takahashi moved to the next shelf.

I pored over the ledgers, my eyes starting to ache. I discovered another Chyōko with a different surname. She'd left the school in 1912... I wrote down her details anyway, struggling to get the strokes of each character right.

It was hypnotic, the rise and fall of pen-nib, the swoop across the paper...

My eyes fluttered. Had I fallen asleep?

I blinked furiously. My hand was moving across the page, and I wasn't moving it. I was watching as if it was at the end of someone else's arm. One character was being written over and over, strokes scored deep into the page.

'Stop,' I gasped. 'I see it, stop!'

My hand was released, aching and cramping. I clutched it to myself. I turned, and behind me was the ghost, so close that I knew she had been leaning over me, holding my hand in hers.

She raised a finger and moved it through the air – and I recognised the motion from before. She was writing a character.

'Did you say something?' Takahashi called.

The ghost dispersed. My hand shook and shook.

Takahashi reappeared with a bundle of papers. 'I have these, but nothing matches exactly.' He spotted the scrawl in my notebook. 'Writing Japanese is difficult, isn't it? We can make copies.'

I trailed silently after him back to reception, gripping my notebook tight. The secretary appeared to be petting the fax machine.

'Did you find what you were looking for?' she asked cheerfully in Japanese.

'We found some Chyōkos, and a few Tairas,' Takahashi replied cryptically, and began photocopying.

'Past students,' I explained.

The secretary picked up one of the freshly printed pages. 'Not Taira Chyōko? The writer?'

'You *know* her?' I cried.

'I went to school here and so did she. I learned about her in literature class. Not history class,' she added unnecessarily. It was plain this was news to Takahashi.

'What else did you learn?'

'I can't remember much but...' The secretary was bemused at my eagerness, and then my disappointment. 'I can show you.'

She brought us back to the records room, to a bookshelf of binders. She scrutinised the dates on the spines, then pulled one out triumphantly, flicking through its plastic pockets until she'd located the right one. She drew out a slim and perfectly preserved newspaper.

'Our school paper! I used to write sometimes.' She spread it out, leafing delicately through it until she found the page.

We stared at it together. There was a short article and a black and white photo: a woman wearing a kimono, hair pinned neatly back, gazing at the camera frankly. She was pretty, but that wasn't what was arresting about her. It looked as though she was about to speak, as if she had something of significance to tell the photographer.

I had to put my hand on the back shelf to steady myself. It was the ghost.

'What does the article say?' I managed.

Takahashi said in English, 'That she studied here, and wrote essays, poetry, stories. She was published in a famous magazine, *Seitō*.'

'Taira was her married name, wasn't it? What was her maiden name?'

'She was from the Harada family. They used to be an important family here.' The secretary pondered. 'I don't think Taira was her husband's name. As a writer she was usually referred to as Chyōko.'

But when she published her first article she hadn't used her real name.

I stared at the character scoured into my notebook.

'What does this say?' I showed the secretary the page.

She faltered at the possessed writing, but replied, 'Kiku.'

'A type of flower,' Takahashi explained. 'I don't know what it's called in English.'

I physically slapped my palm into my forehead. 'Kiku means chrysanthemum.'

'Very good,' the secretary praised, presumably to encourage my kanji study, which I was evidently disturbingly serious about.

This *had* been written in the diary; the kimono silk O-Suzu had thought she would like because of her name.

'Harada Kiku,' I said, at long last. 'That was her real name.'

In my ear came the faint sound of a sigh, of satisfaction.

'I can make you a copy of this,' the secretary said.

I waited in a stupor as she made photocopies of the article.

I bowed as she handed them to me. 'This is... I'm sorry, what's your name?'

'Matsuo Kazue.' She bowed.

'Thank you so much for your help, Matsuo-san,' I said emphatically.

I kept stammering gratitude to her and a disconcerted-looking Takahashi as I backed away, then paused.

'Who was your literature teacher, Matsuo-san?'

'Ah, Ishiguro-sensei. A real Nagasaki woman. She has passed on, sadly,' Matsuo said. 'Why?'

'No reason,' I muttered.

No *reason*, but I wasn't operating on that anymore. I had half-expected the secretary to lead me to O-Suzu...

I was sick and tired of names.

I called Jo as soon as I was outside.

'Jo, you won't believe it. I found the writer's name! I mean – she has *two* names!' I poured out the story breathlessly.

'That's amazing.' Jo sounded sincere and subdued.

'Right? Tell Yuna thanks and thank *you*.'

'What will you do next?' Jo asked.

'Keep looking. It should be easier now.'

'I hope so,' he said.

'Do you want to hang out?' I asked hopefully.

A silence.

'Why won't you play music?' Jo asked instead.

'Your friends don't want me to,' I said. 'I can't play like them, anyway. I'm not good enough.'

There was another silence.

'You can,' he said, 'if you try.'

I stared at my phone after he ended the call, trying to interpret what he meant.

Thirty-eight

At home, I got out my laptop and searched. But I didn't find anything that wasn't already in the secretary's article, and Harada and Kiku were both common enough to throw up a bunch of irrelevant results.

After a couple of hours I had reached another dead end. I knew a bit more about Kiku, yet I'd found no mention of Haru. I turned away from the harsh screen light. My gaze landed on the cello case, unopened since that last horrible rehearsal. I had to return it to Shion sooner or later, and I wanted it to be later.

I took out the cello. From time to time I had a possibly perverted urge to kiss it, the way I kissed Benny – a smack of affection. I resisted, because it wasn't mine, but I put my arms around it. I'd read that hugging a pillow releases the same endorphins as when you hug a person. The problem was that a pillow and a cello couldn't hug back.

Once I'd thought of arms around me, Jo filled my mind. I started playing, not the quartet piece but the Bach I'd tried and failed for my music exam. Jo's voice had been cloudy when we'd spoken. I was sorry, but also angry, resentful. Because he held back? Because he didn't want me in the greedy way

I wanted him to? That was my fault, like everything else. I focussed on the strings beneath my fingers, the angle of the bow, the sound pouring out like the tide.

When I finished I was out of breath. Junko had said she was playing shamisen for herself. I didn't do that often. I was always playing for something else – for class, or a test or for people who needed me to play.

Toshi had said he could hear my style, but I didn't know what he'd meant by that, or how to describe it.

I played on, trying to hear myself.

$\sim$

Next day I returned to frantically scouring the internet, trying to find lieutenants married to Kikus or Haradas. By lunchtime only food could ease the rage and frustration I'd accumulated.

Toshi and Junko looked at me expectantly when I joined them, and I realised why when Toshi picked up an envelope from the table.

'You received a letter,' he said.

My aunt had written back.

The letter wasn't long, but took me ages to read. Mayumi's handwriting was beautiful and even and infinitely more difficult than printed text. A few sentences left me puzzled; I could read every word but couldn't grasp the meaning when I put them all together.

I caved. 'Junko-san, Toshi-san. Can you please help me?'

They both stopped what they were doing and nodded politely, but their eyes were alive with curiosity. Probably no other homestayers had brought as much complicated drama.

They helped with the kanji I couldn't read. Toshi, being Toshi, gave me the English word and Junko, being Junko, glanced at him disapprovingly and wrote out kanji and pronunciation for me to study.

The letter read:

Kai-san,

I hope you are well. The weather is hot, so please take care and keep cool.

Thank you for your letter. I am glad you sent it. I was so surprised when you appeared, and I think I did not stay calm. After you left, I regretted that I hadn't reacted in a better way.

However, I hope you can understand my surprise. I had not seen you since you were a baby. It is rude to say, but I did not think of you often after Ai-chan passed away. You were far away in America with your father.

It's good that your father gave you my information. I thought that he would not do that. I told you it was too late but I hope that was incorrect. There is still time, if you are in Japan for a little longer.

Would you like to visit me again? It may be difficult to speak, but I want to try.

Here is my phone number. I think your father had my old one.

Please stay in good health.

Best,

Mayumi

'What do you think?' I asked Junko and Toshi.

'It's good,' Toshi concluded. 'It is not easy for her, but she wants to meet you anyway.'

'Do *you* want to meet her?' Junko asked.

'I do. But... I'm afraid.'

'Sometimes it is okay to be afraid,' Toshi said.

Junko lowered her eyes.

I picked up my phone.

———

'I'm going to see Mayumi this weekend,' I finished.

'That's good, Adam, it really is.' Even on my phone screen I could see Kate's smile didn't quite reach her eyes.

'What's up?' I asked.

'Benny's on a new sleep cycle that involves waking up on the hour every hour.' Kate showed the screen to Benny. 'There's Adam!'

'Adablrughmadzz,' he burbled.

'My new nickname. Catchy,' I said. 'Dad working a lot?'

Kate dodged this question by saying, 'He's home now. Here he is. It's Adam, say hi.'

It was a command rather than a request.

Dad emerged and we regarded each other. It was the first time we'd spoken since the argument after the atomic bomb museum.

'How's it going?' he asked.

'Fine. Hot.'

Kate frowned at me from behind Dad's back.

'I'm going to visit my aunt again,' I went on.

'That's. Huh. Nice,' he said. 'Send her my regards.'

'I will.' I definitely would not.

'Been doing anything fun?' Dad asked.

'Practising Japanese. Hanging around. Trying to find out about the woman who wrote that diary.'

Dad's face darkened.

'You *could* help me actually,' I said, because our icy silence had at last been broken. I had also exhausted every other resource. 'Remember a while ago I asked you about the lieutenant I was looking for?'

'Ah. Yeah, I got busy...'

I waved away the excuses. 'Can you check now? It's important. He's in the diary.'

'I need more details,' Dad hedged.

'He was a US Navy lieutenant, stationed in Nagasaki in 1911 for around a year.'

'There's been lots of lieutenants,' Dad said.

'He was married to a Japanese woman called Kiku Harada. They had a son. Then he went back to America and married a woman there.'

I hated how similar it sounded to my own story, as if I was inventing it to make a point.

Dad clearly saw the parallels; he had an odd, blank expression. 'It'd be tough to find anything from back then.'

I pressed on. 'When can you look? Tomorrow?'

'As soon as I can...'

'Please, Dad.' I tried out a smile, and realised I hadn't smiled at him in a long time. 'It would mean a lot.'

Dad smiled stiffly back. 'I'll do my best.'

Benny blew me a wet kiss goodbye.

That night the nightmares began. Over and over I saw Kiku's translucent face morph and scream until the sound was loud enough to wake me. Whenever I gasped into consciousness I couldn't tell if the ringing in my ears was from her shrieks or mine. Junko and Toshi didn't mention anything, so I assumed they were hers, echoing inside my head. Which wasn't any better.

'I'll find him,' I promised pleadingly, to my empty room. There was no reply, which should have been a relief, but only added to my growing unease.

That week, I ventured further into Nagasaki, alone. I went to another beach, as beautiful as where I'd gone with Jo, but not as fun. I went to an art gallery. I went to Gunkanjima, an effective illustration of the difference between a desert island and a deserted island. There were ghosts there, among the crumbling remains of a mining town, but I didn't see them. I just knew the place was haunted.

I even went to the Glover Garden, a colonial park where a Scottish businessman had lived. He'd helped found one of Japan's first breweries and was also a sort of arms dealer. A plaque stated that he'd had a common-law Japanese wife. Maybe that's what the Lieutenant had said Kiku was.

I stood on the second-storey verandah of one of the cream-coloured buildings, apparently in a French style, gazing at the tiers of the garden below, but I was suddenly too tired to continue. The bay stretched before me and, behind the mountains, dark clouds were congregating. A single butterfly flitted by, black and sparrow-sized. It didn't die, didn't fade.

Thunder growled. I hurried home. Rain was going to fall, and I could only hope it would ease the tension in the air.

Thirty-nine

♩ ♫ ♪♪ ♩ ♪

I was once again standing on Mayumi's doorstep, only marginally less nervous than last time. I pressed the doorbell and before it finished chiming, she opened the door.

'Kai-san,' she said, calling me by my Japanese name.

Her face mirrored my feelings: trepidation and a smile attempting to cover it. This made me feel a bit better.

Mayumi ushered me into a tatami room with a low table, and I folded myself down onto a cushion. 'Wait a moment.'

She went into the kitchen. There was an old TV, a full bookshelf, a single orchid growing in a pot. The garden outside had curving trees and a stone lantern and a pond. It was the kind of simplicity that spoke of attentive care. Somehow, I could tell she lived alone.

Mayumi returned with a tray of cold tea and a dish of watermelon slices.

'Thank you. Oh, and—' I held out the omiyage.

'Ah, castella. Nagasaki's famous product,' Mayumi said graciously.

I didn't know if this was positive or negative.

'Thank you very much.' She set the castella on the table.

I sipped some tea. We sat there. I stared at the watermelon, then sneaked a glance at Mayumi. She was gazing at the castella, her hands gripping each other tightly.

'Thank you for having me.' My voice came out creaky.

'I'm glad you wrote to me, and came all the way here.' She spoke more slowly now that she was conscious of my level of Japanese. 'I apologise for last time.'

'I shouldn't have arrived like that. It was rude.'

Mayumi inclined her head, not disagreeing. 'Please, tell me about your time here. Do you like Nagasaki?'

I was grateful to have an easy topic to talk about. I told her about Toshi and Junko, sightseeing, eating delicious food.

'That's good,' she said, when my spiel ended.

There was another lull. 'This area is beautiful,' I offered. 'It's nice to be in the countryside.'

'I don't like cities much,' she said. 'I grew up in this house, so I am comfortable here.'

'This is the family home? My mother grew up here too?' I asked eagerly.

Mayumi's expression tightened. 'Until she was eighteen, and then she went to university in Tokyo. I studied in Fukuoka, so I commuted. But Ai-chan wanted to go someplace new.'

'Did she come back often?'

'She returned for each holiday. After she began her job, it was more difficult to take time off.'

'That was when she was teaching English?' That was how Dad had been able to chat her up successfully, he'd told me once.

'Yes. Our parents passed away a few years after she graduated. I think she didn't like to be here, after that. Me, I didn't like to leave.' Mayumi sipped her tea.

'I'm sorry.' I imagined visiting grandparents in this house. Would they have been kind to me? Or would they have felt the same as Mayumi?

'She was lonely, then. Perhaps that's why...' Mayumi trailed off.

That's why she had ended up with my father.

'You must have been lonely as well,' I ventured.

She brightened. 'I was delighted when Ai-chan came back, with you.'

'I was here?' I stared around the room again, hoping to recognise something.

Mayumi's eyes stayed on me. 'I think you are like Ai-chan. You enjoy being with people.'

'I like to be alone too. Well. Alone with my cello. Is that really alone?'

Mayumi said, 'I think an instrument could be another part of yourself. One that makes more noise.'

I agreed. Another spell of quietness, but it was easier. I ate a piece of watermelon.

'You eat the seeds,' Mayumi observed.

'Is that bad?'

'That's what Ai-chan did. I would spit them out. She liked the crunch.' Her face softened.

It was a tiny, silly thing to make me happy.

'Do you remember her?' Mayumi asked.

'Not really.' The feel of arms around me, giggles, long fingers pointing at a green bird in a pink tree. They weren't even complete memories. I could have dreamed them.

'Do you want to see her bedroom?' Mayumi offered.

I said, 'I'd like that.'

I followed her up an almost perpendicular set of stairs. She slid open a door.

It was a small tatami room. The window overlooked the luminous fields, and as I watched, a red train slid steadily across the horizon. One wall was filled with bookshelves. There was an old dresser, and I pulled a drawer at random. There was long flat paper, tied with ribbon. I opened it and colour burst out: vermillion silk patterned with white and sky-blue flowers.

'Ai-chan's furisode kimono. She wore it at her coming-of-age ceremony, when she turned twenty,' Mayumi said.

How funny that this fabric was here, vivid and gorgeous, and my mother was not.

I gazed around, blinking fast. I tried to envision my mother sleeping and waking, lingering over her books as she decided which to read next.

I cleared my throat. 'Mayumi-san, do you remember my mother reading a diary? It looked like a notebook. An old one.' I scanned the bookshelves, hoping against hope there would be another notebook, the end of Kiku's story.

'That sounds familiar,' she said.

'I can show you.'

Jo still had the diary. I hadn't asked for it because once he returned it there would be no excuse to meet him again. But I had photos, and showed Mayumi the cover and the first page.

Recognition bloomed across her face. 'I remember this! Ai-chan said it was the story of a girl's life. A kind of romance.'

I'd thought of it as a tragedy. 'Can you tell me where my mother got it? Did it belong to someone in the family?'

Mayumi half-closed her eyes, remembering. 'No... A neighbour died and a relation gave Ai-chan a box of books that had been stored away in their house. She always loved old books. By the time Ai-chan read the diary, the relation was gone and the house sold.'

A literal dead end.

'I'm looking for the family of the woman who wrote it,' I said.

There was a strange expression on Mayumi's face. 'That's what Ai-chan was doing too.'

'She was?'

'She was searching for someone in the diary. A man.'

I felt an uneasy trembling sensation. All the hair on my arms had lifted.

'Who was the man?' I asked, as calmly as possible.

'An American, a man in the army – no ...'

'The Navy.'

Mayumi nodded. 'Yes, that's right.'

'His name?' I asked urgently.

'She didn't tell me.'

Had my mother seen Kiku? She had looked for the Lieutenant, or even Mr S—. What had she learned?

I almost laughed at the irony. The only Navy man she had found was my father.

There were memories in the air. Mayumi and I stood in silence and let them surround us.

~

My journey back was a blur. In Hakata Station I bought some omiyage – cakes that resembled baby chicks – fell asleep on the train and came to in Nagasaki. I was dazed and groggy rather than refreshed, and now that I was back, the fear came and roosted on me once more. I didn't want to go straight back to Toshi and Junko, so I wandered along Dejima Wharf instead. People were sitting outside, eating and drinking, and a combination of kids and dogs tumbled between tables.

Something portentous was in the atmosphere – or maybe just in the space around me. It was like the time before an exam; a dreaded thing gathering, unknown and unstoppable. I leaned on the railing between me and the water.

'Kiku-san,' I said aloud. 'Please be calm. I have questions. I am trying to help.'

There was no sign that she had heard. The families continued enjoying themselves behind me, and before me, a ship moved placidly on the calm sea.

My phone buzzed. It was Dad. The feeling of foreboding increased. I swallowed and answered.

'Hi, Dad.'

'Adam... How are you?' he asked.

'I'm okay. You?'

'Fine,' he said, in a way that sounded not fine. 'You asked me to track down that lieutenant.'

'Any luck?'

'Luck,' Dad echoed.

'What?' I asked immediately.

'There were a few that fitted the description.'

'That's good. Send me their details,' I said eagerly.

'There was a name I recognised. Pinkerton.'

'Is he famous or something?'

'I don't know how your mother... What she knew...' Dad was troubled. More than that; he was afraid.

'*Tell me.*'

'My grandmother—' Dad began. 'The only time I saw her was at her funeral. Open casket. I was small.'

There was a twisting sensation in my stomach.

'It was my first time seeing a dead body. I was scared. My dad had to take me out of the church. He read to me from the mass booklet – there's always information about the deceased, you see. I remembered...' Dad took a breath.

I wanted to tell Dad to stop speaking, but couldn't seem to form the words.

'Her maiden name was Pinkerton,' he continued. 'Her father was the same man I found in the Navy records. I called my Aunt Ethel to check.'

My brain tried and failed to connect the pieces of information that lay before me.

'I don't understand.'

'That Lieutenant Pinkerton is my great-grandfather,' Dad said. 'So your—'

'Are you sure?' I asked stupidly.

'It might not be the man you're looking for,' Dad replied.

I tumbled through the branches of this family tree. 'He had a daughter?'

'Yes,' Dad said.

'With the American wife? Not with Kiku...'

'Well, my grandmother was fully American—'

'Did he have a Japanese wife?' I asked haltingly.

There was such a profound silence that I had to check Dad was still on the line.

'Nobody knew her,' Dad said distantly. 'It was a different time.'

'What happened to her?' I gripped the railing. 'What happened to their son?'

'Ethel thought she probably died in the war, but she didn't know... They had a son?'

And I started to grasp the enormity of this, the vast and tangled connections of lives and deaths that had reached me and caught me up. I was related to the *Lieutenant*, not Kiku as I'd hoped, not even poor, lovely Mr S—.

'Tell me more about this woman,' Dad said.

'He left her.' My lips were numb. 'She was brilliant and young and had nobody else. He left and she waited for him. He came back and took her child.'

'Adam—' There was real concern in Dad's tone.

'And I'm related to him. So are you. And you...' My chest was empty, as if my heart had left my body.

'It's a coincidence. The world is smaller than we think,' Dad said.

'It's more than that. Am I like him?' We both knew what I was really asking: *am I like you?*

Dad said, brokenly, 'You're better.'

I thought of Jo. 'I'm not.'

Dad let out a ragged breath.

'Can you send me this information? The records, whatever you can.'

'If you want it.' Dad rallied. 'Adam, look. It happened a long time ago.'

'Yeah,' I replied woodenly, because I could see each of us laid out, links that couldn't be broken and me chained to them.

Was this how Kiku had responded to me? But there were other questions, mysteries unsolved.

I didn't know if I wanted any more answers.

Forty

♩ ♫ ♪ ♪ ♩ ♪

'The visit with your aunt didn't go well?' Toshi asked, worried.

My state of shock must have been apparent.

I reassured him. 'It was good. She invited me to return for Obon. She wants to come to Nagasaki too. I'd like you and Junko-san to meet her.'

This pleased Toshi. 'She should come to Shoro Nagashi with us.'

'When is that?'

'August fifteenth,' he said.

A week and a half away.

'How do you write Shoro Nagashi?' I asked.

Toshi wrote out the kanji and I looked up the translation. Spirit Boat Procession. Kiku had gone there. So I would go too.

'After Obon, where do the ancestors go?'

Toshi tilted his head. 'Back to the otherworld, or wherever they are resting.'

Had Kiku ever rested? Had she been waiting all this time for someone to help find what she was looking for? She needed her real family, not *me*. I was seized by an urgency so strong it made me shake. I was the Lieutenant's descendant and I owed it to her.

Before I could do that, I had other wrongs to right.

—

I rang the doorbell and prayed Jo was there. A muffled voice called from inside. I couldn't make out the words.

'It's Adam,' I replied.

The door was opened by a man who must have been Jo's father because they shared the same nose and eyes. 'Yes?' he said gruffly.

'Excuse me.' I introduced myself as politely as possible. 'I'm a friend of Jo-kun. I'm staying with Toshi-san and Junko-san. Is he here?'

Jo's father surveyed me. 'He isn't home.'

A woman popped out from behind him.

'Ah, you're doing the homestay.' Her voice was loud and inquisitive. This had to be Jo's mother. I recognised his energy in her movements. 'Toshi-oniisan is my brother.'

I stared at her, seeing Toshi and Takane-sensei. The shape of their faces could have been cut from the same template. DNA was a funny thing.

'Yes,' I managed. 'Toshi-san is a great host father. And Takane-sensei is an excellent teacher. Very... energetic.'

Even Jo's father snorted at this.

I persisted. 'Will Jo-kun be back soon?'

'He should be. Would you like to come in?' Jo's mother asked.

I hesitated. I doubted Jo would enjoy arriving home to me hanging out with his parents.

'Ah, look!' She waved.

Jo was turning the corner with Sakurako. He looked stricken and Sakurako switched on an extreme mean girl expression.

'Jo-kun, your friend is here!' Jo's mother called, totally unnecessarily.

'Hello,' I said weakly.

Sakurako muttered something which I was actually glad I didn't understand.

'Hi,' Jo said cautiously.

'I'd like to talk to you.'

I waited. So did everybody else. Nobody seemed as though they were going to leave; in fact, everyone had different degrees of interest on their face, even Jo's dad.

'Do you want to go for a walk?' I asked.

Sakurako shook her head. 'I don't think we have time.'

'Are you going on a date?' Jo's mother said hopefully.

Jo and Sakurako blushed. By the heat on my face, I knew I had as well.

Jo's mother glanced between the three of us. I didn't know what conclusion she reached but she backed off. 'Well, nice to meet you, Adam-san.'

'You too,' I said.

Jo's dad turned away, but I caught the appraising look he gave us.

Sakurako didn't move. And Jo...

I'd missed him so much, and seeing him made me conscious of it in a new and fierce way. It was like leaping into cold water and becoming intensely aware of every part of my body, singing with sensation.

Sakurako shifted irritably, and that's when I noticed that Jo and I had been staring at each other.

I switched to English. 'Can we...' I wanted to take Jo's arm, but I settled for beckoning him and taking a few steps away. I glared at Sakurako to prevent her following.

'Are you dating?' I couldn't prevent myself asking.

'No.' Jo blushed deeper. 'My parents think so, but I didn't *tell* them that...'

'I've done that,' I said.

'Really?'

'I even made out with a girl once, where my dad could see me,' I confessed. 'She did it as a favour.' In reality it wasn't a favour; Sylvia had made me do her geography homework in return, until she discovered I was terrible at geography.

Jo cracked a smile.

I glanced at Sakurako over Jo's shoulder. She was poking at her phone as if she was trying to start a fight. 'I think Sakurako *likes* you.'

'She does. But not in that way.'

'Not how I—' I caught myself.

Jo's eyes were glimmering. 'This is what you want to talk about?'

'No. I've learned a lot about Kiku and the diary and... it's weird.'

Jo shivered so slightly that it would have been invisible if I hadn't been watching for it.

I steeled myself. 'If you're seeing things, you're not alone.'

He glanced at me. 'I've been anxious, that's all.'

'You're not going crazy,' I said, 'unless I am too.'

Jo said softly. 'Maybe crazy is better.'

'Have you been scared?' I asked.

'Sometimes.'

'You can tell me. Call me. I'll understand.'

He gave me a long look and didn't say anything to that.

I plunged on. 'My dad tracked down the Lieutenant. His name is Pinkerton. It turns out...' I swallowed. It was harder to say than I thought. I *hated* Pinkerton. 'I'm related to him. On my father's side. He's my great-great-grandfather.'

Jo's lips parted in shock. 'He's your family?'

I shook my head, then nodded. 'I had no idea.'

There was faint sympathy in Jo's eyes.

'I think I have to make things right,' I said.

His sympathy extinguished, became wariness.

'I'm sorry, Jo.' I blurted out. 'Really—'

Jo moved back, though I hadn't tried to touch him. 'We weren't anything.'

'We were, though. I just didn't know what, and that doesn't make it less hurtful. I wish we could go back to... to being friends.'

'I want to,' Jo said, and my heart leaped. 'But it's difficult to believe you. To—'

I finished the sentence. 'To trust me.'

'I'm not like you.' Anger singed the edges of his words. 'You don't hide who you are. You can leave. You *will* leave. I feel... scared.'

I hadn't forgotten that feeling. It was a tension that sank into your bones, holding yourself tight, peering at everyone and thinking, *Do they know, what would they do if they knew?*

'Is it your father?' I asked.

'Not really. My father doesn't care so much.' He said that in a way that hid an old hurt. 'My mother wants a normal family, for me to marry and have children.'

'You can have children,' I protested.

'Not in Japan,' Jo replied.

'Your brother...' I said, a thin comfort.

'But I am part of their future too.' Jo's face was laid bare, sad and resigned.

I couldn't argue with that.

'Jo-kun,' Sakurako called.

I prepared a scowl, but she wasn't looking at me. She was watching Jo with tenderness and worry. 'Would you like to go?'

'Yes,' Jo said, to both of us.

I nodded unwillingly.

'I'll search more for Kiku,' he said, a peace offering. 'I'll message you.'

'I'd like that. The message. But you don't have to investigate anymore if you don't want to.'

'I want to. I think I have to.'

He stared over my shoulder, but when I turned there was nothing there.

—

I returned to Junko and Toshi's house. I was tired. The honesty and emotion and hurt had sucked the energy out of my body. I helped Junko cook. We had become used to moving around the kitchen together.

'My brother is coming to visit!' Toshi announced during dinner. 'Takane-sensei,' he clarified. 'He arrives next week, before Shoro Nagashi.'

'That'll be fun. Sorry, not fun,' I amended. 'It's a serious time, isn't it?'

'Actually, it's lively. There are fireworks, even at the cemetery,' Junko said. 'A tradition from China that we only have in Nagasaki.'

'People make boats – long ago, real boats, but today they are more like carts – and carry them through the city,' Toshi explained. 'They honour people who have died in the past year.'

'So it *is* sad,' I said.

'It can be. It's a good way to commemorate people. It helps those who are alive, as well,' Junko said.

Toshi took a breath before he made his next announcement. 'Our daughter will also come.'

I was happier than I expected. 'That's wonderful! You've been talking to her more?'

Toshi cast his eyes down, slightly shamed. 'Yes. And Jo-kun talked to us.'

'He was in touch with her recently, it seems,' Junko said, giving me a significant look.

Was this because of *me* too? 'Will she stay for long?'

Toshi was smiling. 'For a few days, during the Obon holiday.'

Junko's expression was more apprehensive.

'Then I'll invite my aunt to the festival, like you suggested,' I decided.

'Excellent. It's a good time for families to be together,' Toshi replied.

Junko agreed. 'It makes it easier for the dead.'

A few months ago, that would have sounded chilling; now, it was a comfort.

—

The handle of the cello case slipped in my sweaty hands. I set it down with care and surreptitiously tried to wipe my palms on my jeans.

'Thank you for returning it,' Shion said politely.

'I'm not returning it.' I fidgeted under the collective stare of Shion, Kana and Sakurako. '*I'm* returning.' I tried to sound confident, but my voice wavered as I added, 'If you'll have me.'

Everybody stared, uncomprehending.

'I sincerely apologise for my behaviour.' I bowed low, hoping I was hitting the appropriate angle of regret. 'I acted rudely and thoughtlessly. I understand if you don't want me anymore, but I would be honoured to play with you again.'

'Shit,' said Kana in English, cryptically. She exchanged glances with Shion and Sakurako. 'Can we talk?'

I went into the corridor and tried not to eavesdrop. Sakurako would not vote in my favour.

'Please come back,' Shion called.

I felt like a contestant on a reality show. I mean, I was. It was my reality and lately it had been pretty dramatic.

'We'd like you back,' Kana announced, then added crushingly, 'because we haven't been able to find another cellist.'

Sakurako heaved a sigh.

Kana went on. 'But we need to hear you play again.'

My palms were like taps. I probably had some medical condition. I took out the cello and sat down.

'From the beginning,' Shion said.

I took a deep breath, imagining myself in front of the bedroom window, gazing out at Nagasaki. I played, for myself, not looking at the others.

The last notes melted away.

'You've been practising.' Sakurako was almost offensively surprised.

'A lot,' I said.

'It's not perfect,' Kana said eventually. 'You're a lot better, though.'

I glanced at Sakurako.

'Again,' she said.

When we finished, my shoulders ached so much it was an effort to snap the cello case shut.

Shion said, 'Would you like to get food with us?'

I hadn't expected that. I hesitated. 'Not today. Next time, I'd like to. Sakurako-san, can I please speak to you?'

She didn't say yes, but stayed as the others moved off.

'I want to talk about Jo-kun,' I said in a rush, before she got too scary. 'You care about him a lot. I think you are an excellent friend. I hurt Jo-kun and you're not going to let me hurt him again. But I care for him too. I want you to understand that.'

Sakurako narrowed her eyes. 'You think I'm keeping him away from you?'

'Not exactly. I'm trying to be better. For Jo-kun, for you, as well. And Kana-san and Shion-san. That's why I came back.'

She remained skeptical.

'When I played, I thought about the music, and myself, but I thought of Jo-kun as well. His smile and his laugh. His sadness. Could you hear it?'

Sakurako's gaze thawed. 'I was in love with Jo-kun for years,' she said. 'I confessed to him in junior high, and he told me why he couldn't like me back in the same way. I was upset. I made a joke about it, in front of some other classmates.' Her eyes were wet. 'They hurt him.'

'Oh no,' I said, in horror.

Sakurako blinked furiously. 'I never wanted anything like that to happen. He forgave me. And I promised to protect him. He is the best person I know.'

My fists bunched. 'I want to kill those guys.'

'I tried to.' Sakurako's face was terrifying and serious.

'You failed? I'm surprised.'

'Jo-kun held me back. He saved me from prison.'

I held up my hands. 'Another reason not to hurt Jo-kun.'

'I'm older now. I've learned more,' Sakurako said quietly. 'So I could injure you quite badly.'

I laughed nervously. She didn't.

'I promise I will be good to Jo-kun,' I said hastily. 'I don't want to be anything else.'

Sakurako said, 'I believe you.'

I wanted to be as fierce as her. 'I promise,' I said, one more time.

Forty-one

E ven before I opened my eyes, I knew Kiku was there.

'Kiku,' I whispered. 'Chyōko.'

Her hands stroked the cello strings.

'I found out who I am,' I said, low and bitter.

She glanced at me, almost compassionate. I wished I'd been chosen for a different reason.

Her fingers quickened on the strings and I waited for her to speak through them, but all I made out was:

Ha... ru... Ha... ru...

'What if I can't find him?'

The music was speeding up into a muddle of noise.

'Or can you tell me how you died?' I urged her.

No... No... Do not... know...

She was coming apart in some way, losing her coherence. Her silhouette melded with the shadows but her confusion was clear.

And with that confusion came her fear, and her mouth stretched, wider and wider...

My terror was matched by hers. Her hands clasped her stomach, her neck elongating, lips parting and closing; she was ravenous.

She was becoming a hungry ghost. I scrambled away, and a wind whipped at me – the crescendo of her voice—

She clapped her hands over her mouth. Her eyes wailed. She disappeared, not in a fading or loosening, but as if she had wrenched herself away. She knew; she felt what she was turning into. And she didn't want it to happen.

—

Jo messaged me in the morning, but my delight was swiftly eclipsed by his words.

something happened last night. you said i could tell you.

Had Kiku hungered and howled at him?

are you okay? I replied.

do you want to come over? he responded.

I do and I will

—

I wasn't surprised when Jo told me his parents weren't at home. In the living room was a comfortable couch and comfortable clutter. The diary was on the table.

'What would you like to talk about first?' I asked diplomatically.

'Tell me more about the Lieutenant,' Jo requested.

I told him.

When I finished he said, 'It's destiny.'

'Or justice.' Or retribution. 'I still have to figure out what happened to Haru. And what about her other son, Hiro? That's what Kiku wants. Isn't it?'

'I think so.' Jo rubbed his arms in a way I recognised. 'It's been so strange. I don't want to see her. That's why I wanted to talk to you. To help you end this.'

So it wasn't about me; it wasn't about *us*.

I nodded fast in the hope he wouldn't see me bruising. 'I'll get in touch with my great-aunt, see if she can tell me anything more.'

Jo said, 'At least we have the *end* of the Lieutenant's story – it's in you.'

'I don't want it to be.'

He looked away.

'I kept thinking I was connected to this through my mother's side,' I admitted. 'There's so much there I don't know.'

'Your aunt could show you your family's koseki. They can go back very far,' Jo said. 'I think mine is ten generations.'

'Wow. That's...' I couldn't translate that into time. 'That's a lot of years.'

A silence fell.

When I could bear it no longer, I asked, 'Did you see something last night?'

'A nightmare,' he whispered.

'Do you want to talk about it?'

A muffled voice outside made us startle: one of the occasional announcements from the public speakers, echoing and incomprehensible to me.

'What are they saying?' I asked.

'It's the anniversary of the atomic bomb,' Jo said. 'I forgot. There is a moment of silence at the time the bomb fell.'

'What time was it?' I hadn't retained these details from that sickening trip to the museum.

'11.02 a.m.'

I checked the clock. 'Right now?'

Jo nodded, and the announcement outside fell quiet. I closed my eyes and the moment stretched, from us across the city; the invisible sound of people remembering.

The announcement resumed and finished. We didn't speak. I wanted to return to asking about Kiku but it felt like the dead were too present, full of pain.

Jo must have felt the same. 'Would you like to see a koseki?' he asked.

'Yeah!' A side effect of the diary was that I'd apparently become an old man and was genuinely interested in family trees.

Jo opened a cabinet and rifled through it before moving to another drawer. 'I haven't looked at it for a long time,' he said apologetically.

Eventually, he brought a folder to the table and drew out some documents mainly consisting of vertical rows of handwriting. I recognised Jo's surname but he had to explain most of the first names, the readings of the kanji beyond me.

We went through the generations like this, Jo tapping each name. His finger rested on one longer than the others. Then he read, 'Hirotaka.'

He stopped. We stared at each other.

'There are many names that begin with Hiro,' he faltered. 'Hirofumi, Hiromasa, Hirotomo, Hiroyuki...'

Yet we turned our eyes back to the paper with the same slowness, of dread or anticipation, or a mixture of both.

'His mother,' I began.

A feeling stole over me, the shivering sensation of being observed, of invisible threads tying themselves around me; around *us*.

Jo's hands, spread on the paper, were trembling. 'She married into the family.'

I knew how to read this name.

Jo traced the family lines again, as if to convince himself, and I watched with a sense of unreal inevitability as they led to his own name.

I counted the generations, so many lives. 'Your great-great-grandmother.'

'Harada Kiku,' Jo said, in profound wonder.

A figure coalesced, soft and astonished as Jo's voice. Kiku, behind Jo, reaching towards him. They both stared at me with the same expression; the same eyes.

Jo turned in his seat. I didn't ask if he could see her. I didn't have to.

All I could say was, 'I found *you*.'

Forty-two

♩ ♫ ♪♪ ♩♪

My body was juddering with a feeling of *not-rightness*. Jo and I had parted the evening before, shaken. We had been drawn together by some power that we couldn't exactly name: ghosts, or fate, or blood.

For hours I'd been ready for Kiku to come, but she didn't appear. Was it enough that I had found Jo? He was her son Hirotaka's descendant... But what about Haru? Where was *he*?

I played cello until I went to rehearsal, where I played some more. This time, I accepted Shion's offer to hang out. We went to a café, where we were the youngest people by about five decades, and ate sandwiches. We discussed the concert.

'It won't be big,' Kana assured me. 'We just need performance experience before applying to university.'

'Are you all going to study music?'

They nodded.

'Will you go to university?' Shion asked.

'I hope so. But I haven't decided what I'll do there,' I replied.

'Keep playing,' Sakurako said briskly. 'Don't stop.'

This was the closest thing to a compliment she had ever given me.

'I won't,' I said.

—

I wrote as coherent an email as I could manage to my great-aunt. Dad had given me her phone number but I didn't think I'd make any sense on a call. He had warned that she didn't have much information about Pinkerton but I had to try.

Then I sat down with my cello to practise, and didn't pause until there was a tap on my door.

It was Toshi. 'Adam-san, would you like a bath? And perhaps... sleep?'

'What time is it?' I asked, dazed.

'It's 11 p.m.,' he said. 'You've been practising a long time.'

'The performance is soon, so...' *So that's why I've lost my mind?* It was a believable enough excuse.

Toshi seemed to agree, because he nodded understandingly. 'Okaasan and I are looking forward to it.'

'I'm not that good. It might be boring,' I told him.

Toshi said, enigmatically, 'We have heard you play a lot.'

I was unsure if this was a vote of confidence.

'Is that all you're worried about?' Toshi asked.

I opened and closed my mouth.

'Do you believe in...' I didn't know the word for *reincarnation* and settled for, 'people being born again?'

Toshi adjusted smoothly to this metaphysical shift. 'The idea of living many lives is nice. I would like to be a sea turtle,' he said dreamily.

'Why would people be born again? To do something? To be better?' I asked.

Toshi reflected. 'That's what some people believe. I don't know if being better is from one life to another. It might be best to consider ourselves as we are now, every day.'

'Because we can change in this lifetime, can't we?' I said, half-pleading.

Toshi said, 'I hope we can.'

—

My phone buzzed me awake. I cracked open one eye; it was dark. I answered without checking who it was.

'Hello?' I mumbled.

There was only ragged breathing at the other end.

I sat up. 'Who is this?'

'Jo,' came the whispered reply.

'What happened?'

'Did she come to you?' he asked urgently.

I didn't ask who. 'Not tonight. Why?'

'Be careful—'

'What happened?'

'Adam, she's angry, she was so frightening!'

'She's changing, Jo — but I thought since she found you it would stop!'

His voice was breaking. 'It wasn't enough.'

'I'll come to you!'

'No! It's late, and she's gone, I don't think she will return tonight...'

'She can't stay long, for some reason.'

'Yes.' Jo sounded a little calmer. 'But she might go to you next.'

'She should come to me. It's my ancestor who wronged her,' I said.

'Can we stay on the phone?' Jo asked.

'Of course.' Because now I was afraid too. I put the phone on my pillow and rested my head beside it. 'I'll stay as long as you need me.'

—

Jo smiled wanly when he opened his front door the next day. 'Come in.'

He led me upstairs, and I didn't ask why.

His room was a clean sort of messiness. Unsteady stacks of books and manga, T-shirts flung over the back of a chair. The walls were covered with photos and posters. On the nightstand was the diary.

'Have you talked to your dad?' I asked.

'He was surprised – confused. Kiku died before my father's father was born, so he didn't know anything about her.'

'And her husband died before her,' I said. 'She wrote about that.'

'So much death,' he said softly. 'No wonder she's lost.'

'I didn't think she wanted to hurt us, though. It didn't feel like she was out for revenge.'

'Those kinds of ghosts are common in Japanese stories. If they died in some violent way they would return,' Jo said.

'I don't know how she died... and she doesn't either.' I let out a breath. 'I guess we still have to find Haru. Or *his* descendants.'

'She's been waiting for so long. She can't wait any longer—' Jo broke off. He was distressed, as I had been, but it must be worse for him because she was his *family*.

'She's turning into a hungry ghost, Jo,' I said. 'Like the one she wrote about.'

'Shunkan.' Jo paled. 'Yes.'

'If that happens... what can she *do*? Can she hurt us?' The hungry ghost hadn't hurt Kiku, but she had seemed sure it was going to.

'I have no idea...' Jo shook his head. 'They become hungry if they were hungry during life, or if they did some bad thing – or if there is nobody alive who remembers them.'

Kiku hadn't done anything bad – as far as I knew – and if she'd been hungry it had been for knowledge, or freedom or love... But remembering her; that had to be it.

'We can remember her! Doesn't she understand that?' I asked.

'Maybe we aren't remembering her in the right way,' Jo said.

'What's the right way? Oh – Obon? Is there a... ceremony?'

Jo nodded fervently. 'Yes, there must be...' He turned to his phone. 'Let's ask Google-sensei.'

He read and muttered in Japanese until I nudged him.

'Translation, please.'

'There is something!' he said. 'Called segaki, or sejiki – a special Buddhist ceremony.'

'I'm not a Buddhist. Are you?'

He shrugged. 'I suppose so.'

That wasn't a very religious response, but I decided this was not the best time to question it.

Jo continued, 'There's some prayers, things like that, but it looks like you... feed them. Put food on an altar.'

This was unexpectedly literal.

'You can do it at almost any time,' he went on, 'though most often it's done at Obon.'

'That's good! Can we do it ourselves?'

Jo frowned. 'It might be better if we went to a temple.'

'Do we make an appointment?' I asked.

'I haven't done anything like this before...' Jo started to check the websites of nearby temples. 'I'll call to ask.'

I watched anxiously as he did so. I couldn't follow the conversation, but from the way he asked about days and times in increasing desperation I could tell it wasn't going to be a walk-in situation. He called another and another.

He conceded defeat. 'Obon is a busy time.'

'All booked up?'

'For the next two weeks.'

I thought of Kiku and how she was changing, how frightening and ravenous she had been. 'We don't have that much time.'

'It's expensive,' he added.

'It costs money?'

'It's a job,' Jo replied.

We exchanged looks of mutual confusion at each other's understanding of things.

'I think we might have to do it ourselves,' Jo said reluctantly.

We made a list of what we needed: the types of food, a photo of Kiku, the prayers... and when we would do it.

'We should do it at my house,' Jo said decisively. 'As Kiku is my ancestor.'

'I'm going to my aunt's tomorrow and staying the night... It will have to be on the fifteenth.'

'The last day of Obon... That will work — it will be busy, my parents will probably be out.'

We looked at each other in relief. This wouldn't be so hard.

I smiled tentatively. 'Everything will be okay.'

He came to me, at last, and I put my arms around him. He rested against me, and then his hands stroked my back. I tilted my head so my lips hovered above the delicate skin behind his ear and held myself back. Jo pressed his face to mine, and then his mouth to mine; and all that sunlight came rushing in.

I wanted him and wanted him. We moved to the bed. His fingers twined in my hair as I put my teeth against the smooth skin of his throat. His mouth trailed down my stomach and my hands traced over each miraculous instance of his body.

Yet I couldn't help but think of the ghost and the Lieutenant: Kiku and Pinkerton, and how Jo and I were echoes of them and yet ourselves.

Consider ourselves as we are now.

I touched Jo's face, catching my breath. 'Wait.'

He stopped. 'Is this all right?'

'Oh *yes*, but — I want to talk.'

He pulled back warily. 'Why?'

'I feel I have more explaining to do. I want to tell you the truth, not just apologise for what I've done and pretend it never happened.'

I half-wanted Jo to refuse, say he had already absolved me.

Instead, he sat up so we were facing each other. 'Go on.'

'Things ended – badly – with my ex before I came here. Then we started talking again. It was nice, we were understanding each other better than we ever had before. The first time I went to visit my aunt she didn't want to see me. She turned me away.'

Sympathy passed over Jo's face as I plunged on.

'I felt like nobody wanted me. Then Evan wanted us to get back together, he wanted *me*—'

Jo flushed. 'You thought I didn't?'

'I didn't *know*. I thought you'd show me, tell me...'

Jo said, low, 'I didn't know how to talk about it, any of it.'

'I guess I didn't, either. And I thought: I'll be gone soon and you'll forget about me. You wouldn't—' *You wouldn't wait.*

'You'll be gone,' he agreed. 'I wouldn't forget, but I can't do all the things you can. You will leave *me*.'

'But not...' Not like he left her. 'I won't leave with lies or empty promises.' Words were failing me. I couldn't express everything I wanted him to understand.

'There are different ways to want,' Jo said, his voice hoarse and his eyes dark.

Before I could ask what he meant, he kissed me. Then he froze.

A second later, I knew why. There were voices in the house, footsteps. We pulled on T-shirts, zipped up jeans, combed hands through hair.

'Jo-kun?' It was his mother.

'Yes,' he called.

I randomly picked up a manga as Jo's mother peered into the room.

'Hello,' I said.

Her eyes moved from me to Jo and back again. Her gaze was vaguely disappointed. Almost sad.

It was quietly crushing.

'Your uncle has arrived,' she said.

'Ya-ho!' someone hollered.

Even in this most awkward of moments, I had to smile at the sheer enthusiasm in Takane-sensei's voice.

'Jo-kun, long time no see!' he cried over Jo's mother's shoulder. 'And Adam-san! How... wonderful.'

He took us in: me on the bed, which was unmistakably crumpled, Jo and his mother staring at each other tensely. Takane-sensei knew I was gay, and as far as I knew had no problem with it. In class, if we talked about dating or the type of people we liked, he never mentioned gender. If he hadn't known about Jo before, he was putting two and two together. Putting me and Jo together.

'Shall we have some tea?' he said pointedly.

Jo's mother was roused by the demands of hospitality. 'I have some mugicha.'

'I *love* mugicha! Jo-kun, Adam-san, come join us.' He gave us a meaningful look before leaving.

Jo let out a long breath. 'My mother isn't happy.'

'What will she do?' I asked, afraid of the possible consequences.

'She will pretend this never happened. That's what she does.' Jo paced the room.

I took his hands. 'It could be good to...' Talk about it openly, be your true self. That was easier said than done, like the lyrics to a pop song.

I hugged him tight, and he tensed and then relaxed against me.

'I'm here,' I said.

———

'What time are you going to your aunt's tomorrow?' Junko enquired.

'About 10 a.m.,' I told her.

'Ah, Yuna-chan will arrive later. You will see her the next day, then,' Junko said.

'Looking forward to it,' I replied.

Junko turned away, biting her lip. I was about to ask her what was wrong when my phone pinged.

It was an email from my great-aunt, Ethel. My hope soared and plummeted in the space of a blunt paragraph.

Hi Adam,

Nice to e-meet you. I spoke to your dad and, as I told him, I can't tell you much about Grandpa Pinkerton. He passed before my first birthday. I'd heard rumours about him shacking up with a woman when he was on duty out East but it was a bit hush-hush. You know what it was like back then. Can't say I know much about whether he had a kid with that Oriental lady or whether it was with the wife before my meemaw. She was third-WIFE lucky for him, Meemaw always said, ha ha! She wasn't a woman to dwell on the past. I'll poke around but doubt I'll find anything much. I'm no history nut and these ancestry things are just to get our DNA on file so I don't trust them.

Hope your studies are going well.

Ethel

I felt loose, unmoored. The question following me as if Kiku was whispering it in my ear, ever more distressed: *where is Haru?*

Forty-three

Mayumi was less nervous than before; in fact, she was almost relaxed. So was I, even though I'd left with apprehension, entreating Jo to call if anything happened.

'I thought I would show you around, Kai-san,' Mayumi said.

It was a sweet kind of unfamiliar, being called that. 'That would be wonderful.'

Itoshima was lovely, broad paddy fields and coastline and roads that wound through mountains before revealing views of the countryside.

Inside the car we were mostly quiet, but contented. Mayumi pointed out places: where she and my mother had gone to school, where they learned to swim, the tunnel of trees where they'd hunted for Totoro. We stopped at a factory that sorted salt from seawater and ate jars of purin so delicious I almost passed away.

We drove through both space and time.

We went to a restaurant overlooking a beach, a torii gate and two rocks that rose out of the water. They were connected by a thick, twisted rope, and each was hung with white lightning-shaped papers I recognised from Shinto shrines. Mayumi said they were called Meoto Iwa: the wedded rocks, bound together as husband and wife.

We ate pizza on the terrace, welcoming the fresh breeze from the ocean.

'It's beautiful here,' I said.

Mayumi was proud. 'It's my home.'

I imagined myself moving here, away from Nagasaki and the intricate complications between people. But that's what I had done by going to Nagasaki in the first place.

Mayumi misinterpreted my sigh as tiredness because she said, 'Would you like to go? We can watch the sunset on the way.'

'That sounds amazing.'

Mayumi drove to a spot at a seawall. The sky was a generous blue, rippled with white clouds, and as the sun sank the colours of the sky transformed, lightening or deepening as though the mood of the world was changing. We watched in silence. Nothing needed to be said.

Back in Mayumi's house, we chatted and watched a bonkers variety show on TV.

'I have another room but maybe you would prefer to stay in Ai-chan's room?' Mayumi said.

'I'd like that.'

We laid out the futon together.

'Tomorrow we'll say hello to the ancestors and go to the cemetery,' Mayumi told me.

I didn't know what *saying hello* entailed.

'Goodnight. Tell me if you need anything,' Mayumi said.

I got into the futon and rested my head on the grainy pillow, breathing in the fragrant herbal-tea smell of tatami. The cicadas called yearningly, the frogs a bass harmony. A bird's cry punctuated this symphony of the countryside at night.

My mother had lain in a textured darkness like this. All at once she didn't feel so far away. I sat up and opened the curtains and was dazzled by the moon, full and spilling silver.

The bookshelves were so illuminated that I couldn't help reading each volume title hopefully, just in case. I flicked through some of the older ones, but there was no handwriting, no Kiku or Chyōko.

Vaguely guilty, I slid open the drawers of the wooden dresser, hoping I wouldn't find underwear. There was another kimono, more delicately patterned than the red furisode. There was a high school uniform. There were collections of knick-knacks: figurines, hair accessories, pens. A photo album, which I opened eagerly.

Within were photos of my mother, laughing with school friends; in a hakama at her university graduation; with Mayumi and their parents, the grandparents I'd never met. There was one of my father, in uniform, handsome and so *young*. A photo of the three of us, their arms around me. I saw how I had come from them, a distillation of two humans made into a new person.

On the final page of the album was a single photo of my mother. She was sitting cross-legged; behind her, open doors framed a garden. Her face was serious and concentrating; her eyes were closed. She was holding a biwa.

I inhaled so sharply it was almost a scream. The album slipped through my fingers. I caught it, banging against the dresser in the process. The handle of the bottom drawer rattled, then rattled again. My hands were pulled to it, and I opened it with some effort; it squeaked and stuck from disuse. Inside was a wooden case. I took it out, helpless against this compulsion.

I paused, willing Kiku to appear, for something to guide me. But there was only me. I opened the case warily. The silver light illuminated the biwa inside, the full moon reflecting the twin crescents on the worn wooden body. I laid it across my lap, examining the smooth wood, the strings still taut. I reached into one of the pockets in the inner lid and retrieved the bachi.

Half in a dream, I crept downstairs. I opened the outer doors and sat in the engawa, just as Kiku had described. I held the biwa's neck awkwardly, the bachi in my other hand. I breathed deep and placed my fingers on the strings experimentally. I would never have guessed they were made from silk, thick and woven tight. I plucked a string with the bachi, and the sound was pure and clear, far more than it should have been after being so long alone.

And wisps of shadow gathered. I watched in vain for Kiku – then for my mother – surely she would come to me. But these ghosts had no distinct form, or else I wasn't able to see them. They were waiting, as I was, though I couldn't give them what they'd come for. I could neither play nor sing. I could not placate them – even if I could listen I wouldn't understand what they wanted to tell me. I was gripped by a deep and dreadful fear, like hands landing on my shoulders and tightening. There were lights like flames at the edge of my vision; every time I turned my head to look at them directly, they disappeared. A distant howling stirred up.

'Can you play?' a voice said.

'No,' I half-sobbed.

The ghosts had vanished, and the voice had come from behind me. It was Mayumi. I released a long breath.

'I'm sorry if I frightened you,' she whispered.

'Not you...' I shook my head. 'I'm sorry. I was looking through my mother's things. I didn't know she played biwa.'

'She began to learn not long after you were born.' Mayumi gave a little laugh. 'Who else would take up a hobby with a new baby? She had lessons once, sometimes twice a week.'

'Who was her teacher?' I asked.

'A woman... I can't recall her name. She must have passed on years ago,' Mayumi said.

Had my mother begun to play after reading the diary?

Mayumi's eyes rested on the garden. 'Her teacher was kind. Ai-chan played the biwa her teacher owned. Heike biwa are rare, you see, and expensive. Then her teacher brought this biwa here, saying it would allow Ai-chan more time for practice.'

'My mother must have been delighted,' I said.

'She wasn't here. She had taken you to meet your father. And then...' Mayumi closed her eyes briefly.

'Then she died,' I finished.

'I used to think — if only Ai-chan had been here. She would have picked up the biwa... She might have decided to stay longer and play. So many things might have been different. I wanted to return the biwa; I didn't want to see it or think of it. I had no address to send it to, though. I put it away.'

'I'm sorry,' I said.

'It's fine, now. You're a musician. You should play it.'

The biwa was heavy and uneasy in my arms. 'I suppose so.'

Except I didn't want to; I couldn't. But somebody had to, because it was Obon and the ghosts had returned.

—

Mayumi was an early riser. I avoided the biwa, back in its case. I ate breakfast blearily until the fresh crispness of the vegetables roused me.

'These are delicious,' I said.

'I grew them myself,' she said, satisfied. 'I've been up for a few hours, gardening.'

Maybe I couldn't move out here after all.

Mayumi brought me to the room where the butsudan was, the altar with photos of people. My mother was smiling at the camera, less formal than the other portraits. The scene behind her was newly familiar: where we had watched the sun set. There were fresh flowers, candles, plates of food, an eggplant and a cucumber, each with four wooden skewers for legs. Mayumi explained that the cucumber was a horse and the eggplant was a cow. The ancestors rode them home.

'Don't some swim?' I asked.

Mayumi waved her hands. 'Those are different spirits, from hell.'

I couldn't deal with asking about that further.

I lit sticks of incense as Mayumi directed. We kneeled in front of the altar. Mayumi clasped her hands and closed her eyes. I put my hands together but kept my eyes open, roaming over these people who I had never known, but whose flesh and blood and bone existed in me.

Mayumi eventually got up and I followed suit, wincing at the pins and needles in my legs.

Then we drove up a hill nearby, to an incense-scented temple and the cemetery. We walked down its narrow paths until Mayumi stopped at three gravestones, made of pale-grey stone and as tall as me. We washed them with water, put flowers in the metal vases. We bowed before them and were silent. This was where my mother was.

I put my palm over my face. A hand touched me lightly on the back.

'It's all right,' Mayumi said softly.

'I'm sorry,' I choked out.

I held my breath, trying to cage the sobs in my chest, but I couldn't keep them from escaping. I crouched and braced myself against the ground. Mayumi waited beside me patiently, not touching me, not embarrassed.

When I was calmer, I stood dizzily.

Mayumi put a hand on my arm. To my surprise, she was smiling. 'Ai-chan loved to cry.'

That startled me into laughter.

'At TV dramas, anime, even advertisements,' Mayumi reminisced. 'Afterwards she would say her heart had had a bath.'

I did feel cleansed. Lighter. My heart must have needed to be washed clean.

The puddle of my tears evaporated into the August air.

Forty-four

'This is my aunt, Mayumi,' I said.

Toshi and Junko bowed and introduced themselves. Mayumi presented a gorgeous basket of vegetables from her garden: eggplant, cucumbers, potatoes, goya. Toshi and Junko exclaimed over it and ushered us to sit down.

A woman entered the room, older than in the photos on the wall. Another detail that the photos hadn't captured: the faintest freckles of green in her brown eyes.

'Yuna-san?' I said, 'it's nice to meet you.'

'And you.' Her voice was strong and direct, her smile broad.

A chat about the weather and the journey began among the older adults. Toshi beckoned us to join, but Yuna sat beside me.

'I hope you've been enjoying your homestay, Adam-san,' she said in English.

I replied in English. 'I have. Thank you for letting me use your bedroom.'

'No problem,' she replied. 'When I was small I loved sleeping in the music room. It's cosy. I'll only be here a few days.'

I wasn't seeing the happy reunited family I'd been envisioning. There was tension between Toshi, Junko and

Yuna: a prickling awareness of each other, visible in the way they avoided eye contact and held themselves. Yuna's return hadn't healed the rift; with a sinking feeling I realised that would have been too easy.

'I'm glad you came home,' I volunteered anyway.

Yuna nodded tightly. 'It's been a while. It's good to see Jo-kun. He was the one who convinced me.'

I was taken aback. 'Not your parents?'

'Oh, they wanted me to return. But Jo-kun...' She gave me a look that informed me she knew everything. 'He's been feeling alone.'

'Toshi and Junko have been lonely as well,' I replied defensively.

She narrowed her eyes. 'They told you that?'

'We've talked about our families,' I said.

'I see.'

'Your English is amazing,' I said, filling the silence that followed.

'I lived in Hawaii for a few years,' she explained.

'Hawaii?' I echoed.

Junko, no doubt alerted to the sound of not-Japanese, turned towards us.

'Sorry, Japanese only!' I said hastily.

'Don't be so strict,' Yuna said to Junko, staying in English. 'Can't you give him a break?'

'He's here to learn and I'm here to teach him,' Junko replied.

I nodded weakly, but Junko moved away and went into the kitchen.

'I didn't mean...' Yuna rubbed a hand over her face. 'I thought this would be easier. But I'm still uncomfortable. Angry.'

'I get that.' I thought of Dad, of Jo's parents. 'At least they're trying to understand you.'

Yuna sighed. 'I know.'

'Thank you for helping me, by the way,' I said. 'With going to your old school.'

'I was helping Jo,' Yuna corrected me, but without rancour. 'You found what you were looking for?'

'Some of it, yeah. Did Jo tell you about the diary?'

'He tried... It seems like this – situation – isn't the easiest to explain. So he gave me the diary to read for myself,' Yuna said.

'He did?' I quashed my indignation. It was *his*. 'That's... good.'

'It's not like anything I've read before. It's real, isn't it? But surely not everything in it can be...' She trailed off.

Her arms, tanned golden, were bare, and I watched goosebumps rise on her skin.

'It's all real,' I said in an undertone.

She glanced at me keenly.

'At first I didn't believe the stuff about the biwa and playing for the ghosts, either,' I said.

To my surprise, she said, 'Oh, *that* I believe. That's the strange thing, you see—'

The doorbell rang. Junko answered, voices burst in, and a moment later so did Jo.

'Jo-kun!' Yuna said fondly.

His eyes lit with affection when he saw Yuna, and something more complicated when he looked at me. Jo's parents filed in with Takane-sensei.

Mayumi was alarmed at this sudden influx of people. 'Ah — should I go? I can check into my hotel.'

'We can return at a more convenient time...' Jo's dad offered.

'Oh, we won't stay long!' Takane-sensei said merrily.

Jo, his parents and Takane-sensei went to the altar, decorated for Obon, with white lanterns on either side. They spent a few minutes kneeling in front of it before returning.

'Jo-kun, your brother didn't come home?' I asked.

He rolled his eyes. 'He has gone to Okinawa with his friends.'

Yuna grinned. 'How nice for him. How about we do that next year, Jo-kun?'

Toshi must have overheard her; exasperation passed across his face but Yuna didn't appear to notice.

'It *would* be more relaxing,' Jo agreed.

He was tense, like me, and we were both getting tenser.

'My parents will go out for dinner later, with everyone,' Jo murmured. 'Then we can...'

Yuna was glancing between us curiously.

'Yuna-san, were you going to tell me something about the diary?' I asked quickly.

One of those lulls arrived, when a group falls quiet for some reason. Everyone suddenly turned their attention to us.

In that silence, the now-familiar feeling of profound suspense overcame me.

'Yes,' she said, 'I've been learning biwa.'

In Jo's eyes I saw a reflection of what I felt: an uncanny wonder.

'Why?' I asked.

'It felt as though I should.' Beneath her casual tone was a note of uneasiness.

Jo leaned in. 'Who's teaching you?'

'A biwa-hōshi. She plays in the old tradition, the heike biwa. She came to me...'

Jo, Yuna and I stared at each other.

The biwa-hōshi had gone to Yuna, and another had gone to Kiku and another had gone to my mother. Three players... Into my mind came the whisper: no, *one* player. Of course, it was impossible. The biwa-hōshi was already old when Kiku met her. I almost laughed. What was possible anymore? She was the bridge, as so many biwa-hōshi were; the bridge between this world and the next. And yes, between players, ensuring they had the skills and knowledge and compassion to take up their duty, to sing and to listen.

But I didn't understand why it was Yuna – shouldn't it be *Jo*?

Toshi spoke, breaking the spell. 'You play biwa?'

Yuna gave him a defiant look.

'You told us you wouldn't play any music again.' Toshi's voice was a mixture of anger and optimism.

'Not any music,' Yuna said under her breath. 'The *shamisen*.'

I jumped in. 'Will you play biwa for us, Yuna-san?'

Yuna said regretfully, 'I don't have my own instrument.'

I found Mayumi's eyes, asking for permission. She nodded. 'Please wait, everyone.' I went to my room.

I drew the biwa from its case. Mayumi had given it to me and I had brought it back, in some desperate hope I would magically be able to play it; that Kiku would teach me; that *something* would happen.

And it had. I ran my hands over it lightly, wishing and wishing my mother had had the chance to do the same.

From downstairs came a surge of voices. I picked up the biwa and hurried back to see Yuna putting her shoes on at the genkan.

'Calm down,' Junko was saying.

Yuna shook her head, and then they were speaking in fast, frustrated Japanese that I couldn't follow. I slunk into the living room, where everyone sat in strained silence. I could see Toshi's back in the kitchen.

'What happened?' I whispered to Jo.

Jo kept his eyes down. 'An argument.'

'About what?'

Jo gave me a look that said: *everything and nothing.*

The front door slammed. After a moment, Junko came into the room and murmured to Jo's parents.

'Well, I think I will be off,' Takane-sensei declared.

'Me too,' Mayumi said, standing up.

This wasn't the get-together I had wished for.

Takane-sensei added, 'We will all meet this evening for Shoro Nagashi!'

Everyone nodded feebly.

'And for dinner,' Jo reminded them. 'Grown-ups dinner.'

Takane-sensei said, 'Aren't you and Adam-san joining us?'

'I think Adam-kun and I could spend time with Yuna-chan. Talk to her.' Jo nudged me.

I backed him up. 'Yes! Some time apart to talk and calm down would be good.'

Nobody disagreed.

'I will rest in the hotel,' Mayumi said tactfully, 'and meet you for Shoro Nagashi.'

I saw Mayumi out as the others discussed restaurants.

'I'm sorry,' I said. 'That was a difficult situation.'

She smiled a little sadly. 'Families are difficult, Kai-san. I will see you later.'

Takane-sensei and Jo's parents left next, Jo lingering long enough to mutter to me, 'I'll tell you when they leave.'

I was still holding the biwa. It trembled in my arms. It wanted to be played. It knew the ghosts were here.

Forty-five

Jo messaged to say his parents had left, just as Toshi and Junko were leaving too. They hadn't said much to me – I'd hidden myself away and left them to their muted regretful conversation.

Toshi paused before they went out. 'I am sorry if your aunt was uncomfortable.'

'She understands,' I said. 'So do I.'

Junko sighed. 'Yuna-chan is stubborn. She has no patience.'

'I've learned,' I said cautiously, 'that everyone needs patience.'

Junko bowed her head but didn't reply.

I watched them go. Then I picked up the biwa and headed into the falling evening.

Jo was putting salt out at his front door.

I watched him tamp the salt into a small wooden cone mould, before setting it on a saucer and delicately lifting it away, leaving a perfect conical pile.

'I've seen those outside restaurants and businesses,' I remarked.

'It's called morijio. It's supposed to keep bad energy away.' He straightened up, apparently satisfied. 'I did it at the back door as well.' He went into the house and I followed.

'Yuna-chan was here but has gone again,' he informed me.

'Where to?'

'She didn't say... She is upset. She said she wanted to finish reading the diary.'

'Did you tell her we're doing segaki?' I asked.

'She left before I could. I've messaged her to come back, so I hope she does, soon. I want her to be here, now...'

Now that we knew she played the biwa. Now that we could see a connection.

'I've brought the biwa. I'd like her to have it. She'll return, won't she?'

'Yes.' Jo half-smiled. 'You see, Yuna-chan used to argue with her parents constantly. They would always be fine, in the end. I think they have forgotten that.'

'I heard Yuna-san was stubborn. I didn't know she was a hothead.'

'My mother said she is like Toshi-ojisan when he was young. And Junko-obasan is also strong-minded.'

'Toshi? Really?'

'He grew up, I suppose. But for every argument there was twice as much fun,' Jo said wistfully.

'If they fought about the same things without ever solving them, maybe the arguments got too big,' I suggested.

Jo sighed. 'I shouldn't have told her to come home. It was selfish. I wanted things to be better.'

I touched his shoulder. 'That's what we're going to do together.'

Jo nodded. We went to the butsudan, where he had added a framed photo of Kiku before a low table piled with fruit, rice, wrapped sweets. White lanterns were set on either side.

'I hope it's enough,' he said.

'It looks good,' I told him, though I had no idea really.

We knelt before the table and Jo lit the incense. We both clasped our hands and bent our heads.

'Harada-san,' Jo began haltingly, 'we are here to honour you. I hope you understand that we remember you, and I am glad that you are my ancestor. Please be at peace and continue to watch over us.'

I repeated, 'Please be at peace.'

Jo started to recite a sutra. Even to me, who'd never heard one, it was apparent he wasn't used to this. Still, he was serious and sincere. I prayed to Kiku, or whoever would listen. *Please rest, please be calm, please do not be angry anymore...*

There was a sudden, swift gust, a knife of ice that cut me to the bone. The lights went out as if they were candles. Jo stopped praying. The lanterns flared, lit from within by whirling blue flames. Jo's face was unrecognisable in this sickly glow, and terror laid its hands on me and clenched.

'Please—' Jo began.

A wail swelled, growing as it approached from some unimaginable distance, and then she was there, at the window facing onto the yard. She was barely recognisable as Kiku anymore; she was distorted and wild. Her neck had become long and thin as a spider leg, connecting to a torso craving to be filled, her jaw slack and gaping.

The food on the altar blackened and rotted. Jo was shouting or maybe it was me. We scrambled up and away.

'Kiku,' I imp orec, 'we are trying to help you!'

She only became more furious, her mouth working as if trying to speak.

'Out, let's get out!' Jo pulled me towards the door. I grabbed the biwa and we shoved our shoes on and fled down the street. The morijio had crumbled, the saucer cracked.

I looked back. 'I can't see her – where are we going?'

Jo slowed. 'To a temple? They will have to help us...'

'Even if we just turn up like this?'

'We'll explain—'

'Will they believe us?' I asked.

'They have to!'

We hurried on, casting glances over our shoulders, gripping hands tight.

'Jo-kun? Adam-san?'

We froze, thawed when we saw who it was: Yuna.

'Are you going to Shoro Nagashi already?' she asked. 'I was on my way to your house, Jo-kun. I'm sorry about earlier.' She took us in, panting, dishevelled, full of fear. 'What's the matter?'

'We were trying to do segaki for Kiku,' Jo gasped. 'But it didn't work.'

'Kiku wrote the diary...' I babbled. 'She's hungry, she's become a hungry ghost!'

'She's my relation,' Jo said.

Yuna took a breath. 'That's who she is...'

'And the Lieutenant is mine,' I said.

Yuna turned to me in astonishment.

'We're going to a temple to ask for help,' Jo said.

'Yes, I see.' Yuna's hot head cooled in emergencies, it appeared.

'So we *have* to help her,' I went on. 'Will you come too? Please?'

'Yes. I finished the diary.' Yuna led the way, fast.

Jo and I kept pace, watching for Kiku, feeling watched in return. The streets were busy, people heading to the city centre for Shoro Nagashi, or simply because Obon meant days off work.

'You believe us then?' I asked Yuna.

'I believed the diary,' she said, 'and Jo has never lied to me. And since playing biwa I have learned more about ghosts... I haven't experienced anything like this, but who am I to say it isn't true?'

This was the kind of pragmatic adult response I needed. Even so, we didn't slow down and the stalking sensation of eyes didn't go away. We raced up the steps leading to a red gate flanked by its glaring guardian statues. It was the temple that Toshi had brought me to when he'd first shown me around.

It had been quiet then. Now it had a bustle about it – people rinsing their hands with long-handled ladles, wafting incense smoke over their heads, bowing before the illuminated Buddha. I relaxed; surely this place was safe from vengeful spirits.

The odd thing was the noise: voices, and a pop and crackle I couldn't identify. Yuna went to a low building adjoining the temple, but the shutters were down and nobody answered when she knocked. She made a noise of frustration and tried another building but all was closed.

'We can try the cemetery,' Jo said.

'The cemetery? *Really?*' I hung back.

Jo grimaced, but Yuna said, 'It will be busy tonight.'

They took a path leading behind the temple and, against my instincts and everything I had learned from horror movies, I followed. Yuna was right: the cemetery was lively. There were clusters of people around graves, chatting and not looking very mournful.

'Are those fireworks?' I asked.

'A Nagasaki tradition,' Jo explained. 'We went to our family grave while you were in Itoshima. It's like a party where the dead are the guests of honour.'

'That's... cool, actually,' I replied.

Maybe *that's* what Kiku had wanted, but it was too late now.

'There must be a priest here,' Yuna muttered, casting around.

It was hard to see through the spreading twilight and the hanging smoke of sparklers and fireworks. We weaved between tall headstones, muttering apologies as we dodged past families celebrating relations who had departed. Or who had returned.

'Is that someone? Or more than one.' I pointed to several lights with the official and purposeful beam of torches.

'Yes.' Jo rushed towards them.

'Wait!' Yuna cried, but he didn't.

We chased after him down the twisting narrow paths until, suddenly, we emerged into silence and the almost-dark at the edge of the cemetery. Jo stood before the lights, but there was nobody holding or directing them. They bobbed and swung, orbiting like dreadful little planets burning white and blue.

'Jo, come back,' I called, my voice faint. 'Get away from those things!'

'Onibi,' Yuna said in disbelief. 'Demon fire.'

I ran to Jo and tugged his arm. He was slow to move, the swooping flames mirrored in his transfixed eyes.

I heard it; heard *her*. The wailing rose and the onibi snuffed out as though a huge gasping breath had extinguished them. And she came: Kiku, or what had been Kiku, because all that remained of her was this ragged ravenous thing. She charged forwards and hung before us, mouth splitting wide above her strung-out neck, towing the void of her stomach.

Yuna screamed. I couldn't even do that; I was in a paralysis of terror and perhaps so was Jo because he was motionless beside me.

'Kiku,' I pleaded, 'please...'

She shrieked in rage or in sympathy.

'I am sorry.' Jo stumbled to the ground, kneeling as if he had accepted what was to come.

But I couldn't. Even as Kiku's jaws opened, I lunged to drag him away. The biwa case banged against my side and I flung it off impatiently. It landed on the ground before Kiku.

She halted. Her tormented eyes fixed on the case, so burning I expected it to burst into flames. Her hands reached, and for an instant I saw a flicker of her – the real her.

'We want to remember you, Kiku,' I said desperately. 'Your story, we know it now!'

That wasn't enough; it hadn't been enough for Shunkan either. He'd already been written about in *Heike Monogatari*, recorded for centuries in between but it hadn't satisfied him until...

Until the story was *told*.

'Yuna?' I asked.

'I'm here.' Her shaking hand found my shoulder.

'You have to play!' I tugged the biwa from its case and thrust it at her.

The entirety of Kiku's tortured power fixed on it. Because she *wanted* to be saved; she didn't want this torment.

Yuna took the biwa, crumpling into a cross-legged seat, and I put the bachi in her hand. She was gasping, half-sobbing. 'I don't know what to play.'

'Whatever feels right, a song, a lullaby – anything!'

Jo fell forwards and I caught him. His eyes fluttered, his body frosting over on this sweltering night.

'Yuna!' I cried.

She stared up at Kiku and struck the strings in a frenzied strum, and then another. A third and she had steadied herself. Her voice broke and quavered as she began to sing, a simple melody that didn't have the solemnity of the old songs I had listened to. Kiku paused, leaned down to listen. Her mouth closed.

'That's good,' I breathed.

'It's my school song,' Yuna whispered. '*Our* school song.'

She kept singing and Kiku subsided, just a fraction. Yuna finished the song and kept plucking the tune. I took a hitching breath.

'Kiku-san,' I said softly. 'Let me tell a story. Your story... You were born here in Nagasaki – do you remember the hill you lived on? How you used to watch the sea change?'

She turned to me with a new expression: of need, of yearning. I told the story of her life as she had told it me – her grandmother, her biwa, her marriage, and when I stammered and lost the thread of telling, Yuna played until I found it again. Jo warmed and roused in my arms. He sat up, his fear turning to compassion. When I came to Haru being taken away my throat constricted and Jo took over, his voice tender.

Kiku listened and listened, as if our words were sating her appetite, nourishing her like medicine. Her body shrank to find its form and her mouth returned, lips turned down in sadness.

Jo listed the generations that had followed her and ended with him, and then had no more to tell her. Kiku had diminished, placated into the figure I knew. But for how long? The smoking air sizzled with threat; parts of the story remained unknown and untold.

I tried. 'You won't be forgotten, Kiku. I'll do better than the Lieutenant did.'

'I'll remember you,' Jo promised. 'My whole family will. We're your descendants.'

Kiku looked at him lovingly but spoke with sorrow. Her voice rang out, as distinct as it must have been in life. 'Where is Haru? *Where is my son?*'

We couldn't answer.

The onibi flickered and flared into existence once more. Yuna struck the strings of the biwa but it had an anguished straining sound, suddenly cut off: one of the strings had snapped.

Yuna moaned. 'A string. Is there another?'

We were losing control. Jo scrabbled through the biwa case, through each pocket. He made a sound of surprise, and when I tore my eyes from Kiku I saw he was holding a pale rectangle of paper.

'It's a letter.' He raised his head to Kiku in astonishment. 'It's addressed to you.'

She came closer, and so did the onibi, hovering beside Jo as if they were alight with curiosity.

He opened the envelope. It crackled with age. 'It's in English.' He held it out to me. 'You'll read it faster.'

I took it. The paper shivered, and my voice shivered too, as I read.

To my mother,

I've written you a stack of letters over the years. When I was a kid I used to write them and burn them. I didn't want anyone to find them, and I had nowhere to send them to. I'd watch the smoke blow away and think, maybe this wind will go all the way to Japan. It's for the best they never got to you. I was angry sometimes and wrote pretty horrible stuff. Other times I was sad and I don't want you to read those either.

Even the letter I eventually did send — well, I was mad but it was as polite as I could make it. When we

CLARA KUMAGAI

finally did meet, I could see you understood. It was peculiar, wasn't it? We did understand each other, in the end... I don't know what's happened in the years in between. I wrote to your friend Mr Sharpless and he said he's heard no word from you, that things got real bad in Japan. He told me to keep waiting. I did – I am. I don't think you'd have forgotten me. I don't think you ever did.

Still, this will be the last letter I'll send. I'm sick, you see. I got out of Japan, but a couple years later, America didn't want me either. Didn't care about my passport or my white father – being a Pinkerton didn't help me, after all. That's why I changed my surname when I signed up to fight. I know you wouldn't have wanted me to, but it was that or the internment camps, or prison. And guess what? There was a whole bunch of other Japanese-American boys. Sounds crazy, but some of those times were happy. I'm not going to tell you about the other times.

I got hurt and was sent home, and I never really got well again. The doctors told me to settle my affairs. Good thing I don't take after Pops in that way – no affairs to settle. That's a bad joke, isn't it? I get the feeling you'd get a kick out of it all the same. No affairs but one wife, Roisin. She's Irish and her name means little rose, so my nickname for her is Hanako. She thinks it's cute and so do I. No kids. Never thought I'd care about that but now I think – who'll remember me? It should be the least of my worries but here I am, lying in bed and wondering. I have a half-sister out there somewhere, but I've never met her, and I don't think I will.

You said I have a half-brother in Japan, your other son. When I was fighting I was afraid he'd be on the other side – that one of us would kill the other. Or we'd shoot and then recognise each other too late. Kind of dramatic, really. But they didn't send us near Japan, 'cause they were afraid we might change sides. So I was spared that. I hope your other son was spared too.

And you – I don't know. I hope you're there but to tell the truth, I don't think you are. That begs the question: why the hell am I writing to the dead? I have no answer. Just for myself, I guess. Makes me feel closer to you. As though I'm writing my ending. Not in a bad way; sounds funny but it's making me feel more content. And if you're a ghost – hey, maybe you can read this letter! Can ghosts open letters, though? When Roisin sends for the priest I'll ask him.

I keep thinking of the stories you told me the few times I visited you. There were some funny ones, and weird and sad ones. But a lot of them had something in common: people being separated and finding each other again, even when it was impossible, even if it was frightening or only once a year. That's what I'm hoping will happen. That you'll find me, in the end.

And I'll tell you what I never could before, because sometimes I didn't mean it and other times I was *afraid you wouldn't say it back: you're my mother, and I love you.*

Your son,

Haru

I said his name and could say no more.

There was a murmur around me. I couldn't tell whether it was from the living or the dead.

Kiku was beside me, her poor transparent hands moving over the pages, trying so hard to hold them that they rustled. A damp spot appeared by Haru's name: Kiku's teardrop, her sorrow so deep it was tangible.

'We found him.' I leaned my head on Jo's shoulder and watched as the decades-old paper drank up her tear.

The onibi softened to a warm glow. Kiku wept in a passion of grief, and doused the burning inside her.

'The end of Haru's story,' Jo murmured.

'And Kiku's biwa,' Yuna said in wonder. 'This was yours, wasn't it?'

Kiku nodded.

'The biwa-hōshi must have found it and kept it... and found the letter, but it came too late for Kiku,' I said. And too late for my mother.

'But *how*?' Yuna asked.

I shook my head. I had no logical explanation. It was like the diary; it had wanted to be found, to be read. It had wanted to tell its story.

Kiku bowed to us. 'Thank you,' she whispered.

We bowed back.

Yet she didn't disappear. We still didn't know how she had died... Perhaps this was enough; perhaps she knew we could do no more. She remained, weary and expectant, and behind her other figures took form. The ghosts had arrived.

There was a spare string in the case. Yuna restrung the biwa, and the ghosts – in old-fashioned kimono and western-style uniforms and once-splendid armour of centuries before – waited. They were here to visit the living, to be assured they had not been forgotten.

Yuna plucked the strings and each note hummed and rippled outwards. With a strong strike she rapped the bachi against the wooden body, a call to attention. Her voice penetrating and powerful, she sang the opening of *Heike Monogatari*:

> The sound of the Gion Shōja bells
> echoes the impermanence of all things;
> the color of the śāla flowers reveals the truth
> that the prosperous must decline.
> The proud do not endure,
> they are like a dream on a spring night;
> the mighty fall at last,
> they are as dust before the wind.

Yuna sped up, strumming a galloping and insistent rhythm, and my blood and heart beat in time. This was nothing close to the videos or recordings I had listened to; this music was profoundly in my body, resounding in my soul. Yuna slowed, the last notes drawn out, decisive and final. She strummed once more and the sound echoed and faded.

Like a sigh, the ghosts heard and were content. Kiku nodded to Yuna, proud; to Jo, with affection. And beside Kiku, I glimpsed her; my mother. We gazed at each other, an instant stretched out across years.

'You are my mother,' I whispered, 'and I love you.'

She smiled, brimming with love, and evaporated into the night, or to some other world.

Forty-six

♩ ♫ ♪♪♩ ♪

Jo, Yuna and I were limp with relief and exhaustion when we reached the bridge where Toshi had told us to meet.

We had staggered back to Jo's house after the cemetery, hastily cleaning away dirt, sweat and tears. We reassembled ourselves, piece by heart-aching piece.

Then we went downtown for Shoro Nagashi.

The streets were crowded. Some roads were closed to traffic, and people in happi coats passed us, preparing to bear the boats towards the sea.

We met the group in the middle of a bridge: Jo's parents, and Yuna's, Takane-sensei and Mayumi. We formed a circle and greeted each other. Toshi patted Yuna's shoulder hesitantly and she offered a smile to him and Junko.

'Is everything all right?' Mayumi murmured.

'It's better,' I told her. 'Much better.'

'Are you going to...?' she asked.

I nodded and withdrew a framed photo from my backpack; the one of my mother and the sunset. Jo reached into his own bag and took out the photo of Kiku.

Yuna gazed at it. 'Harada Kiku.'

'Or Taira Chyōko,' I said.

Yuna repeated the name softly. Again the question came to me: *why was Yuna the one who had been called to play biwa?*

'Yuna-san,' I whispered. 'Why did you go to Hawaii?'

Junko heard me. 'She was looking for her family.' Her voice was tinged with hurt.

Yuna corrected her tenderly. 'My *biological* family.' She nudged me. 'I found out I am part American, isn't that strange?'

'Yes.' I stared into her green-flecked eyes. 'And no.'

'That's a story for another time,' Yuna said. 'I have my family right here.'

There was a disorienting sense of an unseen piece clicking gently into place.

Yuna and Jo must have recognised it too; they turned to me and our hands clasped. The three of us – as if we had been here together before.

There was no logic. It simply felt complete. Blood and bonds connected and entwined across time, and Yuna had untangled some of hers. Maybe she would tell us; maybe Mr Sharpless would come to her with his own story.

Yuna and Jo and me. A hundred years ago, Sharpless and Kiku and Pinkerton. Trailing love and hurt and longing across decades. We stood on the bridge, above a river running into the sea.

A sudden series of cracking sounds burst around us. I jumped and we let go of each other. The past released us back into the present.

Jo cried, 'Firecrackers!'

'You will need these.' Junko passed earplugs to us.

A lighted shape came into view: the first boat.

I addressed Toshi and Junko. 'I was wondering, at the end, if I could join the procession?'

Jo stepped up. 'I'd like to remember our relative too. Harada Kiku.'

Next year there might be a photo of Haru. Of Mr Sharpless too...

'People do carry photographs.' Jo's father surveyed the parade volunteers. 'Ah, I know him.' He marched towards a bald guy directing onlookers.

'This is a good thing to do,' Takane-sensei told me.

Jo's dad returned with the go-ahead.

We watched the parade together, the boats decorated with mementos and lanterns, photos of the deceased at the front of the boat. One was in the shape of a cat, another a black ship with a gaping-mouthed face. The firecrackers snapped, raising smoke, half-deafening us.

Towards the end, Jo and I joined in, holding our photographs. The route ended near the docks, where the boats used to be sent out to sea, ablaze. These days they were dismantled and carted away. Jo and I stood together, shoulders touching.

We had remembered the dead and released them, but they lingered, telling us to be good and safe; that we were loved and watched over.

Jo spoke softly in Japanese, to something – someone – that I couldn't see. He touched my arm.

'Give me a minute,' I requested.

He went to where the others had gathered, watching the boats being undone.

I stared at the water. In its reflection I could see Kiku beside me, outlined in light.

'Is that how this works?' I asked. 'We repeat the same mistakes until they're fixed?'

'Some mistakes are not inherited. They are learned,' she answered.

'So we have to unlearn them – or learn *from* them,' I said.

'Yes. That is why we remember. Each story from the past is one for the future.' Her face was full of bright compassion.

'That's why we tell them.'

I turned to her, decades dead and yet living and vibrant in words, in music. In us.

'When does it end?' I asked her.

Kiku smiled. Her eyes were brilliant even as a ghost; how bold and fierce she must have been in life. She looked to the darkness of the ocean. She became part of the saltwater, the boats, the crackling Nagasaki night. Her voice lingered in my ear.

She said, 'It doesn't.'

―

We returned to Toshi and Junko's together, heads ringing from the firecrackers, the roads strewn with their red paper wrappers.

Mayumi hesitated at the doorway. 'Perhaps this is troublesome for us all to be here?'

'No, this is nice, a family reunion! A house party!' Takane-sensei gave Junko a beseeching look. 'Oneesan, I'll order food.'

I wondered if house party reunions were customary in Japan or whether Takane-sensei had been abroad too long.

Either way, Junko surrendered. 'Please, everyone come in!'

And so we did.

Beers were passed out, cool sake poured. Junko pointedly handed Jo and me juice and Yuna sneaked us miniature cups of sake. Platters of sushi were delivered and devoured. Voices rose and fell, with bursts of laughter and gossip, and I was forced into the fastest Japanese I'd spoken yet. It *was* a reunion, more like the friendly one I'd optimistically imagined.

I ended up face-to-face with Jo's mother. I opened my mouth to utter my party safe word – *I need to go to the bathroom* – but she was quicker.

'Jo-kun is a good son,' she said. 'He's important to me and to the family.'

'Yes, definitely,' I agreed.

'You are a good boy too. But you're not like Jo-kun. It is easier for you to be what you want. In Japan...' She trailed off.

'It's not a foreign thing,' I snapped.

'We have different societies. Jo-kun should fit in here. Otherwise...' Fear flitted across her face.

Sakurako said Jo had been beaten up at school, and now I had an idea of how bad that had been.

'Jo-kun *is* different. I don't know anybody like him. I admire your son so much,' I said, more gently. 'He's talked about how important his family is to him. That's why he needs you.'

She listened.

Takane-sensei arrived. 'Praising Jo-kun, eh?' He hustled her away, winking at me.

As I watched, his merry tone became serious and patient. They sat down together. Takane-sensei cemented himself as the best teacher I've ever had.

Yuna came over. 'I'm sorry I won't be here for your concert.'

'It's best you don't see it,' I replied firmly. 'Especially because *you're* a musician.'

Yuna waved her hand. 'Not a professional. Not as good as my parents.'

Jo spoke up. 'Why don't you let us decide that?'

Yuna bit her lip.

Junko said softly, 'Won't you play with us, Yuna-chan?'

And Yuna nodded.

Toshi grinned and disappeared, returning a few moments later with three shamisen cases in his arms. He proffered one to Yuna and she accepted.

Mayumi sat beside me, beaming, and together we watched a family come together once more.

Junko, Toshi and Yuna warmed up, had a brief squabble about what to play, and then began. The tune they struck up was hearty and eager. They played like a true band, offering themselves to each other with each note, conversing through rhythm and beat.

I found Jo. I wanted to kiss him, very much. Instead, we held each other's gaze and around us the music went on.

Forty-seven

♩ ♫ ♪♪ ♩ ♪

Mayumi returned to the countryside. I spent the next couple days with Toshi and Junko and Yuna, eating in Yuna's favourite restaurants, going to an onsen. I witnessed a few other arguments and during a heated one about sweets – takenoko versus kinoko – I burst out laughing. The three of them ganged up on me.

'It's a nationwide debate!' Yuna barked.

Junko frowned at me. 'Please have some respect, Adam-san.'

Toshi just shook his head, looking disappointed in me.

They were healing.

They even planned to go to Heike Odori next year, in Shimonoseki. They would play the shamisen together in the parade, like they had before. But it would be better than last time, Yuna promised.

'I love my parents,' she told me, 'even though we fight a lot. When they told me I was adopted, I was honestly surprised. I had no idea they could keep a secret like that. My first thought was: *this is why they always disagree with me. They wanted something else.* It's easier to see now that I *get* my arguing from them.' She signed. 'I wanted something else too.'

'Did you get it?' I asked.

'I'm not sure yet' she said, 'but I'm glad I came home.'

Before she left, I presented the biwa to her. 'This is for you.'

Yuna's voice was hushed. 'I cannot take this.'

I spoke with some difficulty. 'You must. It needs to be played. It's what Kiku would have wanted. And my mother.'

The past echoed into the present.

Yuna bowed over it. 'Then thank you.'

I remembered the ghosts in the cemetery, listening. 'It won't be easy, playing it. If it's like what Kiku had to do...'

Yuna's gaze shifted beyond me. 'It will be an honour.'

———

Too suddenly, it was the day of the concert. Junko was surprised to see me up so early.

'I'm nervous,' I explained.

Junko was nervous too; my anxiety was infectious. 'Mayumi-san is coming?'

'Yes. She'll meet us at the venue.'

'How is her relationship with your father? Better?' Junko asked unexpectedly.

'It's fine.' I'd told Dad about Mayumi and he'd said vaguely positive things. It didn't matter. She was my family and there was nothing he could do about it.

Junko frowned but didn't press any further.

I attempted to eat breakfast, then decided to go to the venue, which was smaller than I expected but bigger than I would have liked. It was a blessing that this concert was at lunchtime; I'd be a puddle on the ground if it was any later.

Sakurako and Kana were already there.

'I thought I was early,' I said.

'We couldn't wait around either,' Sakurako replied.

Shion arrived later, the only relaxed one.

'A few years ago, I got hit by a car,' he said, by way of explanation.

'I see.' I didn't see.

He went on, 'It's no problem now, I recovered. Since then, I don't feel stressed about anything in comparison.'

'That's good?' I said.

He beamed serenely. I wondered if I had enough time to get hit by a car before the performance started.

We organised ourselves on the low stage, tuned up and ran through a few sections. I felt calmer playing; we all did.

One of the two venue staff came to say they were opening the doors.

Shion and Kana went to greet some of the audience, while Sakurako and I stayed on stage. Jo and his parents came in. Mayumi entered and settled down beside them. I spotted Toshi and Junko, looking positively anxious, and then I understood why. Behind them were Dad, Kate and Benny.

I was momentarily paralysed with shock.

Kate waved. Dad nodded at me. I nodded back and immediately glanced away. Why had they come? Why didn't they tell me? Was this supposed to be a cute surprise? I exhaled my frustration.

Sakurako leaned over. 'You will be good.'

This vaguely threatening assurance dredged a smile out of me.

Kana gave a brief announcement, introducing us and thanking everybody for coming. There was polite applause. She sat down. We met each other's eyes and started the piece: Schubert's *Death and the Maiden*.

I wavered on the first notes, turmoil shuddering through my bow. I looked to Jo and he held my eyes. With that anchor, I let the rest of myself slide into the music. A vision of the sunset Mayumi and I had watched came to me, all those colours blending with each other above the sea. I couldn't tell what colour I was; what I knew was that I was in the sky.

The final notes reverberated away. I opened my eyes. I grinned at Shion, Kana and Sakurako and they grinned back. We had done it. It had been well done.

We rose to bow amid the applause. Kana thanked everybody once more. I put my cello away slowly, collecting myself, congratulating the others.

I steeled myself and stepped off stage.

Jo rushed to me. 'You did so well!'

I grasped his hand, released it. He took it again and squeezed.

Dad, Kate and Benny came forwards. 'How did you get here?' I choked out.

'The usual way.' Kate half-opened her arms, then changed her mind and let them fall to her sides. 'Don't be mad. We worried you'd be more nervous if you knew.'

I hugged her. 'Kate. I love you a lot.'

She sniffed and squeezed me. Benny, who had slept through the entire performance, woke up and gurgled in delight.

I picked him up. 'Hey buddy. I missed you.'

He spat at me gleefully, which I took to mean that the feeling was mutual.

Dad clapped me on the shoulder. 'Adam. Well done.'

'Thanks, Dad.'

'We've never seen you perform before. We thought it was about time.' He abruptly pulled me into a hug.

I saw Mayumi, torn between happiness and old resentment.

'Mayumi-san.' I drew her forwards.

'It's been a long time,' Dad said.

I translated clumsily.

'Too long,' Mayumi replied.

'Yes. I'm sorry.' Dad bowed awkwardly.

Mayumi nodded, accepting.

Benny waved at her.

Kate grabbed this opportunity. 'He likes you! Do you want to hold him?'

Kate put Benny in Mayumi's arms. She held him gingerly, until he giggled and grabbed a chunk of her hair.

'Oh, sorry...' Kate tried to disentangle Mayumi.

Mayumi gently freed herself. 'He must like music.'

'He loves Adam's,' Dad said.

I stammered with surprise as I translated that.

Dad added, 'Now I know.'

Easier conversation broke out, Mayumi and Kate managing to communicate, mainly about Benny. Takane-sensei chatted to Dad in English. Jo stayed close to me. His mother, when I stole a glance at her, was watching him tenderly.

I breathed a long sigh of relief. I had done it. We all had.

Well, almost.

Forty-eight

♩ ♫ ♪♪ ♩ ♪

A
nd to the final question, which had haunted me even though Kiku no longer did, there at last came the answer.

Jo called to say his father had located what we'd asked him to look for, and we met by the fountain before the sizzle of noon.

This time, we bypassed the exhibitions and went directly to the remembrance hall, which I hadn't seen last time. It was pale and calm and serene, lined with columns, coolly illuminated. At one end was a single column which contained shelves, and on the shelves were books, and within the books were names.

Jo spoke to an attendant who showed us to a library room. She invited us to sit at one of the computer monitors and gave us an explanation of what to do before leaving noiselessly.

I watched Jo type and click until we found it: Mori Kiku.

Her final name, the one she'd married into. Here it was, recorded with every known victim of the atomic bomb, written on a page enshrined in that tall and peaceful column. She hadn't known how she died; neither had tens of thousands of others. She'd seen a white light in her dreams, and even in her dreams it had burned her.

But she was resting now. Her death was remembered and so was her life.

We stared at her name for a long time, hushed and held.

We went outside. I heard Jo whisper Kiku's names and then, as if they were a poem, it began to rain.

My last days in Nagasaki whirled by. Kate, Dad and Benny were staying at a hotel, and allowed me space and time together in equal measure. They were leaving the day before me, which I was glad of. I needed to do the journey home alone.

I hung out with Shion, Kana and Sakurako in our newfound lack of purpose, which was far less painful on my arms.

I told Sylvia everything that had happened. She was mildly disappointed the surprise had ended amicably and without a public yelling match.

'I don't think Mayumi will ever like Dad. All I can say for Dad is that he's not going to try to make her like him.'

'That's a truce,' Sylvia said.

'It's the best we can do for now. So... what do you want from Japan?'

Sylvia reeled off a list of snacks so long I told her to message them to me instead.

'If I haul all this back, will you help me with something?' I asked.

'You have to *guarantee* the wobbly cheesecake.'

'Promise.' I would work out how later.

'Go on then, what is it?'

'I need your university admissions skills. I'm going to apply to some music courses,' I said.

A huge grin spread across Sylvia's face. 'That's amazing.' She added, 'But I want to stress that I really do need that cheesecake.'

Jo and I walked over the Spectacles Bridge and stopped on the other side.

This time I located it. 'There's the heart stone.'

He shone a smile on me and, like some growing thing, I leaned towards his light. Waited.

'I like you.' He took a breath.

'But,' I said for him.

'I have a lot to think about. It's been important to me, spending time with you, Adam-kun. I would like us to keep talking, but that's all. For now, at least,' he said.

'I understand. I need to work stuff out too. What I want.' I tried to smile. 'How I want it.'

Too soon, I was hauling my suitcase down the steep street to Toshi's car.

Junko gave me an actual hug. 'Anytime you are in Japan, you must visit.'

Toshi patted my back. 'You can sleep in the music room.'

I couldn't adequately express myself, so settled for, 'Thank you.'

Jo was next, and Toshi and Junko pretended that fitting my suitcase in the trunk was an urgent, two-person job. Jo and I kissed each other one last time, delicious despite its bittersweetness.

'I wish you'd wait for me,' I said. 'But don't. You have a lot more to do than that.'

'I won't,' he replied, and we both laughed, that this kind of promise meant something good for us.

'I'll come back, though. Japan is my home too.' Another new truth for me to tell.

He beamed. His eyes were wet. He held out a bundle – the diary wrapped in its indigo cloth.

'Oh no, it's yours. Let everybody else read it.'

He held it to his heart. 'I will then.'

'You could translate it, Junko-san,' I said.

She tilted her head, considering.

I turned to Nagasaki, the view from the hill that I would miss. I gazed at the city, the mountains, the sea.

I would see this again. The story wouldn't end when I left; it wouldn't end at all. In the west, the sky was turning a heavenly purple. From some other world, there was music. I listened and so did the dead. I thought of Kiku and Mr Sharpless and Pinkerton; I thought of my mother and how they had lived before me.

And how they lived on.

Afterword

Pinkerton:

See, I have caught you...
I hold you as you flutter
Be mine.

Butterfly:

Yes, yours forever.

Madame Butterfly, Giacomo Puccini

The inspiration for this novel began when I saw the opera
Madama Butterfly, written by Giacomo Puccini and first
staged in 1904. The plot centres around a US Navy officer,
Benjamin Franklin Pinkerton, and his 'marriage' to a young
Japanese woman called Cio-Cio-san. After an initially
romantic relationship, Pinkerton leaves, telling Cio-Cio-san
he will return 'when the robins nest', yet two years pass
without sign of him. When he does come back, he asks the
American Consul, Sharpless, to tell Cio-Cio-san that he is
now married to an American woman; he does not want to tell
her himself. Cio-Cio-san reveals that they have a child, who
she has named Sorrow, and Pinkerton and his wife propose
that they will take him back to the US with them. Cio-Cio-san

CLARA KUMAGAI

agrees, asking that Pinkerton return to collect Sorrow. She blindfolds the child and puts a little American flag in his hand, then takes her own life.

The beauty of the music is indisputable, and its themes of love, betrayal and tragedy are shared by many other operas. However, *Madama Butterfly* is significant in that it created a racially reductive narrative that has been replicated and amplified for decades: that of a submissive, self-sacrificing Asian woman. I am not alone in wanting to tell more of Cio-Cio-san – and her son's – story. As early as the 1920s, Japanese and Japanese heritage opera directors, artists and musicians have presented different interpretations of Puccini's work.

If you visit Nagasaki – the real city, outside of the book – you will find many references to *Madama Butterfly*; a house in the Glover Garden was known as 'the Madame Butterfly house', so nicknamed by the wife of a US colonel during the American occupation that followed the Second World War. Nearby stand statues of Puccini and Tamaki Miura, a soprano famous for the role of Cio-Cio-san.

The heike biwa provided a rich nexus of music, storytelling, history and ghostliness. I have fictionalised the powers of the heike biwa, though its spiritual associations are real and rooted in Buddhist beliefs and Shinto and folk religion rituals. The biwa was played mainly by visually-impaired musicians up until the twentieth century – similarly, visually-impaired travelling nuns, called goze, played koto and shamisen. While there was a belief in Japan that visual impairment indicated a connection to spiritual powers, it is of even more relevance that there were few professions open to visually-impaired people.

These musicians, particularly those of low socio-economic status, were often subject to shameful discrimination and marginalisation despite their skills and talent.

The opening of *The Tale of the Heike* which Yuna sings is Helen Craig McCullough's translation (Stanford University Press, 1988). Excerpts of the ballads 'Kumagai to Atsumori' and 'Miyako ochi' are adapted from the Biwa Ballad Collection helmed by chikuzen-biwa player Silvain Kyokusai Guignard; this excellent library can be found online at https://guignardbiwa.com. I am also much indebted to Thomas Ranjo for sharing his extensive knowledge and treating me to a private performance of the satsuma biwa – what a lucky twist of fate to find a biwa player in Ireland!

Ono no Komachi was a real poet and the poem discussed by Kiku and Mr S— was famously anthologised in *Ogura Hyakunin Isshu* by Fujiwara no Teika (1162–1241). The English translation which appears in this book is by Felice Fischer, from *Heroic with Grace: Legendary Women of Japan* (Routledge, 1991), edited by Chieko Irie Mulhern. Kiku and Yuna's school song is 'Kongō-Seki' written in 1877 for a girls' school called Joshi Gakushūin by the Empress Dowager Shōken, which I found in *Satsuma Biwa Songs: An Anthology* by Nakamura Masami (The Nishigai Press, 1990).

Although the opera is set in 1904, I chose to begin the diary in 1911 for several reasons: it was the year that the feminist magazine *Seitō* was founded, and when Japan's imperialism was gaining in intensity. These differing forces represented changes in Japanese society, though unfortunately imperialism was embraced with far more enthusiasm than feminism.

The members of *Seitō*, also known as 'New Women', were considered scandalous and indeed pursued lives and careers in defiance of the 'good wife, wise mother' motto promoted at the time. Hiratsuka Raichō's memoir, *In the Beginning, Woman Was the Sun* (Columbia University Press, 2006), translated by Teruko Craig, and *The Bluestockings of Japan* (University of Michigan Press, 2007), an anthology of writing by *Seitō* members edited by Jan Bardsley, proved both informative and enlightening as I developed the historical setting and characters of my novel.

Japan's military expansion was rapidly advanced by the governments of the Meiji, Taishō and Shōwa eras. During the Second World War, Japan's military seized most of East Asia, invading Korea, China, Taiwan, Hong Kong, Vietnam, Cambodia, Laos, Thailand, Malaysia, Philippines, Singapore, Myanmar, East Timor, New Guinea, Guam and several of the Pacific Islands. Japan's colonisation and occupations there were brutal and affected the lives of millions and caused the deaths of millions more.

Following Japan's attack on Pearl Harbour, those of Japanese heritage in America and Canada were dispossessed of their homes and livelihoods, often separated from family and sent to remote concentration camps for the duration of the war. Given the option, some chose to join the US and Canadian armies, as Haru did; still, some veterans returned home to the US to signs that declared 'No Japs Wanted'. The atomic bombings of Hiroshima and Nagasaki, in which up to 210,000 people lost their lives, marked the horrifying end of Japan's involvement in the Second World War.

There are other stories in this novel, spine-tingling but without the horror of real history; old folk stories, told and retold for generations in myriad different forms and translations. I am grateful to Bon and Shoko Koizumi for their blessing to recount the tale of the ghost and the mizuame, first recorded in English by Bon's great-grandfather Lafcadio Hearn in *Glimpses of Unfamiliar Japan* in 1894. One folk tale that Kiku recounts, however, is an original I wrote for this book.

My aim, with *Songs for Ghosts*, was to create a narrative of echoes, layers and retellings. If you are interested in any of the stories within these pages, I encourage you to explore them – after all, they live on through readers like you.

Clara Kumagai
Ireland
August 2024

Acknowledgements

My list of acknowledgements has grown since my last book, which is testament to the amazing people and organisations who have helped and encouraged me. Foremost among them are:

Angelique Tran Van Sang, my wonderful agent. Thank you for your astute reading and for listening to me list fears—you are always so understanding even when we have vastly different interpretations of films.

Alison Lewis, my brilliant agent across the pond—thank you for your excellent feedback and for always having my back.

Fiona Kennedy, Megan Pickford, Jessie Price and the whole team at Zephyr. Thank you for shepherding my books so beautifully into the world.

Peter Phillips, Samantha Devotta and the team at Penguin Teen Canada. It was a dream to visit PRHC headquarters in Toronto!

Claire Stetzer, Maggie Lehrman and the Abrams Kids team—thank you for bringing my books State-side.

The Irish Arts Council and Louth County Council for their financial aid and support.

Children's Books Ireland, for their tireless work and sheer enthusiasm in fostering children's literature for writers and readers.

Kristin Osani, trusted first reader. Sorry I'm always so sleepy and tardy for our writing dates!

Ami-chan, my brave early reader who gives valued feedback despite my books being "eerily good" at making her cry.

Yutaka Kumagai, for giving such an in-depth critique and making narrative connections I hadn't even noticed.

Kevin and Aris Garcia Byrne, and Good Art Friend Kat Joplin for sharing their experiences of family.

Thomas Ranjo and Silvain Kyokusai Guignard for their wealth of biwa knowledge.

Rui Umezawa for introducing me to Aria Umezawa; and to Aria for her generous sharing of experiences directing *Madama Butterfly*, and who connected me with even more wonderful artists and experts. I hope very much to see one of your productions in the future; I think it's the *Madama Butterfly* that I need.

Musicologist Dr. Kunio Hara, who gave such insight into Japanese music during the Meiji era and beyond, and to designer Yuka Uehara, who provided fascinating historical insight into Nagasaki.

The Nagasaki National Peace Memorial Hall for Atomic

Bomb Victims for answering my questions and curating an essential museum.

Bon and Shoko Koizumi, who run the Lafcadio Hearn Museum in Matsue, and to Makoto Shirai for introducing us.

Studio Kura in Fukuoka, where I could have stayed much longer than a month—Mayumi lives there in my stead.

Hazel Lattimore, my patient cello teacher.

Lucy Smyth, for funny buggers.

The Kakehashi Program and the Asia Pacific Foundation of Canada, for their support of *Catfish Rolling*.

The Irish kidlit community and Discover Irish Kids Books, founded by the irrepressible Sarah Webb.

The Irish Consulate in Chicago and the American Writers Museum for organising and hosting a very fun Halloween event for *Catfish Rolling*.

The booksellers, libraries, schools and literary festivals I have been privileged to visit in Ireland, the UK, Canada, the US. You keep books alive!

Writers and friends who have given advice, consolation and kindness—there are many but in particular I'd like to thank Danny Denton, Lisa McInerney, Nicole Flattery, John Patrick McHugh, Deirdre Sullivan, Traci Chee, Jen Ferguson, Adiba Jaigirdar, Kiran Millwood Hargrave, Katya Balen, Jenny Ireland, Méabh McDonnell, Sarah Suk, Sarah Ellis, Kit Pearson, Hiromi Goto and Ayana Gray.

My family, extended family and in-laws: thank you for all your love and encouragement and for purchasing multiple copies of my book.

Dave, who listened to me read this entire book aloud to

him; thank you for saying things like 'it's all just random!' It really did help me fill in plotholes. Black jeans and a white T-shirt are classic and not boring when you wear them.

The readers I have met along the way—it's all for you.

Clara Kumaga
Ireland
August 2024

INTERIOR ILLUSTRATION CREDITS
Elements taken from the cover art © Cristina Bencina
Full pages designed by Jessie Price | Illustrations: Shutterstock.com /
marukopum, Cadmium_Red, Ikanimo, pixzot, TWINS DESIGN STUDIO, lyubava.21,
Cali6ro, Oleksandr, Poliashenko, 777 Bond vector, Nora Hachio

Magic-realism blends with Japanese myth and legend in an original story about grief, memory, time and an earthquake that shook a nation.

Sora hates the catfish whose rolling caused an earthquake so powerful it cracked time itself. It destroyed her home and took her mother. Now Sora and her scientist father live close to the zones – the wild and abandoned places where time runs faster or slower than normal.

Reviews for *Catfish Rolling*

Zephyr is an imprint of Head of Zeus.
At Zephyr we are proud to publish books
you can read and re-read time and time
again because they tell a brilliant story
and because they entertain you.

𝕏 @_ZephyrBooks

📷 @_zephyrbooks

f HeadofZeusBooks

readzephyr.com
www.headofzeus.com

ZEPHYR